Praise fo...
Dragonfire...

Darkfire Kiss

"Deborah Cooke's Dragonfire novels are impossible to put down. *Darkfire Kiss* is no exception. I dare any reader to skim any part of this terrific story!"
— Romance Reviews Today

Whisper Kiss

"Deborah Cooke has again given readers a truly dynamic story in her Dragonfire chronicles."
— Fresh Fiction

"This is a terrific Kiss urban romantic fantasy. . . . The author has 'Cooked' another winner with the tattoo artist and the dragon shape-shifter." — Alternative Worlds

"A great addition to the *Pyr* story line . . . I recommend Deborah Cooke to those who like dragons and love; this one will be a keeper for your shelves and a reread as you pick up the next book in the line."
— Night Owl Romance

"*Whisper Kiss* by Deborah Cooke is now my unofficial official favorite! . . . Bursting with emotions, passion, and even a real fire or four, I count myself lucky not to have spontaneously combusted! Don't miss this sizzling addition to Deborah Cooke's Dragonfire series—it is marvelous!"
— Romance Junkies

"Cooke introduces her most unconventional and inspiring heroine to date with tattoo artist Rox. . . . Cooke aces another one!" — *Romantic Times* (4½ stars)

continued . . .

Kiss of Fire

Also by Deborah Cooke

The Dragonfire Novels
Kiss of Fire
Kiss of Fury
Kiss of Fate
Winter Kiss
Whisper Kiss
Darkfire Kiss

The Dragon Diaries Novels
Flying Blind
Winging It

FLASHFIRE

A DRAGONFIRE NOVEL

DEBORAH COOKE

A SIGNET ECLIPSE BOOK

SIGNET ECLIPSE
Published by New American Library, a division of
Penguin Group (USA) Inc., 375 Hudson Street,
New York, New York 10014, USA
Penguin Group (Canada), 90 Eglinton Avenue East, Suite 700, Toronto,
Ontario M4P 2Y3, Canada (a division of Pearson Penguin Canada Inc.)
Penguin Books Ltd., 80 Strand, London WC2R 0RL, England
Penguin Ireland, 25 St. Stephen's Green, Dublin 2,
Ireland (a division of Penguin Books Ltd.)
Penguin Group (Australia), 250 Camberwell Road, Camberwell, Victoria 3124,
Australia (a division of Pearson Australia Group Pty. Ltd.)
Penguin Books India Pvt. Ltd., 11 Community Centre, Panchsheel Park,
New Delhi - 110 017, India
Penguin Group (NZ), 67 Apollo Drive, Rosedale, Auckland 0632,
New Zealand (a division of Pearson New Zealand Ltd.)
Penguin Books (South Africa) (Pty.) Ltd., 24 Sturdee Avenue,
Rosebank, Johannesburg 2196, South Africa

Penguin Books Ltd., Registered Offices:
80 Strand, London WC2R 0RL, England

First published by Signet Eclipse, an imprint of New American Library,
a division of Penguin Group (USA) Inc.

First Printing, January 2012
10 9 8 7 6 5 4 3 2 1

For Kon,
as always.

Prologue

Hale'iwa, Hawai'i
January 19, 2011

The *Slayer* Chen settled into a corner table at a ramshackle beach bar on the north shore of Oahu. Here, the surfing season was in full fury, and the waves were high enough to set records.

On this night, the moon would be full. The timing was perfect to move his plan one step closer to fruition.

Next year, 2012, would be the year of the dragon, and time was slipping away. Chen had been compelled to accept that he'd made a slight miscalculation in loosing the darkfire—that potent and disruptive force, legendary among the *Pyr*, and known to turn all assumptions upside down when released. Chen had deliberately chosen to break one of the three crystals that held darkfire captive, and had done so to disrupt the last major firestorm of the *Pyr*. Unfortunately, he'd failed to anticipate that the darkfire could also impact his own situation.

He'd assumed himself immune to such factors.

In fact, "impact" was an understatement. The darkfire

had broken his special tool, the brand he used to enslave *Pyr* and *Slayers*. Although he'd reforged the iron brand, it wasn't the same—and he distrusted the blue-green flame of darkfire that periodically danced around its rim. He wasn't entirely sure what it would do when used, for ancient magic was most unpredictable.

And apparently most susceptible to darkfire's touch.

Instead of working alone, Chen had decided to take on reinforcements. He knew that he needed to have each of the four elements accounted for in order to en-act his plan. He himself had an affinity for fire and for earth. He had mastered some ability to control air and water, but had intended to enslave other dragon shifters with those affinities. Time was passing, though, and the darkfire was loose—Chen was doubling up the options to ensure his own triumph. He'd build a small army, reli-ant upon him, beholden to him, magically bound to him, and guarantee that nothing would fail.

Chen had discovered, to his own surprise, that he rather liked having minions. It was pleasant to sit back, pull the strings, and let others do his dirty work for a change. Viv Jason, for example, was pledged to gather the *Pyr* with an affinity for air, the one Chen had been unable to snatch so far himself.

The party animal who called himself Thorolf.

Chen looked forward to that delivery with anticipa-tion.

Then he'd have to figure out what Viv Jason truly wanted of him. He knew her pledge to bring him Thorolf was but an introductory move in what would surely be a battle for supremacy between them.

Chen smiled at the promise of that.

All in all, he felt that his new scheme was moving to-ward its culmination like clockwork.

Chen sat with his back to the wall in the bar, the corner table allowing him an unobstructed view of the beach. He was in human form, in the guise of an older Chinese man. He liked this form, as people tended to underestimate him when he used it. He ordered a glass of juice from the pretty waitress, ensuring that his English was faulty, then waited.

He felt a thrill when he saw his prey jump out of a convertible, hauling his surfboard and shouting to his friends. This young *Pyr*—powerful, tanned, and confident—was the perfect target.

It was a bonus that Brandon was estranged from his father, unknown by the other *Pyr*, and ignorant of his abilities. None of the *Pyr* even suspected this young one's affinity to the earth.

Chen adored how useful Brandon would be to him.

Never mind how responsive the young dragon was to the Dragon Bone Powder. Chen would bait the trap a little more before harvesting this prey.

Brandon was in his early twenties, his age difficult to guess given his rumpled good looks. His hair was dark auburn and tangled. There was a day's growth of stubble on his chin, and his body was tanned to a deep gold. His smile flashed white, his blue eyes twinkling. He wore only shorts and a Hawaiian shirt that was unfastened, the wind whipping at the fabric and revealing glimpses of his collection of tattoos.

More than one woman watched him walk toward the bar where Chen sat. Brandon smiled only for a dark-haired girl who got out of the same car as he did. She flicked the barest glance at him, then turned away to join her friends. Disappointment crossed Brandon's features.

Brandon leaned his surfboard against the outside of the wooden bar with care, then ducked into the shadows, heading straight for Chen. "Hey, Chen, good to see you." The young *Pyr*'s words carried a subtle hint of Australia, although he sounded more American the longer he remained in Hawai'i.

"I am pleased also to see you again." Chen bowed his head slightly.

"Still into the pineapple juice?"

"You must be my guest," Chen said, knowing that his prey was notoriously short of cash. "I insist." He beckoned to the waitress, then indicated Brandon.

Brandon grinned at the waitress, unaware of his easy charm or his affect upon her. "A beer for me. Thanks, Chen." He leaned over the table then, his expression turning serious as his voice dropped. "You don't have any more of that *stuff*, do you, Chen?"

Chen pretended not to understand, although inwardly he was delighted. Everything was falling perfectly into place.

"You know. Ancient Chinese remedy." Brandon winked. His gaze trailed away to the dark-haired girl he'd smiled at. She was chatting with her friends on the beach, so pointedly ignoring Brandon that Chen knew the attraction was mutual.

The boy had no need of Chen's powder to make this conquest, but Chen would not be the one to tell him so.

"She is very pretty," Chen said, although he thought she was less than remarkable.

"Only here one more day." Brandon grimaced. "Time is of the essence, you know." The hope in his eyes made Chen dizzy. To think that his prey would be so eager to step into the trap. It was beyond expectation.

He had chosen the bait well.

"I have only a little bit of the powder," he admitted. "And you know I rely upon it myself."

"Aren't you going home, soon, though? Can't you get more?"

"Tomorrow, yes. I also remain only one more day."

"So . . . ?"

Chen nodded. "So I can help a friend once more."

"Excellent!" Brandon's grin flashed. His beer came, frost on the bottle, and he drained half of it immediately.

"The usual price," Chen said softly.

Brandon met his gaze, his smile fading. "Again?"

Chen spread his hands, as if the terms were not his to negotiate.

Brandon winced. He eyed the girl. He finished his beer. Then he squared his shoulders and nodded. "Just give me a minute. Watch the board for me, huh?"

Chen inclined his head and Brandon left the table. He heard the young *Pyr* lock himself in the men's room and smiled at the ripple of energy he felt when Brandon shifted shape. Chen closed his eyes and savored the sensation. Soon the young dragon would be completely in his thrall, unable to make the shift without Chen's permission.

He could hardly wait.

Brandon returned moments later, something in his hand.

He laid the scale flat on the table, his hand over it. His fingers were shaking slightly. "Some bitch getting these loose," he said with a cautious grin.

Chen smiled. He glanced around the bar, but no one was paying attention to either of them. The waitress was polishing glasses, her back to them. The bartender was frowning over his inventory. Everyone else was watching the surf.

Chen opened the vial of Dragon Bone Powder over the table and tipped a bit of it into his palm. He blew so that the fine powder took flight and Brandon closed his eyes, inhaling it. He visibly shimmered, so aroused that he was on the cusp of change again.

Chen watched for a moment, transfixed by the power of the powder over the *Pyr*. He felt the pulse of sexual desire as well, but the effect seemed magnified for those dragon shifters who had not yet turned *Slayer*. Brandon's arousal made Chen feel old, in a way, numb.

While Brandon's attention was diverted, Chen seized the scale and hid it away from prying eyes.

"Shit, that's good stuff," Brandon whispered, his doubts dismissed. He opened his eyes and they were bright with anticipation. "And it won't hurt her, either, right?"

"It merely opens the mind to possibilities. You have seen this before."

"Oh yeah."

Chen handed him the vial with a flourish.

Brandon glanced down, clearly intending to pass over the scale. He looked at Chen in confusion. "How'd you do that?"

"Sometimes the hand is quicker than the eye," Chen said with a smile.

Brandon laughed. "Well, have a good trip home, Chen, if I don't see you again."

"Oh, I will," Chen said and shook hands with the *Pyr* who would soon be his to command.

There was no doubt that they would see each other again.

All in good time.

Brandon headed toward his surfboard, whistling. He brushed shoulders with another man on the threshold of the bar, a man in his thirties with dark blond hair and sunglasses. That man eyed Brandon with curiosity before coming to join Chen.

"Fraternizing with the enemy?" Jean-Pierre asked as he took a seat, only the most faint French accent clinging to his words.

"Recruiting," Chen corrected, and smiled. JP looked as if he would ask more, but Chen wasn't interested in sharing all of his plans with his newest acolyte.

JP was merely a pawn in Chen's game, although he was foolish enough to imagine his role to be more significant than that.

Of course, Chen had lied to him to encourage that view. What was important about JP was that he would bring Chen the *Pyr* with the strongest affinity to water.

First, Lorenzo and his link to water.

Then Brandon and his link to earth.

Then Thorolf and his link to air.

Chen would take care of fire himself.

JP shimmered slightly, on the cusp of change himself. Chen was delighted to see the effect of the Dragon Bone Powder, even on the *Slayer*. He would need to replenish his stores soon.

"Something in the air here," JP said, that blue shimmer dancing around his body. He glanced at the beach. "All these kids. Raw testosterone."

"Not quite," Chen said, smiling into his pineapple juice.

JP watched him for a moment. "So, you said you needed me to capture Lorenzo and persuade him to join you," he said, removing his sunglasses. "You haven't told me why it will be worth my while to help."

"The *Pyr* owe you a debt for the murder of your brother."

"That was Quinn and Donovan who cut down Lucien." JP frowned. "I don't see what Lorenzo has to do with it."

Chen smiled. "It is often better to work from the inside. I find the idea of turning one *Pyr* against the others appealing—and potentially very effective."

JP studied the older *Slayer* for a long moment. "Why me?"

"You are the ideal *Slayer* to aid me in this quest, because you appreciate the necessity of stealth," he said, watching JP's gaze brighten. "Have you not watched Quinn and Donovan for years, awaiting the perfect moment for vengeance?"

JP appeared to be uncomfortable. "I thought no one knew that."

Chen smiled again. "Today, we negotiate your compensation." With those few words, Chen knew that he had this *Slayer*'s undivided attention.

Perfect.

Chapter 1

Las Vegas
Wednesday, June 15, 2011

Tacky, tacky, tacky.

Cassie Redmond knew from tacky, but this town really kicked it up a notch. The lights. The velvet paintings. The casinos. The fake attractions and the rhinestones. It was the relentless glitz that drove her crazy. Everything was shiny and everything was an illusion.

Her reaction was probably stronger because of her own current view of the world. Cassie was sick of celebrities and sick of publicity, sick of "spin," sick of everything that pretended to be something it was not.

As a freelance photographer specializing in candid shots of celebrities, illusion was tough to escape. Cassie was part of the paparazzi, one of the best of the best, because she excelled at the hunt and in nailing the perfect image.

In a way, her job was to help to perpetuate illusion — and her current attitude wasn't healthy for business.

Which explained her decision to take her first vacation since, well, since she'd packed up her camera and moved out of her parents' house at eighteen. She'd never looked back. She'd never stopped working either.

And how could she not take a vacation now, when her best friend needed her so much? Stacy had been suddenly, unceremoniously, and undeservedly dumped by that fast-talking loser Cassie had warned her to avoid. Only a month before their planned trip together to Vegas to tie the knot. Despite Cassie's earlier misgivings about Mr. Supposedly-Wonderful, Stacy had been heartbroken.

Cassie and Stacy went all the way back to kindergarten, so one teary phone call had been all that was necessary to have Cassie agreeing to join her pal.

Although Cassie had thought it might be smart to change the destination, Stacy had insisted upon a full-frontal assault on her favorite city in the world, Las Vegas. Stacy's logic was that she wasn't going to lose her deposit on the trip, as well as her fiancé and plans of marital bliss.

Cassie hadn't had the heart to say no.

Even if Vegas was the last place she wanted to be.

Not that she could fault Stacy. They'd gone to two shows a day, were staying at a wonderful hotel, had taken a flight over the Hoover Dam, and had partied like rock stars.

It still felt a bit thin to Cassie. She was fantasizing about hiking through the Grand Canyon, maybe seeing something real.

It was day three of the non-honeymoon and Cassie was trudging down the Strip behind Stacy in the blazing sun. She knew that if she never saw another stage show, silicone-implanted breast, or slot machine in her life, she'd die a happy woman.

That wouldn't be soon, though. Stacy had tickets to every single show playing this week. That was the curse of slot machines—Stacy had won $2,200 on her first pull and was determined to spend it all.

They had gotten tickets for a matinee a bit late and there hadn't been any cabs. Plus the Strip was jammed with traffic. Since they were just going to the next big hotel, they'd decided to walk. It was much farther than either of them anticipated—the hotel properties were enormous—and much hotter than they'd realized. The midday sun was brutal.

"This is going to be the best," Stacy insisted, marching briskly in her fuchsia sling backs.

Stacy, it had to be said, did sparkle. She was already striking, being five eleven, curvy, and blonde, but for Stacy, there was no such thing as too much embellishment. There was no missing her in those shoes. Never mind the low-cut pink camisole—with sequin trim—or the skintight black leather skirt. The glittery nails. The false eyelashes and swinging hoop earrings.

Vegas was Stacy's kind of town.

Cassie and Stacy were as different as two women could be—which was probably why they'd managed to remain best friends for almost thirty years.

Cassie felt positively humdrum in her trademark jeans and cowboy boots. Practical and comfortable, that was her mantra. Forgettable. She could disappear into the crowd at a moment's notice. Nobody would ever catch her in a pair of shoes like Stacy's.

She never knew when she might have to run after a shot.

She never knew when she might need to blend into the wallpaper.

All the same, Cassie was regretting her jeans. She

should have gone with her khakis. She was going to be soaked by the time they arrived at the next hotel.

Her BlackBerry vibrated and she tugged it out of her pocket.

"You're on vacation," Stacy chided.

"Got to stay in touch," Cassie argued as she scanned the screen. It was a message from one of Cassie's favorite editors. This one kept her promises and paid on time.

On this occasion, she was prepared to pay a lot. The number made Cassie's eyes pop. It had to be a typo. She sent a reply to confirm the figure.

"What's up?" Stacy asked. "Are you going to dump me, too?"

It was a joke, but not really.

"Remember those dragon shape shifter guys on that television show by Melissa Smith?" It had been the story of the year, maybe of the decade, for the world to discover that there were dragon shape shifting men living among them.

Assuming that a person believed the story.

Cassie didn't.

Stacy nodded. "There was that hot one on YouTube, too. Yum!"

"This editor wants pictures of one while he's making the change. Man to dragon. Or the other way around. No Photoshop stuff."

Stacy gave her a look. "Do not tell me that you're taking the job."

Cassie shrugged. There was no chance of that. "The shots can only happen if the dragon guys are real."

"Well, of course they are! That guy on YouTube was as real as you and me. I saw him!"

Cassie bit back her skeptical reply as the editor's answer came in. The offer had doubled, just in those few minutes. It had been a long time since she'd seen so much money flashed around over pictures. The money piqued her interest, if not the work itself. "Doesn't seem like she's getting any takers."

"Put that thing away. You promised!"

Cassie read the message again, her gaze lingering on the dollar figure. If anyone could get those shots, it would be her.

If the dragon shifters called the *Pyr* were real.

On the other hand, what if Cassie could prove that they *weren't* real? That was the most interesting idea she'd had in months.

"Vacation," Stacy chided, then spelled out the word.

"I'm not working." Cassie insisted. "I left my cameras at home."

"Uh-huh." Stacy was skeptical.

"Just curious."

"Uh-huh. Look—I promise if I see a dragon shifter, I'll let you know. Now put it away!"

"If I wanted to work, I could have done it already. I've seen Britney Spears and Brad Pitt and George Clooney. Lots of opportunities, but I have no camera."

And absolutely no urge to work.

Which was the strange part. Cassie had never been unmotivated before. Was it burnout? Or something more? She couldn't help thinking that she'd been warned this would happen—and that her mentor, Wade, would have laughed himself silly if he could see her now.

Maybe he could, if heaven had a view.

"Lose the BlackBerry," Stacy advised. "It's going to break you."

"I like to stay in touch," Cassie protested by rote.

"For what? Work you're not going to take?" Stacy did a fingertip wave. "Hello, my workaholic friend. Why *are* you finally taking a vacation anyway? Have you *ever* taken a vacation? Not that I remember. I just about fell off my chair when you agreed to come with me." She leaned closer and her eyes narrowed. "There's more going on than you're telling me. I'm going to force fancy drinks into you until you confess the truth."

"Nothing to tell," Cassie lied. "I'm here for you."

"As if," Stacy retorted. "You never do anything for less than four reasons." She pointed at the BlackBerry with challenge in her eyes.

Cassie deleted the message. She showed the display to her friend. "See? All gone. Temptation denied." She shoved the device back into the pocket of her jeans.

"Keep it turned off during the show," Stacy insisted, and Cassie nodded agreement. "Now, let's hurry."

The offer didn't leave Cassie's thoughts as easily.

A stretch limo drove by and Cassie thought again how odd it was for her to be without a camera. She supposed it was more *real* to just be here, like any other tourist. That thought made her smile.

"What's so special about this show again?" she asked, trying to summon a bit of enthusiasm. The shows were starting to blend together.

"Lorenzo's *Trial by Fire*," Stacy said, awe in every syllable. "It's supposed to be great, absolutely amazing. The tickets were so expensive. The concierge had to get them from a scalper. It's sold out completely this week."

Cassie had the vague sense that she'd heard of this guy. "What does this Lorenzo do for his trial by fire? Walk on hot coals?"

"He's an illusionist or magician. Whatever you call them now."

"We went to a magic show two nights ago. The Cirque du Soleil . . ."

"No, no, no. This is *totally* different. It's just the one guy. Nobody else. It's supposed to be really incredible, with fire and pyrotechnics—a can't-believe-your-eyes kind of thing. Lots of glamour and flash."

Ah. Sparkle. No wonder Stacy was excited. Cassie smiled.

"And he does what exactly?"

"Magic!" Stacy flung up her hands, the rings on her fingers glittering. "I can't wait. He even takes questions from the audience and he knows *all* the answers!"

Cassie tried not to roll her eyes. "That just means it's rigged, Stacy. They're planted props, not actual audience members."

"No, that's not true." Stacy's defense was immediate and vigorous. She was always ready to believe. "This girl I work with, she came here last year and asked him when she'd get engaged. She wasn't even seeing anyone, but Lorenzo said she'd be engaged before Christmas. She met this guy the next week and he popped the question on December 23. Isn't that amazing?"

"Or lucky," Cassie murmured.

"Plus he's supposed to be *gorgeous*." Stacy made a little purr in her throat.

"I wonder whether that's an illusion too."

Stacy stopped in the street to confront Cassie. "You're too cynical, that's what your problem is."

Cassie didn't suggest that Stacy could stand to be a little more cynical. Given the circumstances, it would have been tactless.

She kept her tone level. "Well, what did this Lorenzo guy have to lose? Your friend asked a question, he made up an answer. If he was right, she'd think he was amazing. If he was wrong, well, she'd already paid for the ticket to see his show." Cassie shrugged, inviting Stacy to agree.

Stacy laughed. "Trust you to boil it down to that. You've got to believe in *something*, Cassie."

"Yeah, well, I'm waiting for something that's worth believing in." Cassie didn't want to point out that Stacy kept getting hurt because she kept believing in guys who didn't deserve her faith. It was a lot safer to just refuse to believe in anything.

Work. Cassie believed in work.

Or she had until recently.

"Anyway, he's got this big spectacle coming up on the weekend." Stacy dropped her voice to a whisper. "He's supposed to come back from the dead."

Cassie laughed despite herself and got a look from Stacy. "No, really."

"Yes, really. He's going to get buried alive in the desert for a month."

"Sounds like he will be dead."

"So, this week might be the last chance ever to see his show," Stacy enthused. "No wonder it's sold out. We're *so* lucky."

"It's brilliant marketing," Cassie murmured, keeping her voice low enough that Stacy could just ignore her comment.

She did.

An orange Ferrari swerved past the two women just then, cutting through the traffic to shoot through the intersection on a red light. It looked like a tongue of flame moving down the busy Strip, slipping in and out of traffic with ease. It was moving really fast.

Too fast.

A police cruiser raced in pursuit, lights flashing.

Cassie smiled.

"That was *him*!" Stacy squealed, clutching Cassie's

arm. Her new rhinestone-embellished fingernails dug in deep.

"Who?"

"*Lorenzo*! Didn't you see the custom plates?"

"Didn't you see the cop? Your hero is getting a ticket."

"An escort, more likely." Against all probability, Stacy walked even faster. "Oh my God, I can't wait to see this show. Do you think he'll answer my question?"

Cassie hurried behind her friend, suddenly having a very bad feeling. "What question? What are you going to ask him?"

"When I'll fall in love for real, of course." Stacy rolled her eyes. "Come on, Cassie, what else is there that matters? My stupid job? My mother riding my butt about her lack of grandchildren? *Celebrities*?" This last earned Cassie a look, as if the whole culture of popularity was her fault.

Cassie would have picked her job over love any minute and twice on Sundays, but she knew Stacy didn't agree.

"I thought you were going to take it easy for a while, spend some time alone and all that."

"Right. Then I'd be like you." Stacy grinned, taking the sting from her words. "Nope, I have no desire to ever be alone, even for one day." She lowered her voice to a hiss. "Plus I need sex soon."

"I can help with that," a guy passing them said.

Stacy gave him a cutting look, then looped her arm through Cassie's. "Come on. It'll be fun. Like I said, he's gorgeous." She rummaged in her purse, then shoved a flyer at Cassie.

Cassie studied it as they walked, letting Stacy guide her.

Lorenzo did look like a handsome beast, but Cassie

knew the magic that a good photographer could do. In fact, he was beyond good-looking, with those chiseled features and dark, curly hair. His eyes were hazel with bright flecks of gold, like little lights. His lashes were long and dark, lush for a man, but it was the way that he looked to be on the verge of laughter that made the image so compelling.

Great shot. He looked both mysterious and approachable, trustworthy. Lorenzo had done the smart thing on his promotional shot, and looked directly out at the viewer. It was as if he were making eye contact. A little illusion there, but a good one.

And that half smile was good. Sexy. Sensuous. She'd bet he smiled slowly, like he knew something special about you. All your secrets revealed. She shivered a little.

Then she hoped he wasn't short. Lifts would ruin everything.

"You're probably hoping he isn't short," Stacy charged.

Cassie laughed. "What if I am?"

"So shallow. Love transcends such details." Stacy grinned. "And everyone's the same height lying down, anyway."

"You're terrible!"

Stacy whispered mischievously, her eyes dancing. "No, I'm very, *very* good."

Cassie laughed again.

"I've realized Scott wasn't man enough for me," Stacy said with a confident nod. "You were right about him. All flash, no *delivery*."

Cassie didn't know what to say to that. She tilted the brochure, wondering whether the glints in Lorenzo's eyes had been Photoshopped in. She didn't recognize the photographer's name. Maybe it had been a lucky shot.

Or maybe Lorenzo really was this good-looking.

No. Maybe he knew a good plastic surgeon. She suspected that this much masculine goodness had had a little professional enhancement.

Stacy hurried to the lobby door, leaving Cassie momentarily behind her. That was when Cassie realized something. "Wait a minute," she called after her. "What does it matter whether he's gorgeous?"

Stacy cast a smile over her shoulder and nearly galloped through the doors.

Oh no.

"You're going to ask him more than one question!" Cassie guessed. "Or ask him to help with your, um, agenda item."

Stacy just laughed. "Vacations are supposed to be *fun*, Cassie. And what could be more fun than getting it on with a hunky, rich magician?"

"But . . ."

"It'll be good for my ego, even to catch his eye."

Right. "You can't be expecting forever. . . ."

"No, just *fun*. Remember fun?" Stacy preened a little. "Who knows—I might know a few tricks he doesn't."

Cassie knew when there was no chance of changing Stacy's mind. "This I have to see," she muttered, and Stacy laughed again.

Cassie unfastened her ponytail and redid it as she walked through the lobby, combing her hair into some kind of order with her fingers. As men turned to ogle Stacy, she realized that her friend had deliberately dressed to attract attention.

To stand out from the crowd, as it were.

"Front-row seats," Stacy said, waving the tickets under Cassie's nose. "You won't miss a thing."

"How much *did* those cost you?"

Stacy laughed. "It's found money, so it's guilt-free to spend. Come on!"

"You're crazy," Cassie said lightly. In a way, she was glad to see Stacy ready to take a chance again. And she didn't imagine for one minute that this Lorenzo would take the bait.

Stacy grinned. "No. I'm having fun. You should try it sometime, Ms. Workaholic. You were probably wishing for your camera all day long, even though you said you'd quit."

"Well . . ."

"Then step aside, Cassie Redmond, and watch how it's done." Stacy lifted her chin and squared her shoulders, then sashayed down the aisle of the theater. If the reactions of the people already gathered there were any indication, she'd be stealing the show from Lorenzo.

Cassie smiled to herself at the prospect. Seeing a magician get more than he bargained for just might be fun.

Lorenzo was irritated. He pulled into his parking spot behind the theater and flung himself out of his orange Ferrari. He locked and armed it without a second thought, his hand on the stage door before the car had given its last beep of acquiescence.

Fred was there, sweeping the door open for him with his usual flourish.

At least something was going right.

Lorenzo hated being late. A lack of time before his performance compromised his routine of calming himself before the show. That lack of composure could lead to mistakes. He took the pricing of the tickets to his shows very seriously—he was determined to give each attendee the value he or she had paid for. And that meant a perfect show, each and every time. Perfect consistency. Perfect timing. Perfect showmanship. The way he saw it, he and the humans made an exchange: two hours of magical perfection for one hundred and fifty dollars a seat.

Perfection was only possible with no stress.

Unfortunately, everyone around him seemed determined to generate stress by the megaton.

One more matinee. Three more evening shows. Then the launch of the spectacle, and he'd be done.

Free.

He was counting down the moments.

Lorenzo marched to his dressing room and slammed the door, pressing his fingertips against his temples. He needed to calm himself. He was edgy. Ready to lose it.

Of course, there'd been that argument today at the house, the completely unnecessary drama of his father shifting shape right in front of the staff, and the subsequent need to terminate all employees at the house.

All Lorenzo had done was ask his father what had happened to the darkfire crystal.

Again.

It was still missing. Lorenzo had promised to hold it in trust in exchange for the flashfire song, and he had kept his word. He'd made the deal with Rafferty's grandfather, the Cantor, then dropped the rock into his hoard, content to have what he wanted from the exchange. Six months ago, when he'd been putting the final touches on the plan for his great escape, he'd checked on the crystal.

It had disappeared.

That worried Lorenzo. What would the *Pyr* ask of

him in exchange for his failure to keep the crystal safe? Did anyone know he knew the flashfire song? Could it be wiped from his memory as easily as the Cantor had put it there? It was imperative that he have no more ties to his kind after Saturday, and the flashfire song was key to his disappearance.

Only Lorenzo and Salvatore had access to the hoard, which was secured at his house. Therefore Salvatore must know what happened to it since Lorenzo didn't. But his father was evasive and confused every time Lorenzo asked about the crystal—Lorenzo was certain it was an act. This time, he'd pushed harder, but his father had abruptly shifted shape in the middle of their dispute and gone to sleep.

Of course, the housekeeper and her husband witnessed the shift, which was undoubtedly Salvatore's plan. They would never truly forget seeing a dragon shape shifter in Lorenzo's living room. Lorenzo regretted losing them after so many years of good service, especially due to some game of his father's, although he had paid a hefty severance to each.

Plus the pair had to be beguiled before they left his employment, for their own safety and psychological well-being. Now he had to find another couple willing to work for him under his terms, and for only a few days. It was all very time-consuming and extremely annoying.

Lorenzo couldn't help suspecting that his father was deliberately making problems for him.

Instead of just being old, confused, and generally impossible.

Never mind that there were technical issues with Lorenzo's final spectacle of being buried alive in the desert in his car, a feat of daring that relied upon precise preparation. The modifications to the car were not quite as he had insisted, and he'd have to discuss it with the mechanic again. If Lorenzo had had a dollar for every incompetent human with whom he'd been obliged to work over the past four centuries, he'd be a multimillionaire.

He was one anyway, but he'd earned that money.

And now the eclipse. He could feel it. It had nothing to do with him, because he had nothing to do with his fellow *Pyr*, so it infuriated him that he was sensitive to total lunar eclipses at all. What did he care if another *Pyr* had a firestorm? What did he care if another *Pyr* met his destined mate, whether they conceived another dragon shape shifter? They were just more *Pyr* for Lorenzo to ignore.

Lorenzo had work to do and money to make and obligations to fulfill. He would have appreciated the other *Pyr* ignoring him as thoroughly as he ignored them.

It would only have been polite for the moon to have chosen to not send him notice. But the pending eclipse teased at the edge of his consciousness, making him feel on the cusp of change.

Involuntarily.

Lorenzo hated everything that was involuntary.

And he hated being *Pyr*.

Becoming a dragon was barbaric and primitive. Never mind the fighting, the slashing and ripping and biting. He shuddered. It wasn't clear to him whether the flashfire song would eliminate his shifter powers completely—as well as breaking the connections to his kind—but Lorenzo didn't care.

In this moment, Lorenzo had to put the crystal out of his mind and focus. He preferred evening shows, but that wasn't relevant. Two thousand people had just paid top dollar to see his afternoon performance.

And they would leave his custom-built theater happy.

Lorenzo did his breathing exercises and deliberately lowered his pulse. He steadied himself as well as he was able, under the circumstances, and prayed that all the preparations had been done correctly. On this day, he'd take heads if there was anything less than perfect. He dressed alone, as always, then squared his shoulders and considered his reflection.

He wasn't holding up too badly. He didn't look a day past three hundred years old.

Or in human terms, a day past thirty-five.

The tuxedo fit him beautifully, but that was the mark of a good bespoke tailor. It reassured him to look so polished. Appearances were critical. He straightened his bow tie with a tweak. He swirled the black cape he favored as he swung it over his shoulders. As usual, the glimpse of its orange satin lining lifted his spirits. So beautiful. So elegant. So unexpected. He adored that cape.

Lorenzo scooped up his top hat and turned with a flourish. He strode to the door, leaving his dressing room with purpose. He checked the props and the staff, hearing the chatter of the audience gathered behind the heavy velvet drapes. He felt the familiar tingle that he always felt before a performance—part nerves, part anticipation, part terror.

The lights began to dim. The music began to play.

Showtime.

Cassie had to hand it to this Lorenzo guy. The theater was incredible. He hadn't skimped at all. There was nothing tawdry or tacky about it. The interior was gorgeous and elegant, far more luxurious than any of the other venues they'd visited or glimpsed.

The seats were cushy and upholstered in black velvet.

They were scrupulously clean, as if they'd been upholstered just that day. The carpet was black and thick un-
derfoot, unstained as far as she could see. There wasn't
so much as a stray kernel of popcorn. The curtains on
the stage looked like real velvet, black with a line of metallic orange along the hem. That line etched the glittering outline of flames.

Trial by fire. She got it.

There were sconces spaced along the walls, each
looking like a brass bowl that held a flame. Of course,
they couldn't have been real flames, not with fire codes,
but they looked real. The temperature in the theater was
cool but not cold. It felt like a refuge, both from com-
mercialism and the noisy bustle of Vegas.

She listened to the audience as they took their seats
and murmured to each other. She felt their wonder and
knew that Lorenzo had them believing in him even before he began his show.

Cassie folded her arms across her chest, less willing to
be persuaded. All of this magic stuff relied on trickery,
on making people look left when things happened on
the right, for example. She was determined to see the
truth of whatever this guy did.

Her BlackBerry vibrated again and she glanced at it.
Again they had doubled the price they'd pay for shots of
those shape-shifting dragons. Melissa Smith's television
show about the *Pyr* must have really good ratings. Cassie
scrolled through the message, eyeing the specifications
for what they wanted.

A suite of shots, documenting the change from man
to dragon.

That would be tough to fake.

Of course, if the *Pyr* were real, the shots wouldn't be
fake.

Cassie dismissed that possibility. She wondered what the editor would pay for proof that the *Pyr* were a hoax. Well aware of Stacy's disapproval, Cassie sent a message to ask.

Her BlackBerry received a reply almost instantly. This story was hot. She wasn't totally surprised that the editor would pay the same price for proof of a hoax, but was surprised that the price had increased again.

But where would a person find one of these supposed dragon shifters?

"Off," Stacy muttered. "You promised."

Cassie turned off the device and put it away. It would be enough money to retire. To leave the business of illusion for good.

She was surprised by how appealing that idea sounded.

Cassie was still thinking about that money as the lights began to dim and music started from all sides. The flames in the sconces leapt higher and that line across the bottom of the stage curtains began to glitter.

As if it were burning.

A trick, but a good one.

If she were pretending to be a dragon shifter, where would she hide?

Maybe, just maybe, in a place where nothing was what it seemed to be.

A place like Las Vegas.

Hmm.

Lorenzo nodded at his staff and strode to his place at center stage, where he would await the rising of the curtains. He fought his awareness of the slow burn of the eclipse, teasing at the edge of his thoughts. He felt the firestorm light for some poor *Pyr* and ignored it, just as he had a hundred times before.

Even though it was close.

It was *not* his problem.

Lorenzo was in the act of donning his top hat when the music swelled. One pair of curtains swept back and the other curtain rose skyward.

Right on cue.

Perfect.

The audience stared at him in expectant awe. Lorenzo had a moment to think that everything would be just fine.

Then he raised his hand in a welcoming gesture, and the light of his own firestorm sparked from his fingertips.

Lorenzo was astounded.

His firestorm launched an arc of fire that illuminated the space between him and a woman in the front row. She was lit suddenly with radiant golden light.

The audience gasped.

Lorenzo wanted to swear.

The woman had been sitting with her arms folded across her chest, reluctant to be impressed. Her skepticism would have made his eye skip over her under other circumstances. The blonde beside her was more typical of the women Lorenzo took as lovers.

But the bright glimmer of the spark startled her.

And it compelled Lorenzo to look. Her bones were good. She could have been attractive if she'd chosen to do anything other than tug her hair back into a sloppy ponytail. She wore no makeup and was dressed in jeans, a cotton shirt, and hideous red cowboy boots.

Lorenzo couldn't stand cowboy boots.

Even on cowboys.

Women certainly shouldn't dress like cowboys, not if they wanted to show their glory to advantage. Women should wear skirts and high heels, lacy little bits of nothing, and lipstick. They had serious assets and they should use them.

This woman apparently didn't bother. Her hair was reddish blond, her skin fair. She jumped when the spark struck her shoulder, and the golden light revealed that she was young and pretty. There was intelligence in her expression, wariness and interest mingled together.

Despite that, there couldn't be a woman on the face of the earth whom he was less likely to find intriguing. She seemed to feel the same way about him. Lorenzo didn't find it promising that they had that one thing in common.

Meanwhile, he smiled at the crowd and bowed, as though everything were going according to plan.

Far from it! Curse the firestorm, its timing and its choices. Curse his *Pyr* nature and everything that came with it.

Lorenzo was just going to have to work with the firestorm.

Somehow.

Cassie jumped when the spark struck her shoulder. She'd assumed it was an illusion, but the collision of that flame with her skin gave her the strangest sensation.

She was hot.

She was simmering.

No, she was *aroused*. The electric heat of desire slid through her body, turning her mind in earthy directions, making her fidget in her chair. She was consumed with lust, which was about as far from her usual frame of mind as possible.

She stared at Lorenzo, wondering what the hell he was pumping into the air in this place. He smiled at her, as slowly as she'd anticipated. Like he knew what she was thinking. He was suave and confident, and she wondered whether he made love slowly, too.

In fact, she tingled at the very idea.

He was manipulating her, but she couldn't figure out how.

Lorenzo was gorgeous, but Cassie saw lots of hot guys up close and personal in her line of work. Genuine or augmented. She talked to them, she cajoled them, sometimes she even shared a joke with them. Not a one of them had ever made her feel like this. Not a one of them had ever made her mouth go dry, or made her panties wet with a single glance.

She wasn't sure there had ever been anybody who had made her feel like this.

And she didn't like it one bit.

"Welcome, ladies and gentlemen, girls and boys." Lorenzo's voice was low and rich, the kind of voice a woman could listen to all day long.

Or all night long.

Cassie stifled a shiver and folded her arms more tightly across her chest. Charisma. He had charisma. Buckets of it. That was all. And he knew how to work a crowd. He had each and every one of them in his pocket already.

Maybe there were vibrators in these chairs.

Or just in hers.

"I hope you are prepared to be amazed!"

A flick of his wrist and the stage erupted in flames. They were brilliant orange and waist high, surrounding Lorenzo. He stood, smiling, in his tux, untouched by the fire. Maybe he was Faust, completely at ease with the heat of hellfire. Certainly there was something wicked in his smile.

With a gesture from him, the flames were all extinguished, the stage still looking like wooden boards.

Unburned.

The audience applauded wildly, but Lorenzo was already on the move.

"Yum!" Stacy whispered, and Cassie nodded agreement.

Okay, she wasn't just burnt out. She was going insane. Cassie felt like a besotted teenager, but she couldn't take her eyes off Lorenzo.

This was not good.

Chapter 2

Cassie didn't know much about the specifics of magic shows, but Lorenzo made it look effortless. The pacing was relentless, one trick slipping right into the next. The whole presentation was slick and sexy.

He charmed and chatted all through the show, which was longer than Cassie had anticipated. He made a joke of the sparks that kept flying from him to her. The way he incorporated that spark into his patter convinced her that it was a regular part of his show. She'd just gotten the wrong seat.

The hot seat, as it were.

All the same, she wondered how the hell he was doing it. There had to be something in the chair, a magnet or something.

She couldn't figure it out—she was becoming so aroused that she couldn't even think straight. Worse, the target of her desire was Lorenzo. She noticed the sweat on his temples and felt an uncharacteristic urge to wipe it away. She watched his hands, liking their elegant strength, wondering how those fingertips would feel sliding across her skin. When he strode across the stage, she watched his hips and her breath caught. The man moved like a sleek and powerful panther.

She was sure he paid a fortune to make himself look this good. She was sure he spent hours at the gym. She was sure he was a complete narcissist, one accustomed to attracting women with the crook of a finger, then casting them off when he was done.

But she was finding serious appeal in Stacy's idea of fun.

It wasn't just because he wasn't short.

Cassie watched, transfixed, as he spoke, achingly aware of the sexy timbre of Lorenzo's voice and the firm line of his lips. How would this man kiss? She wanted to know, and she wanted to know now.

What was wrong with her?

She liked his easy humor and obvious intelligence, his deliberate management of the audience's attention. She wondered what it would be like to have his undivided attention—even the glimpses he cast her way, the smiles he bestowed upon her when he was toying with that spark, filled her mind with lusty possibilities.

She kept her arms folded across her chest, as if her body language could stave off her reactions.

Or contain her imagination.

She felt as obsessed as a fan girl for the first time in her life, and she couldn't explain it. One glance at Stacy was enough to confirm that Cassie wasn't the only one in Lorenzo's thrall.

That wasn't the most reassuring realization. She was supposed to be immune to this kind of spectacle. She was supposed to be the smart one, the one who saw behind the facade.

But on this afternoon, Cassie was snared by it.

Completely.

It was warm in the theater, all the use of flames and pyrotechnics heating the air. The tricks and illusions blurred together for Cassie, becoming a stream of impossible feats. In a way, they were irrelevant. She only wanted to watch Lorenzo, and couldn't have cared less what he was doing.

She would have watched him brush his teeth.

For hours.

It would have been best if he'd been brushing them while naked.

He did have an uncommon flair. He started fires and extinguished them. He burned items with the point of a finger and those flames rose and fell from the stage several times. The whole time he spoke in that low, melodic voice.

He brought a python on stage soon after the intro, a massive yellow-and-black-patterned serpent that Cassie would have been happier to see as a pair of boots. She hated snakes, but he handled the reptile deftly. He dropped it into a basket, then made it disappear. It slithered down the main aisle a moment later, heading directly toward him as the audience shrieked. It coiled itself obediently into its basket on his command.

Checking on the snake and making it appear elsewhere was a recurring theme, one that the young boys in the audience seemed to especially enjoy.

The tricks became increasingly elaborate and showy, until the two female assistants rolled a huge clear box onto the stage. They were attractive women, beautiful blondes who could have been models.

Cassie figured they were glad to have a job in this town that let them keep their shirts on.

The cube looked to be filled with water and must have been twelve feet on a side. The assistants turned it on the stage, rolling it around on a shiny silver frame with casters, letting the audience see all sides.

Or think they could see all sides. It had to be an illusion.

A shiny ladder was rolled into place and attached to the cube. Cassie ignored the patter as Lorenzo climbed it to a small platform at the top. He went on and on, something about water extinguishing flames, about the human body being able to last a certain number of minutes without air.

One assistant rolled a massive timer onto the stage and stood ready to start it. The other followed him and stood beside him on the platform.

The music began to build momentum.

Meanwhile, completely at ease, Lorenzo removed his short cape with a flourish, doffed his gloves. He talked all the while as he handed garments to the blonde. Cassie doubted she was the only audience member interested in seeing how naked he'd get.

He shed his tuxedo jacket and handed it to the assistant. He stepped into a cloth sack, then halted to take off his shoes.

Then he was handcuffed and his ankles locked into shackles. He made jokes about being at the whim of the blonde and she mugged a bit for the audience. His ankle shackles and handcuffs were hooked together, so that he squatted before them. It was impossible not to note the breadth of his shoulders or the ripple of muscles visible beneath the cloth of his shirt.

He blew a kiss to the crowd and said, "*Au revoir.*"

The bag was pulled up over his head and knotted. The assistant grinned at the audience, then pushed Lorenzo into the water with one foot. He splashed, then struggled like a fish as the lid locked down on the cube. The timer started. The assistant scampered down the ladder and rolled it away from the tank, even as the cloth bag churned.

The audience leaned forward in dismay.

The assistant crossed the stage and dropped the keys to the tank into the basket with the snake. The snake roused itself in apparent annoyance and had to be forced back into the basket by both assistants. Cassie knew she was supposed to be watching their antics with the snake, so she watched the tank instead.

It was a clever trick because the locked tank was clear. It did appear that Lorenzo was struggling in his bonds in the water. She couldn't see anything odd about it.

The keys deposited and the timer running, the lights dimmed to a single spotlight locked on the tank and Lorenzo's struggling form. The timer was illuminated, its letters the same orange-red as the flames that leapt higher in the wall sconces.

There was no sound except the relentless pound of a drum, marking the passing seconds. Cassie could feel the audience's concern. She was leaning forward herself. Stacy clutched her hand in terror.

There had to be mirrors. Cassie looked for them without success.

The timer ticked past the two-minute mark.

Lorenzo's body suddenly went still in the water.

Had the trick gone wrong?

Or was this part of the illusion?

Cassie was surprised by how worried she was.

Cassie wasn't alone in her reaction.

There was a collective gasp from the audience

A ripple of fear passed through the crowd. The assistants eyed each other in obvious consternation. They raced to retrieve the keys to the locked tank, but the snake hissed at them. It coiled itself up and looked dangerous. They retreated, conferred, then tried to approach the snake again. It was apparently too annoyed to let them get close.

Meanwhile, the audience became more agitated. Some people rose to their feet. The motionless canvas bag was a chilling sight. Cassie couldn't look away from it.

Surely he couldn't be dead?

It had to be a trick.

But as the seconds passed and the assistants visibly panicked, she had a harder time believing it.

"Hurry!" shouted a man at the back of the audience.

His cry was taken up by the crowd, as they urged the assistants onward. The man shouted again, his voice louder than the others.

Cassie had a vague sense that something didn't add up. She felt the shimmer of heat on her skin, as if there were a forest fire raging all over her body. In fact, when she looked down, it appeared that her skin was glowing with an inner fire.

Radiant.

Just the way it had when he'd launched those sparks. She thought of Lorenzo's lips and his hands and his drop-dead hot looks, and shivered. Could a man so vital really have died in front of them? That sack didn't move.

The man shouted again.

Cassie recognized his voice.

She spun in her seat, incredulous, only to see Lorenzo himself striding down the main aisle of the theater.

He was dripping wet and wearing only a black bathing suit.

A very tight black bathing suit.

Her mouth went dry at the sight of him.

His eyes were twinkling as he called again for his assistants to hurry. The crowd gasped in astonishment as they saw him, silence rolling from the back of the house.

Followed by a tidal wave of applause.

Cassie just stared. Lorenzo was a pure and perfect male specimen. He had muscle definition that would put a Chippendale dancer to shame. His wet, curly hair hung over his forehead, making him look mischievous and boyish—an appealing contrast to his very masculine physique. It was a Superman kind of look and it worked in a very big way.

All while being PG-13.

"Oh. My. God." Stacy spoke in a whisper.

Lorenzo leapt up to the stage, an elegant move of pure power. He pivoted and bowed, muscles flexing. He winked at Cassie, then blew her a kiss, his gesture launching another spark in her direction. The crowd hooted with delight.

Cassie didn't join in. She was annoyed. Not only had she been tricked, along with everyone else, but he was making it look as if she worked for him. That spark and the way he played it made it appear that she was part of the show.

His use of her as a prop made her want to challenge him.

She wanted to destroy at least part of his illusion.

The applause, meanwhile, was deafening. The flames in the sconces leapt high, flickering as if they too would salute him. Lorenzo bowed a few more times, managing to look both cocky and modest.

"I could eat him up with a spoon," Stacy murmured.

Cassie simmered. She crossed her legs, wishing this tingling would stop. That last flame had only made it worse. It was almost impossible to think about anything other than sex.

Wild, endless sex—with Lorenzo.

Every woman in the audience was captivated. Lorenzo shook hands with his assistants, gestured the snake back into its basket, and pulled the key out of his swimsuit. He ascended the ladder, unlocked the box, and pulled out his soaked shirt and trousers with an expression of regret.

He cast them to an assistant, then strode to center stage, still wearing only that black swimsuit. He held up his hands for silence and had it instantly. The tank was wheeled away, and a ruffled black satin curtain descended behind him. He was alone on stage, apparently without props or aids.

Cassie didn't believe it for a minute.

"And so we come to the most popular part of the show," he said, that low voice doing dangerous things to her equilibrium. "The real *Trial by Fire*." He gestured and the house lights turned up slightly. "As usual, I'll take three questions today, and I hope you've brought your most challenging ones. Who will be first?"

That was when Cassie knew how she was going to show him up. She was a hunter, and she liked to expose frauds. This guy was manipulating everything in this theater.

She'd give him something he couldn't manipulate.

She'd prove that she wasn't part of the illusion.

She'd ask him a question he couldn't answer.

Cassie hunkered down in her seat. She wouldn't be first. She'd gamble on being chosen third. Lorenzo was using that spark for a reason, and she knew he'd want to end the show with a flourish. She'd bet it had something to do with this hot seat.

Well, two could play that game.

* * *

The firestorm was more infuriating than Lorenzo could have imagined.

It had only just ignited, but already it burned with an insistence that drove every other thought from his mind. He could think only of Ms. Practicality, sitting there with her arms folded around herself. Everything about her said "prim." Everything about her was a denial of pleasure and passion, the two things he found most important in life.

The firestorm ensured that he wanted to change her view. He wanted to coax her to relax, make her smile, make her shiver. He wanted to peel off her jeans, unfasten that ponytail, and run his fingers through her hair. He wanted to see her naked. He wanted to caress her skin. He wanted to hear the sound of her laughter.

Of her orgasm.

The firestorm was messing with him by partnering him with a woman so vastly different from himself.

And Lorenzo didn't appreciate it.

He very nearly screwed up the escape, he was so distracted by the simmer lit by her presence. The persistent lick of the firestorm's flames drove every thought from his mind except the prospect of sex.

Lots of it.

He could only work with the heat of the firestorm by persuading himself that a brilliantly executed finale might earn her smile.

Even Lorenzo didn't truly believe that.

It would take more than that to make Ms. Skeptical crack a smile.

Unfortunately, his imagination was more than ready to conjure possibilities.

None of which had anything to do with executing a flawless illusion.

He silently cursed the firestorm.

It made no difference.

When Lorenzo strode down the aisle and found his destined mate still scowling—obviously doubtful of his skills—he nearly roared with frustration. His irritation only heightened his reaction, making him more aware of her. If anything, the firestorm burned hotter, taunting him.

It was enough to tempt Lorenzo to take a real risk. He wanted to provoke a reaction from her.

Any reaction would do. Lorenzo was sure that it was her composure that grated upon him. He was consumed with her and she was completely indifferent to him.

The part of his mind that remained rational—instead of rapturous—recognized that this was a problem. He knew that a distraction could completely condemn his scheduled feat at the end of this week. If the firestorm continued to burn hotter with every passing moment, he'd be a disaster by the next morning.

When Lorenzo invited questions with his usual aplomb, he knew with sudden conviction what he had to do. He had to satisfy the firestorm. Immediately. If not sooner. He couldn't afford to make a mistake with this upcoming spectacle, the planned pinnacle of his career. He couldn't afford to lose control of the variables at this precise moment in time.

Perfection demanded the elimination of distractions.

If Lorenzo was to be cursed with a firestorm, he wasn't going to waste any more time than was necessary in seeing it satisfied. He knew all the stories. He knew that the firestorm only burned hotter and hotter the longer it remained unsated. He knew that it was supposed to be the mark of a *Pyr* meeting his destined mate. He knew that Erik argued in favor of creating a lasting partnership with the woman in question.

Lorenzo didn't care about any of that. His firestorm was an obstacle and a problem. The sooner it was satisfied, the better. It wasn't as if he believed that this woman would go home from vacation pregnant with a baby dragon shifter. That was just *Pyr* superstition, perpetuated and buttressed by romantic idiots like Erik, leader of the *Pyr,* who encouraged the *Pyr* to make permanent relationships.

He worked alone and always would.

Lorenzo knew he would have been kinder if his apparent mate hadn't been so determined to believe him a fraud. If she had been softer, more feminine, more alluring, more his type of woman—well, he might have been more inclined to seduce her and savor a few weeks together.

But this one, this one could undoubtedly deal with anything life dealt her and could do it all by herself.

Maybe she preferred it that way. Her hands were devoid of rings and she wasn't with a partner.

Lorenzo eyed the woman and smiled at her, just as he launched another firestorm spark in her direction. Those sparks annoyed her and he liked ensuring that he wasn't the only one annoyed. The crowd oohed and aahed at what they thought was an effect.

Lorenzo watched his mate. He saw the quick tightening of her lips, saw her irritation rise. She glanced around herself, assessing perhaps whether other people thought she was in his employ. The notion didn't seem to please her. He saw her jaw set and knew that she had made a choice, as well.

He doubted it would be very interesting. Humans were terribly predictable. But no matter what she did, this woman—his destined mate—was going to get more than she anticipated.

And she was going to get it within the hour.

Lorenzo didn't have time to mess around with a firestorm. It would be sated, and it would be sated ASAP.

After Lorenzo had answered the second question from the audience, Cassie raised her hand and rose smoothly to her feet.

Cassie wasn't the only one who had a question. Stacy waved hard enough to bring the house down. But Cassie knew that Lorenzo was watching her. She could tell by the way the hair was prickling on the back of her neck.

He was good. Most people wouldn't have noticed the focus of his attention, but Cassie was keenly observant. Her ability to interpret small signs and guess what any given person would do—or where he or she would go— had contributed to her success.

And she knew Lorenzo would take this bait.

He did. He turned to her with a dazzling smile. His gaze locked on hers and she suppressed a shiver. She couldn't stop herself from standing taller beneath his attention, or from licking her lips.

He smiled slowly at that, his eyes gleaming with intent.

It was really hot in the theater and it seemed to get hotter just because Lorenzo was looking at her.

Cassie held her ground and smiled back at him.

"Our third question, from the lady who sparks the flame," Lorenzo said, as smooth as butter. The audience cheered.

"Ask him about me," Stacy insisted in a whisper.

Cassie couldn't say a thing. She was staring at Lorenzo, her mouth dry.

He spread his hands as he walked toward her, all masculine grace, then dropped to one knee at the closest point on the stage. His gaze locked on her and he arched his brow, inviting her question.

Cassie thought she might spontaneously combust. There was a trickle of perspiration running down her back, but the more disconcerting heat was the one that simmered beneath her skin. Proximity only made him more alluring. She noticed the even tone of his tan, the muscled strength of his thighs, the grace of those strong hands. She saw the taut muscles of his chest—and the quirk of his smile just about dissolved her knees.

She wondered again how he'd kiss.

She wondered whether his skin was as warm as hers.

She wondered how those hands would feel, sliding over her naked body.

She wondered just how she had managed to lose her mind in an hour and a half.

Then that spark leapt between his hands, seeming brighter than ever, blazing an arc from one palm to the other. Its golden light only made him look more hand-some, dancing over the planes of his face and glinting in his dark hair. His eyes shone gold in the light of the flames and she had the sudden sensation that she was his prey.

And that she didn't care.

He lifted his hands and the spark shot toward her in a massive arc of orange flame.

The other flames in the theater leapt for the ceiling, blazing in unison. The entire theater was filled with the crackle of flames, the brilliant light of fire, while Cassie was filled with a simmering throb of desire.

She had no idea how he did it, but it was impressive.

The spark was hotter than it had been before, more sensual, and its impact nearly melted Cassie.

Or was that the effect of having Lorenzo's undivided attention?

She halfway wished he'd put on some more clothes.

The other half of her liked the view just fine.

"And so, we have our third and final question," he said in that dark chocolate voice. "From the lady who has lit my fire this afternoon."

The audience chuckled and Cassie felt herself flush.

She could lose herself in those eyes. He watched her, unblinking, just his gaze making her mind turn in very basic directions. The reflection of the flames in his eyes would have made for a great photograph.

"My question is this," she said, speaking clearly and slowly. "Where would I find one of those dragon shape shifter guys, the *Pyr*, the ones Melissa Smith has been profiling on her television show?"

There was one beat of silence.

She heard Lorenzo catch his breath.

Then his smile broadened.

There was something calculating about that smile, something that might have worried Cassie if she'd been anywhere else in the world than in front of two thousand witnesses. A light dawned in Lorenzo's eyes that was both wild and unpredictable, one that made her catch her breath at his raw sexuality. She sensed that he was about to surprise her.

And she was excited by the prospect.

Then he threw up his hands. The stage erupted in flames, as it had at the beginning of the show. This time, though, the flames burned as high as his shoulders.

He repeated her question in his deep voice.

Cassie was sure Lorenzo was stalling. She stared at him, not willing to back down. When he smiled at her again, she held his gaze, silently daring him.

She expected him to come up with some palatable story.

She expected him to try to fake out the audience.

She expected him to do pretty much anything other than what he did do.

Lorenzo's eyes flashed. There was a strange shimmer of blue light around his body. The flames on the stage leapt even higher, as tall as him. He was obscured, except for that blue light. The shimmer became a glow, like a brilliant pale blue aura.

"Right here at the *Trial by Fire*!" he cried, then leapt into the air.

And disappeared.

In the blink of an eye, a massive gold dragon appeared above the audience. Cassie gasped. The dragon's scales could have been made of hammered gold, each embellished with cabochon gems. It looked as if the dragon had been made of medieval reliquaries.

But it wasn't mechanical. It moved with a lithe grace, a sinuous power that reminded Cassie of the swing of Lorenzo's hips. And it was more than smoke and mirrors. Its golden wings flapped, ensuring that it hovered above the crowd, and Cassie felt the wind they created. The dragon breathed a plume of fire that crackled over the heads of the assembled crowd and Cassie felt its heat.

"Amazing," Stacy whispered.

To Cassie's surprise, the dragon even flew out over the astonished audience. She couldn't see wires or mirrors anywhere, although there had to be some. She couldn't see an image being projected from anywhere, either. She turned with everyone else, and watched the dragon in wonder.

She felt its gaze lock upon her, as if it were real, as if it were a conscious creature, and her heart leapt. She was reminded of the way she'd felt when Lorenzo looked at her.

Prey.

Or treasure.

The dragon swooped down over Cassie and snatched her off her feet in one great claw. She cried out in shock as she was swept into the air. It had to be a trick, but she couldn't imagine how it worked. Dragons weren't real.

But this one felt real. She fingered its talons, the ones locked around her waist, and they felt solid. The dragon wasn't cold either, but warm.

And his eyes were a rich hazel, filled with humor.

She looked down and she was definitely flying above the enraptured audience.

When she touched the dragon's nails, just to check, he laughed a deep dragon laugh.

She saw his array of sharp white teeth and the dark hole of his gullet. She had an instant to dread the direction of this trick, and to fear that she might be a disappearing lady.

Then there was another blinding shimmer of blue.

Cassie opened her eyes when she felt something solid beneath her feet. She was standing on the stage. Lorenzo, the nearly naked sexy guy, had his arm around her shoulders. The flames had died down to nothing again. His grip was firm and possessive, a clear message that she shouldn't move.

Not that she wanted to. It wasn't all bad being pressed against his strength. That simmering heat was rolling through Cassie, weakening her knees and making her keenly aware of the man who had her locked against his side. She could even see orange sparks dancing between them, vivid orange flames that seemed only to make her burn with lust.

It looked as if her skin were on fire.

Apparently, she was becoming delusional as well.

Of course, it had been a while since she'd been caught against the chest of an incredibly hot and charismatic man. Her awareness of him was a natural reaction.

Even though she'd never burned with a desire like this before.

His thumb was tracing a hypnotic circle against her shoulder, one that seemed to sear through her shirt. She was tempted to wrap herself around him, or rub herself against him, or otherwise surrender to a temptation that she wasn't used to feeling.

She had to get out of this theater before she did something she'd regret.

Lorenzo smiled at the audience, and his appeal was even more powerful at close range. Cassie wiggled a little to extricate herself from his embrace, but his grip tightened slightly.

Then Lorenzo looked down at Cassie and she saw the reflection of flames in his eyes. At least, it had to be a reflection, because otherwise there would have been flames burning in his pupils.

It had to be an illusion.

Cassie looked closer, trying to discern the trick.

"A man can wait a lifetime to meet a woman who kindles his desire," he murmured with a smile. His voice was rich and melodic, the kind of voice a woman could listen to all night long. "Surely love is the true trial by fire."

"Love is the true trial by fire," Cassie heard herself say. A part of her mind was incredulous that she had uttered any such garbage aloud.

On the other hand, it seemed inevitable.

Right.

Uh-oh.

The flames in Lorenzo's pupils danced higher. Another trick. One she could surely figure out. She leaned closer and he lifted his other hand, his fingertips touching her chin. His hand was warm, his caress gentle.

Cassie wanted more.

No, she burned for more.

"To surrender to the heat of the moment," Lorenzo said.

"To surrender to the heat of the moment," Cassie said, her gaze falling to his firm lips, then back to those amazing eyes again.

"Without regret."

"Without regret." These words left Cassie's lips like a sigh, a concession, a surrender to whatever he was going to do.

Lorenzo's eyes gleamed with mischief and the heat of desire redoubled, rolling through her body with urgent demand.

Then Lorenzo pulled her to her toes and kissed her.

Cassie heard the audience go wild. She heard the music soar and felt the curtain shut. She was sure she heard Stacy squeal.

But she was too busy returning Lorenzo's kiss to care. Pragmatic Cassie Redmond was overwhelmed by sensation for the first time in her life, and she didn't want to change one thing. Lorenzo's kiss was potent, both enticing and demanding, the kind of kiss that should close a show.

Or bring down the house.

Cassie slid her arms around Lorenzo's neck and kissed him back. She twined her fingers into his hair and pulled him closer, crushing herself against him. She heard Lorenzo's possessive growl, and she felt his reaction against her hip. His arm locked around her waist and his mouth slanted over hers to deepen the kiss. The sparks leapt high all around them and the audience seemed very, very far away.

She was more interested in the way Lorenzo's tongue danced with hers. Cassie was feeling impulsive and in need of some fun.

She was pretty sure she'd found it.

Chapter 3

Lorenzo was shocked, and it was a novel sensation. He'd been surprised by Ms. Practicality's question. Whether there was more to this human than met the eye, or whether she was so caught in the spell of his beguiling that she'd given him the perfect question was irrelevant. He had no idea what she knew about the *Pyr*, much less why she was interested, and he didn't care. Her query had given him the ideal way to close the show.

Spectacularly.

Always his favorite choice.

What shocked Lorenzo the most, though, was this woman's reaction to him. She'd witnessed his shift to dragon form and back again. She'd fingered his talon—no surprise, given her obvious skepticism—to check whether his dragon form was real. Yet she hadn't screamed. She hadn't run. She hadn't turned away from him in revulsion.

Far from it. She was no fainting damsel, and although he generally preferred meeker women—they were easier to leave behind when the time came—he was aroused by this woman's passion.

He'd expected—no, he'd *known*—that her reaction would be the complete opposite of what it was. Being wrong about this woman and his own reaction to her threw his game slightly.

In a most delicious way.

Erik would be livid that Lorenzo had broken the Covenant—that no *Pyr* should reveal himself to any human in both his human and dragon form—but Lorenzo would be only too happy to remind the leader of the *Pyr* that he had not actually sworn the Covenant. He couldn't be berated for breaking a pledge he hadn't made. Besides, he was consummating the firestorm, which was always a significant agenda issue for Erik.

That might take the spark out of the inevitable argument.

Lorenzo was ever so slightly troubled that he had shifted shape for the first time in centuries, and done so by choice, but he blamed that on the firestorm. The ends justified the means. He'd be back to normal in no time.

Lorenzo was doubly relieved that the woman had been so readily beguiled. She must have found him attractive, which made it so much easier for him to seduce her. A human could only truly be beguiled to do something he or she already had some yearning to do. Her surrender made the matter much simpler.

It was about time that his life became less complicated.

When she kissed him back with such ardor, his hopes for an entertaining interval were increased. He'd never expected her to have any passion. They couldn't extinguish the firestorm without surrendering to its demands, and Lorenzo had been afraid it might be a task.

Instead, it promised to be a delight.

After the curtain closed, Lorenzo swept the woman

into his arms and headed for his dressing room. He broke a kiss only to dismiss his assistants with a single lethal glance. They scurried out of sight, already knowing it was smarter to keep their thoughts to themselves.

Ms. Practicality, meanwhile, was pulling his head down for another soul-searing kiss. Her lips were swollen and red, and her face was flushed. The sparkle in her eyes and the hint of a smile was alluring. He smiled at her, then kissed her again. He kicked the door to his dressing room shut behind himself, locked it, and carried the woman to the bed in the back corner.

She looked more irresistible by the second.

There was no need for conversation. The firestorm's flames flickered between them, setting the space between their bodies alight with orange light. The radiance of those flames touched the woman's skin, gilding her cheeks, making her look more beautiful than he had expected.

He was enchanted by her.

Lorenzo rolled onto the bed, impatient to see the firestorm resolved, yet wanting to linger over the pleasure it promised. Once again, he was glad he had not skimped. This was no flimsy cot, but a queen-sized bed with a luxury mattress and sheets of finely woven cotton. It was stacked high with pillows and a wonderful duvet. He didn't sleep here often, but Lorenzo saw no reason to ever make do with second best.

The woman twisted in his arms and wrapped her legs around his waist. Even with her jeans and his swimsuit between them, he was well aware of the softness that denim hid. He braced himself over her and broke his kiss. She smiled up at him, her eyes sparkling. The flames of the firestorm licked and danced between them, sizzling his skin and coaxing his desire to an inferno.

"Wow," she said and he liked the sound. He'd noticed when she asked her question that her voice was low and sultry, unexpectedly so for a woman who looked so practical. At closer proximity, he could see that she was very pretty, her lashes a dark copper and her eyes a clear blue.

That voice could persuade him to linger.

That voice could persuade him to unravel all of her secrets.

Lorenzo had no time.

"No words today," he murmured, dropping a finger to her lips to silence her, then slid his fingertips along her jaw.

"But . . . ," she began, but Lorenzo didn't want to argue. He didn't care what tools he used to achieve the end he desired.

"But time is of the essence," he murmured, letting the flames light in his eyes, the flames that persuaded humans to believe.

"Essence," she echoed.

He could guess that she wasn't one to act on impulse. This was a faster seduction than she would have preferred.

But Lorenzo had no time to court her surrender.

And he already knew that she wanted him. He was just being expedient, not changing the inevitable result.

She stared at his eyes, apparently transfixed by the flames. Her lips parted in wonder, looking ripe and soft and tempting. Her ponytail had come loose and her hair was wavy and wild spread across the pillows. The sight of her reminded him of paintings of sirens and temptresses.

He was tempted to make more of this than simply the firestorm's satisfaction. He wanted her to have the best sex of her life. The firestorm might have drawn his eye to her, but now that he had looked, he wanted more than one quick interval.

Temptation, indeed.

Lorenzo coaxed the flames in his eyes to burn higher and her lips parted in awe as she stared.

"Feel the heat between us," he murmured, watching the firestorm's flames dance between her skin and his fingertips. To his surprise, she reached up and slid her own fingers over his shoulders. He swallowed at the demanding heat she sent through his body.

Maybe he wasn't the only one casting a spell.

He kissed her again, and she wrapped herself around him. The power of their kiss left him dizzy, and the insistent demand of her caressing hands prompted him to forget everything other than this woman.

He opened her blouse and was astonished to find that she wore a lacy bra of dark purple satin. The choice seemed out of character, making him wonder what else he hadn't imagined about this woman. Was there more to her than met the eye? He was tempted to believe it, but knew it would be foolish to become involved.

Instead, he let his admiration of her choice of lingerie show. He traced a fingertip along one edge as she blushed. She was slender, but her breasts were a generous feast. He would never have guessed that her jeans and practical shirt hid such ripe femininity, but she was as curvaceous as a goddess.

Maybe closer to being his kind of woman than he'd guessed.

Again, he was surprised.

"You are beautiful," he said, and meant it.

She might have protested, but he brushed a light kiss across her mouth. She sighed as the firestorm's flames danced between them.

Then she touched her tongue to his.

Lorenzo thought he would explode.

"Beautiful," he whispered into her ear, letting his fingers slide along her throat. She arched her back beneath his caress and he smiled at her loveliness. He slid his palm over her breast, loving how she caught her breath when he touched her taut nipple. "Exquisite," he added, then pinched that turgid nipple.

She gasped; then he kissed her again. He unfastened her jeans, discarding the boots and masculine clothing that hid her many charms. His fingertips told him that her panties matched the bra. And her skin was so fair—the contrast would be gorgeous.

Lorenzo had to see.

He sat up and surveyed the perfection of her lounging on his bed, the red-gold waves of her hair in disarray, the purple lingerie making her skin look like flawless ivory. He was astonished. He would never have guessed that such a gem was hidden by her armor.

She reached out, smiled, and hooked a finger into the waistband of his bathing suit. Lorenzo smiled, shed it, then returned to the bed. Her eyes glowed with anticipation as he took her in his arms again, and their kiss fired his blood even more. He removed her panties and caressed her, loving how she caught her breath at his first touch.

And after that, there was no time for conversation. The firestorm drove them to erotic heights, pushing them to satisfy each other over and over again. Lorenzo had never had such a coupling. Her passion challenged all of his assumptions about humans—and her unexpected laughter provoked a reaction deep within him that he would have preferred not to feel.

*   *   *

Hours later, Lorenzo stood beside the bed, watching the woman sleep as he dressed. He was both exhausted and yearning for more. He was physically sated, but still there was more he wanted to know about this woman. He couldn't reconcile her no-nonsense appearance with her luxurious taste in lingerie, her apparent pragmatism with her passion. She had surprised him more than once, which was a novelty to him.

He didn't even know her name.

He reminded himself that he didn't want to. Such curiosity was dangerous. More information could only lead to more entanglement between them. They'd done what had to be done. He would leave it at that.

He had beguiled her, Lorenzo reminded himself. Just because she'd found him attractive didn't mean that she'd intended to do anything about it, either today or any other day. He felt a twinge of guilt about his decision, but couldn't regret all that had happened between them.

That was when he realized he'd forgotten to feed the flames in his eyes after he'd been startled by the sight of her lingerie. Beguiling had gotten her into his bed—the seduction that had followed had been by mutual choice. Some other sorcery had unfolded between the two of them then, some other magic that had surprised him with its ardent heat.

He'd probably never see her again.

And even though that was exactly what he had thought he wanted, Lorenzo was disappointed by the prospect. Unlike most women, one interlude with this one hadn't been enough.

That hadn't happened to him since Caterina.

Which should have been warning enough.

Lorenzo stretched out one hand—hoping on some

level that he hadn't been thorough enough, knowing that he had. There was no flame between them any longer.

The spark was dead.

The firestorm was over.

Lorenzo would not be disappointed.

He sighed, even so.

He should be relieved. He should be glad that there would be nothing drawing him to this woman again. He told himself that the only good news was that he'd been smart enough to not fall under the firestorm's spell. He'd acted quickly, solved the issue, and now could push it—and the woman—from his thoughts. It was exactly what he wanted.

Even if he felt cheated.

Even if he felt once again the hope that Caterina's betrayal should have killed forever.

It wasn't smart to yearn.

And Lorenzo was smart.

Even if he had to remind himself—twice—of that.

Lorenzo took one backward glance from the threshold, unable to resist the sight of her, then left the theater.

Cassie awakened alone in Lorenzo's dressing room.

She was naked, her clothes folded neatly on a nearby chair. Her lingerie was on top. She certainly hadn't left her clothes that way—they'd been flung in every direction when she'd peeled them off. She had also been tucked into the bed by somebody and she could guess who it had been.

Why would that surprise her? Lorenzo had been a thoughtful lover.

A thorough one.

If one she hadn't planned on having. Cassie sat up in

a hurry and shoved a hand through her hair. She looked around once more, this time with alarm.

What the hell had happened here? Where was Stacy? How could Cassie have abandoned her? What time was it? How had she ended up being impulsive when she was normally cautious about sex?

Cassie felt as if an alien had taken possession of her body and mind. She *never* did things like this. She never would have willingly left Stacy alone.

On the other hand, Stacy had always insisted that she should have more fun.

When she stopped to think about it, Cassie felt pretty good about taking her friend's advice.

This interval with Lorenzo made her wonder whether she'd missed out on a whole range of experience. It had been, without a doubt, the best sex she'd ever had. Was that because it had been impulsive? She was both exhausted and stimulated. She'd been not only more impetuous than usual, but had felt more comfortable with her own body. She'd felt sexy. She'd felt powerful. And what they'd done to pleasure each other had been phenomenal.

Stacy was the one person who would understand a desire to be impulsive about sex. She'd probably congratulate Cassie on finally loosening up.

But still. She'd met her share of charmers in her time, and nobody but nobody had ever gotten her into bed on the first date.

Never mind *before* a first date.

The whole thing was surreal. There'd been that leaping spark between them, the one he'd launched in her direction over and over again. She had felt raw lust every time he'd stepped onto the stage. Again—Lorenzo was gorgeous, but Cassie dealt with gorgeous hunks all the time. None of them had ever had this effect on her.

Then there'd been the dragon snatching her up. The burning heat everywhere they touched, like little armies of flames, and the glow of fire on her skin. There had been those flames in Lorenzo's eyes.

Had they been a reflection?

How had he made her burn with desire?

Cassie didn't doubt that all women found him attractive and liked the eye candy he offered, but her reaction had been a bit vehement. How had he so entranced her?

Was it legal?

Or was he a hypnotist?

The scary part was that Cassie didn't regret a thing—well, except leaving Stacy alone. She didn't doubt that she'd do it all over again given the chance. Whatever it was that Lorenzo was serving in this theater, Cassie needed to get away from it and recover her senses.

Well, five of her senses were present and accounted for. He'd experimented with every one of them. It was her common sense that was AWOL.

Cassie got out of bed, intent on leaving right away.

She listened but couldn't hear anything outside the room. It might be soundproofed. (She hoped so, given the noises she'd made.) She also couldn't tell what time it was. There were no clocks in the dressing room, which struck her as an odd thing.

There was a connected half bathroom, which she made use of. She was amazed by her own reflection. She looked sparkly, which was a change from her usual world-weary expression. Younger. More vibrant.

Whatever Lorenzo had going on, he should bottle it and sell it.

On the other hand, he probably made enough money using it to enhance his show.

Just as Stacy had said, he was amazing.

He'd been amazing after the show, that was for sure.

Cassie laughed. She started to whistle as she dressed. She felt good. Really good. And that couldn't be all bad.

There was a soft rap at the door while she was tugging on her boots. One of the stage assistants smiled at her when she answered the door. "Good. You're awake," she said. "Will you be leaving now?"

It wasn't exactly subtle. Cassie flushed a bit, realizing that everyone backstage knew what had happened in the dressing room whether they'd overheard her enthusiasm or not. "What time is it?"

"Just after six." The woman fidgeted a little, in a hurry to get something done.

"Is there an evening show?"

"At ten," the woman answered with a nod. There was concern in her eyes. "Will you be going now?"

Cassie understood. "Is that what he likes . . . ?" She gestured when she left the question hanging, inviting the woman to share her name.

"Ursula." She smiled a little. "He's very concerned with his preparations, with ensuring that each show is perfect."

Cassie knew then that the woman feared she would be blamed if Cassie was still there. And she wasn't quite ready to face Lorenzo herself. What kind of power did he have that he could make her forget herself so easily? Could he do it to her again?

Besides, Stacy would be concerned.

"I've got to find my friend," Cassie said, to Ursula's obvious relief.

"He always arranges for a limo," she said. "Just ask at the concierge for Lorenzo's car."

Right. *Always.* Lorenzo did this so often that he had a system. That took a little of the afterglow away. Cassie had been right—she'd sat, literally, in the hot seat.

Well, she wasn't going to be just another one of the women seduced by Lorenzo and cast aside. And she wasn't going to let everyone in the place know that she was the woman who had gotten it from Lorenzo after the matinee today. "Right. Thanks again."

"Bye." Ursula smiled, her relief clear. "Take care."

Cassie started to head for the lobby, trying to convince herself that a nice dinner would set her to rights. Maybe a drink. Maybe three. Of course, she didn't need to lose any more inhibitions.

She stopped partway, belatedly deciding to be unobtrusive again. "Ursula, is there a back door?"

"Sure. Right this way." Ursula smiled and gestured.

A heavyset man smiled at Cassie as he opened the door, ushering her out of Lorenzo's little world.

Cassie heaved a sigh of relief when she stepped into the rear parking lot. The sky was beginning to darken and she could see a few stars coming out. The air was cooler too. Beside the stage door was a parking spot, labeled "Lorenzo." No surprise there.

The spot was empty, which worked for Cassie in a big way.

She darted down the back lane, scooting around Dumpsters and employee cars, feeling as if she was on her usual turf. She wasn't really surprised that the distance to her own hotel was shorter this way. She figured Stacy had headed back when Cassie had disappeared backstage. She walked quickly, refusing to name the source of her new optimism and energy.

Stacy was going to gloat, but Cassie was okay with that.

She was okay with pretty much everything at this moment in time.

Thanks to Lorenzo and his *Trial by Fire*.

Cassie decided that she really needed a drink.

Lorenzo parked his car, sliding to a halt in a flurry of red dust. He got out, locked and armed it by habit, then strode closer to the site of his upcoming feat. The sun was just setting, its orange light and the long shadows making the rock formations look eerie and exotic.

He should have been soothed by arriving here. That was why he had stopped on his way back to town.

But he was still edgy.

Where was the stupid crystal?

As was his practice when he felt agitated, Lorenzo reviewed the long list of things that he controlled—or which were turned to his advantage.

He liked the setting for his spectacle. It would occur at almost exactly this time of day. Lorenzo considered the striped sky with the rocks silhouetted against it and liked the visual effect. That view would make a stunning backdrop to his spectacle. Even on a small screen, it would be impressive.

He'd checked the weather again, and it was still supposed to be clear. Of course, it was usually clear in Nevada at this time of year, which was why he'd scheduled a June date, but still—having the weather on his side was good.

There were no snoops or paparazzi poking around the site. It was still a relative secret, which was good.

He forced himself to exhale. He'd gotten that last detail on the car modification fixed to his satisfaction, after all.

He wouldn't think about how much extra he'd paid for the mechanic's silence.

Or that he'd beguiled the man, just to guarantee his word was kept.

Preparations here at the site were going well. The foreman was excellent and his attention to detail was extreme. Lorenzo walked through the site again, reviewing a thousand details, and was pleased by their progress.

The equipment had arrived for lowering the car into the hole and looked impressive, just as he had ordered it. The chains were large, and powerful in appearance. It was all too big and too much. The stainless steel would all have to be polished again, right before the show, but the sun shining on the polished metal would look good. The hole was massive and deep. Impressive.

Lorenzo shook hands with the foreman and congratulated him on the near-completion of the job. He met with the security personnel, reviewing their duty roster, emphasizing that security must be complete.

Even after all that, Lorenzo was agitated.

Matters had been subdued at the house, which was good. His father had retired to his rooms, which meant one less confrontation for the day. The old man still hadn't packed, but they would argue about that later.

The employment agency, well aware of his needs, had sent a new couple as potential employees. Of course, no one knew that they'd soon be looking for employment again. Lorenzo made a mental note to ensure that they were compensated for their trouble. He had been pleased by the pair, especially as they'd been readily beguiled.

He'd satisfied the firestorm. He knew it wasn't burning anymore.

The preparations would be made for the evening show already. His assistants were excellent.

The incident with the woman and his dragon form should make for good publicity. Such coverage was always welcome before a big spectacle. If it didn't appear in the news media tonight, he'd leak it through his usual channels so it would make the morning news. He made a mental note to check.

The sex had been great.

Unexpectedly great. He could have closed his eyes and relived every moment of it, but Lorenzo didn't have time for such indulgences.

The crystal was still gone, but so far, no one was attempting to collect it—or demand a due for him losing it. Would his luck hold until Saturday?

Something else wasn't right.

Lorenzo reviewed his list again. He sat in the car and drummed his fingers on the steering wheel, listening to the satisfying thrum of the engine. And that was when he knew.

He sensed trouble approaching. He could smell the proximity of Erik Sorensson and knew that they would argue about the firestorm.

Of course. It was inevitable.

He hoped they wouldn't argue about the crystal.

Either way, they would argue on Lorenzo's terms.

Lorenzo hit the gas to leave the site of the scheduled spectacle. He loved how the engine roared and the car fishtailed in the red dust. It lunged for the road, the tires squealing as they gained traction on the asphalt. He glanced up and grinned, barely discerning the distant silhouette of a pewter dragon.

Lorenzo floored the accelerator and the car raced toward the distant lights of Vegas.

If Erik wanted to give him shit, he could work for it.
And he could do it on Lorenzo's turf.

Cassie was relieved to step into the air-conditioned comfort of the hotel where she and Stacy were staying. She was even more glad to spot Stacy perched on a stool at the bar in the lobby. Her friend had a large pink drink in front of her, complete with paper umbrella, and was flirting with a handsome stranger.

No wonder she looked so happy. This guy's attention was exactly what Stacy needed.

Never mind that the drink matched her shoes. That kind of detail always put Stacy in a good mood. Maybe it hadn't worked out so badly that Cassie had been a crappy friend.

Cassie debated the merit of just going up to the room and leaving the pair alone, but Stacy spotted her and waved. Her smile got wider and brighter.

"There you are!" she said, jumping from her stool to give Cassie a hug. "Isn't he divine?" she whispered, then stepped back, continuing in a normal tone. "Cassie, this is Jean-Pierre. He's visiting from Paris. Jean-Pierre, my friend Cassie."

"Pleased to meet you," Jean-Pierre said, bending to kiss the back of Cassie's hand. Stacy rolled her eyes and fanned herself when he couldn't see her face. Cassie fought her laughter, trying to turn it into a polite smile as Jean-Pierre straightened. "You must call me JP, as all my American friends do."

Cassie had a strange and sudden dislike of JP, although she couldn't say why. He was handsome and he was charming, but something felt off.

On the other hand, her judgment was seriously questionable on this day.

It might be the heat.

It might be that she was feeling protective of Stacy, who did have terrible taste in guys.

Not that Cassie was picking any long-term players herself.

"Sorry . . . ," Cassie started to say, but Stacy just grinned at her.

"It's easy to get separated here," she said breezily, then winked when JP looked away. It was clear that Stacy had no hard feelings, even if Cassie felt guilty.

She still couldn't figure out what had made her act that way.

"Cassie's a photographer," Stacy said, then hopped back on to her seat.

"Really?" JP was being polite. Cassie knew it. He wasn't interested in her, and that was just fine. He smiled at Stacy and Stacy smiled back.

"She's really good at it," Stacy said, and Cassie saw JP's flicker of annoyance. Maybe he'd rather they talked about him.

Well, she knew how to remove the spotlight from herself.

"'Paparazzi' is maybe a better term for photographers like me," Cassie said. "It's not like I have shows in galleries or anything." She flagged the bartender and ordered herself a glass of wine.

Surprisingly, her attempt to deflect attention from herself only had JP turning toward her with interest.

"So, you must know a lot of celebrities," he said.

"You could say that." Cassie smiled. "Some throw rocks at my Jeep when they see it."

His eyes sparkled. For a second, it looked like malice, not humor. But she must have been mistaken. "Do they ever hit it?"

"Not often, but I had to get the windshield replaced last month."

"And it doesn't bother you, taking pictures of people who don't want to be photographed?"

Ah, so this was his issue.

Cassie was used to this question, and had made her peace with the concept a long time ago. "It comes with the territory, don't you think? Some people think that to be famous, they need to be in the news all the time. They're the stars who actively cultivate every kind of exposure. I don't think it's reasonable for them to expect to be able to turn that on and off to suit their own convenience. You go around lighting fires, you're going to get burned."

It was an unfortunate choice of analogy, one that reminded her of where she and Stacy had been that afternoon.

"But those who don't look for the exposure?" JP persisted.

"They want to be left alone." Cassie shrugged. "I usually leave them alone."

"Other photographers don't, though," Stacy said.

JP nodded. "I've seen them, at Cannes. It's quite vulgar how aggressive they can be."

Cassie heard the judgment in his tone and didn't blame him for it. The pursuit of a coveted shot—and the money it would pay—could get ugly. "Sure. There's often more money offered for shots of reclusive celebrities." Cassie smiled and firmly tried to close the subject. "I work freelance. I choose my own jobs. We all do. I can't answer for every other photographer and his or her choices. I try to make choices I can live with."

Which was exactly what she had done recently, which was the core of the problem. That, however, wasn't JP's business.

Stacy was watching Cassie, probably having guessed something from her friend's tone, but Cassie looked away. She wasn't ready to talk about her crisis of faith yet.

And certainly not in front of JP.

The conversation died as the waitress brought Cassie's wine. She thought she might just disappear with it, so these two could get back to their private conversation.

"And so?" Stacy prompted, leaning closer to Cassie. "Did he tell you what you wanted to know?"

"Who?" JP asked.

Stacy told the story when Cassie might have swept it aside. "Cassie asked the illusionist Lorenzo where she could find one of those dragon shape shifters that have been mentioned on TV." She nodded with excitement and sipped her drink. "It was amazing."

JP swallowed a smile, his eyes twinkling as he lifted his drink to his lips. Cassie interpreted that as skepticism and smiled at him. "I know," she said. "It's crazy. The whole dragon shape-shifter gig has to be a trick, but Lorenzo pulled a great one."

JP put down his glass. "I don't understand."

"His answer was 'Right here!'" Stacy contributed, flinging her hands up in an echo of Lorenzo's move. Fortunately, she'd already put down the pink drink. "Then he turned into a dragon and flew over the crowd. It was incredible!"

"It was an illusion," Cassie said. "I'm sure he does it every night and twice on Wednesdays." She took a sip of her wine, hoping Stacy didn't feel compelled to share the rest of what had happened.

JP frowned. "But I don't understand," he said. "I saw his show the other night. He didn't turn into a dragon."

"It was the big finish," Stacy insisted. "After he got out of that tank, then answered three questions."

JP shook his head. "No. He disappeared in a pillar of starlight. That was the big finish. There was no dragon. I would have remembered that."

No dragon?

Cassie and Stacy exchanged a glance. "Maybe it was an addition to the show," Cassie suggested, sensing that wasn't the answer.

"A new trick," Stacy agreed with a nod. "We were just the first to see it."

"Do you think so?" JP asked. "I thought these shows ran for years, essentially the same, then were renamed or even relocated when the performance changed."

He was right. Cassie thought about the magnitude of the illusion and couldn't imagine that it would just be added into the act without fanfare. Lorenzo seemed to have a flair for publicity.

"Ah, look at the time. No wonder I'm hungry. Would you ladies join me for dinner?" JP asked, his gaze fixed upon Stacy.

Cassie got the message and declined his invitation, but Stacy accepted with a smile. There was no sign of the waitress, so Cassie said she'd stay to finish her wine. JP gave her some cash to cover the bill for all of their drinks, plus a nice tip.

He wasn't cheap, which was a good change for Stacy.

Stacy tucked her arm into JP's elbow as they walked away and Cassie watched him lean closer, put his hand over hers, say something that made her smile. And maybe he was a bit of a gentleman, too. Stacy could use a bit of that.

Stacy gave Cassie a fingertip wave and smiled; then they were lost in the throng.

Maybe Cassie had judged him too quickly.

She sipped her wine and wondered some more about the dragon.

The obvious conclusion was insane. There had to be another logical explanation.

And Cassie would find it.

Chapter 4

"Another round?" the waitress asked, startling Cassie.

"No, thanks. I'll settle up." Cassie watched the woman as she produced the tab. She paid the bill, appreciating JP's math skills again.

"Thanks!" The waitress smiled and started to turn away.

Cassie had an idea. She called after the waitress. "By the way, have you seen Lorenzo's show, the *Trial by Fire*?"

"Several times," the woman acknowledged, her smile genuine. "It's fabulous. My kids want to go all the time. We've seen it maybe eight times this year, whenever I manage to snag some comps." She winked. "Funny, but I don't mind going either, given the view after that water tank trick." She smiled, then scanned her section.

"That and the dragon trick," Cassie said.

The waitress glanced back at her in surprise. "What dragon trick?"

"When he turns into a dragon, right at the end."

The waitress frowned. "Are you talking about Lorenzo's show, the *Trial by Fire*?"

Cassie nodded, her excitement rising. "We just saw it this afternoon and he turned into a dragon at the end of the questions. It was incredible."

"No kidding." The waitress pursed her lips. "Well, that's funny. I can't imagine that he'd add a new illusion without advertising it, much less that he'd do it right now."

"Right now?"

"Lorenzo has that big spectacle coming up on the weekend." The waitress rolled her eyes as Cassie recalled Stacy's brochure. "He's going to be buried alive in his car for a month. My kids are beside themselves with anticipation. There was *no* chance of our watching it on HBO—even though the tickets cost me the earth and I had to seriously negotiate for a Saturday off." A patron at a nearby table raised a hand and she flashed one last smile at Cassie. "Gotta get back to it."

She left Cassie, moving toward the patron with a smile.

Interesting. The dragon trick *was* new. Had it been in response to her question? But how could he have prepared for it, if it had been done just by chance? How had he done it anyway?

It had to be a new trick, maybe one he'd been testing out for the first time today. That was the only thing that made sense.

Cassie finished her wine and put the empty glass on the bar. The obvious way to find out whether Lorenzo had added a new illusion or whether it had been a one-off was to go to the evening show.

Even though she didn't want to see him again.

No, this was pure research. The resolution of an intellectual question. Solving a puzzle, hunting down something that didn't add up. This was completely characteristic of her.

Even if her pulse was leaping.

She'd go up to the room, shower and change, grab something to eat, then head back for the evening show. It would be sold out, like the other performances this week, but maybe Ursula would let her into the theater.

Lorenzo would never even need to know that she was there.

Besides, if he repeated the trick, images of the show might satisfy that editor's craving for photos of the *Pyr*. It wasn't quite what she wanted, but that didn't mean she wouldn't pay for them anyway. If dragons were hot, dragon shots would sell to someone.

Cassie decided to buy a decent camera before the show.

Just in case.

She'd better pick up a present for Ursula, to smooth her own entry into the theater. She congratulated herself as she left the bar, glad to find her usual workaholic spark back in play. Maybe a little fun had been all she needed to reenergize. Maybe she'd been making too much of that troublesome incident. Maybe Wade hadn't been right about an inevitable crisis of faith.

Cassie strode toward the elevators, telling herself that her rising sense of anticipation had nothing to do with the prospect of seeing her passionate lover again.

Even she knew a lie when she heard one.

"I don't have time to discuss this with you," Lorenzo told Erik.

The leader of the *Pyr* didn't look inclined to leave Lorenzo's dressing room. In fact, Erik appeared to be supremely pissed off. Given that he was characteristically grim, principled, and inclined to irritation, that wasn't much of a surprise.

Lorenzo was pretty sure that Erik hadn't liked him choosing the venue, or the fact that Ursula had met him in the lobby and escorted him to the dressing room. Like Lorenzo, Erik preferred to keep the element of surprise on his own side.

Lorenzo wasn't happy with the situation himself, but he hid his reaction. He had no idea how much Erik knew or suspected about flashfire, but he could guess what the leader of the *Pyr* would think about it. Lorenzo didn't intend to share any information.

His dressing room was filled with the woman's scent, which distracted him mightily. It took considerable effort to think of anything other than the silk of her skin beneath his hands and the way her lips parted in surprise.

He wanted to surprise her again.

He wanted to repeat that particular performance.

And the realization was killing his composure.

"I'm not going to simply forget about this, Lorenzo," Erik insisted. "I've been patient, but I need to you to rejoin the *Pyr*. I need every talon . . ."

"Rejoin?" Lorenzo scoffed. "I've never been part of your team."

Erik's eyes flashed. "You're not *Slayer*."

"I don't play on anyone's team. Period." Saturday could not come soon enough.

"You must!" Erik became more agitated. "We are in the midst of the final reckoning with the *Slayers* . . ."

"Blah blah blah. It's always a crisis." Lorenzo eyed the other *Pyr's* reflection in the mirror and forced a smile. "You need to get out more," he suggested, calmly fastening the front of his white shirt. "Find some entertainment. Enjoy life. You're in the perfect place for such an endeavor."

Erik's lips tightened. "There is a firestorm, and it is my responsibility . . ."

"There is no firestorm," Lorenzo corrected in that same mild tone. He made a show of checking his reflection as if unconcerned with Erik's presence. He could use a bit more color, he decided. It had been so busy that he hadn't had time to bask in the sun this week, and he could see that his tan was starting to fade.

He was livid that Erik would dare to come to the theater and challenge him. Lorenzo answered to no one, man or *Pyr*, and the one individual who should have understood that was Erik. Lorenzo *invited* Erik when he wanted to talk to him, and not one minute before. And he didn't want to talk to Erik now. Lorenzo took a steadying breath and forced the light of anger out of his eyes.

The less Erik knew of his true feelings, the better. He must not even think about flashfire lest Erik catch wind of Lorenzo's real intent.

Lorenzo, fortunately, could feign indifference better than most.

"Of course there is a firestorm," Erik argued with impatience. He started to pace the width of the room, always a sign of a pending lecture. His British accent was stronger, too, which meant he was even more annoyed than he looked. "It was launched by the eclipse earlier today and I followed its heat to you. You are having a firestorm, whether you like it or not."

"No, I'm not," Lorenzo said calmly.

Erik's eyes flashed. "You don't have a choice in the matter. . . ."

"The firestorm is sated," Lorenzo said, interrupting him. He gestured to the unmade bed, then picked up his tie. "She was most enchanting." He examined the tie, as if it were fascinating.

He was actually recalling the sight of her.

In that purple lingerie.

The memory stirred him more than would have been ideal. Far more. He always forgot women as soon as he had them. Why did he keep thinking about this one? Why was he wondering what lingerie she was wearing now? Why was he tempted to find her and seduce her again? Why hadn't he learned his lesson?

Why did he have to endure this complication now?

Erik opened his mouth and closed it again. He looked at the bed, then at Lorenzo, his displeasure clear. "You have already satisfied it? It's only hours since it sparked."

"I thought you'd be pleased," Lorenzo said coolly, then chided the older *Pyr*. "Actually, I thought you'd already know. Are you losing your edge?" It amused him to remind Erik of his connection with all of the *Pyr*, right before Lorenzo and the flashfire severed that connection.

A charged silence was his only reply.

Lorenzo smiled at his reflection, exuding a calm he didn't feel. The knot of his tie didn't come out as neatly as he wanted, so he unfurled the tie and started over. Lorenzo wished that hadn't happened—it was random chance, but made it look as if he were rattled. He knew Erik would notice.

His game wasn't slipping that badly.

Not quite.

Even if he couldn't stop thinking of the contrast between the woman's luxurious, feminine lingerie and her practical, easy-to-overlook clothing. Which was the real woman? The hedonist or the pragmatist? Which was the illusion? Which was the truth?

What was her name?

Why did he want to know so badly?

Erik folded his arms across his chest and leaned against the doorframe. "Why would I be pleased?"

Just as anticipated, Erik's tone had changed. Instead of being confrontational, he was composed, curious. Lorenzo stifled his annoyance. Erik *had* noticed Lorenzo's agitation, which meant that the illusion was not perfect. Lorenzo turned from the mirror to confront the man who had once been his friend.

"It always pleases you when a firestorm is satisfied," he said, his tone challenging.

"True enough. But that was a quick seduction, even for you." There was a taunt in Erik's tone and Lorenzo chose to take the bait.

"I beguiled her. Of course." He smiled as Erik inhaled sharply. So he had still managed to needle the leader of the *Pyr*. He turned back to the mirror and adjusted the length of his tie, feeling more in control of the situation. He could hear the audience filing into the theater and needed his composure. "It was a question of expediency."

Erik arched a brow. He flicked a glance to the door, then switched to old-speak. *"Does she know there will be a child?"*

Always concerned with discretion and the long-term view. Always convinced of the *Pyr* mythology, which Lorenzo thought was a lot of wishful thinking.

Erik's problem was that he was risk-averse.

While Lorenzo thrived on risk.

Lorenzo snorted, then spoke aloud. He would not resort to the old-speak of the *Pyr*. With any luck, sating the firestorm meant that he could forget the most tedious details of his dragon nature. "We had better things to do than chitchat."

This time, Lorenzo did a perfect job of knotting the tie.

"Not all women are like Caterina," Erik continued in old-speak.

Lorenzo refused to answer in kind. Erik had found a nerve, though, and Lorenzo fought to hide his reaction. He kept his tone level. "But some are."

"But . . ."

"I don't believe the stories. Save them for your children."

"You're wrong . . ."

Lorenzo put on his tuxedo jacket, then straightened the lapels with a tug. He smiled at Erik. "If so, you've always been fond of responsibility. You can assume this one."

Erik's eyes flashed.

Lorenzo swirled his cape over his shoulders and fastened it, well aware of the expectant murmur of the gathering crowd. He picked up his top hat, rapping its brim against his other palm.

It irked him that he'd had no time to make his usual preparations, to check and double-check, but he'd have to make do.

"But . . . ," Erik began to protest.

"But I have other obligations in this moment," Lorenzo said. He indicated the door that Erik was blocking. "If you will excuse me, I have a performance to deliver."

Erik didn't move.

His resistance was infuriating.

For a moment, Lorenzo let the mask slip. He couldn't help it. He'd been pushed too far. For one heartbeat, he showed Erik the simmering heat of his anger. He let the fury rise to his eyes and blaze there.

Just one glare had the leader of the *Pyr* stepping aside.

"You are more committed than you realize," Erik

murmured in old-speak as Lorenzo stepped past him. *"She has snared you."*

The words echoed in Lorenzo's thoughts, mingling with his own, resonating with the clarity of truth.

No. He would not permit this to be true.

Lorenzo halted beside Erik and hissed his reply. "You see only what you wish to see," he said, holding Erik's gaze.

Erik smiled, his confidence unshaken. *"Caterina . . . ,"* he began.

". . . did me a favor," Lorenzo concluded flatly. He felt his nostrils flare, for he had been provoked and his performance had been compromised.

He had no time for this meddling.

"I thought a firestorm would bring you back into the fold," Erik said, and Lorenzo remembered why he'd come. *"I can use every talon . . ."*

Lorenzo laughed at the very idea. He wished he would be able to see Erik's expression on Saturday when Lorenzo completely disappeared from his awareness.

Erik fell silent. Was he suspicious?

"Ursula will see you out," Lorenzo said tersely. "No one is permitted backstage during the show, except my assistants. I ask you to respect that much, at least." He treated Erik to one last glare, then strode into the wings.

He knew that Erik did not move. He struggled against his anger at that. He had a performance to deliver. Lorenzo took a deep, steadying breath.

It didn't help.

It was her scent, he decided as he took his place on the stage. He felt surrounded by her scent, as if he had been dipped in it, as if he would never be able to remove it from his skin. It had thrown him off balance in the dressing room, had been strong enough to fill his mind with images of their afternoon interlude, and persuasive enough to tempt him to sample again the pleasure they'd shared. That scent had followed Lorenzo from the dressing room with unexpected strength, as if she would haunt him forevermore.

No.

That wasn't it.

A shiver slipped over his skin as he realized the truth.

Lorenzo could smell the woman's scent because she was *back*.

She'd followed him. She'd returned. And Erik's mood had changed because he had caught a whiff of her arrival. He'd known that she was backstage and he'd deliberately steered the conversation, ensuring that the woman would hear that she had been beguiled.

Lorenzo had condemned himself with his own words.

The trickster had been tricked.

Lorenzo pivoted from his mark on the stage and glared into the wings. He caught a glimpse of Erik's confident smile, that old dragon more than happy to see Lorenzo's game compromised by the firestorm.

Erik hadn't left, as instructed, which was audacious enough, never mind that the woman was backstage as well. Every principle that Lorenzo held dear was compromised.

And he would be the one to pay the price.

Rage rolled through Lorenzo. Erik had no idea what was at stake. He was playing with fire, all for the sake of the cursed firestorm and his precious *Pyr* team.

Lorenzo would not let chance ruin his plans.

He couldn't see the woman, although he looked for her. He could certainly recognize her scent. His body betrayed him then, the pervasive power of her presence making his imagination run riot. There were so many things they hadn't yet done, so many possibilities yet to explore. They could part sweetly.

After another interval in the dressing room.

The prospect inflamed him, which was exactly what he didn't need in this moment when concentration was critical.

He could have spit sparks at Erik.

Or at her. He wasn't truly surprised that she had come back—actually, he was flattered and excited—but he sensed that she was backstage. How had she managed that? Why hadn't he noticed her arrival? What did she really want from him? Was Erik intent upon telling her the truth?

That *Pyr* smiled, serenely content with whatever he had done.

The curtains rose and parted, and there was no time for such distractions. Lorenzo turned a confident smile on the gathered audience. As he bowed, he said a small silent prayer that he could perform well under pressure.

With the knowledge that she was watching.

Probably composing her accusations.

He simmered. He fumed. He seethed.

Then he pushed everything out of his mind except his show and went to work.

Perfection seemed a lofty goal on this night, but Lorenzo was still going to reach for it.

There was nothing else he could do.

For the moment.

Turned out Ursula loved French perfume. Cassie was backstage in no time at all.

The bottle of Scotch for the burly doorman hadn't hurt, either.

The guy with the British accent was watching Lorenzo

from the wings, his arms folded across his chest. He wore a black leather jacket, black jeans, and black Blundstone boots. The dark clothes provided a striking contrast to the silver hair at his temples. He had a slim, athletic build, but Cassie couldn't have guessed his age. Although his posture was casual, Cassie sensed the tension in him.

And she'd overheard the argument.

She didn't want to surprise him, but she had questions too.

Lots of them.

"What's beguiling?" Cassie asked in an undertone as she quietly took a place beside him.

The stranger didn't glance her way and he wasn't startled. She realized that he'd known she was there.

For how long?

He answered in a similarly low tone, his gaze locked on Lorenzo. "It's a kind of hypnosis, one particularly effective on humans."

So that was why she'd acted like someone else. She'd been hypnotized by Lorenzo. He'd used a trick to make her fall into bed with him. It explained everything.

Except how much she'd enjoyed it.

And how she'd felt as if she'd been set free of her inhibitions.

And how good she'd felt afterward.

Now she just felt stupid.

Like a pawn.

And that made her angry.

"Flames in the pupils of his eyes," she guessed, forcing her voice to remain low.

The man nodded once.

"It's a great illusion." One that must get him laid all the time. Cassie seethed. "How does he do it?"

"It's no illusion," the man said flatly. "It's an ability of our kind." Cassie stared at him, unable to compute his meaning. *Our kind?* What kind? Was he an illusionist, too?

The man nodded toward Lorenzo. "He is very good."

Cassie didn't know whether he was talking about Lorenzo's skill with beguiling or with the current illusion on the stage. She folded her arms across her chest, echoing the man's posture. She reminded herself to take advantage of this opportunity to gather information.

Why had this guy even challenged Lorenzo? What would he care about his amorous adventures? She had a feeling that his presence wasn't common—otherwise, Lorenzo wouldn't have been so annoyed to find him here.

How long had this man known of her presence?

Had the argument been prompted for her benefit?

Cassie tried to pick the best question. "What's a firestorm?"

"You should take that up with Lorenzo."

Wrong question.

"You knew I was listening," she guessed and was rewarded by a quick sidelong smile.

Right direction.

"You tricked him," she said. "Why?"

"It was for his own good."

This guy's answers didn't exactly make things crystal clear.

"How so?"

"Lorenzo was being irresponsible. I dislike that."

Which didn't answer the question as to why this man should be entitled to straighten out Lorenzo. Was there a code of ethics among magicians? Cassie couldn't imagine Lorenzo answering to anyone, but he seemed to answer to this guy. Sort of. There had to be a reason.

"You're his boss?"

The man shook his head. "No."

Cassie glanced at the theater and wondered who paid for it, and for the fancy car. "Loan shark?"

He shook his head again, flicking her an assessing glance. "No."

"Big brother?"

Again there was that mysterious fleeting smile. "Something like that."

"I don't see the resemblance."

His smile lingered this time. "Perhaps it's better that way."

Cassie frowned. The stage was in flames now, just as it had been earlier. From this angle, though, she could see that the flames ran in lines, several feet of wood between each one. There were gaps in the stage flooring, gaps with gas burners embedded in them.

Next question. Cassie couldn't pick just one.

Her companion turned away from the stage abruptly, his sleeve brushing against hers as he moved. "If you will excuse me," he said, polite to a fault. His eyes glittered in a way that made her think of the dragon Lorenzo had become, and his cool smile made her shiver. He looked dangerous and unpredictable.

Still, she had more questions and he was most likely to provide answers, given present company. Cassie trailed behind him. "You're leaving? Just like that?"

"Yes." He had his hand on the door. The burly doorman hovered in the shadows, pretending not to see. "I've done what needed to be done. The rest is up to you." The stranger opened the door, admitting a waft of night air, then turned back to her, eyes gleaming. "Good luck."

That sounded ominous.

Cassie looked back at the stage, just as the house

erupted in applause. She glanced at the crowd, then at Lorenzo with the large snake. When she turned back to the stranger, there was no sign of him.

As if he'd never been.

He'd wished her luck. Cassie didn't believe much in luck. She preferred to make her own luck. She preferred to have a plan, to do the footwork and align the variables and see what evolved naturally from her efforts.

Okay. Time for a plan.

Her fingers slipped along the edge of the new digital camera in her pocket. She still needed to know whether Lorenzo had a new illusion in turning into a dragon. She still wanted to know how he made those sparks leap between them. She still needed to check out the hot seat and compare the two shows.

But given his power to seduce her at will and forget her own principles, it would be better to do that from another vantage point. Cassie didn't want to be found very easily by this dangerously persuasive man.

Who could hypnotize her into bed with a sizzling glance.

Even if the prospect of doing it with him again made her tingle.

She knew from the lethal look Lorenzo cast into the wings that he'd realized she was there.

Cassie wasn't a gambler, but she'd have bet every dollar she possessed that Lorenzo was going to want to talk to her, right after the show.

And she wasn't ready to talk to him.

Not yet.

The show went well enough. It wasn't perfect, but the flaws would be imperceptible to anyone other than Lorenzo. The fact that he had been less smooth than usual rankled, but it was done and the crowd was happy. He stood before them in his swimsuit and bowed, his sodden prop tux dripping from his hand.

Where was the woman? Her scent muddled his thoughts. Her presence made his attention stray from the business at hand. What gave her such power over him? Erik was gone, which was a relief, but she was still in the theater.

No longer backstage.

Where had she gone?

He'd overheard their conversation, of course, given his sharp hearing, although Lorenzo would have preferred to have not had the distraction. What would she do with the information Erik had compelled him to reveal?

More important, what kind of lingerie was she wearing now?

Was it possible that the firestorm awakened a hunger that took more than one interval to satisfy? Lorenzo was starting to believe that it did. His curiosity about the woman was not a good sign.

A distraction.

An obstacle to perfection.

A problem he *still* had to resolve.

It didn't help that in his mind's eye, he could see Caterina in that last moment, the truth finally clear in her eyes.

Diavolo. That's what she had called him.

Right before she revealed him. He should never forget it.

Especially as the woman who had sparked his firestorm hadn't been surprised that he'd shifted to dragon form. Did she already know his truth? Was that why she'd returned? Lorenzo was keenly aware that a woman had betrayed him before, nearly costing him his life, and that it could happen very easily once again.

It wasn't a reassuring thought.

Cassie didn't get it. She watched the show from a seat at the edge in the second to last row, the best Ursula had been able to arrange for her. She hunkered down low, hoping Lorenzo wouldn't see or recognize her. She'd slipped into the seat during a dark phase in the show.

But she was confused. There were no sparks leaping from Lorenzo's fingertips.

Not one. Not during the entire show. That array of sparks that he'd launched at her and toyed with, bouncing it between his hands, was completely missing from this show.

And apparently there was no hot seat. An attractive brunette sat in the seat Cassie had occupied earlier, practically drooling as she watched Lorenzo, but he didn't even glance her way.

Why had the show been different earlier?

Firestorm. What did that word imply? Did it have something to do with those flames? Lorenzo had used the word.

What did it mean?

The show was impressive, as it had been before, and Lorenzo was every bit as elegant and gorgeous as he had been earlier. She certainly still thought he was a prime specimen. But there was another difference. Cassie didn't feel that simmering heat beneath her skin. She didn't yearn and burn with desire. She didn't want Lorenzo with every fiber of her being.

Was that because he'd had what he wanted of her?

She remembered those flames in Lorenzo's eyes. He'd hypnotized her with them, then seduced her. "Beguiled" was the word the stranger had used, and it certainly described the way she had felt. Enchanted. Dazzled.

And not, if she were honest with herself, entirely unwilling to surrender.

But she'd felt that burning desire as soon as the first spark had danced between them, and that had been the moment he'd been revealed on the stage. That had been long before she'd seen the flames in his eyes.

Way before the dragon bit.

Was it all about proximity?

Cassie didn't think so. There was something else going on.

She couldn't help remembering what the stranger had said.

An ability of our kind.

What kind?

Cassie had a bad feeling about that comment. The obvious conclusion—the insane conclusion—was that they were both of the dragon shape shifting kind, of the *Pyr* that Melissa Smith had profiled on her show.

The very idea made Cassie squirm.

But what if Lorenzo had answered her question honestly? He'd said "Right here!" then became a dragon, after all. She nibbled her lip and thought about that weird blue shimmer that had surrounded his body.

What if that *was* the truth?

The idea defied probability. It spat in the eye of logic. It challenged everything she knew to be true in the world. There could not truly be dragon shape shifting men. Cassie knew that, in her heart and in her mind.

Even if bunches of people did believe in them.

Even if Melissa Smith had them on her television show.

Even if one of them was on YouTube.

She sat in the theater and wrestled with the improbability of it all. If she was understanding the guy in black correctly, that would mean that she had met two dragon shape shifters within hours. There was a coincidence that blew the probabilities right out of the water.

Or confirmed the theory. Wouldn't it be reasonable that they would know each other? Maybe hang out together? Argue?

Cassie watched Lorenzo perform and she wondered. What other explanation could there possibly be? How could he have pulled off such an illusion?

What if Lorenzo's changing to a dragon hadn't been a trick? What if he was a *Pyr*?

How could she find out for sure?

Cassie held her breath moments later when Lorenzo took the third question from the audience, certain he would end the show the same way.

But there was no dragon.

Just as JP had said, Lorenzo took his final bow, then disappeared into a pillar of starlight. The flames in the wall sconces leapt high; then the house lights came up.

The audience was on its feet, clapping wildly.

The show was over.

The encore, in fact, encouraged her that her skepticism was right. She didn't understand how the pillar of starlight trick worked either. Just because she was ignorant about illusions didn't make Lorenzo a dragon shape shifter.

She needed more information about magic tricks—or about one in particular—but she already knew that illusionists were proprietary about their secrets.

One thing was for sure. Watching Lorenzo made her want him all over again. There might not be flames, and she might not have quite such a vehement desire, but the man had a potent effect on her.

One that messed with her usual clear thinking.

Cassie ducked out of the theater and cut through the lobby of the hotel, snagging a cab and heading directly back to her hotel. Lorenzo didn't know where she was staying. He'd never find her again in this crazy town. She had time to regroup and make a plan.

All roads led to Lorenzo, whether she wanted more sex or more info about illusions. Cassie wanted to confront Lorenzo on her own terms, with a plan.

Because the trick was going to be getting any information out of him while keeping her panties on.

Cassie was crossing the lobby of her hotel when someone tapped her on the shoulder.

To her surprise it was JP.

And he looked to be in a state.

"I am so relieved to have found you," JP said, his agitation clear. He was far less smooth than he had been earlier.

There was no sign of Stacy. Had she found someone more fun? "Why? What's wrong?"

JP passed a hand over his brow. "Stacy became ill in the restaurant." Cassie was immediately concerned. "I think it was the shrimp. She went back to your room."

Cassie turned to stride toward the elevators. JP matched her pace. His concern was palpable. "I've tried to call her, but she's not answering the phone."

"Don't worry," Cassie said, hoping to reassure him. "I'm on my way upstairs myself. I'll check on her."

His grip tightened on her elbow. "And you'll let me know that she's okay? I feel horrible. I recommended that she try the shrimp." He shoved a hand through his hair, which made him look disheveled and very cute.

There was no mistaking his distress, though, and Cassie found herself liking him more than earlier. "It's not your fault," she said.

"I had them last night and they were marvelous, but now I feel responsible." JP forced a thin smile. "I am sorry to trouble you, but I could not bear for her to be sick because of my suggestion."

Cassie hit the button for the elevator.

"Why don't I let you know." Cassie rummaged in her pocket for a scrap of paper. She only had the brochure for Lorenzo's show that Stacy had given her earlier. "Just give me your cell phone number. . . ."

"I haven't got a cell phone," JP said, then corrected himself. "Actually, I have one, but it doesn't work in America." His smile was rueful. "A miscalculation on my part."

"But you said you tried to call her."

"From the house phone."

Of course. "Okay." Cassie went for a backup plan. "Why don't I meet you down here in ten minutes or so? I'll check on her, then come back and tell you what's going on." She smiled for him. "She's probably just fallen asleep. If she's not feeling well, that would be the best, anyway."

"I hope so!" The prospect seemed to encourage him. JP surveyed the lobby. "How about there, in the bar, where we met earlier?"

"No problem." Cassie tugged out her room key. "I'll see you in a few minutes. Don't worry," she added to reassure him. "Maybe you should have a drink while you wait. Calm your nerves."

"A glass of wine, perhaps." JP smiled then and took a deep breath. "I am sure you're right, but I'll be glad to know for certain." He waited with her, hovering by her side until the elevator came and she stepped inside.

JP was still standing there, watching, when the doors slid closed. Worry lined his brow and there was tension in the line of his shoulders. For all that, he was one attractive man.

Maybe Stacy had found a keeper.

What Cassie didn't see was JP taking a seat in the bar after she'd gone upstairs. He glanced around, then reached into his pocket. He removed a silver vial, the exterior covered with strange markings.

He rolled it in his hand, deliberately recalling Chen's precise directions. Cassie would meet him here shortly. The fact was that wherever Cassie was, Lorenzo would inevitably follow.

And then he'd smell this.

Which would open the minds of both of them to *possibilities*.

JP tipped out a pinch of the dark powder within, then capped the vial tightly. He blew the dark dust off his palm into the air.

It twinkled, dissolving into nothing before his eyes.

But the invisible cloud it created was palpable.

JP felt a flush of heat.

Followed by a tightening in his groin and a hunger that only a great deal of sex would satisfy. This was every bit as potent as Chen had warned.

The waitress wiped the table in front of him and for a heartbeat, he thought of jumping her bones.

"Drink?" she asked with a smile.

JP took a steadying breath. He tucked the vial back

into his pocket, smiled at her, and ordered two glasses of the wine Cassie had been drinking earlier.

Chen had been convinced that the Dragon Bone Powder heated a firestorm to a fever pitch, even after the firestorm was satisfied. He'd said that the powder sharpened the desire of all *Pyr*, making them insatiable.

JP, even having changed to the *Slayer* team, was feeling more insatiable himself than he could ever recall. He felt all tingly and could hear his blood thumping. He was aware of the scent of women's perfumes mingling in the hotel bar. He noticed the curves of cheeks and buttocks and breasts and wanted to claim them all. He wanted to go upstairs and check on Stacy himself.

No, he wanted to do more than check on her.

He decided that his reaction was a good sign, and that Chen's plan would work.

So JP waited, and played his role.

He reminded himself that his reward would be worth any short-term sacrifice. To be Chen's right hand when that *Slayer* ruled the world would be no small thing.

He could do whatever he wanted to the *Pyr* then.

He could avenge his brother Lucien.

He could make those *Pyr* who had killed Lucien pay. With interest.

The prospect made JP smile.

Chapter 5

Cassie heard her friend's snores as soon as she unlocked the door. The sound made her smile with relief.

The lights were still on in the room, and Stacy was still dressed. It looked as if she had staggered through the door, dropped her purse, and landed—mostly—on the mattress. One foot dangled in the air, a fuchsia sling back hanging on for dear life.

Cassie tugged off her friend's shoes and put them in the closet. She picked up Stacy's purse and put it on the dresser. She considered her friend, debating the merits of getting her undressed against potentially waking her.

Stacy stirred and moaned, then rolled to her back. "Owww."

"Too many frilly drinks?" Cassie asked, her tone teasing. They'd been through this scene before a few times, and for years had taken turns playing the lead.

"Just two," Stacy said with a grimace. She peered at Cassie from behind her hand. "What do they put in those things?"

Cassie smiled. "Some of the recipes look like they clean out the bar."

"You're smarter to stick with wine."

"Live and learn. You okay?"

Stacy sat up carefully but still winced. She pressed her fingers to her temples. "I think so. What time is it?"

"Just before midnight."

"Is that all? I'm exhausted, like it's three in the morning."

Cassie sat on the edge of the bed, making sure it didn't bounce beneath her weight. "How were the shrimp? Is your stomach okay?"

Stacy peered at Cassie again. "How do you know about the shrimp?"

"JP. He pounced on me in the lobby. He's pretty worried about you."

That news seemed to perk Stacy up. "Really?"

"Really. He's pacing like a caged tiger down there, chewing himself up for recommending the shrimp and getting you sick." Cassie considered her friend. "He seems like a nice guy."

"So I get falling-down drunk the first time he takes me for dinner. Doesn't that figure?" Stacy reached out a hand and Cassie helped her to stand. "No wonder my track record with men sucks so much. I'm my own worst enemy."

"I said I'd come back and confirm that you'd survived. I'll put in a good word for you."

"It's official: you are the best friend ever."

"Hardly!" Cassie protested. "Not after the way I bailed on you this afternoon."

Stacy shook a finger at her. "Which reminds me—you owe me the whole story."

"It was just, um, fun," Cassie said, and her friend laughed.

"I don't think so. There was something really strong between you two. Maybe it's kismet. Or true love. I couldn't blame you for going after that."

Before Cassie could think of what to say to that, Stacy headed for the bathroom. She made a sound of distress when she saw her reflection. "I look like a wreck!"

Cassie followed her after the toilet flushed, then watched from the doorway as Stacy removed her makeup. Better to stick to safer topics than Lorenzo. "Did the shrimp make you sick? If so, maybe I should tell someone."

Stacy paused, one eye devoid of mascara and the other still thick with it. She turned to look at Cassie. "You know, it was weird. I thought the shrimp were great. In fact, I thought everything was going really well. I didn't even feel drunk. Just happy. I was having a great time." She frowned. "This is going to sound stupid, but then I saw these flames reflected in his eyes. And I looked closer, and I ended up repeating everything he said. I sounded like some kind of moron."

Cassie straightened. "What did he say that you repeated?"

"That I was tired. That my stomach was upset. That I had to go back to my room and sleep." Stacy shrugged. "And I did feel sleepy. Really sleepy. Just like that." She snapped her fingers. "I could barely keep my eyes open. I don't even remember coming up here. It was weird." She grimaced at her reflection. "He must be thinking I'm some kind of nutcase."

Cassie was pretty sure that wasn't what JP was thinking.

He was doing the same hypnosis trick that Lorenzo had done on her.

It was a heck of an illusion.

Did they know each other?

They must at least know *of* each other, if they knew the same trick. *Our kind.* They must all be magicians. That was it!

"Do you think he thinks I'm nuts?" Stacy asked, interrupting Cassie's thoughts. "You look as worried as I feel."

"Sorry. Lost in thought. I'll go talk to JP, defend your honor and all that." Cassie smiled to encourage her friend.

Stacy gave her a hug. "You are the best, Cassie."

"No problem."

"I owe you big time."

"Okay. I'll start thinking about what I want in exchange," Cassie teased. Stacy made to swat her, then winced again, clutching the bathroom counter to steady herself. "You okay?"

"I'll be fine. Go save the best date I've had in years, please." She shook a finger at Cassie. "And remember what I said about giving true love a chance."

Cassie didn't roll her eyes. She ensured that she still had her room key in her purse. The camera was still there, too. In the elevator, she checked that the flash was charged, more from force of habit than anything else. She took a breath and squared her shoulders as she eyed her reflection in the polished elevator doors.

She noticed in the reflection that her eyes were sparkling. She knew that look. She had a lead and she was going to follow it.

Looked like a little "fun" had restored her mojo.

Or maybe it had been Lorenzo himself.

Lorenzo flung himself out the stage door, keys in hand. He had time to savor a deep breath of cool night air before he caught another scent.

Slayer.

There was a red Ferrari parked next to his own, a 360 Spider. Rental. Lorenzo knew this car. He'd seen it around town. A man was crouched down, admiring the lines of Lorenzo's car, the sight sending a ripple of annoyance through Lorenzo.

Because he knew this *Slayer*.

Suddenly Lorenzo was living in Grand Central Terminal. Was every dragon shifter on the planet going to drop by to chat? Lorenzo sincerely hoped not. He had a policy of avoiding his kind as much as possible—which was quite a lot. It would have been courteous of them to return the favor.

He hated that there was nothing he could do about it.

Except get rid of each arrival in turn, as quickly as possible.

It bit that the part about the firestorm attracting all dragon shifters appeared to be true.

On the upside, he was looking forward to invoking the flashfire more and more with every passing hour. He couldn't wait to be lost to his own kind.

Lorenzo strode to his car, clicking the button that unlocked the driver's side door. "I already declined," he said to Balthasar, not bothering to hide his impatience.

"I thought you might have changed your mind." Balthasar straightened as he spoke. He still had a slight limp and a scar on his cheek, but the combination gave him a rakish charm. Especially when he smiled, as he did now. He looked like a handsome pirate. Lorenzo wished he'd go swashbuckle and pillage somewhere else. "They say a firestorm changes everything. Perspective, especially."

"I wouldn't know anything about that." Lorenzo hauled open the door and got in. He took a deep breath, liking the car's familiar embrace. It soothed his nerves, made him feel in control again.

Was that just another illusion?

This car certainly couldn't hold a candle to his all-time favorite, his baby, the 1963 Lusso that was locked away for its own safety.

The Lusso was already "sold" to his next identity of choice, just waiting for him to be "reborn" into a new identity one more time. It became tedious to create new identities every twenty or thirty years, but longevity was one facet of being *Pyr* that Lorenzo did like.

Even with the inconvenience of staging his own death.

The difference this time was that Lorenzo intended to disappear not just from human society, but from *Pyr* society. It was high time his life was entirely his own. He didn't care what price the flashfire demanded. Losing his shifter powers would be no great loss if it meant Erik and Balthasar could never find him again.

Three more days—then freedom.

Balthasar caught the door before Lorenzo could close it and leaned in to continue the conversation. Lorenzo snarled a little, but Balthasar ignored the hint. "Don't be stupid. We can all feel the heat of the firestorm." Lorenzo glared at him, but Balthasar didn't even blink. "You must feel it yourself."

Lorenzo knew his eyes flashed. "I choose to not involve myself in other *Pyr*s' business." He grabbed for the door handle. "It would be touching to see that courtesy reciprocated."

"Exactly." Lorenzo seethed as Balthasar made his argument. "You don't follow Erik. You avoid the *Pyr*. You hate humans. And now you've had your firestorm. There's no reason *not* to join me."

"Except that I don't want to." Lorenzo shut the door with force, tugging it out of Balthasar's grip. He turned the key savagely in the ignition, letting the engine roar.

Balthasar had made these arguments repeatedly, and Lorenzo was bored with them. Why didn't any of the dragon shifters—*Pyr* or *Slayer*—understand that Lorenzo wanted to be alone?

"It's not complicated," Lorenzo said, speaking slowly and deliberately. "I don't play team sports."

Balthasar stood back and smiled, switching to old-speak. *"Engine has guts, I'll give you that. Does yours slip a bit between third and fourth?"*

Lorenzo growled as he put the car in reverse. He wasn't interested in doing an automotive review with Balthasar.

"Could be a rental issue," Balthasar mused; then his voice deepened. *"Having your firestorm means you'll start to age, Lorenzo. I thought immortality might have more allure for you now."*

It was a reminder that Lorenzo didn't need. He scoffed instead, taking defense in a good offense. He lowered his window, speaking aloud. "You don't have immortality to offer. I know a con when I hear one. The Elixir is gone and so is Magnus."

Even then, that *Slayer's* version of immortality had been burdened with tedious conditions and liabilities, being as it was an addiction to the life-renewing Elixir. The Elixir hadn't ensured that Magnus could survive a dragon fight, either. Magnus was dead, his ambitions with him.

This plea was about leadership of the *Slayers*. Balthasar wanted the job, but leaders need followers.

Lorenzo wasn't interested in following anyone.

Balthasar smiled. "But I have his library and his hoard."

"So what?" Lorenzo said. "You don't know what it means. It might as well all be gibberish."

Balthasar's gaze was steady. "Are you sure there's nothing in there of interest? He did have several millennia to build his collection."

"And the best he could do was make a disgusting Elixir that didn't save him from dying by Rafferty's hand in the end." Lorenzo sighed with forbearance. "Let me guess—the price of a peek is turning *Slayer*." He shook his head, bored by it all. "No sale, Balthasar, just as I told you before. I do not join anything or anyone, as a matter of principle."

"Still pretending to run solo?"

"There's no pretense about that."

"No, it's just illusion." Balthasar smiled, looking unpredictable again. "How's your dad, anyway?"

"You will leave my father out of this discussion."

Balthasar's smile broadened, just long enough to give Lorenzo the creeps. "Well, I think you're making a mistake," he said, stepping back from the car. He surveyed Lorenzo, smiling with an oily confidence that was reminiscent of Magnus. It made Lorenzo want to injure him.

They were all the same, these self-motivated *Slayers* who pretended to have something to offer—but in truth were manipulative and self-motivated. Lorenzo could teach them a thing or two about looking out for oneself.

Or at least about baiting a hook so it was tempting.

Balthasar's smile broadened. "Which just means I'll have to find another way to change your mind."

"There is no way to change my mind." Lorenzo spoke with resolve, even as he feared the opposite was true.

He had to survive only until Saturday.

The days couldn't pass quickly enough.

After the spectacle, none of these fools would ever find him again.

"Isn't there?" Balthasar turned and inhaled deeply of the wind. "Her scent is distinctive, don't you think? Even for a human." His eyes glinted as he smiled again. "I'll bet I could find her *anywhere*."

Lorenzo's heart clenched, but he hid his reaction. The trick was ensuring that someone like Balthasar never knew that he had found a nerve.

Lorenzo smiled coldly. "And you're welcome to her," he said, as if he were far more cavalier than he was. "I've had my fun." He shook his head, as if weary of humans and their supposed charms. "Forgettable, really, but the choice is yours."

Balthasar's eyes glinted, but he had no chance to reply. Lorenzo backed out of the spot, the tires almost smoking against the pavement.

"If you'll forgive me, I have other obligations." He peeled out of the parking lot without waiting for a reply.

Lorenzo fumed as he took the turn onto the Strip. The nerve of his kind, coming to meddle in his life. Drawn to the firestorm and determined to make trouble. How many of them were in town? How far would each pursue his own agenda, careless of the price to Lorenzo?

It wasn't as if he had nothing else to do.

He ripped down the road, intent upon getting home as soon as possible. Responsibilities beckoned, unwelcome responsibilities but obligations all the same. He still had to persuade his father to pack, which promised to be a wearisome battle. He halfway expected Balthasar to follow him, but there was no sign of the other Ferrari.

Where had he gone?

Not that Lorenzo cared.

The light turned red at the entry to the next hotel,

and mindful of how much he'd been pushing his luck with the cops lately, Lorenzo squealed to a stop. His window was still open, the night air a balm to his sour mood.

Balthasar was right. Her scent *was* distinctive.

It led right here.

Just this waft of it flooded his mind with images of the afternoon they'd spent together. The pleasure they'd shared. The desire he still felt.

His need for more.

Abruptly, Lorenzo's thoughts were filled with flames, the crackle of heat and the sound of a woman's screams. He caught his breath, terror flooding him all over again.

Just as it had in the past. He could not logically remember that night—he'd been too young—but his nightmares had always been filled with smoke and fire and suffocating darkness. He could smell the ash. He could hear the chants. He could sense the hatred.

He could taste his mother's fear.

He could hear the chanting of the crowd, mingling with the accusation from Caterina's lips decades later.

Diavolo.

The two incidents had blended together in his memories, potent experience—and reminders—of the destructive fear of humans.

Lorenzo shoved the memories out of his mind just as the light turned green. His mouth dry, he recalled Balthasar's threat and target. He would be a devil if he let a *Slayer* have his way with this woman.

She deserved better.

Lorenzo swore, then turned hard into the hotel entrance. He'd thought that the firestorm was the last thing he needed, but the truth was that Balthasar's arrival was the straw that broke the camel's back.

As much as Lorenzo might have preferred otherwise, he couldn't let this particular human be endangered.

His reaction was fortified when he caught the distinctive whiff of *Slayer* drifting from the hotel lobby. Not Balthasar—another *Slayer*. Worse, the scent entwined with that of the woman with the alluring lingerie. Lorenzo even let the valet park his car in his haste to get to her side, a fact that astonished both of them.

He strode into the hotel with determination, his gaze scanning the interior. What Lorenzo saw in the lobby bar did precisely nothing to reassure him. His temper flared.

Enough already.

As soon as Cassie stepped off the elevator, she saw JP stand up in the bar. He even waved to get her attention, as if anyone would miss such a gorgeous hunk.

"She's fine," Cassie said to JP before he could even ask.

He pulled out her chair, his eyes filled with concern. "Are you sure?"

"She was asleep. I woke her up and we talked for a bit." Cassie smiled at JP. "She feels really bad about messing up your evening together."

"I shouldn't have suggested that she have the shrimp." JP spoke with obvious irritation. "What was I thinking? Shrimp in the middle of a desert? It would have to be flown in, and it's like an inferno out there every day. The chances of the shrimp getting warm are so high—"

"She's fine," Cassie interrupted. "She'll be back to normal in the morning. She just wanted me to apologize to you." She smiled, then leaned closer to whisper, "I think she really likes you."

JP relaxed then, his own smile widening. "I suppose it's no secret that I like her, too."

They smiled at each other, Stacy's admiration society, and JP gestured to the wine. When she sipped, Cassie realized he'd ordered the same one she'd had earlier.

Stacy could do with a man in her life who was attentive.

They sat in silence for a minute and Cassie wondered how she'd steer the conversation to the illusion of those flames. Without seeing them, of course. She didn't want to get hypnotized herself again.

To Cassie's surprise, JP gave her the opening she needed. "And how was Lorenzo's show tonight? Did he turn into a dragon again?"

He looked like he was fighting the urge to laugh.

As if she'd made it up.

Cassie found that reassuring. "No. I guess that was a one-off illusion." Cassie smiled. "Still a good show, though."

"Yes, I thought it was quite a spectacle." JP sipped his drink and glanced over the bar, his interest wandering.

Cassie hauled it back with her next question. "Do you know anything about magic at all?"

JP looked at her in surprise. "Me? Why?"

Cassie let her gaze slide over the occupants of the bar, as if she were less interested in their conversation than she was. "I was just trying to figure out one of his illusions, that's all."

"Let me guess—the dragon one."

"No. That's got to be all smoke and mirrors. It's the little tricks that intrigue me." She tried to sound offhand. "The way it looks like there are flames in the pupils of his eyes, for example."

If JP was startled, he hid it well. He smiled. "You saw him close up?"

"Yes, after the show. Didn't I mention that? I talked to him backstage, but he wasn't interested in sharing the secrets of any of his illusions." She let her eyes widen. "Certainly not in being photographed."

JP laughed. "He does seem to have a control issue."

"Many celebrities do," Cassie acknowledged. The manipulation and management of a public image was old news to her. "Those flames, though, they looked real, as if there were fires burning right in his eyes." Cassie shrugged and shook her head. "I can't figure out how he did it." She took a sip of her glass of wine. "Unless, of course, the beguiling has something to do with the firestorm."

"It's totally unrelated," JP said, then fell abruptly silent, as if realizing that he'd said too much.

Cassie looked at him.

He looked back.

"Caught," he whispered, and smiled. JP toasted Cassie with his drink. "Well done." He considered her for a moment. "Do you have any idea what you just asked me?"

"Not really. I was hoping you'd fill me in."

JP nodded, then leaned forward. "I'm sure you've heard about these *Pyr*, the dragon shape shifters."

Cassie nodded in turn. "Are they real?"

JP grimaced. "Who knows? But the stories are persistent, and there are elements in those stories that make for a great show. Like beguiling." He smiled at her. "It's a type of hypnosis that these *Pyr* are supposed to be able to do, by conjuring flames in their eyes."

"But others can learn the trick, too," Cassie guessed,

remembering what Stacy had said. "Like you and Lorenzo."

JP nodded again. "Probably other illusionists, as well."

Cassie found this conversation reassuring. She could imagine that Lorenzo would learn illusions from anybody anywhere to use in his show. She was more ready to believe in a group of magicians who guarded the secrets of their illusions jealously than a team of dragon shape shifters.

If JP was one of them, he might be able to tell her more.

"So why did you hypnotize Stacy?"

JP winced. He ran a finger around the base of his wineglass. "It's very tempting, you know, to use hypnosis as a tool to get what you want," he said quietly, then flicked a look at Cassie. "But in my experience, this kind of hypnosis, this beguiling, works on a person only once." He sighed. "So I thought I would remove temptation and hypnotize Stacy over something ridiculous and small. That way, if anything happens between us, it'll be what we both want."

Cassie was liking JP more by the minute. Given her own experience of the afternoon, she could relate to what he was saying. Imagine having the power to make people do what you wanted them to do? Cassie could believe that it would be easy to use that ability to expedite things.

She admired JP's foresight.

She was glad to know that Lorenzo wouldn't be able to beguile her again.

JP sipped his drink thoughtfully. "As usual, Lorenzo is pushing the edge. He likes to take risks. That dragon illusion that you saw will just perpetuate the idea that he's more than human. Did you see the papers tonight?"

Cassie hadn't, but she could guess by JP's attitude that Lorenzo's feat had made the news. "So you don't actually think Lorenzo is a dragon shifter?"

JP laughed. There was a lingering twinkle in his eyes when he met Cassie's gaze. "So much is manufactured for effect in an illusionist's biography."

That was true of any celebrity's bio. "You're right. But maybe you can fill me in on some of the other stories about the *Pyr*."

He watched her with a bit of wariness. "Why?"

"There's a big photo assignment available, to get shots of them. It's because of the all the interest in Melissa Smith's shows."

JP nodded his understanding.

"I wouldn't mind scooping up some of the cash." That wasn't all of Cassie's motivation, but JP didn't need to know that she just wanted to know more about Lorenzo.

"Yes, material goods are always tempting, aren't they?"

It was a strange comment, but Cassie chose to ignore it. "What is the firestorm exactly?"

JP leaned toward her, as if sharing a secret. His voice was low and his gaze was intent, but there were no flames dancing in his pupils. Still Cassie could feel the considerable influence of his charm. "The firestorm is a sign that a *Pyr* has met his destined mate. Sparks fly between them, so neither can miss the presence of the other."

Cassie thought of those strange flames that had jumped between herself and Lorenzo at the afternoon show. She didn't believe for a minute that the effect wasn't under his complete control, even if she couldn't explain it.

Had Lorenzo conjured the effect to seduce her?

Seemed improbable.

It was a lot more likely that he'd mastered the trick of those flames and incorporated them into the show on purpose. Right before he did that transformation trick, it might buttress the idea that he was *Pyr*.

That would be fabulous PR.

She made a mental note to check the papers herself.

"And they say that the firestorm lights desire within both the *Pyr* and his mate." JP smiled. "They are said to burn with lust for each other, until they consummate their relationship."

"Who's they? Who says this?"

"The dragon shifters, of course." JP widened his eyes. "At least that's what one hears."

"Right." Cassie considered this information. "But once the *Pyr* and his mate do the wild thing, the firestorm is over?"

JP smiled. "Except for the mate's little souvenir."

"What souvenir?"

"She conceives a child. That's the point." JP shrugged. "At least, that's the story they tell."

"Do you think they're real?"

JP's smile turned enigmatic. "Who's to say what's real and what's not? Particularly in a place as filled with illusion as this one?"

Fair enough. Cassie sipped her drink, her thoughts racing, and tried not to panic. The conversation had made her realize she and Lorenzo hadn't used any protection that afternoon, and she wasn't on the pill anymore. She hadn't really thought about precautions. That wasn't like her, either.

But then, it was long odds to conceive in one try. It was the prospect of other little souvenirs that made her wine taste sour. How could she have been so impulsive?

She had been *beguiled*.

Manipulated by the master of illusion.

Hypnotized.

She was starting to give serious consideration to the prospect of getting even.

"So what about beguiling?" she asked JP, keeping her tone light. "Can anybody do it?"

But JP wasn't listening anymore. He had turned to glance toward the hotel entrance. His nostrils flared in the strangest way, as if he were smelling something he didn't like. Cassie couldn't smell anything distinctive. JP's eyes glittered and there was a faint blue shimmer around his body.

The same kind of blue shimmer she'd seen around Lorenzo before the dragon trick.

Cassie blinked and the blue light was gone. Had she imagined it? Or was it another illusion from the magician's society?

JP faced her again, looking perfectly normal once more. "I'm sorry," he said with an easy smile. "What did you just say?"

Cassie had a very unsettled feeling, all of a sudden, that JP wasn't quite who or what he seemed to be.

She had no time to think about it, though, because a man stormed toward their table.

Not just any man—Lorenzo.

And he was furious.

Cassie felt a flush start at her toes and spread slowly upward as she watched Lorenzo approach. Apparently one wild naked afternoon hadn't been enough to diminish her attraction to him. What was it about this man? Did the effects of beguiling last? She knew Stacy couldn't be right about kismet. But the fact was that Cassie couldn't think of anything beyond repeating the afternoon's festivities.

This was not good.

Lorenzo's hair was unruly, as if he'd been shoving his hands through it. It was sexy to see him looking so agitated. Out of control. She'd bet he wasn't distracted very often.

He moved with a powerful grace that was mesmerizing. He strode through the lobby like he was parting the seas: people stepped aside and watched him with awe. Cassie found the sight of him pretty riveting herself.

It wasn't just that he was tall.

It wasn't just that he was so incredibly good-looking.

It wasn't even that he projected an aura of authority.

Lorenzo had presence anyway, but it was multiplied by a factor of ten because he was angry. His eyes blazed; his attention was completely fixed upon Cassie. It was clear that nothing was going to stop his progress.

And everyone knew it.

There was something of the avenging angel about him.

And Cassie was his destination. Her mouth was as dry as the Nevada desert.

It was a fact—Lorenzo was the sexiest man alive.

Period.

A secret part of her quivered in anticipation that he was targeting her.

But at the last second, his attention flicked to JP. His gaze locked on the other man. Lorenzo seemed to get even taller, and there was that bizarre blue shimmer around his body.

"What the hell do you think you're doing?" he demanded, grasping JP's shoulder.

A jealous rage? Cassie was astounded. He certainly hadn't given the impression that he was possessive of her.

After all, he'd left while she was asleep.

She winced at the sight of his fingers gripping JP's shoulder. She would have bet his hold was tight, but JP didn't flinch.

In fact, JP regarded Lorenzo steadily, despite the crackle of tension between the two men. Here was proof positive that they not only knew each other, but that they didn't like each other.

Antagonism snapped in the air for a long moment.

So maybe things weren't so friendly in the secret society of stage illusionists tapping into the mythos of the *Pyr*. Was that why JP was here? To nick secrets from Lorenzo? Just how competitive were magicians anyway?

That would explain Lorenzo's attitude, at least.

Then JP slipped out from beneath the weight of Lorenzo's hand in one elegant move. He brushed the shoulder of his shirt with fastidious care. "I'm having a drink with Cassie," he said calmly, as if daring Lorenzo to make an issue of it.

Lorenzo's gaze flicked between Cassie and JP, and she nearly flinched at the heat in his gaze.

"Cassie," Lorenzo murmured, her name like a caress on his tongue.

Cassie tried to hide his effect upon her. She stuck out her hand and forced a businesslike smile. "Cassie Redmond. Cassandra, actually." Her smile turned more genuine when she decided to tease him. "I don't think we actually did introductions earlier."

Lorenzo inhaled. He looked her up and down, but didn't

take her hand. Did he recognize her name? She didn't think she was that high profile, but then, Lorenzo probably knew a lot of people in the celebrity media game. "A photographer," he murmured, his eyes glinting dangerously.

"Paparazzi, really," Cassie admitted, and his nostrils flared.

"And your assignment?" His voice was low and velvety, filled with a threat that made Cassie shiver.

She had the definite sense that he knew the answer already.

"She's chasing shots of the *Pyr*," JP contributed, his tone gleeful.

Lorenzo gave Cassie one last glare, then pointed a finger at JP. "You're trying to meddle where your interference is not welcome. You should know better than that."

"You make assumptions."

"You make presumptions. Did Erik send you here?"

JP shook his head, his calm manner in complete contrast to Lorenzo's anger. "Why on earth would Erik hold any sway over me?" He sipped his drink. "He holds none over you."

Who was Erik? Another competitive illusionist?

Lorenzo simmered. "Who then? Jorge?"

JP's gaze flickered. "I don't know anyone named Jorge."

He was lying and Cassie knew it. Why? Who was Jorge? This was starting to sound like a big club.

"Balthasar?"

JP blinked and lied again. "Who?"

Lorenzo braced his hands on the table and glared at JP. His manner was so intense that even though JP clearly wanted to ignore him, he couldn't. He glanced up at Lorenzo, his expression sulky.

The force of will between the two men was enough to make Cassie dizzy. It could have been flattering to believe that they were arguing over her, but Cassie knew their animosity had a different root.

She watched, intrigued.

"The real question," Lorenzo said, his voice low and silky, "is why are you even here?"

JP averted his gaze with an effort and put an increment of space between himself and Lorenzo. "No, the real question is, what do you think you are doing?" he said, no real question in his tone. "This bar isn't your property, nor is my lovely companion."

Lorenzo's eyes flashed. "You're insinuating yourself into a situation that is not your concern. I'm asking you to leave."

JP smiled. "And I'm declining to do what you *request*." He sipped his drink again, but Cassie saw that his hand wasn't as steady as it had been.

So, Lorenzo spooked him.

Interesting.

Lorenzo straightened and turned a glance on Cassie, imperiously offering her his hand.

His eyes were still dark and glittering. She knew instinctively that he wouldn't hurt her—she also understood that he wasn't thrilled to learn her occupation.

Of course, that wasn't surprising, given how he preferred to manage his public persona.

If he intended to lecture her on her choice of work and ethics, he could think again.

If nothing else, this was just a reminder that what was done was done, and that there was no future between them.

Too bad his proximity made it hard to remember that.

"I'm fine right here, thanks." Cassie smiled, as if his

very presence wasn't turning her thoughts in a predictable, sensual direction. She was thinking she could
change his mood, put all that passion to better use than a
lecture. The idea made her all warm inside. "Just started
my drink, actually."

"I'll buy you another, just to get you away from this
snake."

"Hey! That's a little strong," JP said, rising to his feet.
He was several inches shorter than Lorenzo, but just as
muscled. His gaze turned steely. "I might take exception."

Lorenzo smiled coldly. "And I might enjoy it, if you
did."

They glared at each other, sizing each other up. Cassie
had a feeling they'd fought before.

Physically.

And she'd put her nickel on Lorenzo if they fought
again. The world of stage magicians and illusionists was
a lot more interesting than she'd ever imagined.

Yet the argument was about nothing. These two were
going to brawl over stage tricks and sleight of hand that
they each perceived to be proprietary. How ridiculous
was that? Even if there could be a lot of money at stake,
none of it was real.

None of it *counted*.

And Cassie was fed up with illusions of all kinds.

It was time to leave.

A photographer? Paparazzi? And hunting images of the
Pyr? Every detail Lorenzo learned about the woman
who fascinated him just made the situation worse. How
much did she know? Did she have other plans for her
evidence beyond selling the images?

Cassie stood up, her expression grim, and Lorenzo

knew it was up to him to change her mind about her intentions.

And he knew exactly how he'd eliminate any suspicions she had about the truth of his nature. He'd prove to her that he was one hundred percent man, in the most fundamental way possible.

The very idea inflamed him, even as he looked down into her eyes.

What lingerie was she wearing tonight?

How long could he delay her orgasm with pleasure?

"Do you have to act like children?" she demanded in her most disparaging tone. "What are you going to do? Have a fistfight in a bar like a pair of morons? Over a stage trick? How juvenile is that?"

So she thought they were competing illusionists. Lorenzo smiled, liking that angle just fine.

JP didn't smile, his gaze remaining locked on Lorenzo. He was utterly still.

"You disapprove?" Lorenzo asked her.

She surveyed him, sensing the change in his mood but obviously not knowing the reason for it. He liked that she was observant, that she was always thinking.

"I always disapprove of stupidity." She looked between the two of them with disgust. "What are you going to solve by beating each other up?"

"Ascendancy." JP bit off the word.

"Don't hold your breath," Lorenzo murmured.

They glared at each other.

Cassie flung out her hands. "Why does everything have to be a contest for men? You're all the same!"

Lorenzo glanced at her with interest. "You're not competitive?"

Cassie flushed and he knew the truth. "That's not the

point. You're not going to solve anything with physical force. Give it up and shake hands."

"I don't think so," Lorenzo said.

"Why not?" she asked and they both ignored her. The bouncers moved closer.

Cassie spoke to Lorenzo, her eyes flashing in a most enticing way. "You might be in charge of everything that happens on your stage, but in the real world, there are lots of choices. I *chose* to have a drink with JP."

That caught Lorenzo's interest. He respected people who were self-determining—people who made active choices, like himself. Did he and Cassie have more in common than great sex?

She grabbed her glass and finished her wine, the alcohol making her flush even more. Lorenzo watched, convinced that she was the most alluring woman alive.

"And now I choose to leave you both," she announced. "Maybe you can sort out your differences in a reasonable way, whatever they are."

Cassie pivoted and marched out of the bar. Lorenzo chuckled. He really liked her spirit. Did she know that she had just chewed out two dragon shape shifters? That her opinion of brawling was the same as his? Did she have any idea how refreshing she was?

She glanced back, blushed crimson, then stumbled on the steps that descended from the bar to the lobby.

Lorenzo knew exactly what he was going to do. He looked JP right in the eyes steadily. *"Don't come near her again,"* he murmured in old-speak. *"Or you'll have to answer to me."* He didn't blink, just held the *Slayer's* gaze.

"I'm not afraid," JP replied with defiance.

Lorenzo smiled. *"You should be. Maybe you're not*

that smart, after all." He waited for the flash of doubt in JP's eyes, then pursued his mate with purpose.

He was looking forward to driving every doubt about his nature out of Cassie's mind.

It would be hours before he realized he'd chosen to use old-speak again.

Chapter 6

Lorenzo was suddenly beside Cassie, his hand cupping her elbow with a protectiveness that made her heart flutter. "Unbelievable that you could trip in those boots," he said in an undertone. She could hear the laughter underlying his words.

Cassie pulled her arm from his grip easily. "There's nothing wrong with my boots."

He rolled his eyes. Apparently his dangerous mood had passed. "Except that they're ugly."

"They're practical."

"For what?" Lorenzo glanced pointedly around the lobby. "I see very few broncos in need of breaking."

"Except you and JP."

He chuckled then, his eyes dancing. She liked her sense that she had surprised him and fought her answering smile.

"I'm not leaving with you, so don't get any ideas."

Lorenzo countered smoothly. "I'm not leaving you with him."

Cassie stopped to argue. "I don't have to choose one or the other...."

"Yes, you do." Lorenzo smiled, making it impossible to think of anything or anyone other than him. He leaned closer, fixing his attention upon her and locking his hands on her shoulders. Cassie's mouth went dry. He exuded a heat and a sexual energy that left Cassie yearning to have him all over again.

Even though there were no flames in his eyes.

Was JP right that the trick could work only once?

Lorenzo didn't need to hypnotize her to catch her eye, to ensure that she saw only him in a crowded bar. He didn't need to create the illusion of sparks between them for her skin to burn at his touch, a flush of desire to glow inside her, or her mind to turn to infinite variations on the theme of sex. He certainly hadn't needed any crazy story about the *Pyr* and their firestorms to get her into bed.

He just had to look at her with those hazel eyes, smile that slow, crooked smile, murmur something in that seductive voice, and she was lost.

Had their interval been completely a trick?

What if she chose to do it again with him? Would it be different? Better? Would her taking the lead surprise him—or please him?

Cassie suddenly wanted to know. It was an impulsive urge, but she had the feeling that she'd always wonder if she just walked away from him.

"Do us both a favor and forget JP," Lorenzo said in that seductive voice. "Nothing good will come of spending time with him."

Cassie was so lost in the intensity of Lorenzo's gaze that for a moment she wasn't sure who he was talking about.

JP! Right. She glanced back to the bar, but the other man had disappeared.

"He's gone."

"No surprise." Lorenzo was dismissive. "He mostly bluffs."

She looked back at Lorenzo, considering his confidence. He'd left her alone, as if he'd had all he wanted of her, but now he was tracking her down at her hotel. It made no sense. It would be easy to be flattered, but Cassie needed more than that.

"Why are you even here?" she demanded. "Just come to save me from bad company? Or did you follow me?"

He dropped his gaze, and she had the strange sense that he didn't know the answer himself. He swallowed and actually looked awkward.

Was it possible that she wasn't the only one feeling this powerful attraction?

Lorenzo impaled her with a hot glance. "I might as well admit it," he said, as if he'd rather do anything else. "I couldn't *not* see you again." The steadiness of his gaze convinced her that although the confession might be reluctant, it was true.

Cassie suddenly found it very hard to catch her breath.

"I thought that was what you wanted," she managed to say. "A single virtuoso performance."

That bemused smile tugged at the corner of his mouth. "Was it that virtuoso?"

Cassie blushed. "I thought it was awesome," she admitted.

He bent toward her and whispered, those eyes gleaming wickedly. "So did I. I thought you were awesome."

He'd followed her.

He couldn't stop thinking about her, either.

Incredibly, they had something in common.

Cassie's heart galloped. Lorenzo's gaze warmed and his smile broadened. "Maybe that's why I want more."

His gaze slid over her, admiration in his expression, and he shook his head slightly. "Against all odds."

Cassie bristled. "What's that supposed to mean?"

"That nothing about you is as anticipated." He lifted a hand, apparently helpless against his own reaction. "And everything about you is enchanting."

Cassie didn't know what to say. She could completely relate, both to his interest and his confusion. She'd never been attracted to a man who was so gorgeous, let alone one so enamored of control. And yet, and yet, she had a feeling she'd never forget Lorenzo.

But there were still issues. If she was going to do this again, this time it would be on her terms.

"Let's remember that you tricked me," she said, challenge in her tone. She thought she'd have to spell it all out, but he immediately looked contrite.

"I did. I am sorry." Lorenzo heaved a sigh and shoved a hand through his hair. "Passion overwhelmed good sense." His smile was rueful. "Any chance of you forgiving me?"

"Are you going to beguile me again?"

"No."

Cassie's annoyance melted. This man could play her like a cheap guitar.

He bent then, and touched his lips to her cheek, his gentle touch making her shiver. "Passion is doing it again," he whispered.

"Doing what?"

"Overwhelming good sense." Lorenzo didn't move, just kept his lips against her cheek. The feel of them moving, of his breath on her skin, made Cassie tingle from head to toe. "I should have gone home, gotten some sleep, and prepared for my next show. Instead I'm standing in a hotel lobby, trying to make you smile."

Cassie pulled back to look into his eyes and her heart skipped a beat. Maybe two.

Lorenzo arched a brow. "Forgive me?"

Oh, she was in deep trouble.

"I'm not sure I should." She glanced at him, expecting sad puppy eyes or a plea for mercy. Instead, Lorenzo was grinning at her, as if she was unpredictable, enticing, refreshing.

Maybe women never said no to him.

She was pretty sure she shouldn't either. But she'd do it because she chose it, not because he tricked her.

Lorenzo arched that one brow higher and smiled, a move that made him look mischievous and impossibly sexy. "Give me a chance to make it up to you?"

"How?"

He laughed, a good, rich laugh. His hands rose to capture her shoulders. Then he bent and whispered in her ear, gathering her closer in a move that dissolved her resistance. "I'll show you. Let's get a room."

Cassie's eyes closed as his teeth grazed her earlobe and she sighed when he kissed her neck right below her ear. She was filled with a warm desire that she knew he could sate, but she took a step back to meet his gaze.

"Condoms this time," she said firmly, adding another condition.

Lorenzo's smile was so fleeting that she thought he'd argue. But he laced their fingers together and strode toward the shop in the lobby that sold toiletries. She had to hurry to keep up with his long-legged stride, but his obvious anticipation made her pulse skip.

Because it seemed to be as high as her own.

Cassie expected Lorenzo to be such a gentleman. He didn't drag her to the desk like some guy panting to get lucky—he urged her to take a seat in one corner of the lobby while he swept to the counter alone.

She eavesdropped shamelessly.

Lorenzo was clearly recognized, but he worked with it. He professed to being too tired to drive home and the staff scampered to find him suitable accommodation. She saw the flash of his gold card snapping onto the counter before she glanced away.

A man with that much charm should be classified a dangerous weapon.

There was no sign of JP anymore and Cassie half wondered where he had gone. Bed, probably. It had to be close to one in the morning.

Then Lorenzo stood before her, his smile making her forget everything but him.

They rode the elevator together in silence.

She shouldn't have been surprised that he'd rented a penthouse that had to take up half of the top floor of the hotel. Did he do everything full-out? Cassie was thinking so.

Which was both exciting and daunting. After all, he'd compromised—a little—to accommodate her demands.

Did he ever compromise on the big stuff?

Then he unlocked the door to the room, gestured her in, and Cassie froze in the foyer in astonishment. This suite was bigger than her entire house in California. The view was stupendous, the rooms enormous. Lorenzo wandered through it, a panther at ease in his new den. He flicked on lights, checked locks, ensured that everything was just as he wanted it to be.

She was amused that his need for control extended to every corner of his life.

"Stars or drapes?" he asked from the window, giving her the choice.

The room was on a curved corner, and the windows ran from floor to ceiling and wall to wall. The view seemed to go on forever. Even the lights of the Strip looked glamorous from this vantage point, like fairy lights on an over-the-top Christmas tree. The sky was a deep indigo dotted with stars, stars that couldn't compete with the neon and flashing lights on the ground.

Cassie smiled at Lorenzo. "You're not deciding?"

He smiled back. "There's an old joke that what a woman likes best is the chance to choose."

She could have listened to his voice all night long. It was so rich and deep, the way he spoke so measured and deliberate. He could read the telephone book to her and she'd be enchanted.

The idea made her smile broaden.

"There are things I like better than that," Cassie said. She put her hand on his arm and let her fingers slide up to his shoulder. He was as muscled and strong as she remembered, but stood still, watching her.

He really did intend to let her choose this time.

She was amazed by this concession from a man who liked very much to be in charge. But he knew that he'd betrayed her trust by letting his desire get the upper hand—and he was choosing to prove to her that it didn't have to be that way.

That he would act differently just for her was enough to trash the last of her inhibitions.

There was more to Lorenzo than the illusions he cultivated.

"Stars," she decided. "It's beautiful."

"Stars it is." Lorenzo turned from the window then, bent and caught her lips beneath his. His kiss was initially gentle—if persuasive—again giving her the choice.

Cassie chose. She leaned against his chest and slid her arms around his neck. She knotted her fingers in his hair, opened her mouth, and pulled him closer. Lorenzo made a sound like a growl; then his hands locked around her waist and he lifted her to her toes. He deepened his kiss with an ardor that Cassie echoed.

This was honest.

This was a decision on both their parts.

And the passion they felt was mutual.

There was no better aphrodisiac than that.

Their embrace quickly turned hungry. Cassie opened Lorenzo's shirt and peeled it off his shoulders, running her hands over the muscled strength of his chest. He tugged the fastener out of her hair, loosing it over her shoulders, then ran his fingers through it. He kissed her ear, her neck; then his hands slid beneath her shirt. Her shirt was untucked, the heat of his hands roving over her skin.

Cassie kissed him all the while, wanting to taste every inch of him. He was so warm, his skin so firm and golden. She ran her hand over his nipple and liked how he caught his breath. She pinched it then, and reached for the front of his jeans. His smile flashed; then he tossed her over his shoulder and headed for the bed.

The bed was enormous. She had time to bounce; then Lorenzo was beside her, peeling off her shirt and unfastening her jeans. He flung her boots aside with a disdain that made her laugh.

He stroked her endlessly as he undressed her, the glow in his eyes enough to make her preen. The sheets were pink satin, and they felt sinfully soft beneath her. On impulse, Cassie posed like a pin-up model, and loved how his eyes flashed with desire.

"White lace," he muttered through his teeth, as if her

lingerie was the most provocative possibility. She had a thought that she could show him a whole lot more interesting lingerie than this; then he reached for her and she forgot everything except his touch.

His kiss was demanding and wonderful, making her want everything he had to give. She pushed him to his back before he could unfasten her bra, and tugged off his jeans. He wore silk boxers, the black contrasting with his tan, but she tugged them off. He smiled at her, posing in turn. She eyed him as he lounged on the bed like a great lion, and his eyes gleamed as he let her look.

Lorenzo was as sculpted as a Renaissance statue. She reasoned that he must be working out all the time that he wasn't working. Cassie knew a thing or two about plastic surgery and couldn't help but look for the evidence. She couldn't see a single scar.

This was Lorenzo's original equipment.

She met his gaze, knowing that her reaction showed. His eyes flashed and he reached again for her. He caught her in his arms, his lips in her hair, his hands sliding behind her. "My turn," he murmured, then kissed her all over again.

When she was nude, he looked, that smile making her blood simmer. His kisses slid down her throat, tracing a burning line as he explored her body. He cupped each breast and tasted the nipple, ran his tongue down to her navel, spread his hands over her thighs. Cassie closed her eyes and savored. The satin was smooth against her back, and his caresses were seductive. She'd never felt worshipped before and decided she could get used to it. She didn't know what he was going to do next, but it was all good.

Cassie caught her breath when she felt Lorenzo's tongue slide closer to her heat. She arched her back, luxuriating beneath his caress like a cat in the sun. When he touched her clitoris, her eyes flew open.

She saw then that there was a mirror inside the canopy over the bed. She was impressed by the sight of Lorenzo, his muscles moving as he tormented her with pleasure. She was amazed by the reflection of herself, her hair spread over the pillows and her face flushed.

She looked about as different from her usual practical, tidy, and unobtrusive self as possible. She looked like a wanton nymph.

In the midst of her seduction by a Greek god.

And loving every minute of it.

Cassie was sure she didn't usually look like this, even in bed.

How did Lorenzo do this to her?

Watching their lovemaking in the mirror was unexpectedly arousing. Cassie reached to fondle Lorenzo's hair, watching her fingers tangle in his dark curls. She closed her eyes as he coaxed her closer to the summit, then felt his hands beneath her buttocks. He lifted her up, bracing his weight on his elbows, feasting upon her. She watched his tight butt and wanted to grab it.

Her breath caught as his teeth grazed her unexpectedly. Probably deliberately, given his quick chuckle of satisfaction. She'd never felt such pleasure, never had such a determined and deliberate lover.

She was going to have to get even.

Cassie gasped at the power of his tongue. She watched her nipples bead. She saw the flush grow around her breasts as her pulse started to pound. She saw her own breath catch. She saw the flush rise over her skin, suffusing her throat and her cheeks. She saw her eyes sparkle and her toes point. She felt the tide of heat surge through her and heard herself cry out with pleasure.

She opened her eyes to find Lorenzo grinning at her. She crooked a finger at him and he started to ease his weight over her.

"No," she said, pushing his shoulder. He rolled to his back easily, waiting for whatever she wanted. "You'll miss the show that way."

He glanced beyond her, grinning when he spied the mirror. Cassie knelt over him, sitting astride, then lowered herself onto him.

He moaned and bared his teeth at the first touch of her skin to his. "Slower," he whispered as his hands fell on her waist. "I want this to last."

"Don't worry," Cassie whispered against his throat, stealing a kiss as she took all of him inside her. "We can always do it again."

He smiled at her then, his eyes startlingly bright at close proximity. He pushed a hand through her hair with possessive ease, then cupped her nape. "Why do I think that twice isn't going to be enough?" he mused, then pulled her closer for a kiss.

Cassie didn't answer, because she was starting to think the same thing. Then he moved his hips, filling her with his strength, and there were better things to think about.

The digital clock on the nightstand read four thirty.

Cassie could have been content to stay in bed with Lorenzo for the duration. There was something appealing about his determination to savor every pleasure they could give each other, to take all that life had to offer and be ready for more.

He lived in the moment, wringing it dry of sensation.

It was exhausting, and exhilarating.

It felt real.

She watched him sleep, and let her fingers slide through the darkness of his hair. Even in sleep, he was exquisite.

But it was more than his looks that snared her. She liked that he was clever. She liked that he didn't mind when she teased him. She suspected that he probably could laugh at himself.

She loved that he'd given her a choice and also that he'd admitted that he was caught in this spell of attraction as surely as she was. She knew that he created illusions, but this desire wasn't manufactured.

No. He'd as much as admitted that it was inconvenient.

Then he'd seduced her all over again.

Cassie sighed and nestled against his warmth. The sky was starting to change color as the dawn came closer. The strip still twinkled below. They were sprawled across the bed, pink satin sheets smooth beneath them. Cassie turned to her side, facing the windows, and Lorenzo moved to curl behind her, his warmth at her back and his arm around her waist.

As if they'd slept like this a thousand times.

She thought she'd awakened him, but it must have been an instinctive move. She could feel his breath on her neck, hear the slow, rhythmic breathing of sleep.

And no wonder. She recalled their energetic lovemaking and smiled. No sparks. No flames. No beguiling or supposed firestorm.

But fireworks all the same.

Cassie smiled at that. She looked at his fingers, the weight of his hand on her hip, and wished the interlude hadn't ended so quickly. She didn't imagine for a minute that there would be a third such interval between them.

Lorenzo had practically told her that he was interested in single performances. This was already an exception for him. Cassie wasn't stupid enough to expect a man to change for her.

Cassie was also pragmatic. There was no point in making this an awkward parting. They'd had great sex, twice, and it had been a bit of fun for both of them. Unlike Stacy, Cassie didn't believe in kismet and happily ever after.

She sighed in reluctance, then slipped from beneath the weight of Lorenzo's arm. He didn't stir. He must be exhausted. She surveyed him from beside the bed, and thought she saw a glimmer beneath his eyelids, but he seemed to be asleep. His breathing didn't change either.

She went to the bathroom, shaking her head that it was larger than the bedroom she and Stacy were sharing, then returned to the bedroom to dress. He still hadn't moved.

He wouldn't miss her. Not today and not ever.

That was a fact, even if she didn't like it much.

Maybe he'd remember her.

She was never going to forget him. Lorenzo was larger than life, an epic lover, a man no woman would ever erase from her memories.

Great. She was back to being a groupie.

On the other hand, it was better to leave at a high point, to part with a good memory, than to descend into all the fighting and disagreements that characterized an ill-fated match.

As theirs had to be.

Cassie picked up her boots, then paused on the threshold to look back. She could just see the sculpted muscles of one calf from here and the sight was enough to make her reconsider leaving.

Cassie shook her head and slipped quietly into the corridor.

Maybe Stacy wouldn't notice her late return to their room.

As soon as the door closed behind Cassie, Lorenzo rolled to his back. He folded his arms behind his head and considered his reflection.

How could one woman be so irresistible?

How could he have achieved precisely what he'd hoped to achieve and be disappointed? He wished Cassie hadn't left.

The firestorm was supposed to make a *Pyr* desire a specific woman, but his firestorm was satisfied. And the memory of this woman was still tormenting Lorenzo. He could have spent the entire day in bed with Cassie, inundating himself with her scent, caressing every increment of her skin, making her eyes dance with unexpected humor. He liked that she wasn't afraid of him, or even entirely under his spell.

She surprised him and intrigued him.

The firestorm was trying to tempt him to make a mistake.

He thought of Caterina and the lesson she'd taught him, the way she'd tried to trap and expose him. It was no coincidence that the firestorm tempted him to make the same mistake, right before a similar disappearance.

Lorenzo reminded himself that he never made the same mistake twice.

Humans were deceitful. Humans lost their conviction in key moments—when they felt the heat of the fire, for example—and betrayed whoever they so chose. Or whoever they had to betray to save their own skins. Humans were unreliable.

Diavolo.

In the bathroom, Lorenzo reminded himself of all of those things, repeatedly, and to no avail.

He still wanted Cassie.

He was still in big trouble.

This particular human was enticing.

And simultaneously dangerous. Was that her appeal?

What spell had she cast over him? He had no desire for a connection with a human woman, much less to make a partnership of any kind. He had obligations and responsibilities and deadlines. He was scheduled to die in less than three days, to be reborn in a new secret identity and disappear from the world of the *Pyr* once and for all. The success of that endeavor relied upon a lack of personal ties.

Or distractions.

But still. He could have followed her scent to her room; he could have found her in this massive hotel in ten minutes or less; he could have persuaded her to go home with him. He could have confided in her, precisely as he had confided once in Caterina, but he knew what the result would be.

All the same, it took everything he had to resist the urge to follow her.

He was losing his edge.

The firestorm was, he reminded himself savagely, just sex.

Even if JP was here.

Even if Balthasar was here.

Even if Erik was here.

At least none of them appeared to know about the flashfire. Or had come demanding the darkfire crystal. He decided to be grateful for small mercies.

Lorenzo took a scaldingly hot shower, telling himself that none of this was his responsibility.

He didn't believe it.

He could take her with him, invoke the flashfire, have something like a normal human life together. The idea was enticing beyond expectation.

It was insane that he was even tempted. Confiding in others was a risk. It was a loss of control. It opened the door to the possibility of betrayal.

Of failure.

He knew better than that.

Diavolo.

Lorenzo marched out of the bathroom, impatient with himself. He had been sure that another seduction would satisfy him. He had been positive that he just had to get Cassie out of his system, that repeated exposure would diminish her allure.

But as Lorenzo dressed, he was haunted by memories of the lush tangle of her hair—the way she gasped when surprised, the way she flushed with pleasure—and he wondered whether he was wrong. He thought of the contrast between her outward manner—tough, practical, pragmatic, blunt—and her attitude in private—coy, seductive, soft, feminine.

They had at least one thing in common—they both loved lingerie.

Lorenzo could sense a huge error on his own horizon. His plans always included every eventuality.

But he hadn't planned for Cassie Redmond. She excited him, distracted him, turned him inside out and upside down. And each time they parted, he just wanted more.

Not just sex, although that was fabulous. He wanted to get to know her. It had taken everything within him not to stop her from leaving, not to linger over breakfast together, not to learn more about her.

But he didn't do long-term connections. He didn't do intimacy and he didn't do entanglement.

Lorenzo did sex.

Then Lorenzo moved on.

That was Caterina's lesson to him, that expecting more—given what he was—was impossible. He wasn't going to forget that simple truth now.

Lorenzo had worked his system for centuries and it was fine. No, it was *good*. It gave him what he needed from humans and risked nothing. Every few decades, he staged a disappearance, preparing with his usual care, then started over again with a new identity. It worked.

Even if this time, he meant to slide even deeper into obscurity than ever before.

Why a firestorm now? Lorenzo had the startling thought that Cassie could have been sent to distract him right before his big spectacle. Could Balthasar or the other *Slayers* deliberately spark a firestorm?

No, that was nonsense.

It wasn't encouraging that he was getting paranoid.

He paused, glanced out the window. He was being manipulated. The firestorm had occurred of its own volition, but other dragon shifters were using it against him—each for his own agenda.

Lorenzo didn't like that Balthasar had arrived, that Erik had come to nag him, that JP had made Cassie's acquaintance already. He felt as if the entire *Pyr* world—the one to which he vehemently didn't want to belong—was gathering around him, conspiring against him.

But it was just that. It *was* a conspiracy, a plan to throw his game right before he disappeared forever. Everyone was gathering to take one last shot at cornering Lorenzo. Perhaps somehow they sensed his intent, even though he had confided in no one.

And somehow, Cassie was a pawn in that game.

Well, Lorenzo had never done what was predictable. He'd never been malleable, and he'd never subscribed to the *Pyr* perspective.

He would not create a partnership out of his firestorm.

He would not change his plan.

He could still hear Caterina spitting that word.

Routine was key. He had to get home. He had to check on his plans. He had to secure his perimeter and guard his valuables. He had to persuade his father to pack, and he had to get some sleep. He had to continue with his scheme and not be distracted.

Cassie had made her choice. She had left this morning.

And Lorenzo told himself that that suited him just fine.

It was perfect, in fact.

Best for everyone.

Even though he guessed that, this time, the person he was trying to persuade was himself.

There was someone in Lorenzo's car.

The valets had been sleepy and disorganized. Lorenzo had demanded his keys when his impatience reached the tipping point, then marched out in the early morning to the valet lot. His car was distinctive enough—with the custom paint job done at the factory, there couldn't be two.

He'd paid to ensure the specific shade of orange was never used again.

He was just acknowledging that he was going to miss this car after it was destroyed, when he saw the silhouette in the passenger seat.

Lorenzo tried the driver's side door, but it was still locked. The man in the passenger seat glanced idly in Lorenzo's direction, as if he broke into locked cars, sat in them, and locked them again all the time.

One breath proved that he was *Pyr*.

Of course.

Lorenzo should start an appointment calendar. Or a waiting list. A convention, maybe. If nothing else, they could form a line. *Pyr* to the right; *Slayers* to the left. He wasn't joining either team, and the sooner he disappeared from their view, the better.

Lorenzo disengaged the alarm—which apparently hadn't noticed this intruder—unlocked the door and opened it with somewhat less than his usual smooth style.

"What the fuck do you want?" he demanded by way of greeting. He flung himself into the car, took a deep breath, then glared at his unwelcome companion.

A stranger.

The dark-haired, dark-eyed *Pyr* smiled serenely at Lorenzo. "The darkfire crystal," he said and Lorenzo's heart sank.

The reckoning had come.

He'd feared it would, but had hoped otherwise.

There was a glitter in this dragon's eyes, though, a glitter that belied his easygoing manner.

Despite his apparent serenity, this *Pyr* understood force.

And persuasion. He put out his hand, as if expecting Lorenzo to surrender the crystal immediately.

As if he carried it around all the time.

As if he still had it.

While Lorenzo respected that his guest didn't beat around the bush, he still couldn't give him what he wanted. He was terrified at what this stranger might demand in exchange.

This did nothing to improve his mood. He went with an aggressive tone. It couldn't hurt, and he had been known to intimidate some of his kind. "I don't have it."

"Of course you do. You have been its custodian for centuries."

"Well, it's gone." Lorenzo started the engine. "I can't help you. Get out of the car."

His companion didn't move. He merely blinked at Lorenzo. "Gone where?"

"I don't know." When his companion said nothing, Lorenzo gave voice to the most plausible theory. "Someone must have stolen it."

"Your lair doesn't have locks and alarms?"

"My *car* has locks and alarms, but that apparently didn't stop you."

The other *Pyr* smiled fleetingly at that. "I don't think we've met."

"This is not a cocktail party. I'm sorry the gem is gone, but I don't know where it is and I'm late."

"Marcus Maximus," the other *Pyr* continued as if Lorenzo hadn't spoken. "They call me Marco." He shrugged. "They used to call me the Sleeper."

Lorenzo recognized the title with a pang. This was not good news. The Sleeper was the one *Pyr* who had a legitimate claim to the darkfire crystal, as the heir to the Cantor. He didn't just have a rightful claim, but potentially some of the Cantor's powers.

He'd have to bluff.

"You're wasting your breath and my time," Lorenzo said. "I don't have what you want and even if I did, I know it's too precious to just hand over to the first *Pyr* who asks for it."

Marco frowned. "Am I really only the first?"

Lorenzo pinched the bridge of his nose and wished heartily that at least one of his fellows could take a hint. "Get out of my car."

"I could prove my claim to it, if you showed it to me. The darkfire trapped within it will respond to my presence."

That was the test Lorenzo had been taught, but with the crystal vanished, it didn't much matter. It was imperative that he ensure this Marco never demanded the flashfire song—maybe he didn't even know about it. Lorenzo could hope.

And terminate the exchange as quickly as possible.

"I told you. It's gone. I'm sorry. That's that."

"No." Marco looked out the window. "I'll ride to your lair with you and check."

Lorenzo's temper—and his terror—flared. "My word should suffice. I am not going to permit you to search my lair. . . ."

"I won't have to," Marco said mildly. "I'll be able to feel whether it's there or not."

"If that were true, you would have known already that I don't have it."

"I did." Marco smiled, unsurprised. "But it could have been an illusion."

Lorenzo exhaled, practically ready to breathe fire and smoke. "Fine. You'll come to my lair; then you'll get out of my car and leave me alone."

Marco's smile didn't falter. "If I don't sense the crystal, yes."

It was the best offer Lorenzo was likely to get. He put the car into gear and shot out of the parking lot.

The sooner he was home, the sooner he could get rid of this particular *Pyr*. In an ideal universe, he would have been happy to keep his promise and surrender the stone to its rightful keeper.

Lorenzo was increasingly aware that he did not live in an ideal universe.

What could Salvatore have done with the crystal?

He drove fast, really fast, but Marco didn't seem troubled by the speed. The other *Pyr* looked out the window, his expression serene.

Lorenzo was not serene. In fact, he couldn't recall ever having been so riled up. Two *Pyr* and two *Slayers* had poked into his life in less than twelve hours. It defied probability. How many more of them were going to show up to waste his time?

What could he do to stop them?

Why hadn't he disappeared sooner?

And what about Cassie? What about her future? Letting her leave him was precisely what Lorenzo had wanted to happen, but now it felt wrong. Lorenzo took the curve into the driveway hard and fast, disliking the sense that he was making a mistake.

A big mistake.

"*Diavolo*," Marco murmured softly and Lorenzo nearly drove off the road.

Chapter 7

Thorolf decided he liked Bangkok.

The city's hustle, bustle, and color reminded him of the market cities he'd known centuries ago, places where you could buy or sell pretty much anything.

For the moment, he stuck to beer and shooters.

And eye candy.

Thorolf didn't realize that he offered a kind of eye candy himself. Well over six feet tall with dark blond dreadlocks, several tattoos, and the raw muscle of a dragon shape shifter, Thorolf was unlikely to blend into the wallpaper in any city. He did better at being overlooked in Manhattan than in Bangkok — at least he had until he'd been filmed shifting shape in DC during another *Pyr*'s firestorm.

When that video had appeared on YouTube, Erik had hit the proverbial roof. Thorolf had decided to make himself scarce for a while. Bangkok seemed like a good choice, if only because he had never been there and he had heard that it was a good place to party.

Thorolf pretty much lived to party.

He sat at the end of a bar in a disreputable part of

town and watched the action in the street. It was late, but far from dark where he sat, given all the sparkling lights and neon signs. He listened to the hawkers and smelled the street food and watched the parade of people looking for someplace to party.

It was hot, the smell of the jungle underlying everything. His T-shirt was stuck to his back and he could taste sweat on his upper lip. The skin of the women surrounding him glistened in a way that he liked.

The beer was cold. He didn't understand much of what the bartender said to him, but the shooter had been recommended with sign language. Thorolf didn't know what it was and didn't much care—it had a kick like lightning. That worked for him.

This bar was noisy and crowded, which was why he had chosen it. The music was loud, familiar, and its beat had him tapping his toe. The women were gorgeous, independent of their prices.

Thorolf was in his element.

This was his kind of place.

Even though he was theoretically hunting the *Slayer* Chen, Thorolf wasn't in a hurry to get started on that quest for vengeance. He wasn't sure exactly where to start anyway. Chen was in Asia somewhere. That didn't exactly narrow things down. And Chen had made it clear he didn't want to be found.

Each beer made hunting Chen sound more like work. Each shooter made Thorolf more convinced to just hang out for a while. He'd told his friend Rox for years that he was allergic to work, and in this place, he could believe it himself.

Thorolf ordered another round. He decided he'd begin with the vacation part and get to the quest bit later.

That was when he noticed her.

How could he *not* have noticed her? A slim woman with ivory skin and red hair was sitting at the opposite end of the bar. She ordered a glass of wine, so she must have just arrived.

Thorolf listened to her voice over the din of the bar, glad of his keen senses. He liked that she had a husky voice. That was sexy. Her hair was cut really short, but she was so pretty that it just emphasized her femininity. The dangling silver earrings and eyeliner didn't hurt either.

She had curves in all the right places.

Thorolf straightened a bit, tugging at the hem of his T-shirt. Her gaze danced over the occupants of the bar, then landed on him.

He smiled.

She looked.

She smiled.

He looked.

And when her glass of wine came, she lifted it toward Thorolf in a silent toast. She smiled a little bit more before she sipped.

Definitely his kind of place.

Thorolf echoed her salute with his beer. He was thinking of sauntering over there, but she glanced away, speaking to the guy who was sitting beside her. That guy laughed at whatever she said—it wasn't in English—and then she laughed, too.

But she smiled at Thorolf again as she sipped. Her eyes half closed, showing off her long lashes. The gesture made her features look exotic.

Oh yeah.

Her gaze slid away coyly, then back to Thorolf, as if she hoped she'd catch a look at him while his gaze was averted. Thorolf was perfectly willing to be checked out.

He stood, flexed his muscles, and lifted his beer, peering over the crowd as if he were expecting a friend.

He felt her watching him. He smiled, knowing that he was premium goods himself.

The night, in fact, was showing unexpected promise.

When he sat down again—apparently resigned that his friend was delayed—he glanced her way once more. What he saw had him on his feet once again.

A guy was behind her, like a shadow against the night. There was something furtive about the guy, who had his hood pulled over his head and tugged over his forehead. It was way too hot for such a thick sweatshirt, never mind a hood.

The woman was oblivious to the guy's presence, just nodding to the music. The guy eased closer. He looked left and right. He reached.

Thorolf knew instantly what was happening. He saw the flap of the woman's bag move and shouted.

"Hey!" he roared, his call lost in the music.

Sure enough, the guy flitted away, something in his hand.

"Thief!" Thorolf bellowed and lunged out into the street after him. He knocked over three chairs but kept on going.

It was a lanky kid, dressed all in black, and he was fast.

Thorolf was right behind the kid, fury giving him speed.

He would have loved to shift shape, but he knew Erik would be angry if he revealed his dragon form. Instead, he used his dragon senses to ensure he didn't lose the thief.

The kid ducked through stalls and Thorolf followed.

The kid slipped down dark alleys and Thorolf followed.

The kid leapt over a fence, raced through a tiny yard, and catapulted into the street beyond. Thorolf followed.

The kid also knew the streets in the area, which was like a rabbit warren to Thorolf. Thorolf realized that the thief was trying to make his way to the left. He guessed that the kid had a partner, and wanted to drop the goods.

Thorolf ensured that the kid couldn't turn left. He drove him steadily to the right, heading off every attempt to veer left.

He heard the kid start to panic. His breath hitched and his heart was thundering.

Good. He'd make a mistake if he was freaked. Thorolf stayed close.

The kid jumped to a roof, scrabbling for a grip on the corrugated metal before hauling himself up.

Thorolf followed.

The kid leapt to the next roof, Thorolf hot on his heels. They raced across a series of roofs, each slanted in a different direction, some metal, some wood, some plastic.

Then suddenly the kid skidded to a halt, arms windmilling to keep himself from falling forward.

There was a gap ahead and Thorolf smelled water.

A canal.

Nowhere to jump.

Oops.

Thorolf stopped to stalk his prey more quietly. He wasn't entirely sure the kid still had the wallet. He might have to interrogate him.

It was dark here, quiet. Every window was shuttered against the night, despite the heat. Not a safe area, then.

The kid was panting, scanning his surroundings in desperation, his fingers moving on the wallet. So he did have it. Thorolf respected that the kid was still trying to figure out a way to save the situation.

Not stupid, then.

Just desperate. Thorolf noticed now how thin the kid was and how dirty his clothes were. He probably needed the money, and that realization sent a pang through Thorolf.

Been there and done that. In a place not that different from Bangkok. Thorolf could remember being that hungry and that reckless.

He could remember having nothing left to lose.

The kid pivoted, catching his breath when he saw Thorolf still behind him. Thorolf smiled. He took slow steps closer, then extended his hand for the woman's wallet. The kid's hood was still up, against all expectation, his face in shadows. The kid looked left and right. He checked out the canal. He watched Thorolf nervously and backed to the lip of the roof.

Thorolf took another step, then let his eyes change to dragon eyes.

The kid gasped.

He flung the wallet at Thorolf. In the same moment, he took a flying leap off the roof.

As if he were diving into a pool, an Olympic contender.

Thorolf snatched the wallet out of the air. He lunged after the kid, peering over the side of the roof. He halfway thought he'd see the kid turn three graceful somersaults in the air, but instead he saw a splash into the dark canal.

The kid sank and Thorolf gripped the edge of the roof in fear. A wallet wasn't worth dying for.

Unfortunately, Thorolf couldn't swim, so he'd be of no help.

He was thinking of diving in anyway—how deep could it be?—when the kid suddenly came to the surface again, sputtering. Thorolf watched until he had hold of a fishing boat. He hung there, most of his body still in the water, and struggled to catch his breath. He stared up at Thorolf.

Uncertain.

On impulse, Thorolf pulled out his own wallet. He tugged out an American fifty dollar bill, folded it into a paper airplane, and launched it at the kid. The kid hauled himself out of the water in a hurry to catch it. He clearly hadn't guessed what it was when he snatched it out of the air—after he unfolded it, he looked up at Thorolf in astonishment.

Thorolf waved, then loped back to the bar.

His *Pyr* sense of smell helped him out big-time, making it reasonably easy to follow their convoluted trail in reverse. Within moments, he was sauntering down the street toward the bar.

The redhead was arguing with the bartender, and she looked shaken. Even though Thorolf still didn't understand exactly what the bartender was saying, he could guess what the fight was about.

She was unable to pay.

She was trying to explain herself, showing a dexterity with language that Thorolf lacked, although the bartender wasn't interested in excuses. Thorolf leaned on the bar beside her and she gave him a quick glance.

Then a smile.

Then she turned to argue her case again.

"Lose something?" Thorolf asked, offering her wallet.

"Oh!" Her features lit with relief and she really smiled at him this time. "Thank you!" She quickly opened the wallet and paid her bill, stopping the bartender's tirade in midsentence.

Then that man eyed Thorolf, a frown creasing his brow. He pointed at the half-empty beer glass and the shooter where Thorolf had been sitting, but before he could complain, Thorolf handed him some cash.

Within moments, Thorolf was sitting with the red-head, fresh drinks in front of both of them.

"Pickpockets," Thorolf said, feeling quite the man of the world. "There are thousands of them here. You've got to be more careful."

"How did you know?"

"I saw him behind you, knew you didn't see him."

"And you chased him. Wow. Most people wouldn't have bothered. I owe you big-time. Thanks so much." Her eyes glowed with gratitude and Thorolf noticed they were a wonderful shade of green. Sexy. She smiled again and stuck out her hand. "I'm Viv Jason."

"Thorolf." He shook her hand, liking how soft and finely boned it was. Delicate. Feminine. He wanted to pull her closer instead of releasing her hand, find out maybe just how soft those lips were.

Her eyes twinkled as she looked up at him. "Thorolf what?"

"Just Thorolf."

"All right, Just Thorolf, I need some advice, and since you seem to know your way around, you get to advise me."

"Ask away." Thorolf treated himself to a long, cool sip of beer.

"Know any good places to stay?"

Viv was still looking at him as if he were a hero, so

Thorolf took a chance. He was feeling pretty lucky. He grinned. "How about you stay with me?"

She smiled. She blushed a little.

Then she leaned against him, her voice dropping even lower than its usual husky tone. "Thanks. I'd like that."

"Me, too."

When Viv slipped her hand around his neck, the move pressing her breasts right against his side, Thorolf figured his evening couldn't get a whole lot better.

That was even before she kissed him.

Chandra was soaked to the skin, but she didn't care.

She thought about the guy who had pursued her, and the way his eyes had changed. She had a pretty good idea not just what he was but who he was.

She thought about the woman she'd been following in the first place, the woman whose aura told a thousand tales.

Dark tales.

Old tales.

Twisted tales.

One of the Liliot, Lilith's Daughters. Parasites and vermin. Chandra spat, feeling dirty just for thinking of their name.

Chandra had lifted the woman's wallet to find out what name she was using this time. Upon reflection, though, she didn't think it was a coincidence that the woman had been in the same place as the dragon shifter.

She fingered the fifty, knew he could have done far worse to her.

Which just meant that she owed him.

Fortunately, a huge guy with tattoos and blond dreadlocks would be reasonably easy to follow in Bangkok.

Chandra went home to change, then slipped back to

the vicinity of the bar. The *Pyr* and the witch were still there, laughing together. Neither noticed her in her changed clothes, but she was used to that.

Chandra sank back into the shadows to watch.

She might have to save the dragon from his own mistake—and repay her debt to him—sooner than expected.

Chapter 8

*D*iavolo. How had Marco known that Lorenzo had been thinking that word? How much more did the Sleeper know? For the first time, Lorenzo cursed himself for not paying much attention to *Pyr* lore over the years. He didn't know what the Sleeper could do, much less why—all he knew was that this *Pyr* had a claim on the darkfire crystal.

Actually, Lorenzo didn't even know what that stone could do or what its importance was. That had been before the blue-green flame of darkfire had rippled in the core of the stone, before Rafferty's own firestorm had been touched by the challenging force of the mythic darkfire.

Once upon a time, none of this had been Lorenzo's business. It wasn't unreasonable for him to yearn for that to be his situation once again.

Saturday. He'd be done with all of them on Saturday.

He didn't dare even think about flashfire, much less the song the Cantor had given him.

He slanted a sidelong glance at his passenger and wondered how much the other *Pyr* knew about him. He wasn't sure he wanted to know.

He hated that Marco smiled right then.

Lorenzo didn't make conversation. He drove. He wasn't fooled by Marco's calm demeanor. The Sleeper was a *Pyr*, which meant he was a dragon, which meant the fire burned hot within him. It might be banked, or he might simply be disguising its heat, but if cornered or vexed, Marco would fight.

Just like all the *Pyr*. They were primitive creatures. Dangerous. Violent. Inclined to anger and destruction.

He could only hope his companion didn't do something absurd, like toss a challenge coin at him and demand a duel to the death over the crystal. Such practices were barbaric.

Lorenzo drove and acknowledged that he loathed his dragon nature. He was good with the longevity and his control over the element of fire. He liked having the ability to beguile—mostly because those powers had ensured that he'd been able to live as luxuriously as he desired.

But the ripping, tearing, fighting, and biting side of his nature he found vulgar. Ill mannered.

That was why he never shifted shape.

Except for the incident the day before—provoked by Cassie's presence and her question—he couldn't recall the last time he had let himself shift.

It was a point of pride that he never lost control, but he *had* lost control in the theater.

And he'd threatened JP in old-speak.

Lorenzo frowned and accelerated, telling himself that it wouldn't happen again.

"Yes, it will," Marco murmured beside him.

Lorenzo glanced at his companion in wary surprise. Had he heard Lorenzo's thoughts?

"I did," Marco supplied, with a serenity that annoyed

Lorenzo. "Again. It's the legacy of the darkfire, I think. I can hear the thoughts of all the *Pyr*."

"I am not on Erik's team."

"But you can't deny your own nature," Marco said, watching the scenery with apparent fascination. "You have tried to do so for enough time that you should know that."

"What I know is that I *can* deny it."

Marco's smile broadened. "The way you denied the firestorm?"

"I satisfied the firestorm, to rid myself of its inconvenience."

"Ah." Marco was clearly not persuaded. "Then why did you pursue your mate to her hotel?"

Mate. Lorenzo wanted to snarl at the choice of word. "I smelled *Slayer*," he confessed through gritted teeth.

"And isn't it our nature to defend our mates from *Slayers*?"

"Believe what you need to," Lorenzo said. "I do not adhere to Erik's philosophy and I will not be governed by base instincts."

"I see." Marco nodded. "Why the second interlude, then? The firestorm was satisfied, so you should have had no need or desire for her—unless she really is your destiny."

"There is no such thing as destiny."

Marco smiled. "Perhaps your so-called base nature is more a part of you than you think."

Lorenzo felt his own banked fire begin to simmer. "I owe you no explanation."

"True." That maddening smile curved Marco's lips even wider. "I note only that you can't deny what you are." He gave Lorenzo a look. "You can't run from it and you can't hide from it."

Lorenzo turned savagely into his own driveway. "You *were* sent by Erik! You can tell him that I'm not signing up. I'm not joining the *Pyr*!"

"Believe what you need to," Marco said mildly.

"Why can't you leave me alone? Why can't you all go and harass another *Pyr*, one who actually wants to be involved with you?"

Marco smiled. "Because you need us, Lorenzo, whether you realize it or not."

"I don't need *anyone*!"

Marco chuckled.

Lorenzo fumed. He didn't slow down as he approached the closed gates, knowing the timing perfectly. If he'd thought to spook his companion, he was doomed to be disappointed. He saw a slight glitter in Marco's eyes, no more than that; then the gates swung open in the nick of time. He squealed to a halt before his own front door, just as the gates clanged shut.

"You're wrong," Marco said. "But the good thing is that when you ask for the help of the *Pyr*, we will come — despite your attitude."

"I will never ask for the help of the *Pyr*."

Marco smiled that infuriating smile. "We'll see."

Before Lorenzo could argue with him, the Sleeper got out of the car. He stood staring at the house, his eyes narrowed as he scanned its height and breadth.

It was magnificent. Lorenzo looked at it with admiration and knew he would miss it, as well.

On the other hand, the one he was going to occupy had its own charm, and its own challenges. He knew he would love living there, as well.

Life was to be savored in the moment.

But Marco wasn't impressed by the house. He flicked

a glance toward Lorenzo, and smiled again. "It is gone, after all," he murmured. This time, humor danced in his eyes. "I should have known it would choose its own destination."

"Who took it?" Lorenzo demanded. "And how?"

Marco smiled again. "Ask your father." Before Lorenzo could ask, the other *Pyr* inclined his head slightly. "I thank you for your assistance." Marco shimmered blue, shifted shape, then took flight in Lorenzo's courtyard.

In broad daylight.

Right in front of the new housekeeper, who had opened the door to greet Lorenzo and stood there, astonished.

Lorenzo could have spit sparks in frustration.

Not *again*.

But the housekeeper's mouth fell open and her eyes went round and Lorenzo knew he had more beguiling to do.

At least Marco hadn't demanded the flashfire song. Lorenzo could still remember it, much to his relief.

Something was going right.

"So?" Stacy was bouncing on Cassie's bed, an activity guaranteed to ensure that Cassie woke up.

She did. She sat up, noted that it was almost lunchtime, and was surprised that she felt as good as she did.

"So what?" she asked, noting that her friend was showered, dressed, and pretty in purple on this particular day.

Stacy's eyes shone. "Soooooo, you never told me and I couldn't ask because JP was there and later I was too tired to grill you for details. Tell me! Did you have *fun* yesterday afternoon?"

Cassie blushed. She tried to hide it by heading for the bathroom, but no luck—Stacy followed her. "You've already guessed."

"But I want all the details!"

"Well, you're not getting any." Cassie met her friend's gaze. "Look. I feel really bad about leaving you at the show."

Stacy waved this off. "I'm a big girl. And you were past due for some fun. Now, *dish*!"

"No!"

"Come on. Was it fun? Was he amazing?" Stacy's eyes shone. "Is it true love forever?"

"Okay." Cassie froze in the act of brushing her teeth. "Yes. And yes. And no, absolutely not. Satisfied?"

Stacy laughed. "No!" She leaned in the doorway and grinned. "Enough fun that you had to go back for more?"

Cassie continued brushing, ignoring Stacy's pointed remark. A person couldn't be too careful with good dental hygiene.

Stacy laughed again. "Good. I'm glad. When you can't get enough, it's a good sign, you know. Kismet." Cassie rolled her eyes and Stacy sobered. "Is sex with Lorenzo fixing whatever's been bothering you?"

Cassie was going to deny that anything had been bothering her, but she met her own gaze in the mirror, surprised by Stacy's intuitive response. She turned to Stacy. "You know, it is."

"Great! Then I don't mind that you've been too busy to tell me all your secrets. We can catch up later."

Cassie felt guilty at that. "Let's grab some lunch together. . . ."

"Not today. I have a date and he's good for what ails me. I told you years ago that you needed a vacation. I've been telling you for months that a little fun would set you straight. Maybe you'll believe me from now on." Stacy left the doorway, and Cassie heard her rummaging in the closet. She reappeared, posing with a pair of metallic purple sandals with stiletto heels. "What about these shoes?"

"Who's the lucky guy?"

"JP." Stacy inhaled and closed her eyes, as if she were giddy at the prospect. "Gorgeous man with gorgeous taste."

Cassie recalled what JP had said about temptation, and decided not to tell Stacy what he'd said. It sounded as if he was serious about her friend, and she liked that he was thinking of the longer term.

Stacy made an appreciative purr in her throat. "I could just pack him in my suitcase and take him home."

"You might get the chance."

Stacy grinned. "Don't tempt me. Your Jeep could be full of yummy men when we head home. We'll grab Lorenzo on our way past his show."

Cassie laughed at the very idea of getting Lorenzo out of Vegas. She laughed harder at the idea of JP and Lorenzo jammed into the back of her Jeep for the long drive back to L.A. Which illusionist would make the other disappear?

"What's so funny?"

"I don't think they like each other. I was imagining them both locked in the back of the Jeep together."

Stacy laughed then too. "Don't worry. Lorenzo can ride in the front with you and I'll hop in the back with JP." She winked and grabbed her purse.

Cassie supposed her interludes with Lorenzo had served their purpose. She felt more invigorated. Still not ready to rush back to work, but happier.

She indicated Stacy's choice of shoes. "Those look good, especially if you don't have to walk far." Cassie knew better than to expect that Stacy's interrogation was done. She turned on the shower and pretended not to notice that her pal was hovering.

"So, are you seeing *him* today?"

"I don't think so." Cassie tried to sound casual. "It was *fun*, you know, and that's that."

"It was kismet. I saw you two together," Stacy said, and Cassie tried to not roll her eyes at Stacy's favorite word. Or maybe it was her favorite idea. "Did he tell you about your dragon dudes?"

"No, actually, he didn't. There was just that illusion."

"See? He wants you to come after him."

"I don't think so."

"Do you think he did that illusion again at last night's show?"

"He didn't. I guess it was a one-off."

"He didn't? How do you know?" Stacy grinned. "You went *back*!"

Cassie felt herself blushing. "I wanted to know."

"Uh-huh. Don't go getting married while I'm having lunch. I get to be a bridesmaid."

"Not a chance of that happening."

"So maybe Lorenzo knows more about the *Pyr* than he's admitting." Stacy grinned. "Maybe he *is* one. How else would he have done that trick?"

"He's an illusionist," Cassie insisted. "It's his job to make people believe things that aren't true."

Stacy smiled. "Are you sure?"

"Yes! The *Pyr* don't exist."

"Lots of people think they do. Remember YouTube."

Rather than keep arguing, Cassie shut the door, peeled down, and got into the shower instead. She realized that Stacy had followed her when her friend abruptly pulled back the edge of the curtain. "Maybe you should find out for sure," Stacy whispered.

"I don't think Lorenzo's going to play Twenty Questions with me."

"Maybe Truth or Dare," Stacy teased. "Or Spin the Bottle." She primped in front of the mirror. "Maybe you just need an excuse to see him again."

"Maybe I don't."

"Maybe you *should*." Stacy disappeared, her heels clicking on the bathroom floor. "Seeing as he's going to die on Saturday. Make every moment count and all that."

"What are you talking about?" Cassie ripped open the shower curtain and looked after her friend, who smiled.

"The spectacle." Stacy reminded her, waving the brochure with Lorenzo's picture on it. "Didn't you read the brochure? Oh no, I forgot, you were too busy ogling his picture." Stacy rolled her eyes to show her skepticism. "Checking on the competition in the photography game."

"I'm sure it's a stunt. He's not going to die."

"That's not what the bookies are saying. You should see the odds. If he survives this trick, Lorenzo could be a kabillionaire."

Cassie eyed the shower and thought about Lorenzo dying.

It wasn't a good thought.

She was sure that he would work out the illusion so he survived—but what if he was wrong? Anyone could miscalculate.

Stacy grabbed her purse and flashed a smile. "Gotta go. Be good—or if you can't be good, be careful."

"Right back at you."

Stacy laughed, and then she was gone.

Cassie stood under the deluge of hot water. Was Lorenzo's feat going to kill him?

Or was there more going on than anyone—even the bookies—realized?

By the time she got out of the shower, Cassie was determined to find out.

Not because she imagined that she had any future with a sexy illusionist. Cassie knew better than to believe in the long term.

But she still wanted to know. Maybe she just wanted to know that Lorenzo himself had a long term. Maybe she just liked the idea of a world with one very sexy magician in it.

Yes, that was it.

She knew Lorenzo wouldn't tell her outright. He was a man who prized his secrets and his privacy, maybe to preserve a bit of mystery about himself, maybe because he had something to hide.

Unfortunately for Lorenzo, Cassie was the one woman who could find out anything about anybody.

In another time and place, Lorenzo would have already been positive that his father had a talon in his current misfortunes. It was the kind of meddling his father most enjoyed.

But even Marco's conviction of that couldn't persuade Lorenzo of his father's involvement. The old *Pyr* was just too feeble to make trouble.

After convincing the housekeeper that she couldn't possibly have seen what she had seen, Lorenzo strode to his father's apartment at the back of the house. He stood outside the door, listening.

All he heard was the steady rhythm of his father's breathing. It was very slow, evidence that the old man was essentially hibernating again. He'd been like this since the death of Lorenzo's mother, but it had gotten worse in recent years.

As if Salvatore was avoiding life.

As if he couldn't face it without Angelina.

He certainly had aged to a state of frailty that was shocking to Lorenzo.

Lorenzo entered the security code that kept curious eyes from peeking in on his father's privacy and opened the door silently. He stepped into the darkness beyond, closing the door behind him and leaning back against it. The room was dark, the windows shuttered against the sun. The air was cool here, the stone floor exuding a familiar chill. Lorenzo checked, but his dragonsmoke boundary mark was intact.

His father was safe.

Lorenzo only ever breathed dragonsmoke for Salvatore. Dragonsmoke was a perimeter mark, one that was invisible to humans but a barrier to other dragons. A *Pyr* or *Slayer* could only cross the dragonsmoke boundary of another dragon with explicit permission.

Lorenzo breathed his dragonsmoke so that only he and his father could cross it without being burned to a crisp.

His father slept in dragon form, sprawled across an antique Persian carpet, the red and gold of the rug making a good contrast with his pale scales. He could have been made of hammered silver, or alabaster carved so thin that the light shone right through it. His scales shone even in the dim light, aglow like faceted quartz or diamonds. His tail unfurled across the carpet, magnificent and powerful.

Unlike Lorenzo, his father preferred his dragon form. And why not? Salvatore had fought battles in this form. He had conquered villains in this form. He had won the heart of a courtesan in this form—although he'd seduced her in his human form. Lorenzo smiled, imagining the sight of his father carrying his mother on one of their night rides over the Veneto. His father had given her an experience that no other man could offer, and she, by all accounts, had been a sophisticated woman with a taste for the unusual.

Lorenzo had never seen them together. He had few actual memories of his mother, since she'd died when he was so young. One painting of her was all that he had, and over time, he'd become uncertain how much of what he thought was memory was shaped by the painting.

Did he really remember the curl of her hair touched by sunlight? The way her eyes had shone before she laughed? The whisper-soft caress of her fingertips on his cheek? The sweet rhythm of her voice? He'd been so young when she died that it seemed impossible he'd remember anything of her—and yet those snippets nudged at his thoughts.

Lorenzo was convinced, though, that his parents' romance was a relic from another era.

He wasn't at all persuaded that Angelina wouldn't have tired of his father, his habits and his abilities, given time. They had been in the first flush of romance when she died, for it had been only two years after the firestorm had sparked.

And they—two passionate people—had already been arguing.

Immediately after Angelina's death, Lorenzo's father had been wild, drinking and gambling and carousing at a manic pace. Then abruptly, after fifty years, he'd just stopped. As if he had no more taste for life anymore.

Since then, he'd steadily become more pale and more feeble. His fire might not have been extinguished, but it was certainly dimmed. Even with all that had passed between them in Lorenzo's first fifty years, he hadn't been able to leave his father alone after that.

The firestorm had launched his aging process, and life without his mate had only sped it along. Salvatore slept more every year, to the point that he could seldom be awakened for anything these days.

Lorenzo stepped closer, shaking his head that his father continued to sleep, apparently unaware of his presence. He could see that his father's scales had become thinner, that there was less muscle in his body, that he was slipping away.

He'd been slipping away for most of Lorenzo's life.

He wondered why his father hadn't yet gone.

In a way, it was unkind to make demands of him, to trouble him with the details of life. Lorenzo had tried to rouse his father, tried to make arrangements for his future, but Salvatore would not prepare to move from this house.

He could barely be roused.

If Salvatore had been responsible for the disappearance of the darkfire crystal—and who else could be?—Lorenzo wasn't convinced that his father would even remember what he'd done with it. He could have given it to one of the staff as a tip, a pretty bauble from an eccentric old man.

Did it really matter anymore? The stone was gone. Lorenzo's promise to keep it safe was broken. Marco knew the gem wasn't here anymore. In fact, Marco seemed to know where it was. Mercifully, no one had demanded compensation for the stone's disappearance, so Lorenzo's disappearance could continue as scheduled.

He definitely had the sense of having made a miraculous escape.

Lorenzo stood and watched the old *Pyr*. He didn't want to abandon his father, but he couldn't move him like this. And apparently he hadn't been very persuasive in arguing his case for them leaving together.

Or maybe his father simply didn't have the will to live anymore.

Maybe Lorenzo should make alternate plans. He could let his father remain here, at the house. He could will the house to Salvatore, ensure that there was enough capital to support him for another hundred years. The dragonsmoke would dissipate, of course, but maybe that didn't matter as much as Lorenzo had thought. His father could live out his days in comparative tranquillity. It was a compromise, but maybe it would be more kind.

Maybe Lorenzo didn't have a lot of choices.

He pivoted with purpose, his decision made. He'd have to contact the lawyer right away to ensure that everything was arranged in time. He wished there was another option, but he couldn't see his initial plan working now.

He paused on the threshold to look back one last time. The old dragon slept on, blissfully unaware that the perimeter of his lair had been compromised and Lorenzo's dragonsmoke had been breached, even if it had just been by Lorenzo himself.

Lorenzo's lips tightened in dissatisfaction and he left, intent on the arrangements that had to be made.

Lorenzo didn't see his father's eyes open after he left the apartment.

He certainly didn't see his father's slow smile, much less the glint of mischief that lit Salvatore's eyes.

Stacy had—very helpfully—left another copy of Lorenzo's brochure on the dresser, prominently displayed. Cassie read it while she dressed and learned the details of Lorenzo's upcoming stunt.

On Saturday, Lorenzo was going to be buried alive in Valley of Fire State Park. He'd be seated in his orange Ferrari, which would be buried in the desert. He'd be left underground for an entire month, longer than any person could be expected to survive with such limited supply of oxygen—never mind in the desert in the summer.

No wonder people thought he wouldn't survive.

The whole idea gave Cassie the creeps. She didn't like the dark much and she hated being enclosed in small spaces. Even elevators were endurance tests for her if they stopped too many times. She shuddered as she read the brochure again. She was sure there had to be a trick, and that Lorenzo had planned somehow to ensure his own survival.

She was sure he wasn't the kind of man to have a death wish.

But he could make a mistake. It wasn't as if he could practice this one, while doing a performance every day and two on Wednesday. How far would he go in pursuit of spectacle and a hit of publicity? Too far? The very idea made Cassie nervous.

She dressed practically, packed a bag with a few essentials, and headed out to hunt for details.

This was, after all, what Cassie did best.

In the lobby bar, Cassie struck up a conversation with that same waitress, the one whose kids were intrigued with Lorenzo. It didn't take much prodding to learn from her where Lorenzo lived—in a gated compound about forty-five minutes out of town. Cassie left the waitress a good tip and headed out to do research.

She doubted he'd be in the phone book—on the other hand, she didn't even know his surname so she couldn't be sure. She went to the library and looked him up on the Internet.

Cassie started with the accounts in the morning papers about his new dragon illusion the night before. Evidently the audience would be full of reporters for the remaining performances. As a result of the excitement, scalpers' prices for Lorenzo's final shows this week had gone even higher.

It took her most of the day to read all the articles about Lorenzo—he had a good publicist—and despite all the articles she never found his surname or his date of birth.

She didn't find any personal details, either. No stories leaked by former staff. No unauthorized photographs. No gossip or trivia. Nothing about blood relatives, lovers, ex-wives, or kids. Cassie was impressed by his ability to stay on top of the information generated about him, especially given his level of fame.

That only made her more determined to know more.

Because it convinced her that he had a secret.

It was probably something mundane. Maybe he had a lot of illegitimate children. A criminal record. Or maybe he just liked his privacy. Cassie couldn't fault him for that.

She still wanted to know.

Cassie didn't imagine that she'd be able to breach Lorenzo's security system, but she could head out to the house and have a look. She'd do it while Lorenzo was involved in his evening performance, so she'd know for sure that he wasn't home.

She wouldn't have an address, per se, but it sounded as if the house was distinct. One thing was on her side— famous people like Lorenzo never did their own laundry or took out their own trash.

Maybe she'd find a staff member willing to talk.

She called Stacy and learned that her friend was going to dinner and a show with JP. Cassie smiled at Stacy's warning that she should call before letting herself into the room, and was glad to hear her friend so excited again.

It sounded like JP was exactly what Stacy needed.

Cassie waited until twenty minutes before Lorenzo's show started. She could have gone sooner, but hadn't wanted to risk passing Lorenzo on the highway heading out of town.

She found her Jeep in the hotel parking lot, then drove past the back of Lorenzo's theater just to be sure. She was relieved to see his orange Ferrari parked in place.

He was there and inside.

Busy.

Cassie did some quick calculations. The show would last two hours or maybe a bit more, which meant Lorenzo could be on the road home by eleven. She should be able to get to the house by nine thirty, but to ensure that they wouldn't pass on the road when she returned to town, she'd have to leave by ten fifteen. Make it ten for insurance.

She didn't have a lot of time.

Cassie headed out of town, pushing her Jeep to its limit once she was on the open highway. She rolled down the window, liking the wide horizons, and ignored the unhealthy vibration of the engine. She liked that she was leaving Las Vegas behind, with all its hype and sparkle. These canyons and sweeping vistas of the desert touched her in a way that was surprising. She'd never been a nature fiend, but she liked the raw power of stone and sand.

They were genuine.

To her relief, even without an address, Lorenzo's house was obvious. The only thing real about it was that it must have cost a fortune—it was evidence of his success. Beyond that, it was pure Vegas, another spectacle. The house could have been a piece of Renaissance Italy transplanted. In the midst of cacti and dust, after passing scattered adobe buildings and sixties ranches, the Venetian palace caught the eye.

It was massive, all arches and golden light, a fountain dancing in the front courtyard. It was two stories in height, judging by the lines of windows, but each floor must have fifteen-foot ceilings.

The driveway was long and straight, and she was sure that there were lots of cameras to track anything that moved on that length of pavement. There was a high fence surrounding the house and several acres of grounds, with large wrought-iron gates front and center.

They were closed.

They were embellished with a shield, a coat of arms, and lots of frilly curlicues.

A capital L right in the middle.

She smiled. Lorenzo didn't do subtle.

The land was rocky, both inside and outside the fence. The size of the lot would give a certain amount of privacy, and Cassie thought that the windows probably had sheer blinds. She could see light behind them, but it was diffused and there were no distinct shadows. The property backed against a rocky rise, one that looked red against the night sky.

Cassie drove past the house, slowing down only a little bit. She continued until the road finally curved, then turned off the asphalt. She took the Jeep off-road and circled back to the house from behind.

She turned off her headlights when she could see the house and was glad that there was enough light from the moon to mostly see her way. She drove slowly, aware of the press of time, but not wanting to kick up any dust that might be noticed.

She parked the Jeep when she'd driven as close as she dared, grabbed a flashlight and her camera, and crept closer. She hunkered down behind a cactus about twenty feet from the house and had a better look.

There were fewer lights at the back of the house, just as she'd suspected. Light showed in only one window. It looked as if a blind was pulled down, the light showing only around the perimeter of the window.

Good. No one to witness what she was about to do.

She could spot just two security cameras, one on each corner pillar of the fence. They moved in a steady rhythm, sweeping the area. Their paths were synchronized so that one or the other always had the back fence in its field of view.

Cassie tugged out her new camera and used the zoom to get a better look. The gardens were extensive and formal, laid out in succulents and stones. Another smaller fountain chortled here, nestled between a pair of benches. There was a stone gazebo close to one corner. The yard looked tranquil and it was quiet other than the sound of the fountain.

She wondered whether this was where Lorenzo did his sunbathing. Not many gawkers would make it around the back of the house. It was easy to imagine him sprawled out beside the fountain, dozing in the sun.

There was no sign of any staff members at the house. Just those relentless security cameras. And the house was located so far within the fence that she wouldn't even have been able to intercept anyone taking out the trash. Cassie sat for a while in her hiding spot, checking out the house through the zoom on her camera, and hoping for a miracle.

No luck. She just got chilled.

And time was slipping away.

Cassie was just about to call her mission a failure when she noticed that the far camera had frozen in place. Its lens was fixed on the desert in the opposite direction of where she was.

It defied belief that it should break right when she was thinking of approaching the house.

The light flickered at that window, as if someone had moved the shade. Cassie swallowed and braced herself to run back to the Jeep. She expected dogs to be released, or guns to be fired, or security men to chase her away.

What she saw instead was the other camera freezing in place, its view fixed on the distant road.

The shade opened abruptly, and the entire square of the window was illuminated. Cassie saw the silhouette of a figure.

It beckoned to her.

She wasn't sure who it was or what that person wanted—much less how that person had seen her—but Cassie wasn't going to look a gift horse in the mouth. She ran for the fence, unable to see whether it was electrified or otherwise booby-trapped.

Was she just being tricked into exposing herself? Lorenzo had taken measures to ensure his privacy.

Who was in the window anyhow?

She looked back at the silhouetted figure. The man pointed and Cassie followed his gesture. There was a service gate disguised in the pattern of the fence. She never would have seen it if it hadn't been pointed out, not at night anyway.

It had an electronic lock.

But there was no light on the display.

No power.

Cassie looked up. The man in the window beckoned once more. She touched the gate with a cautious finger-tip and it swung inward.

Unlocked.

Deliberately, she was sure.

Okay, she had an ally, and maybe a source of information. Cassie slipped into the courtyard. She glanced at the window, just as the light winked out.

The man was gone.

The closest camera clicked as if it was going to start moving again.

Unable to stifle the sense that she was stepping right into a trap, Cassie raced toward the house. She was wondering which door exactly she should target when one opened, throwing a patch of light into the yard.

A man gestured from there, urging her to hurry. It looked like the same man. She realized as she got closer that he was older, although he still stood tall. She ducked into the house and he closed the door behind her, sharing a conspiratorial smile.

"So, you are safely inside the lair," he said, his dark eyes twinkling. He had an accent, maybe Italian. It sounded exotic. His hair was silver, a luxuriant wavy mane. "Lorenzo will have a surprise!" He laughed at the prospect, so delighted with himself that Cassie was tempted to smile. He surveyed her, then turned with surprising speed, beckoning her again. "Come, come."

Her unexpected accomplice looked to be quite elderly, but he moved with the spry energy of a young man. The twinkle in his eyes made him look irrepressible.

"You turned off the cameras?"

"Of course. Lorenzo would be notified the moment there was a trespasser noted on the premises." The older man shook his head. "He likes to know everything. He thinks he knows everything." He rolled his eyes, showing his opinion of that.

Cassie instinctively liked him after that comment. "But he doesn't."

"He knows *nothing*! But we shall teach him, you and I together. Every man learns what he needs to know either from a woman or from his father." The older man laughed, and Cassie had to admit that the prospect of teaching Lorenzo anything made her smile, too. Then he offered his hand. "I am Salvatore di Fiore. Lorenzo's father."

Cassie was surprised that Lorenzo's father lived with him. She admired that Lorenzo took care of his father, and that the fact had never once been mentioned in any of the biographies and articles she'd read. She respected that he did the right thing but didn't expect credit.

She liked that. A lot.

"Cassie," she said with a smile. "Cassie Redmond."

Salvatore bowed low over her hand, a courtly gesture, and touched his lips to its back. Then he looked up at her, that mischief dancing in his dark eyes.

"You are the one," he said with a confidence that made Cassie's heart skip. "I like you already. It is time Lorenzo had a woman who challenged him, made him work. The others make it too easy for him." He shrugged. "He does not respect them."

Cassie appreciated the idea of being different from the other women Lorenzo seduced, the ones who used his limo service. "Is that why you helped me?"

He smiled. "What do you think?" Salvatore gave her a look then, one that hinted at a considerable measure of determination, then gestured her onward.

"Welcome," he said as they stepped into a large and gracious room.

Chapter 9

Cassie was astonished. It could have been a living room, but like everything else about Lorenzo, it far exceeded any expectations. The room was large, partly because the ceilings were so high, but sparingly and elegantly furnished. A pair of velvet-upholstered sofas with curved backs faced each other, beneath a massive glittering chandelier. It must have been hung with a thousand faceted crystal teardrops.

The floor was dark wood inlaid with a circular flourish that could have been ivory, and the plaster moldings on the ceiling were elaborate. For all that, the surfaces were painted in solid colors, not the gilt or filigree that Cassie might have expected. One entire wall was composed of arched windows, which faced a private courtyard. She could smell exotic flowers, which must be in bloom in that garden.

She understood then why the house seemed so large. It probably had more interior courtyards like this one, garden spaces that provided privacy to Lorenzo and his father.

Even she would have a hard time getting an unapproved and candid shot of the great illusionist at home. He'd sunbathe in a courtyard, secured from prying eyes.

The room was dominated by an enormous painting that hung opposite the windows. It was framed in gilt and almost filled that wall. The paint was flaking slightly and Cassie guessed that it was very old. The colors had the luminosity that she remembered from art history class, like altarpieces by Titian.

But this was no altarpiece. There were no saints shown in this image and not a Madonna to be seen. The painting showed a room remarkably similar to this one, so similar that she wondered whether this room was supposed to be a replica. The main difference was that the windows in the image opened onto a canal lined with other houses, not onto a desert courtyard. She recognized the architecture characteristic of Venice, but this time from her own travels.

The scene seemed to be one of a house of pleasure, for the women—with their splendid long hair and rosy breasts—were naked. They wore only jewels, at their ears, on their fingers, pearls around their necks and waists. The men—who admired them, fed them, were fed by them, lounged on couches—wore Renaissance garb. There was food on every surface, as well as great goblets of wine, dogs, parrots, a monkey, and a group of six musicians. The night sky beyond the windows was filled with stars, and Cassie thought it was probably quite a party.

There was a date inscribed in one corner—1586—and a signature she couldn't decipher. Whoever had painted it had been very good, though.

The composition was unusual because one woman, a great beauty with a knowing smile, stood to one side of the painting. She was almost life-sized and looked out at the viewer as she apparently pulled a velvet drape aside.

With her free hand, she gestured to the room behind her. Her expression was daring and mischievous, as if she revealed a secret. She wore only a long string of fat pearls, a golden bracelet set with rubies, and embroidered slippers. Her hair was long and red-gold, hanging in glistening waves past her hips.

That figure's pose created an intimacy with the viewer, putting Cassie right in the scene—as if she were a guest in that house, being shown its true business.

And being invited to join the festivities.

Cassie thought it an odd choice for a room where one received guests, and gave her accomplice a considering glance.

What exactly were Salvatore's expectations?

She realized that she'd been staring and he'd been watching her.

And he didn't look so mischievous anymore.

Had she made a big mistake?

Salvatore laughed heartily as if he'd read Cassie's thoughts and found them ridiculous. Then he gestured to the couches in invitation. "Prosecco, perhaps?"

"That would be nice."

"Prosecco is always nice," he said, moving to a silver champagne bucket filled with ice.

And one bottle. There were two flutes there, as if he'd expected guests.

Expecting her?

How?

Salvatore eased the cork out of the bottle with his thumbs, a man who had performed this task a thousand times, then poured the sparkling contents. He offered one glass to Cassie with a slight bow.

"And so we drink to the successful seduction of my son," he said, eyes dancing with merriment. "Yes, Lorenzo is my son." He indicated the painting, his smile fading as he eyed the figure on the right. "And this, this is his mother, Angelina." He raised his glass to the painting and toasted her image.

He drank a great swallow of the Prosecco and Cassie felt obliged to do the same. It was cool and effervescent on her tongue, the perfect refreshment after her time in the desert.

"Lorenzo was born in that house," her companion said gruffly, turning back to retrieve the bottle.

Cassie eyed the date in the corner of the picture, confused. "When?"

"In 1585," Salvatore said, as if there was nothing unusual about it at all.

Cassie didn't want to be rude, but she'd heard enough propaganda in her time. She smiled at Salvatore to soften her words. "But that's impossible."

He was unruffled. "It cannot be impossible, for it is so." He smiled. "I remember the night very, very well." His gaze slid to the painting again, locking on the image of the woman who held the drape.

Cassie sipped her Prosecco, keeping silent while he visited his memories. Whatever they were. She didn't believe for one minute that Lorenzo was four hundred years old, or that he was the son of a Venetian courtesan. That made no more sense than him being a dragon shifter. It was just part of his patter, part of the illusion of his show. And his father, evidently seeing which side his bread was buttered on, helped support the illusion.

She got that far in her thinking before Salvatore turned his bright gaze on her. He glanced up and down, then inhaled slightly, as if he did not like what he saw.

Then he met her gaze steadily. "You think I am old

and confused because I tell you something you choose not to believe. We shall have honesty between us."

Cassie was startled that he would be so direct. Were her thoughts that obvious? "Okay." She agreed cautiously, not certain she had much choice.

"I am old but not confused."

Cassie smiled at his indignation. "Fair enough."

"While you are young and beautiful, but hide your truth. Why do you dress like a boy? Do you not wish to win my Lorenzo for your own? Are you ashamed to be a woman?"

"No, of course not." She gestured to the painting. "Jewelry and slippers isn't a very practical outfit in my line of work."

Salvatore moved quickly to flick the clip out of her hair while she was looking at the painting. She was startled, but he fluffed it loose around her face.

"Better," he said, approval in his eyes. He gestured to the painting again. "You must understand a secret. This place is in Lorenzo's heart. This is what he knows. And femininity, raw and potent, is his weakness."

Cassie considered the painting, and had to admit that what she knew of Lorenzo certainly included a taste for luxury.

She recalled his admiration of her lingerie.

"You cannot catch a fly with water, Cassie Redmond," Salvatore whispered close beside her. "It has never yet been done. Honey is how you must bait the trap."

She wasn't sure what to say to that, but by the time she was ready to look the old man in the eye, she turned to find him gone. She was alone in a beautiful room, alone except for the knowing gaze of the woman in the painting.

Angelina.

That was when she heard the throaty rumble of an approaching Ferrari.

Cassie glanced at her watch and grimaced.

She'd lost track of the time.

Or Salvatore had ensured that she would still be here when his son returned. She had a feeling that the old man wasn't entirely innocent in this—and he had said that Lorenzo would be surprised to find her here.

She was pretty sure Lorenzo wouldn't be happy to find her in his home, uninvited. He liked his privacy too much.

Cassie was tempted to run. The logical way out would be just as she'd come in, but she knew she couldn't clear the fence without Lorenzo seeing her departure. The cameras were probably back on, as well. She doubted she could get back to her Jeep, let alone all the way back to Vegas, without him catching up to her.

Femininity, raw and potent, is his weakness.

Okay. Maybe the best choice was to brazen it out. She liked when she surprised Lorenzo. Maybe he'd answer her questions if he was caught off guard.

Cassie heard a door opening and the beep of an alarm system.

Then footsteps coming closer.

Lorenzo appeared in the doorway.

He froze.

He stared.

He dropped his car keys.

The world stopped cold as they eyed each other.

Lorenzo was wearing a tuxedo shirt, the front unfastened, and a pair of black jeans. He had the tuxedo on a hanger, hooked over his shoulder, as if he intended to take it to the dry cleaners. He looked good enough to eat, even without his gaze dancing over her.

Or the heat that lit his eyes.

He opened his mouth to say something, then closed it again without speaking a word. Cassie loved that she had surprised Lorenzo so much that he was struck speechless. She had a feeling that didn't happen very often.

Lorenzo's hands clenched and unclenched, and she saw him swallow. There was a faint shimmer of blue around him, which was odd, and an obvious sign of interest in his jeans.

Cassie knew right then and there that he was glad to see her. She smiled, feeling that she had more in common with the woman in the picture by the minute.

And all the questions she'd just had didn't seem that important anymore. Cassie rose to her feet, feeling the heat of his perusal.

There was no doubt that she had Lorenzo's undivided attention. He watched her hungrily, his eyes darkening.

Cassie felt powerful and sexy, which was a pretty good combination. She was sure the temperature in the room had tripled, maybe even quadrupled.

"Maybe you should get another glass," she suggested. "Before the Prosecco gets warm."

Lorenzo flung his tuxedo on a chair and stepped toward her, his eyes gleaming with intent. He smiled that slow smile, the way his gaze roved over her so obviously appreciative that Cassie's blood simmered. She felt tingly all over and knew that their lovemaking would be fabulous again.

She didn't know what had turned her into a woman who couldn't get enough, but she didn't care.

Lorenzo was the sexiest man alive, and he wanted her.

Then she understood—he was what had changed her perspective.

And, for the moment, Cassie liked that just fine.

Cassie's heart had time to flutter with anticipation; then Lorenzo inhaled sharply and pivoted to look toward the courtyard. That blue shimmer around him brightened to blinding intensity; then he leapt for the windows in a blaze of light.

Cassie had seen that weird blue light before, in his theater and again in the bar with JP. She squinted, refusing to close her eyes completely, lest she miss something.

She never expected to see what she did.

Right before her eyes, inside the halo of blue light, Lorenzo changed shape. He became the same massive gold dragon that had appeared in the finale of his show. She saw the wings grow out of his shoulders. She saw his hands extend into claws. She saw the tail unfurl from his back and the scales erupt all over his body. She saw the ferocious teeth form. It happened in a flash, but she saw it all.

There was no smoke.

There were no mirrors.

The change was real.

Cassie was stunned. Even though she'd speculated that this might be his secret, it was astounding to witness the truth. It hadn't been an illusion, not here and not in the theater. Lorenzo really was a shape-shifting dragon guy.

He hadn't lied in the theater when he'd said "Right here!"

She'd uncovered his secret and it was the last one she'd expected him to have. She sat down just as her knees gave out beneath her.

Cassie had actually found a *Pyr*.

Lorenzo was astounded by Cassie.

Again.

He was shocked to find her in his home. She shouldn't have been able to breach his security system, but evidently she had.

He was also astonished to realize that she was already pregnant, just as the *Pyr* stories insisted. He could smell the difference in her body. Were all the old myths true?

And he was surprised by how well it suited her. She looked relaxed and confident, aware of her femininity in a way that was new. Her hair was loose and her eyes were sparkling. Was that the Prosecco? The child?

Or because of him? Lorenzo knew which answer he liked the best.

Mostly, though, Lorenzo was shaken by how glad he was to see Cassie. He'd spent the evening trying to convince himself that she had no place in his life, that it was better she had left, that they had no future together. Just one glimpse of her lounging on his couch with a glass of Prosecco was enough to completely trash his rationalizations.

And make him realize that he wanted her all over again.

But Lorenzo had only had time to savor the fact that Cassie was waiting for him before he'd caught the scent of *Slayer*.

Balthasar.

Lorenzo reacted immediately and instinctively. The change ripped through him with primal force, his need to defend Cassie so overwhelming that there was nothing he could do to stop his shift.

That would have worried him, if he'd had time to think about it.

As it was, he was remembering Balthasar's threat to change his mind about joining the *Slayers*.

Lorenzo knew whose mind was going to get changed and it wouldn't be his. All he wanted was to be left alone—right now, he wanted to be left alone with Cassie. If Balthasar found that concept elusive, Lorenzo would ensure the *Slayer* followed it anyway.

With pure unadulterated dragon emphasis.

Nobody but nobody was going to lay a talon on anyone in Lorenzo's lair.

Cassie watched in amazement as Lorenzo kicked out the glass in the window, shattering it with one blow from his massive tail. He raged into the courtyard, leaping through the broken pane as he breathed fire. She had a heartbeat to wonder what his issue was—then she knew.

Another dragon swooped over the roof, coming at Lorenzo with talons extended. He exhaled a plume of bright orange fire and Cassie heard a sound like thunder.

He obviously hadn't stopped by for a glass of wine.

Lorenzo must have heard him coming.

But Lorenzo wasn't glad to see this dragon. The antagonism between the two crackled in the air. The sound of thunder was relentless if inexplicable. The sky was clear overheard, some stars glittering in the darkness. There was more thunder; then they began to fight.

Hard.

The two dragons collided, biting and slashing at each other with ferocious strength. They pounded each other, thrashing with their tails and breathing fire.

Cassie knew a grudge match when she saw one. Neither one gave the other any quarter.

The dragon that was Lorenzo appeared just as he had at the theater the other night. His scales looked like they were made of hammered gold—maybe they were—but now she could see that there were different hues of gold in his scales. She saw red-gold scales, white-gold ones, and yellow-gold ones. They glinted, each looking as if it had been pounded to its shape, catching the light as the dragons fought. She could see the powerful muscles moving beneath them, and was awed by the line of what looked like cabochon gems adorning the scales on Lorenzo's chest and tail.

He really did look like a medieval reliquary.

But a dangerous one.

Where was Salvatore? The thought struck her suddenly.

Cassie winced as Lorenzo flung the other dragon into the side of the house and the whole building shook with the impact. The other dragon snarled and leapt for Lorenzo, fury in his eyes.

This other dragon's scales could have been carved of agate or jasper. They were veined with russet and gold and green, each one rimmed in gold. His talons looked to be gold, too, although they were viciously sharp.

Did Lorenzo know him? Cassie had to believe that the party circuit for shape-shifting dragon men had to be pretty small. They probably all knew each other.

She heard the crash of them colliding again and more thunder and winced. It seemed as if they hated each other.

Although she wouldn't have been a fan of anyone who came raging into her own private patio to start a vicious fight. Cassie winced as Lorenzo took a hit. His eyes flashed and he breathed a brilliant plume of fire at his opponent. There was a smell of burning flesh as the other dragon yelped and retreated.

Cassie pulled her camera out of the pocket of her jeans, but hesitated to use it. Instinct told her to grab the shots and run, but Cassie wasn't sure.

She knew Lorenzo prized his privacy.

She was pretty sure she now knew why.

The thing was that Lorenzo was a publicity hound. He cultivated media attention, but this detail of his life—which would have put him on the front page of every publication in the world—had been one he'd chosen to hide.

She'd bet that there had been extenuating circumstances of some kind the night before when he'd shifted in the theater—but even then, he'd done it during his show, so people assumed it was an illusion.

Cassie had to believe that there was a good reason for that. Lorenzo didn't do anything by accident, and he wasn't stupid.

Which meant there was something she didn't know about these dragons. She heard the crackle of fire and the sound of crunching bones and guessed it might be something that could get a puny human like herself killed.

Cassie wasn't stupid either.

She turned off the camera and put it on the end table. The fact was that she didn't want to betray Lorenzo. She'd think about why later—for the moment, she'd go with her instinct.

Which was to get out alive while it was still possible.

Cassie crossed the floor, making herself as inconspicuous as possible, and picked up Lorenzo's car keys. The Ferrari would be faster than her Jeep, and closer, too. In the doorway, she looked back and hesitated.

She couldn't leave, not without knowing that Lorenzo

survived. Even knowing that she could end up getting fried, she couldn't help but watch.

Behind the couch offered a better view. She ducked back down there, shoving the car keys into her pocket.

Lorenzo loosed another torrent of dragonfire at his assailant and Cassie smelled burning flesh. She saw the other dragon's agate scales blacken and begin to curl.

The other dragon backed into a corner, but Lorenzo went after him, spewing fire every step of the way. The agate dragon howled when Lorenzo cut open his shoulder with a ferocious slash from his claws. Black blood spurted onto the stone patio. That blood sizzled on contact, a plume of steam rising from the puddle.

Cassie's eyes widened. These guys were toxic in more ways than she'd expected.

The other dragon bared his teeth and rallied, lunging at Lorenzo. Lorenzo punched him in the gut and in the face, a quick volley of five fierce blows that left the other dragon staggering. Lorenzo was savage and he was thorough.

And he was kicking butt.

He thrashed the other dragon with his tail and his opponent fell to the ground.

Lorenzo hovered over him in flight, waiting, perhaps fearing a trick. Cassie saw his eyes narrow as he circled his fallen foe. The other dragon didn't move.

Was he breathing? Cassie thought so.

Suddenly Lorenzo pounced on the other dragon, locking his claws into his opponent's body and hauling him into the air. Lorenzo's massive wings gleamed, beating with power as he carried the other dragon into the night sky. Cassie left her hiding place and followed into the atrium, watching from below as Lorenzo soared high into the night sky.

He was magnificent.

She saw Lorenzo fling the other dragon into the desert, casting him away from the house. His power and strength left her in awe.

Cassie heard a scream; then the house jumped with the impact of the dragon's fall.

There was no sound of him returning.

Cassie's heart stopped when Lorenzo reappeared and looked down at her. She saw his eyes glitter and swallowed. He descended with easy grace, his gaze locked upon her.

Cassie couldn't read his mood, not when he was in dragon form. She retreated into the elegant room again, wondering how exactly she would plead for mercy.

Or whether she needed to.

Lorenzo landed in the courtyard, his glittering gaze still fixed on Cassie. She stood by the couch and held her ground, reminding herself that Lorenzo had never hurt her. The air practically sizzled with his fury. But then, she would be pretty ticked if someone invaded her home to try to beat her up.

He folded back his wings with deliberate care, his gaze unblinking. In fact, he showed similar traits in dragon form as in human form. Cassie sensed that he was gathering his composure. She watched him control his passion, exactly the way he did in human form.

Then his gaze fell on the camera.

She saw his eyes flash. She saw the puff of smoke flare from his nostrils. She saw him take a step toward her, talons extended, and had a second to panic. There was a shimmer of blue light, a glimpse of Lorenzo nude; then Lorenzo was striding toward her in his jeans.

With purpose.

The thing was, he didn't look significantly less pissed off.

* * *

Lorenzo was livid.

He couldn't recall ever having been so furious. How dare Balthasar attack him in his own home? How dare Balthasar threaten the safety of Lorenzo's elderly father? How dare he taunt him that he would kill his mate?

Barbarians! *Pyr* and *Slayers* were all barbarians, savage and bloodthirsty and primitive. It didn't matter what their objectives were—their basic nature was consistent. He was glad he had so little to do with them.

But he'd already sated the firestorm, and that had evidently made no difference. The notion of his kind infecting his life from this point onward was so intolerable that Lorenzo wanted to rip something to shreds.

Preferably Balthasar.

Which meant that he was no better. The fact that he'd been unable to keep himself from shifting shape when he'd smelled Balthasar was what made him angriest of all. They were awakening his dragon tendencies, against his own will. He was becoming prey to his own passions, despite his every attempt to master—or eliminate—his nature.

Never mind that Cassie had witnessed it all.

The only thing that had stopped Lorenzo from killing Balthasar then and there—as that *Slayer* so rightly deserved—was the fact that the deed would have verified his own base nature. It would have proven that he was no better than the crude reptiles from which he was descended. It would have proven that he was an animal. A beast. A throwback to a less civilized time.

And it would have horrified Cassie to have seen him be so brutal.

All the same, it hadn't been easy. Lorenzo hated that

he'd had to fight his impulses so hard. He could only hope that the flashfire *did* eliminate his dragon powers.

Although they had been quite useful of late. For the first time, he felt a shiver of dread. Could he survive without his shifter abilities? Without the ability to beguile? Of course he could!

The firestorm was proving to be far more trouble than he'd ever expected. And now his dragon nature was riding ascendant. He had shifted without making the choice to do so. He had fought. He had triumphed and was virtually unscathed. He knew that it was the presence of his mate that had made him so vicious and decisive.

Biology had him in its clutches.

And now his body wanted to celebrate. He wanted to eat, to drink, to lose himself in the beguiling softness of Cassie. He wanted to spend the night making love, forgetting everything else in the world except her.

It was a treacherous and dangerous impulse. He had no time for the demands of his dragon nature. He had no time for such primitive nonsense.

Even though he knew that, desire had Lorenzo sizzling.

And keenly aware of Cassie. He heard her erratic pulse. He saw the flutter of it at her throat, so achingly vulnerable. He smelled her anxiety, even though she hadn't heard what Balthasar had threatened to do to her.

He admired that Cassie didn't run, although he had to acknowledge that she might be too terrified to do so. She watched him, unblinking, and he knew she had seen and understood every facet of his truth. There could be no facile story now. There could be no excuse, no claim that it was an illusion.

She knew.

And he was, for the second time in all his life, exposed.

It was not a good feeling, especially given what had happened that other time.

She carried his son. That fact was humbling and changed everything.

Lorenzo had no idea what to say to her, didn't want to lie, didn't want to hear her make the same horrified judgment. At the same time, he didn't want to just walk away. He was snared by her, just as Erik had suggested, snared by Cassie's passion and her beauty and her ability to surprise him.

So he waited for the inevitable condemnation, wishing it wouldn't come, hoping that history wouldn't repeat itself. The air crackled between them, his fists clenching and unclenching with that rampant desire.

Then he saw the camera.

His temper flared to new heights. How could he have forgotten her occupation?

Lorenzo marched through the broken glass and snatched up the camera. He might have destroyed it, but he saw that it was turned off. A flick of his thumb revealed that the memory card was empty.

He looked at Cassie, uncertain what to think.

She was a professional photographer. He knew that pictures of the *Pyr* were worth a fortune, thanks to Melissa Smith's television specials. He had spent his entire life convinced that humans were self-motivated and untrustworthy. He was so convinced of it that the empty memory card shook his world.

Was it possible that there were humans who were different? Was Cassie different from Caterina?

Or was this an illusion?

"I didn't take any pictures," she admitted quietly.

"Why not? Isn't that your job?" His tone was sharp, but Lorenzo couldn't help it. He felt vital and alive, but also within a hair of losing control.

Again.

Cassie exhaled. "I'm on vacation." She smiled.

"Don't shit me." Lorenzo spoke with force, having no patience for games. He could have guessed that he was shimmering around his perimeter, hovering on the cusp of change. His eyes were probably glittering, half dragon, his body coiled to fight again.

He knew he was right when Cassie's smile disappeared. She looked him over, then swallowed. She took a shaking breath and glanced around the room before meeting his gaze again.

But she answered him. She wasn't a coward. He liked that.

His dragon loved it. He'd never been much for fainting virgins or damsels in distress—and princesses were generally too much trouble.

"It would be great publicity for you to reveal what you are, but you haven't done it," she said. "In fact, you've hidden that truth really carefully. I have to think you have a good reason for that, that you know more about the risks than I do." She shrugged. "You're not stupid, and neither am I."

Lorenzo was astounded by her observations and how much they revealed her understanding of him. "You trust me?"

Cassie's smile was quick and genuine. "I guess I do." If he was shocked by the prospect of a human trusting him, her confirmation amazed him even more. "So what don't I know about all of this dragon stuff? Will you fill me in?"

It was a fair question. A fair exchange.

Even if answering her defied every choice Lorenzo had made in over three hundred years.

Was she tricking him?

Did he dare to trust her?

What about their son?

Lorenzo put down the camera with care, shaken by his emotions. He wasn't used to being overwhelmed, not by detail or by passion or by his own base instincts, but he was certainly shaken in this moment. He wasn't thinking clearly, his body still demanding pleasure with such vehemence that his pulse was pounding.

She trusted him.

He wanted to reciprocate in kind.

"You don't know anything about it," he admitted with quiet heat. "And you're right—it is dangerous." He met Cassie's gaze, knowing that she was strong enough for the truth. "Especially for the woman who is the mate of a *Pyr*. Humans are fundamentally fragile, in comparison to us."

As he anticipated, she made the connection. And she didn't like it much. "Mate. I'll guess that could be me." Lorenzo braced himself for a discussion about the conception of *Pyr*—never mind the fact that she had already conceived his son.

He didn't want to think about the fact that Cassie would—quite reasonably—lose any trust she had in him with his confession that he hadn't told her all of the truth.

He'd been sure at the time that he was doing the right thing, but now, now he felt mounting guilt.

Diavolo.

It appeared he had more wicked tendencies than he'd previously believed. He recalled only now that humans were supposed to go insane if they witnessed the shift of a *Pyr* from man to dragon. He'd never believed that either—although there hadn't been time to think about protecting Cassie from the sight when Balthasar attacked—but he was relieved to find that that bit of lore was nonsense.

Or was there more to Cassie than met the eye?

Cassie kept surprising him, forcing him to reconsider his assumptions. Humans might be merely useful, but that perspective was based upon them being self-motivated vermin.

Lorenzo eyed the camera. What if his mate was not?

What if the firestorm was right?

No. He wouldn't think about that. Firestorms were doomed, as were all partnerships with human women. His nature would betray everything. It was kinder to step away, to let her think badly of him, to deny himself whatever she offered.

And yet . . .

Lorenzo glanced at her again. In her presence, it was hard to think about anything other than seducing her again, especially when his body longed to do just that.

Was that part of the firestorm's power?

Cassie surprised him one more time. "How'd you know he was coming? Can dragons see the future?"

"No."

"Well, that's a relief. I can have some secrets, at least." The sparkle in Cassie's eyes, the fact that she had recovered from the sight of his dragon, made him think that celebration might actually be possible.

He swallowed, choosing his words with care. "Our senses are sharper than human senses. I smelled him."

"So you know him?"

"Unfortunately." Lorenzo grimaced and she smiled again.

"Not friends?"

"No." An explanation of Balthasar and his objectives was not what Lorenzo wanted to talk about. He dropped his voice to a murmur. "I prefer to keep my privacy."

He let the simmer of desire grow, and took a step closer to Cassie. She didn't run. In fact, her smile broadened, turned a little bit mysterious. He liked how her gaze slipped over him, the way she bit her luscious bottom lip. He wanted to bite it himself.

Cassie caught her breath, that tempting flush staining her cheeks. "Maybe that's not such a bad thing," she whispered. She glanced at the broken windows. "Do you think he'll come back?"

Lorenzo shook his head. "Not tonight. Maybe not ever." He felt his eyes narrow. "I made him regret the intrusion once. Don't you think I will again?"

Her flush deepened with her obvious pleasure and Lorenzo felt his pulse leap. "You were amazing," she murmured, surveying him with awe.

That was exactly what his dragon yearned to hear. Lorenzo wanted to preen. He took a step closer, was surrounded by her scent, and lost the battle against her allure.

"Where were we, before we were so rudely interrupted?" he murmured.

Cassie smiled and beckoned for him to come closer. "You were just about here," she said, her eyes shining. "Although you hadn't said anything. I'm not sure what you had in mind."

"Aren't you?" Lorenzo moved to that spot and raised his fingertip to Cassie's cheek. He felt her shiver in anticipation. He smelled the heady scent of her arousal. He kissed her beneath her ear and glanced down her shirt at that delicious pink bra.

He knew he'd never been so tempted by a woman before.

And his dragon's needs weren't entirely responsible for that change.

He parted the front of her shirt and bent to kiss between her breasts. He heard her sweet gasp of pleasure, smiled against her skin, then unbuttoned her shirt. Her breasts filled his hands, the nipples taut with a desire that echoed his own. Lorenzo took one peak in his mouth and surrendered to Cassie's allure.

The celebration had begun.

Chapter 10

An hour later, Cassie awakened from a luxurious doze. She was lying naked on the creamy leather couch, the cool night air of the desert wafting through the broken windows to the atrium. She could see the moon riding high overhead, surrounded by stars, and sighed in contentment.

Lorenzo dozed beside her, his legs entangled with hers and his hand on her hip. Her pink bra and panties were on the floor, discarded along with his jeans. She ran her fingers through the thick waves of his hair, felt the stubble on his chin against her shoulder, and wondered what kind of magic had allowed this man to turn her into a glutton for sex.

Cassie didn't much care.

Maybe it was one of the secret powers of dragon men. She felt alive, vibrantly alive, for the first time in years. Maybe ever. She also felt as if she had a connection to a man, a romantic connection like nothing she'd had before.

Like nothing she'd let herself have before.

That was new and it was surprisingly reassuring.

She also couldn't figure out how Lorenzo managed to

please her even more each time they made love. There wasn't anything routine about Lorenzo in bed. Each time was like a new discovery, a deepening of their understanding of each other. No wonder it was so addictive. She smoothed the hair back from his temple, loving the heat and the strength of him against her.

She wondered whether she would ever get enough of Lorenzo.

And she didn't mind one bit if she didn't. Cassie couldn't remember feeling such passion for anyone in her life. She didn't really believe that she was going to fall in love with a dragon shifter—or anyone, for that matter—but even being in lust was very, very good stuff.

Lorenzo stirred then, tipping his head back to give her a sleepy smile. His hand slid over her skin, his fingers cupping her breast. He watched her as he eased his thumb over the nipple, and she knew he noticed how she caught her breath. "Okay?" he murmured in that deep, rich voice.

Cassie nodded, liking his concern. "And you?"

His smile broadened with satisfaction; then he nodded, too. Now that she knew to look, there was something of the dragon in his slow assessment of her, in the way his gaze simmered when his passion was roused. He had an intensity she could easily associate with dragons.

It was sexy, sexier than she might have expected.

Which reminded her. "You haven't told me any more about dragons," she said.

He bent and took her nipple in his mouth, driving her crazy with his tongue. When he released her, she was gasping with pleasure. "What do you want to know?"

"How do you become one?"

Lorenzo moved, bracing himself on one elbow and smiling down at her. His free hand danced over her skin, sliding toward her navel. He twirled his fingertip in it, tickling her a bit. "You don't. Dragons are born, not made."

"But why?"

"Dominant gene, runs in the male line, finds expression in the male progeny." He bent and kissed her ear, his caress making Cassie close her eyes in delight. His fingers meanwhile slipped through the tangle of hair at the apex of her thighs with purpose.

"Sons," Cassie gasped. "Baby dragon boys."

"No. Manifests at puberty." Lorenzo ran his tongue under her ear, exhaling slightly against her skin. Cassie shivered, and turned her head to kiss him. His kiss was as potent as ever, leaving her sizzling with desire and dizzy all over again.

"Tell me something else about dragons," she managed to say. "Something else you can do."

"Our senses are more keen than human senses," Lorenzo said, his eyes doing that glittering thing as he smiled down at her.

"You said that already."

His voice dropped to a seductive whisper. "But that means I can hear your heartbeat across the room. I feel you gasp, even when you're not beside me. I taste your passion."

"That's why you're such a good lover," she whispered.

"Longevity means that there's never a reason to rush through anything. Especially not pleasure." His fingers slipped over her clitoris, teasing and touching once again. Cassie heard herself moan as she parted her thighs, then saw him smile.

"Not immortality?"

"No. Forever is not our thing."

Cassie closed her eyes and almost lost the thread of

the conversation, his fingers were doing such interesting things. "You can't tell what I'm thinking, can you?"

"I just pay attention, to all the little signs, and home in on what gives you the most pleasure." He gave her an intent glance. "You do much the same."

Cassie looked at him, liking that they were both observant. "What gives you pleasure?"

Lorenzo's smile flashed; then he was atop her, his weight braced above her. "Don't you know?" he asked. Then his heat and strength were inside her again.

Cassie clutched his shoulders as he kissed her again, kissed her thoroughly and deeply. He moved more slowly this time, seeming to luxuriate in their lovemaking, his deliberate caresses exciting Cassie in a new and different way. He braced himself above her, watching her as he moved, and his intensity made her pulse flutter.

"I liked watching you fight," she admitted.

He smiled and the warmth of his fingers slid into her hair. "It was my pleasure to defend you."

Was that all of the truth, though?

He leaned down to kiss her again, but Cassie turned her face away. Lorenzo watched her, his gaze searching hers. "Something wrong?" he murmured.

The fact that they were both observant meant no secrets.

Cassie liked that honesty. She wanted his kiss, but she wanted some information, too.

"Maybe you have someone else to defend," Cassie said, her words coming out breathless. "I'll guess that your dad doesn't kick butt the way he used to." Lorenzo pulled back to meet her gaze, his own turning wary. "Because if the ability passes from father to son, he must be a dragon shifter, too."

Lorenzo moved like lightning away from her to sit on

the coffee table and consider her. His expression was imperious as he looked down at her, and Cassie sensed that she'd crossed a line. He seemed to be filled with coiled strength, like a cobra ready to strike.

She'd spooked him, but wasn't sure why.

"What do you know about my father?" he asked softly.

Cassie refused to be daunted. "Not much." She sat up, as well, but remained on the couch. There was an increment of distance between their knees, but she could feel the heat of his skin. "He didn't have time to tell me much."

Lorenzo spoke with precision. "You can't have talked to him. My father is ill, and he hasn't left his room in decades. . . ."

Cassie smiled. "He looked pretty frisky to me. I liked him." She gestured to the painting. "He told me about your mom, although I didn't believe him when he said you were born in 1585. Were you?"

Lorenzo looked as if he'd had the rug pulled out from beneath him. "No one could have told you that," he murmured, horror dawning in his eyes.

Cassie remembered his love of privacy, but didn't want to have any lies between them. She arched a brow. "Don't you mean no one but your dad?"

She saw him realize the truth.

She saw his displeasure.

Did he really think his dad was so ill as that?

Shouldn't he be relieved to learn otherwise?

Lorenzo got up, tugged on his jeans and shirt, then marched out of the room without saying another word. Cassie saw the anger in every line of his body, and hoped he was in a better mood when he came back.

He was halfway out of the room when an explosion

rocked the house. It was close, but seemed to have come from outside the house. Several alarms sounded, but Lorenzo didn't slow his pace.

"What was that?" Cassie demanded, in the midst of tugging on her own jeans.

Lorenzo glanced back, as composed as ever. "I assume you drove a vehicle here."

Cassie blinked. "My Jeep. I parked it in the desert. . . ."

"I will buy you another." Lorenzo turned to continue, leaving her to work it out.

As if the loss of her vehicle didn't matter.

"What?" Cassie cried in outrage. "That's my car. . . ."

Lorenzo pivoted, eyes blazing as he came back into the room. The sight of that blue shimmer dancing around his body made Cassie shut up.

"Balthasar is a poor sport," he declared, his manner intense. "He knew that your presence gave me more incentive to win, so once he recovered sufficiently, he retaliated for his loss. We *Pyr* are fundamentally primitive creatures." He arched a brow. "And poor losers."

With that, Lorenzo pivoted and was gone.

Just like Cassie's Jeep.

Salvatore had deceived him!

Lorenzo stood in the foyer of his father's suite, narrowing his eyes against the darkness as he watched his father sleep. Salvatore's breathing was slow and rhythmic. He was in exactly the same pose and position as the last time Lorenzo had visited.

But it was a lie.

His father was messing with him.

In a way, this was the reminder he needed. This was the inescapable truth. It didn't matter whether Cassie trusted him. It didn't matter whether he trusted her. In the end, his own nature would ensure that any partnership between them would come to grief.

That had happened to his parents.

And the injustice of it made Lorenzo more angry than he had been in centuries. What was the point of this genetic curse his father had passed to him? What was its merit, if the firestorm taunted him with a promise of a partner, then cheated him of any future with her?

He knew he could have no happiness with a woman, and no permanent partnership with anyone human. He'd learned that *Pyr* matches were ill fated, even if well intentioned. And no son needed a devil for a father. He'd grown up with that burden himself and wouldn't put it on any child.

What was the point of the firestorm, if it changed his perspective but his own nature ensured that he couldn't accept the firestorm's promise?

Lorenzo couldn't remember ever being so furious. He couldn't remember ever hating the fact that he was *Pyr* as much as he did in this moment.

Yet his father still feigned sleep.

Had he provoked all of this by giving away the darkfire crystal? Had his father loosed the darkfire in the first place? Was that what was changing everything?

"I know you're awake," Lorenzo said, using the Venetian dialect he had learned as a boy.

His father started slightly, a sign that he'd been surprised by Lorenzo's assertion, but made no other sign that his slumber had been disturbed.

"I know you let her in." Lorenzo strode into the suite, not bothering with the lights. "I know you got rid of the darkfire crystal." He walked around his father as he continued to speak. "I know you are meddling again." He paused in front on his father's face, then crouched down before the enormous dragon nostrils. He switched to old-speak, just for the sake of surprise. *"You should know that it won't make any difference."*

His father snorted, releasing a single puff of smoke.

"You won't change my mind," Lorenzo added. *"Because you can't change what I am."*

His father smiled slowly, the way a crocodile might smile, the move revealing several sharp teeth. He smiled knowingly.

Lorenzo simmered.

Usually, Salvatore's smug confidence in his own perspective didn't bother Lorenzo. Usually, he could shrug it off, let the old dragon believe what he wanted to believe, and move away. But on this day, in this moment, he was too riled up to let it go. There was too much at risk, including his father's safety.

It was time they got things straight.

It was time he made himself clear.

Lorenzo roared and let the dragon take ascendance, shifting shape in a brilliant shimmer of blue light. He reared back and bared his teeth, then dropped to his belly and lay utterly still. His nostrils were only inches from his father's.

His father's eyes had opened and Lorenzo glared at him.

"You won't change me. You won't compel me to believe that I can partner with a woman any more successfully than you did."

"Yet you just defended her."

"From an assault that would never have occurred without your interference! I will not subscribe to your romantic nonsense."

Salvatore tut-tutted. "The firestorm drew Balthasar. Not me."

"The firestorm is sated."

Salvatore shrugged. "It has yet to be extinguished." He eyed Lorenzo and switched to old-speak. *"Your desire for her still burns hot. It is a sign."*

His assertion echoed in Lorenzo's thoughts, showing a disconcerting ability to merge with them and tempt Lorenzo with possibilities. "It is mere circumstance," Lorenzo corrected with anger. "It is not destiny and it is not kismet and it is not love. Do not pile all your nonsense on my back. There is no future in it."

Salvatore smiled.

Lorenzo could have decked him. "What did you tell Cassie?"

"What she needed to know." Salvatore's smile broadened.

The sight sent Lorenzo straight to the moon. "How dare you interfere?" His father didn't reply, but didn't avert his gaze either. He was still convinced he knew better than his son. "Don't you understand how much is at risk?"

Two days until his major spectacle. Two days until he ensured his own security and seclusion for the future. Two days to change the arrangements for his father's survival.

Two days to figure out how to ensure Cassie's safety and silence.

And all this time, his father had been deceiving him, undermining his efforts.

"Where is the darkfire crystal?" Lorenzo demanded. "What did you do with it? Tell me that, at least."

"I ensured its safety." His father's tone was untroubled. "I put it where it belonged."

And risked someone demanding the flashfire song as the price of Lorenzo's failure. His father could have ruined everything!

"How dare you?" Lorenzo roared. Now Salvatore added insult to injury, scheming against the son determined to protect him. Lorenzo had to hold back his urge to simply incinerate the entire suite.

And its contents.

He'd paid for it. It was his to destroy.

But before he could vent his anger, Salvatore shifted shape. He became an elderly man, one who stood undaunted before the ferocious dragon that was Lorenzo.

"I dare," Salvatore said softly, "because I understand exactly what is at risk."

His father reached out one hand and laid it on Lorenzo's scaled chest, right over the thunder of his son's heartbeat.

"This is at risk, no more and no less than the most precious treasure in your hoard." Salvatore spoke in the Venetian dialect, the one that flowed more smoothly from Lorenzo's tongue than his own. His gaze was unswerving as he switched to old-speak. *"I promised your mother that I would ensure your happiness. I keep my promises."*

There was no other claim that could have made Lorenzo more angry. His father had condemned his mother, as surely as if he had struck the first match himself.

"The way you ensured hers?" Lorenzo roared. "She *died* because of you! Don't think I've forgotten. I was there." He shifted to human form himself, seizing his father's hand and casting it away from him. He leaned closer to snarl. "Just as you were not."

A shadow touched his father's face. "Don't throw that old detail at me again."

"Detail? You betrayed her! You endangered her and left her undefended." He lowered his voice, leaning close to his father. "You might as well have struck her dead with your own hand."

His father tilted his head to regard Lorenzo. "And what exactly are you doing differently with the delightful Cassie?"

Lorenzo's heart stopped cold.

But he knew he was being manipulated. He would have none of such accusations. "Keep your romantic notions to yourself. There is no bond between *Pyr* and human that endures and I know it as well as you do. You proved it to me. This proves it to me. It's all an illusion."

Even as he said the words, Lorenzo suddenly wished they were not true.

His father watched him steadily, untroubled by his outburst. "You could love this one," he said finally.

Lorenzo chose not to argue that point. "But I will not. I keep my promises, too, and I won't make one doomed to be broken."

With that, Lorenzo turned his back on his father and left the suite, his footsteps pounding even on the carpets. He was seething again, his blood thundering in his ears and his body itching for another fight. Whatever *Pyr* or *Slayer* crossed Lorenzo's path on this night would sorely regret the choice.

"Yet you defend her," his father mused in old-speak. *"Repeatedly and in dragon form. You assume your true shape and use your powers, after denying them for so long. I find all of this most telling. Will you really use the flashfire?"*

Lorenzo pivoted and glared back down the hall toward his father's suite.

And his father, curse him, chuckled with that smug confidence.

Lorenzo inhaled sharply at the sound.

But he didn't turn back.

He had to ensure Cassie's safety. His father wasn't going anywhere, but Cassie just might.

Cassie sat down heavily, not entirely certain she had a choice. Her knees just gave out beneath her. Lorenzo had said he'd had more motivation to win because she was here.

He'd called her his mate.

The chemistry between them wasn't the only thing making her heart leap and her thoughts spin. The man's words were pretty potent, too.

Cassie had never expected to have a dragon as her champion, much less one who could turn her inside out—and set her passion alight—so easily as Lorenzo.

She also hadn't thought she'd ever get into a long-term relationship, much less be involved with a man who challenged every expectation.

Even that of his being a man all the time.

Cassie had never expected that she'd be flung into a world of mythical creatures, like dragons, who fought each other with such force. And who knew what else they did?

Cassie remembered the blood she'd seen and took a gulp of Prosecco. She knew Lorenzo would be back soon. She probably could leave, but she wasn't in a hurry to be in the desert alone at night.

Without a vehicle. Her Jeep was gone.

Because there was a dragon out there who wanted to kill her.

Balthasar. Wounded but not dead, and clearly pissed off.

No, staying put and facing Lorenzo had far more appeal. He might yell or be evasive, but he'd never hurt her.

Cassie drained the glass and knew she needed a distraction. She tugged out her BlackBerry and saw that she had a couple of messages. She ignored the one from the acquiring editor, but opened the one from Stacy.

R U OK?

Cassie smiled. Of course, it was the middle of the night and they were sharing a hotel room. It was nice to have someone be worried about her—and not fair to leave Stacy worrying. She chose to be positive and heavily edited her current reality.

MORE THAN OK. HAVING FUN.

She sent the reply before she had time to second-guess it. Stacy replied immediately with a smiley face.

Cassie made to shove the device back into the pocket of her jeans, then had a thought. That dragon Balthasar was after her. A little insurance wouldn't be remiss.

She updated her location on foursquare, changing her settings so that only Stacy could see her data. She got another smiley face reply in acknowledgment of that.

If something happened, Stacy would have a clue where to start.

But what was going to happen? Cassie heard a door slam somewhere in the house and the solid tread of Lorenzo's footsteps. She shivered in anticipation of seeing him again, in recollection of the way his eyes had blazed.

But she shouldn't forget he'd fought a dragon to defend her. That fact was unassailable, and it did make her feel all tingly.

He'd looked amazing while he'd done it, too.

She eyed the broken window glass on the floor and the black blood that was still smoking on the patio stones. It looked to be eating its way through them. She figured that things couldn't get any more weird.

Then she turned around to find the woman in the painting—the one who was supposed to be Lorenzo's mother, Angelina—beckoning to her.

As if she were alive, not the subject of a painting.

Cassie blinked. She hadn't had that much to drink.

Angelina crooked her finger and smiled.

Cassie figured she didn't have a lot to lose. She stepped across the room and Angelina's hand came right out of the painting. Cassie stared, then took Angelina's hand.

Which was warm and soft. Angelina's grip was firm, which was a good thing because she tugged Cassie right into the painting alongside her.

She'd been wrong: things *could* get more weird.

They just had.

Lorenzo was furious and agitated. Too many items were slipping from his control. He was vulnerable, as he had never been before. His secrets were exposed and time was of the essence. He couldn't begin to imagine how he would guarantee Cassie's silence, but he had to try. He took the stairs three at a time to get back to the room adjacent to the atrium.

Only to find that room empty.

Where had Cassie gone?

Lorenzo checked the courtyard, but there was no sign that Cassie had ventured over the broken glass to explore it. He couldn't detect her scent there, and there was no escape from the courtyard other than the open sky.

One thing this woman could not do was fly.

Although it was possible that Balthasar had returned for her. Lorenzo checked again, his heart pounding in trepidation. No, he was certain she hadn't stepped into the courtyard—there was no trace of her scent there. And Balthasar's scent was fading.

What if Cassie had left the house by more conventional exits? He strode through the quiet house, checking the alarms on every door. Nothing. There had been no exits or entries since his own return. The housekeeper and her husband were secure in their suite, sleeping.

Thank goodness for soundproofing and beguiling.

At the back door, he detected a trace of Cassie's scent, mingled with his father's. The alarm indicated that it had been turned off several hours before, for an interval of five minutes.

Salvatore had let her in this way, then.

Lorenzo opened the door and peered into the night, seeing only the smoking wreckage of the Jeep far off to one side. He narrowed his eyes but discerned no signs of life other than the usual activity of the desert at night.

He shut the door and leaned back against it, thinking. Cassie hadn't left the house, but she had disappeared all the same. He returned to the room adjacent to the courtyard where he had seen her last. Her clothes were gone but her scent trail did not leave this room.

Was she hiding? Hoping he'd track her down? He prowled the perimeter, then surveyed the room again. There was nowhere to hide within it.

That was when he realized that the massive painting had changed.

His mother no longer stood to one side, holding back the curtain and smiling at the viewer. She was gone, and the curtain hung slack.

Lorenzo blinked. It was impossible. Paintings didn't change. This one had never changed before. Why now? Was this another legacy of darkfire and its power to turn assumptions upside down?

Lorenzo didn't know.

He did know that the painting was different.

He eased closer to the massive work, not trusting his own eyes. He scanned it, seeking what other details had changed. It took him only a moment to spot Angelina, now in the middle of the painting. She stood before a man with a pointed beard, and gestured to the woman at her side.

Who wore jeans and red cowboy boots.

Cassie.

Lorenzo rubbed his chin. He watched the trio intently, but the figures didn't move at all. He studied the rest of the painting, confirming that its surface didn't appear to have changed. Just the imagery was different. When next he looked at the trio, Angelina was smiling at Cassie, her fingertips brushing Cassie's stomach.

Cassie appeared to be shocked.

Lorenzo had a very bad feeling about that. He could make a good guess as to what his mother had just told her. His ability to control all the variables in his life seemed to be disappearing fast.

Thanks to unexpected interference from his parents.

One of whom was dead.

Both of whom meant well, but both of whom were wrong.

If he was going to regain control, Lorenzo needed a plan. He poured himself a glass of Prosecco, sat on the couch, and thought furiously as he waited.

For whatever would happen next.

If nothing else, Cassie was keeping him on his toes.

In fact, when it came to variables, Lorenzo had a feel-

ing Cassie Redmond wasn't one who could be easily
controlled anyway.

And in a strange way, Lorenzo had to admit that he
was stimulated by his firestorm. It had been a long time
since he'd been surprised by anything—or anyone. He
never would have anticipated that he would find it so
intriguing to be involved with someone who challenged
his assumptions, like Cassie. He just wished the firestorm
hadn't happened now, right when so much hung in the
balance. He wished he did have a future to promise her.

Was it possible that Cassie was different from Caterina?

Was it possible that his father was right?

Two days ago, Lorenzo would have insisted that was
impossible. Now he felt the lingering glow of the firestorm, watched the painting, and wondered.

The room depicted in the painting was as lush as it appeared. Cassie wasn't sure how she had become part of
it, but she was. She could smell roasted meat, as well as
the salt tang of the sea drifting through the open windows. Curtains fluttered and women laughed. Lilting
music came from one corner of the room.

If she had stepped into the painting, did that mean
she was in 1586?

If this was a dream or a hallucination, it was a pretty
vivid one.

She turned to find Angelina smiling at her. Angelina
said something to her, something she didn't understand,
something she assumed was in Italian. Cassie figured
her incomprehension showed, because Angelina shook
her head.

She grasped Cassie's hand and tugged her toward a
tall, slender man who sat at a table, watching the crowd

and stroking his beard. He looked Cassie up and down and shook his head, clearly disinterested in her charms. Cassie would have protested, but Angelina did it for her, explaining something rapidly and with gusto. Her voice was lovely, and melodious, which maybe explained why the man stared at her in wonder.

He smiled when Angelina was done, then looked Cassie in the eye. "So, you are the choice for Angelina's son," he said, his British accent strong. "Do you not think he is rather young?"

Salvatore had said that Lorenzo had been born in 1585. If she was in 1586, he'd been an infant still. That sounded so crazy, even within her own thoughts, that she didn't say it out loud.

Angelina, meanwhile, was explaining something to the man, something that required a lot of gesticulation.

"Angelina has some advice for you," the man said. It was clear to Cassie that he found the situation quite strange as well. She realized that he was staring at her boots. They were pretty remarkable boots in the twenty-first century, but she supposed they were even more so in the sixteenth.

"She says you have felt the firestorm."

JP had mentioned that word, although he had dismissed it as dragon lore. If it were true, though, and she had had a firestorm with Lorenzo, that would explain the sparks in the theater.

There were, after all, more things that were proving to be true than Cassie had ever expected.

Angelina said something low and fast, and the man smiled. "She says it makes sense that Lorenzo did not tell you the details, that he, of course, will resemble his father in many ways."

Angelina gave Cassie a hard look and she nodded,

knowing that the other woman was referring to Lorenzo's dragon powers—and his resulting desire for privacy.

"The firestorm is a mark of a man like Lorenzo meeting his destined mate," the man explained, translating as Angelina spoke. "When sparks fly between lovers."

The sparks had gone away after she and Lorenzo had made love the first time. Cassie had a funny feeling about that.

Meanwhile, translator-man smiled and ran a fingertip down Angelina's arm, his expression so ardent that Cassie understood he was smitten with Angelina.

Angelina smiled, but her expression was tight.

So, the feeling wasn't reciprocated.

But then, wasn't Angelina supposed to have been a courtesan?

Cassie glanced around the room but couldn't see any sign of Lorenzo's father, even in younger form. "Salvatore?" she asked, and Angelina caught her breath. Cassie saw tears glistening before Angelina shook her head and began to talk to her chosen translator again.

"You cannot escape the power of a destined love," he said, his gaze locked upon Angelina's face. "You cannot evade the fact that you are destined to bear your lover's son, a child who will carry his father's mark."

Cassie recalled that Lorenzo had used the word "mate," too. Could she really be pregnant? After just that one time? The very idea made her queasy.

"When the firestorm is sated, the child takes life. One spark feeds another."

Cassie touched her stomach, knowing her expression was questioning.

Angelina smiled. She placed her hand over Cassie's and pressed it lightly against her stomach. Then she made a cradling motion with her hands.

"Already?" Cassie asked, and the man translated.

Angelina smiled with confidence and said something.

"The child takes root when the sparks of the firestorm fade," the man said, translating so she could understand.

"But wait a minute," Cassie protested. "I'm not going to have a baby, not now. . . ."

Angelina shook a finger at her in warning. She tugged Cassie away from the man, who watched them go with some confusion. Angelina gestured to him, rolled her eyes, then spoke rapidly to a servant. Cassie heard the word "porto."

A moment later, that servant carried a carafe of red liquid to the man who had spoken to Cassie. He explained the situation, and the man rose to his feet to bow in appreciation of the gift.

It was a really big decanter of port. Cassie looked to Angelina to find her smiling. She folded her hands together, miming sleep, then pretended to awaken in confusion.

Cassie laughed. She would bet that this guy wouldn't remember anything of their conversation the next day.

Angelina laughed and kissed her cheek with obvious affection. "*Pyr*," she murmured, placing a hand over her heart. Her expression turned rapturous, and Cassie felt herself blush.

She nodded agreement, which clearly pleased Angelina.

Angelina tugged her toward a smaller room off to the side, one filled with books and ledgers. She reached up to one shelf, where a small leather-bound book rested alone. She opened it quickly, almost furtively, and removed a slip of parchment. There was something written on it. It looked like a verse.

Angelina put the parchment in Cassie's hand, then placed her other hand on top of it so that the parchment was completely hidden. She said Lorenzo's name several times, squeezed Cassie's hands together, and Cassie understood that she was to take this sheet. She looked at it and realized it was written in a language she couldn't read. She gestured to the man who had translated, but Angelina shook her head.

"Lorenzo. Lorenzo!"

Lorenzo would translate it for her.

Maybe because he'd knocked her up and owed her one.

No. That couldn't be true. Not after one time.

Even though everything else that couldn't be true was turning out to be so.

Cassie nodded agreement. She was enfolded in a tight embrace then, one that was all softness and perfume. Angelina's touch caught at Cassie's heart, made her remember her own mom's affectionate nature, and had her tears rising.

Angelina had tears in her eyes, too, when she pulled back. She kissed Cassie's cheeks, then framed Cassie's face in her hands. She smiled at her, blinking back her tears. Cassie sensed that there were a thousand things Lorenzo's mother would have liked to have told her, but more than the language barrier stood between them.

A clock chimed.

Angelina's eyes widened. She kissed Cassie again, whispered something to her in a husky voice, then gave her a resolute push.

Exactly the kind of push Cassie's own mom had given her once or twice.

Chapter 11

Cassie stumbled as she fell back into the room in Lorenzo's house. He was standing there, two sparkling glasses of Prosecco in his hand, watching avidly. As if he were waiting for her. Did people walk into his artwork all the time? He stepped forward to catch her elbow and steady her, his touch making her pulse leap.

"I wondered how long you'd stay," he murmured, his eyes glinting. He was wearing only his jeans and his muscles were pumped as if he'd been working out, his hair tousled. He looked vital, larger than life, more powerful than your average hunky guy. He was completely composed, which made Cassie feel only more disheveled.

More like Alice down the rabbit hole.

Or spit back out of it.

"Welcome back." Lorenzo handed her a glass, letting his fingertips brush hers in a way that left Cassie tingling. He arched a brow and toasted her, his gaze unswerving.

Cassie took a gulp of wine, trying to work out what had just happened.

Never mind what she had learned. Had this been another trick? A dream? It had certainly felt real.

Lorenzo appeared bemused.

Cassie looked back at the painting. She looked at him. "You're not surprised."

"Very little surprises me anymore."

"Does this happen all the time?"

"No." He spoke with such resolve that Cassie believed him. His scrutiny of her was intense, as if he was waiting for her to say something.

"How did you know, then?"

"I didn't. I guessed." He shrugged, seemingly at ease with the weirdness of it all. Maybe being a dragon shifter gave a person the ability to take things in stride. Maybe being over four hundred years old gave a person the ability to take things in stride.

She looked more closely and realized that he wasn't as hard to read as she'd initially thought. If she paid attention, she could make a pretty good guess at his reactions.

Lorenzo was relieved, although he would have preferred to have hidden it. She could tell by the way his gaze clung to her and by the way he stayed close.

He'd been worried about her.

Because it *was* weird for people to disappear into his paintings.

That made Cassie feel a bit better.

She threw back half of the glass of Prosecco. It was a bit warm, but it still helped soothe her. She was rattled by the exchange with Angelina and the reminder of just how much she'd lost.

Never mind whose fault that was.

"You were gone, yet the alarm system indicates that no one has left the house." Lorenzo smiled slowly, his expression making Cassie think of more interesting things than paintings. "I realized that Angelina had moved, and that her new protégé was wearing a most unusual outfit for the time."

"I think that guy, the one up there with the beard, wanted my boots."

Lorenzo winced. "You should have given them to him."

"I like these boots!" Cassie protested, then saw the twinkle in his eyes.

Lorenzo lifted a hand as if heralding peace. "We have other things to discuss than your unfortunate choice of footwear."

"What's wrong with them?"

"You have gorgeous, feminine feet." His eyes shone with conviction. "The boots don't do you credit."

Cassie wasn't quite ready to be charmed by Lorenzo all over again. Since he was giving her a hard time about her boots, she'd give him one right back. "Does the fact that the sparks of the firestorm aren't burning anymore really mean that I've conceived your son?"

Lorenzo's features set, his change of expression telling her that it was true.

And that made her mad.

"How could you not tell me?" she demanded. "You can't just knock someone up without discussing it first!"

"I didn't believe it." He grimaced, looking rueful. "I've never had a firestorm before and not all legends are true, you know."

That took the wind from Cassie's sails. "But you have to believe it. It's a story of your kind."

Lorenzo sighed and grimaced. "I don't believe half of what is said about the *Pyr*. There's so much myth mixed in that it's hard to find the truth. And really, I don't want to have anything to do with it."

"Why not?"

He shuddered. "It's primitive. It's involuntary. I dislike being out of control."

Cassie shrugged. "It worked for me that you convinced Balthasar to leave."

He sighed and frowned, suddenly finding the bottom of his glass fascinating beyond all else.

But he didn't leave.

And he didn't shut her out.

Cassie dared to be encouraged. "So, that was a firestorm? All the sparks and flames between us?"

Lorenzo nodded. "Indisputably." He shoved one hand through his hair, drained his glass, and fixed her with a look. "I thought that sex might quench the flames. That's the story, so it was worth a try. The flames were inconvenient."

"You didn't control them?"

"If I had, I would have put them out." He looked so irritated that she started to feel a bit sorry for him.

"Messed with your concentration?"

His sidelong glance was fierce. "Yes." He grimaced. "But the part about the woman conceiving the first time she's intimate with the *Pyr*? That defies belief, don't you think?"

Cassie dared to feel relieved. "Then I'm not pregnant?"

"No, you are." Lorenzo spoke flatly, with no joy. "I was wrong to be skeptical."

"You can't know, not yet. . . ."

He interrupted her tersely. "You taste different. You smell different." His eyes flashed. "Trust me. You're pregnant."

And he wasn't happy about it.

Cassie sat down with care because she did trust Lorenzo when it came to minute observation. "And if it's a boy, it'll be another *Pyr*."

"It will be a boy. We only have sons." Lorenzo held up the bottle of Prosecco against the light. There was still some in the bottom. He offered it to Cassie.

Pregnant?

"I probably shouldn't," she said, touching her stomach.

Lorenzo followed her gesture, then inhaled. There was an awkward pause between them, one that persuaded her that he really hadn't believed she'd get pregnant.

He sat down heavily beside her. "You're right, of course," he agreed. If anything, he looked more shaken than Cassie felt. He poured the remaining wine into his glass and drained it immediately.

"You should have told me about it first," Cassie suggested. "Or at least before the next time."

Lorenzo's eyes darkened when he glanced her way, and he bit out his next words. "Maybe I haven't been thinking too clearly in your presence."

Cassie's breath caught. That was another hint that she might have as much effect on Lorenzo as he had on her. He looked grim, but his gaze was simmering still.

She needed more than implication. "What's that supposed to mean?"

He leaned closer, his gaze so intent that her mouth went dry. "That I have never found a woman so distracting in my life." He glanced over her, and his eyes brightened. "That I have never been in the situation of not being able to get enough, of not being able to think of anything else."

"Me neither," Cassie admitted, and saw his relief. "Is that what the firestorm is supposed to be like?"

He frowned. "Only until it's sated."

"But we did that right away."

He smiled crookedly. "Pretty much."

"So what's going on?"

His eyes glittered as he regarded her, and he arched a brow. "Kismet?" He seemed to be making a joke of it, which was perfectly consistent with Cassie's view of destined love.

Even if it might have been nice. . . .

"I don't believe in kismet," she said flatly, and he toasted her with the empty glass.

"Perfectly rational," he agreed, then looked at the painting.

It occurred to Cassie that there wasn't much going on in this place that was rational. She tried to steer the conversation back to practical matters.

Like her having Lorenzo's baby. She'd never expected to have kids, and certainly had never intended to have an unplanned pregnancy. The prospect was unnerving.

"So what happens now?" she asked, hearing her own trepidation.

"What do you mean?"

That he could even wonder what she wanted to talk about was irritating. Cassie heard her voice rise. "I'm just supposed to go back to my life and have a child in nine months, one that's incidentally going to be a dragon shape shifter? And you'll carry on as if this firestorm never happened?"

Lorenzo winced and she knew he wasn't as indifferent as he might have liked her to believe. He tapped his fingers on his knee, as if trying to find the words.

Cassie couldn't wait. She got up to pace.

"This is about you being buried alive Saturday night for that spectacle, isn't it? Well, here's something else to think about. After you're buried in your car, I'll be out here, on my own, with this Balthasar guy waiting for a chance to fry me."

"But—" Lorenzo would have interjected, but Cassie was on a roll.

"I don't even have a car anymore, thank you very much. I'm thinking he can fly faster than I can run—especially if I shouldn't strain myself for the sake of the *baby*." She spun to face a watchful Lorenzo. "Who will defend me when you can't?"

That he didn't answer her directly wasn't a really good sign, in Cassie's opinion. She felt her heart skip a beat or two as he regarded her.

Then he stood as if they'd been talking about the weather, put the glasses and the empty bottle on a side table, and turned to face her.

"Well? I'm ready for answers."

"I was just waiting for you to finish," Lorenzo said, his composure making her want to shake him.

Except he was putting it on. She would have bet her last dollar on that.

"Is it just Balthasar you're worried about?" he asked.

"No! I'm worried about having a dragon baby alone. . . ."

"I told you. Our powers don't manifest until puberty."

"But what happens then? Who's going to tell him how to do what he can do? And how am I going to manage this, if I survive? Having kids was never part of my plan."

"Why not?"

Cassie might have brushed off the question, but Lorenzo looked surprised. He looked as if he really wanted to know her answer.

"I don't believe in the whole married-with-kids thing," Cassie said.

He arched a brow, waiting for more.

Cassie folded her arms across her chest. "What happens when people decide to get married and have kids and buy a house and get a dog is that the guy carries on doing whatever he wants to do and the woman gives up everything. She becomes the baby maker and the maid and the cook and the housekeeper and has nothing left for herself anymore."

Cassie would have liked to have stopped there, but it seemed she couldn't. Angelina had opened an old wound. "And then one day, the kids leave the proverbial nest, and she's left with nothing at all. Maybe not even a husband, if he's decided that she's as boring as she looks. That's not—and never has been—my plan. I want to achieve something other than adding to the world's population count."

Lorenzo was watching her carefully. "Sounds like a personal experience."

"My parents divorced in their fifties." The words were bitter on Cassie's tongue. "It killed my mom. I knew before then that I didn't want to live her life, but that drove the lesson home." She couldn't hold back the words she'd never said aloud. "My mom was just *useful* to my dad. She gave him kids. She kept the house. She cooked and did the laundry. She did *everything*. And when she wasn't useful anymore or young anymore, he chucked her out. Oh, they talked about love fading and all the rest of it, but that was a lie."

Lorenzo nodded thoughtfully, as if he was really listening to her. But then, he always did. "You said it killed her?"

"She was devastated. I think she really did love my dad. She died within two years." Cassie sat down, wanting to cry all over again. "He destroyed her, and he didn't even care."

She felt Lorenzo watching her. "Anything else bothering you?" he prompted softly.

Cassie couldn't understand his mood. "Aren't you worried that I'm going to die right after your car gets buried?"

Lorenzo shook his head. "No. Because you aren't going to die."

"How can you be so sure of that? Maybe you're going to die!"

Lorenzo smiled. "I'm not."

His confidence wasn't good enough for Cassie. "You could be wrong, you know. I'll guess that you have a trick planned, but whatever it is might not work."

His smile broadened.

Cassie stared at him. "Do you have other superhuman powers I don't know about?"

Lorenzo thought about it for a moment, then shook his head. "No. I think you've seen everything I can do."

He was so calm that Cassie wanted to provoke him.

"Then unless there's something I don't know, you *are* going to die," Cassie insisted. "You're going to get buried in that car and you're going to suffocate, no matter how slowly you breathe or how well you meditate, and when they dig you up in a month, you'll be dead. But that won't bother me because Balthasar is going to kill me before the week is out."

He watched her for a long moment. "Finished?" he asked again.

Cassie remembered the piece of parchment in her hand and thrust it at him. "No. What about this? The only clue I have and it's written in a language I don't understand!"

Lorenzo took the piece of parchment with care, his gaze dancing back and forth as he read it. Whatever it said didn't please him. His lips tightened, but he folded it carefully before shoving it into the pocket of his jeans.

"Aren't you going to tell me what it says?"

"No. It's nonsense." His eyes glinted, making him look dangerous again. She saw a faint shimmer of blue around his body and realized he wasn't just hiding his reaction—he was a lot more annoyed than he wanted her to realize. That message was important. "Anything else?"

Cassie stared around the room, back at the painting, then at him. "No," she said. "I think that pretty much covers it."

Lorenzo gestured to the couch. "Then let's talk about the future."

Cassie didn't trust his calm attitude one bit. It was another illusion, but she was learning to look behind the mask.

Lorenzo had a plan. And he was going to share it with her. Unless he was going to do that flame thing again. JP had said it would only work once, but Cassie wanted another guarantee.

She lifted a finger in warning. "No beguiling," she decreed. "If I see one flame in your eyes, I'm out of here."

A muscle tensed in Lorenzo's jaw. "I thought you trusted me."

"You have a scheme. Until I know what it is, I reserve the right to not be beguiled."

His eyes flashed; then he nodded tightly. "Fine." He bit off the word and gestured again to the couch.

Cassie didn't move. "Promise me."

Lorenzo glared at her and the blue shimmer became brighter. "I promise." His words were hard. This time, when he indicated the couch, his manner was more imperious.

He wasn't nearly as tranquil as he wanted her to believe.

That was very reassuring. She crossed the room and perched on the couch, waiting for whatever plan he intended to propose.

She would never have expected Lorenzo to say what he did.

Cassie took his suggestion worse than Lorenzo had hoped.

"You've got to be insane!" she protested. "There is no way that anybody is going to bury me alive in the desert, not for one minute, never mind one month."

Lorenzo gritted his teeth and fought for control. "If you would just let me explain...."

"No! I don't care what your plan is. And hey, I've got a passenger to think about now, too." She patted her stomach. "Whether his arrival was planned or not doesn't matter anymore. He's here, so I'm going to take care of him."

Lorenzo sat back. "So you won't listen to the rest of my idea?"

"No! Forget it."

Lorenzo inhaled sharply and schooled his temper. "The other option is that you remain here for a month with my father. The house is fully alarmed and apparently my father is more agile than I had believed...."

"No way," Cassie said, her tone filled with challenge. "You have to cancel your spectacle."

"Nonnegotiable," Lorenzo said without hesitation.

"I'm going to have to change my plans in the next nine months. It won't hurt you to make some revisions, too." Cassie's lips set. "It's only fair."

"You don't understand," Lorenzo argued. "Everything has been arranged. It has taken almost a year to put all the pieces into place, and the fact that there's so much trouble from my kind proves that I might have waited too long. The spectacle will proceed as planned. You can join me or not. It's your choice."

The fact that Cassie carried his son just made his disappearance more imperative. No one was going to use Cassie or their son as a point of weakness to manipulate him.

No one.

Cassie looked at him, her intense scrutiny almost making him flinch. He was aware of the crackle of the parchment in his pocket, of the dire prognosis in that prophecy. It couldn't have anything to do with him.

Could it?

Even if it mentioned flashfire.

Where had Angelina gotten it, anyway?

"Wait a minute. There's more to this than the illusion of survival." Cassie was staring at him, and he could almost hear the gears turning in her mind. "It's a *disappearing* act. You're going to make it look like you *do* die in that car."

Lorenzo was only mildly shocked that she'd pieced the plan together. He figured the moment he suggested she come with him, he'd given it away.

Cassie got to her feet. She began to pace the room in agitation. "It's a vanishing act, isn't it? You're just going to disappear. You're going to bail on everything and everyone! You're going to start again somewhere else, with a new name and nice Swiss bank accounts."

She nodded to herself, walking more quickly as his sense of vulnerability grew. "You'd have to do that regularly if you lived for centuries. It's the only way to ensure that there are never any questions about your longevity. It makes perfect sense." She pivoted to confront him, daring him to toss his secrets at her feet. "That's why you don't care what happens to me."

"I do!"

"Prove it!"

Lorenzo couldn't think of a thing to say.

"Of course," she said, nodding. "You leave *nothing* to chance!" Cassie shook her finger at him. "Which means you're not risking anything this time either." She folded her arms across her chest, looking so determined and volatile that Lorenzo wanted to seduce her all over again. Her voice had dropped even lower than its usual husky tones, once again messing with his composure. "Especially not anything important to you, like your life."

Lorenzo felt himself shimmering on the cusp of change. He was that annoyed and alarmed—and aroused. Damn it. He hadn't expected her to figure out every single detail on the spot—and look so good doing it. She was everything he could want in a mate.

If, in fact, he'd ever wanted one.

Cassie tipped her head to regard him, fearless in challenging him. Her tone was fierce. "Who will be the corpse? Your father?"

"No!"

"You're not going to just bail on him, too?"

"I have made arrangements for him to remain here."

Lorenzo didn't like that plan any better than Cassie obviously did, but his father's lack of cooperation had necessitated compromise.

"Uh-huh." She gestured to the atrium. "What if Balthasar comes back? Who will defend Salvatore? Your dad looks like his fighting days are over, I have to say."

Lorenzo's temper flared. She was itemizing the weak points in his plan, identifying the precise areas that troubled him, and forcing him to confront them all over again. "He won't follow the plan!"

"So you're just going to leave him behind." She gave him a hot look. "I have to say that I expected better of you. I thought you had some ability to care. But you're going to look after number one, cut and run for your own convenience. You're just like my dad. There's nothing special about you at all."

Her disgust was clear, and it angered Lorenzo. He'd seen how hurt she was by her father's behavior and how deep the wound was from losing her mother.

He was not like human men, or her rat of a father.

He was not selfish and heartless.

And he couldn't bear to have Cassie think as much.

It would have been nice if she'd at least listened to his plans to save her! Lorenzo got to his feet and jabbed a finger through the air in her direction, wanting all the while to do something better than argue. "I don't owe you any stories. . . ."

She seized his arm, completely unafraid of him. Didn't she understand what he was? "Wrong! You're planning to fake your own death, to head off secretly to start your life anew someplace else, with as little baggage as possible. But this baby is baggage you can't leave behind. What if I terminate the pregnancy?"

Lorenzo was shocked. "You wouldn't!"

"You're not doing a whole lot to change my mind about the importance of having more dragon shifters in our world."

That was it.

"*Your* world?" Lorenzo demanded. "We *Pyr* are the custodians of the earth and the guardians of the four elements. We are the ones who keep the balance and ensure the future. You humans are the vermin intent upon destroying everything you touch. . . ."

Even as he said the words, he knew he didn't believe them any longer.

But what did he believe?

He was talking about the *Pyr* as if he was of their number. And yet he had never been willing to follow Erik.

What was the firestorm doing to him?

He thought of the prophecy again—his father's assertion and the fact that Marco had peered into his thoughts but had not wiped out the flashfire song from his memory—and fell silent.

Was the firestorm going to make a dragon out of him?

The idea astounded Lorenzo, partly because it made such unexpected sense.

"Vermin?" Cassie echoed, her eyes narrowing. He saw the flash of her anger and didn't blame her one bit.

He had acted shamelessly.

But he couldn't just abandon everything in a heartbeat, not after he'd spent nearly a year preparing for this spectacle. . . . He had to think. He had to regroup and modify his plan. He needed a bit of time.

Cassie continued, not interested in giving him one minute to think. "I don't see you defending anything except yourself. Selfishness is the definition of *vermin* in my book."

Lorenzo knew he couldn't think fast enough to save the situation. "You don't understand. . . ."

"No, but I know you won't tell me," she retorted. "And if you won't confide in me, I won't play along." He admired that about her, that she gave as good as she got, that she was unafraid of him or his truth.

No. Lorenzo more than admired Cassie.

He loved her.

She was the one turning his world inside out, not the firestorm.

Erik, to Lorenzo's chagrin, had been right that Cassie had already captured him. As much as Lorenzo would have preferred otherwise, his father had been right about his ability to fall in love with Cassie.

It was breathtakingly inconvenient. He could only have her if he trusted her with all the details of his escape plan.

Which looked a whole lot like repeating the past. Hadn't he confided in Caterina at exactly the same point in his first escape? He could be setting himself up for the same disappointment all over again.

Cassie glared at him. "You want me to cut you some slack, feel free to share the details that will change my mind." She eyed him, expectant, toe tapping, but Lorenzo couldn't find the words.

It was all happening too quickly, the net of his assumptions collapsing around him like a house of cards in a stiff breeze.

Was this what Angelina had done to Salvatore?

Now that he knew her, what would be the point of his life without Cassie? He glanced at the painting of his mother's home and a lump rose in his throat at the notion of his own future.

Alone.

Aging.

Fading, because the firestorm had come and gone.

"What happened to her?" Cassie asked quietly.

Lorenzo started. She must have followed his gaze.

Trust Cassie to find the heart of the matter. Trust Cassie to guess what he was really thinking. For centuries, he'd believed himself inscrutable and untouchable. For centuries, his shields had been impenetrable. He'd thought himself above it all, invulnerable. But it had only taken the right woman and the heat of the firestorm to prove just how wrong he had been.

Lorenzo couldn't summon a word to his lips.

Cassie smiled, although it was a sad smile. The sight wrenched Lorenzo's heart. "Right. You owe me nothing, seeing as how I'm just the vehicle to bear your son and human vermin besides." When she met his gaze, her eyes were cold. "So, men are all the same, after all."

She pulled her hand out of her pocket, spun his car keys on her finger, then turned to leave. "You owe me a car, so we'll just call it square. Have a nice spectacle, Lorenzo."

With that, she marched out of the room, fury in her every step.

Leaving a very astonished dragon behind her.

Cassie wasn't happy to learn—again—that men took what they wanted, conceded nothing, then moved on. What a moron she had been to think that Lorenzo might be different. Humans were vermin, were they?

Well, bad things happened to everyone, but only stupid people blamed an entire species for their problems. Cassie was completely disappointed in Lorenzo. She'd been sure he was smarter than that.

She'd been sure that she was smarter than this.

She blinked away her tears, telling herself that he wasn't worth mourning. No, what she'd glimpsed in him had been the illusion. His tenderness, his humor, his intelligence—that had all been the trick.

And the idea that he was bailing on the world, intending to start over somewhere else with all his money but not with her or their child, was just salt in the wound. She didn't know that they could make a permanent relationship, but it would have been nice for him to *try*.

It would have been nice of him to care.

Cassie heard Lorenzo behind her as she marched out of his house and his life. She heard him calling after her but didn't slow down. She couldn't have cared less what he had to say. As far as she was concerned, he'd said plenty. To the left of the front door was another door. Cassie guessed that it led to the garage.

Perfect. She ripped it open, not caring that the security alarm went off. Lorenzo could deal with that—it was small potatoes compared to raising a child alone.

"Cassie!" Lorenzo swore and quickened his pace, shouting her name again. If he wanted something else from her, he could wait. Cassie hit the unlock button on the key for the car as she walked into the garage.

The Ferrari beeped obediently.

"No!" Lorenzo bellowed.

Cassie glanced back to discover that he was right behind her, shimmering blue.

Cassie leapt into the car, locking the doors as soon as she was inside. Lorenzo fell against the outside of the vehicle, his weight making it rock. He didn't shift, but leaned close to the window, still shimmering blue as he looked to be wildly negotiating.

Well, she'd cracked his composure, at least.

But it was too late.

She knew he wouldn't rip open the door: the car was too precious to him to risk damaging it.

Cassie, unfortunately, didn't hold the car in quite as much esteem. She ignored him and whatever he was promising. It was probably all bullshit anyway.

Or beguiling. She didn't dare listen to him, lest she be seduced by the appeal in his words. She didn't dare look at him, lest he try to enchant her all over again. She knew he could get to her, and knew herself well enough to recognize that she hadn't completely turned against him.

Cassie was pretty sure his earlier promise not to beguile her again was moot at this point.

He pivoted and raced back to the house. Cassie really hoped he didn't have a second set of car keys.

He probably did.

She wasn't going to wait to find out.

Her heart was pounding as she started the engine. She gave it too much gas and it roared. She found the button for the garage door opener, and at her touch, the door slid upward, revealing an inky square of desert night.

Lorenzo shouted at her.

Cassie turned up the music to block the sound and fastened her seat belt. She'd driven a flashy car like this once, when pursuing a shot of a celebrity who raced cars. He'd offered her the photo she wanted if she won a race against him on a closed track. She hadn't won, but she'd done well enough that he'd posed for the shot.

Cassie surveyed the dash and the gearbox, pushed in

the clutch, and put the car in reverse. The gearbox was as smooth as butter, the gear engaging with a sweet snick.

Piece of cake.

And just the thing for escaping dragons.

She took off the emergency brake just as Lorenzo came back into the garage. She gave him a fingertip wave more characteristic of Stacy, and hit the gas. The car rocketed backward. She turned and braked to a smoking halt.

She really liked how the tires squealed.

As a bonus, the sound disguised Lorenzo's roar of rage. He erupted from the garage, with something that looked suspiciously like another set of keys in his hand.

Cassie didn't wait to chat.

She was racing down the driveway when she realized the gates were still closed. There wasn't another control button, at least not one she could see. She had an instant to panic; then a sensor on the gate evidently recognized the car.

The gates began to swing open.

Cassie smiled and accelerated.

Her eyes widened when the gates changed direction and started to close again. Lorenzo must have an override at the house.

She was not going to get trapped in this compound.

She knew he wouldn't hurt her—she just didn't want to argue anymore.

No more false promises.

No more illusions.

Reality started now.

Cassie gauged the distance to the gate opening, geared down for a burst of speed, and put the gas pedal to the floor. The car lunged forward, like a cheetah on the hunt.

It slipped through the closing gates with the barest sliver of space.

In fact, one gate caught the rear right fender. She heard the sound of metal scraping against metal, and winced at the grinding sound. The car's trajectory twisted slightly, but Cassie didn't slow down.

So now something precious to him was damaged. She could just imagine how Lorenzo was roaring now.

But Cassie had gotten away. She turned onto the highway, fishtailing a bit on the last of the gravel, and tried to figure out exactly where she was going to go.

A bit too late, she looked skyward for Balthasar. There was no sign of him. Maybe her luck was changing for the better.

Either way, Cassie needed a plan before Saturday.

Sooner would be better.

Chapter 12

Lorenzo was right behind Cassie. He took the bold chance of shifting shape as he leapt out of the garage, unconcerned with who saw his change. It was reckless and uncharacteristic.

Lorenzo had no time for artifice.

He had to ensure Cassie's safety.

Even if he would have liked to have given her a good shake. How could one woman turn him so inside out and upside down? How could he be simultaneously infuriated with her and worried about her? How was it that he couldn't get enough of her?

He ground his teeth as he flew low and fast after her, not wanting to risk having her out of his sight. He raced after the taillights of his car, knowing what the firestorm and Cassie were conspiring to make him do.

And with every beat of his wings, Lorenzo wondered: Could the prophecy be right?

How could a ditty scrawled on a piece of parchment have any relevance to real life?

There were too many questions, too many variables,

too much information missing for Lorenzo to make a good choice. And no time. He had no time.

What was he going to do?

Even as Lorenzo flew, he knew the answer. He wasn't at all persuaded that he and Cassie could have a future together, but he wanted her to have one. He'd seen the depth of her hurt and she'd told him the reason for her distrust of men. He wanted to prove to her that he was different.

Fortunately, he had an idea how to do it.

But he'd need help. Even as he trailed behind Cassie, Lorenzo understood why Erik was in town.

Lorenzo was going to have to ask the leader of the *Pyr* for assistance. And Erik, with his gift of foresight, had known it.

Lorenzo was pretty sure the words would stick in his throat.

But it was clear that his established tendencies weren't going to ensure Cassie's safety. If she wouldn't trust him and join him in his plan, then he couldn't defend her and his son. And no matter what she thought of him, he wasn't prepared to lose her.

His sense that he had become a kind of focus for *Slayers* and *Pyr* alike wasn't paranoia, after all. They were attracted to him for some reason, and intent upon using him for something. And the only way to foil whatever their scheme might be was to surprise them. A little sleight of hand was required.

Lorenzo could only hope that Erik wouldn't turn him down.

Cassie saw the sign for the national park on her way back to Vegas. It gave her an idea.

After all, she didn't really want to go back to the hotel. Not with Balthasar hunting her. It would be bad enough if he took her down, but she wasn't going to lead him straight to Stacy, too.

She didn't want to go back to Lorenzo's place.

But the state park was where Lorenzo's spectacle was supposed to be held. She turned into the park on impulse, slowing down only slightly on the smaller road. There was no one at the gates to the park, but she could see spotlights far ahead and off to one side.

She'd guess that was where Lorenzo's preparations were being made. She drove directly toward the bright lights, not really surprised to find the site busy despite the hour.

And defended. There was security staff everywhere, probably ensuring that no one got into the site before the big day. She might have turned back, but the first guard obviously recognized the car.

He gave her a salute and opened the gate, well in advance of her arrival. Cassie realized the windows of the Ferrari were tinted quite dark.

And they must be used to Lorenzo driving fast to open the gate so early.

Cassie went with the assumption and roared through the gate, as if she'd expected nothing else. She drove on as if she knew where she was going. There was a big pit in the middle of the site, with lots of bleachers for spectators. Enormous light standards had been constructed, and three massive screens stood to display video for the crowd. There was a big silver crane poised to lift something into that hole.

The car.

Cassie shuddered at the thought. The men glanced toward the car, then continued their rounds, as if accustomed to Lorenzo making unannounced visits.

As long as she stayed in the car, no one would realize he wasn't the driver.

Cassie wondered whether the cloak of Lorenzo's protectiveness extended farther than that. Could Balthasar tell who was in the car? Maybe not. She parked the car at one end of the space, choosing a shadowed zone that didn't seem very busy. She killed the engine, watching the men work and patrol the perimeter.

Cassie was as safe here as anywhere.

For whatever that was worth.

At least she wasn't alone. If Balthasar attacked, surely Lorenzo's employees would call the cops. She didn't doubt that Balthasar could gobble her up before anyone could arrive to intervene, but this was probably as good as it got.

And Cassie was exhausted. Now that the adrenaline had abandoned her, she was completely wiped. She might see a plan for her future more clearly in the morning. She supposed she should start taking better care of herself, to ensure the health of her unexpected arrival. Vitamins. Better insurance. She could repaint one of the bedrooms in her house, turn it into a nursery.

Give her neighbors something to talk about.

Cassie locked the doors and armed the alarm. She reclined the seat slightly and saw that Lorenzo's leather jacket was on the passenger seat. She tugged it over herself like a blanket and stared at the stars through the sunroof. She could smell his scent on the jacket and, as much as she would have liked otherwise, it reassured her.

As if he had her back.

Even though she knew he didn't.

A baby.

On her own.

Crap. That wasn't the way she'd thought her story would shape up. That was even worse than her mom's story. She didn't entirely blame Lorenzo—she'd been a pretty active participant in the process, herself. But she was disappointed in him now.

She could have loved him, if the illusion had been the reality.

But it wasn't.

She'd believed too easily.

Maybe she wasn't that different from Stacy after all.

Cassie leaned her head back against the headrest and let herself cry, just a little, for what would never be.

Lorenzo was surprised when Cassie turned into the park, even more surprised when she headed for the site of his spectacle. He told himself that he shouldn't be surprised by Cassie anymore, but the truth was he suspected that would never change.

He was surprised by how much he wanted to make a permanent connection with her.

Why would she choose to visit this location? A cautious bit of him wondered if she was after some shots to sell, but that made no sense. She'd chosen not to photograph him and Balthasar. Cassie deserved more of his trust than that.

Then why here?

Lorenzo recalled suddenly the presence of JP. Why was that *Slayer* in town? And what had he wanted with Cassie? Lorenzo had been sloppy with regards to JP, and carelessness always irritated him. It didn't matter that he'd been distracted by Cassie's presence. Was that what the firestorm did? Ensure that *Pyr* screwed up? Why hadn't he found out more? Was JP manipulating her, maybe into leading him into a trap?

Lorenzo felt his temper flare and he scanned the site, seeking some trace of *Slayer* presence.

Meanwhile, Cassie parked the car and killed the engine. Lorenzo scanned the grounds, but no one approached the vehicle. The shadows were empty and still. He patrolled the area with vigilance, but found nothing out of order. He kept to the darkness so that the security staff wouldn't notice him and clung to the shadows, hoping Cassie wouldn't see him either. He avoided the bright security lights, certain he was missing some key detail.

And he heard Cassie begin to weep.

It shattered something deep within him.

He had made her cry.

He felt like vermin.

Lorenzo landed on a cliff above and behind Cassie, hiding himself in the rock formations ground out of the earth ages ago. He shifted back to human form and stood in the darkness, focused on his mate. He had his eyes closed and his fists clenched as he listened.

Her tears halted sooner than he expected.

He felt her breathing and her pulse slow.

And he knew the very moment when she fell asleep.

There were worse places she could have taken refuge than in his car. Lorenzo scanned the cliffs silhouetted against the night sky, once again seeking any sign of *Pyr* or *Slayers*. He found none.

So far.

He climbed to the top of the outcropping and laid on his belly on the rock. He had a perfect view of the entire site for his spectacle, as well as the car parked beneath him. He could see to the horizon in front of him and to either side.

As much as he would have preferred to remain in human form, he knew he had to breathe dragonsmoke to defend Cassie, and he could do that fastest in dragon form.

Once again, he was shifting for the sake of the firestorm. The security staff changed shifts and he took advantage of their distraction to shift shape.

The glimmer of pale blue light might draw their attention otherwise.

Then Lorenzo stretched out again, vigilant. He slowed his own breathing, let his eyes narrow, then began to breathe a web of dragonsmoke. He wove it around his car, around Cassie and his unborn son, around everything he had belatedly realized was important to him.

Tomorrow, he and Erik would create a plan.

Tonight, he had to ensure that there was a tomorrow. For both of them.

When his dragonsmoke was thick and deep and tightly interwoven, Lorenzo took a deep breath and dismissed his pride. He closed his eyes, winced, then sent a message in old-speak to Erik.

"I need your help."

Short and sweet. Lorenzo wasn't going to beg.

Not yet anyway.

It was four in the morning when JP awakened in Stacy's hotel room, feeling both satisfied and proud. He didn't much mind humans, especially the women, especially after one had sated him as well as this one.

Stacy had been everything he'd hoped she would be.

He was certain that he had surpassed her expectations. That powder Chen had given him had been ferocious stuff, all right. He hadn't been able to stop thinking about sex since he'd gotten the first whiff of it in Hawai'i, and when he'd loosed it at Cassie and Lorenzo, his mind had lodged completely in the gutter. He knew he wouldn't be able to do anything until he had Stacy a good six or seven times.

And Chen's plan could wait a day.

The old *Slayer* had probably anticipated that JP would be distracted by the powder and factored its effects into his plans.

JP was feeling too good to worry about it.

He had watched Stacy sleep and thought about taking her an eighth time. The powder seemed to shimmer in his blood, as enticing and distracting as the firestorm he'd never had. He couldn't get enough.

He wanted more.

Stacy was snoring slightly when JP finally summoned the will to deny his desire and leave. He had to think about Chen's scheme. He had to claim Lorenzo before his spectacle. There was no point in lingering here—it was clear that Cassie wasn't going to return to the room before morning.

She was probably with Lorenzo, stamping out the last sparks of the firestorm.

JP was in too good of a mood to resent anyone getting any of what he'd had. There was lots of time to put the final step of his plan into action. JP couldn't deny the doomed *Pyr* one last night of great sex.

Chen would never know the difference.

There was a woman in the elevator when its doors opened, an Asian woman in high heels and a tight dress. JP assumed she was a hooker, having finished with her client of the hour. She stood in the back corner and avoided his gaze, as if slightly nervous.

Maybe this hotel routinely tossed hookers out.

He turned his back on the woman, not wanting to start a conversation, and hit the button for the lobby.

The doors closed and the elevator began its smooth descent.

He had a moment to catch a whiff of the woman's perfume and realize it was quite arousing before she moved. She leapt forward and slammed her hand against the stop button.

The elevator lurched to a halt.

"What the hell are you doing?" JP demanded. She turned on him with a snarl, the irises of her eyes changing to vertical slits.

His mind stalled. She was *Pyr*? She was *Slayer*? Why hadn't he been able to smell her nature? And how could a woman even be a dragon shifter? This was no Wyvern, the only female dragon shifter in the *Pyr*.

She jumped him when he gaped, hauling a piece of metal out of her sparkly purse. She slammed him into the wall of the elevator with astonishing strength, bashing his head against the hard wall. JP went down, dizzy from the impact, and her talons locked around his neck.

How could such a tiny woman be so strong?

Even if she was a dragon shifter.

She turned and bared her teeth, breathing a stream of fire at the piece of metal she held. JP couldn't make sense of what he was seeing. Her fingers became talons, her mouth was a dragon mouth. She was hovering between forms, flickering between dragon and woman.

Old man.

Young man.

Then he guessed the truth. His attacker was Chen.

And JP was in deep trouble.

"*Where is the offering I sent you to collect?*" Chen hissed in old-speak, his words searing JP's brain.

"*Tomorrow,*" JP replied, struggling in desperation. "*I'll spring the trap tomorrow.*"

"*Wrong answer,*" Chen said. "*I want him* now."

"*But, but . . .*" JP tried to save himself, even knowing it was too late. He lunged to his feet, but Chen decked him. He fell against the back corner, the *Slayer* landing on top of him with such force that the breath was driven out of his lungs. Chen ripped JP's collar downward, either with a long red nail or a golden talon, JP couldn't be sure.

Then JP screamed in agony as Chen's red-hot brand was pressed against his neck.

"*Now you're mine,*" Chen murmured, his words echoing in JP's mind as everything around him faded away. "*Now you'll never defy me again.*"

JP had a vague sense of the elevator beginning to descend again, of the doors opening to the quiet hush of the lobby in the middle of the night. He heard those heels as Chen stepped smartly over him and marched across the tile floor.

And he knew that his life had changed forever.

Salvatore was trespassing.

He knew it, and he knew the price for his transgression could be high.

If he were caught.

Salvatore didn't intend to be caught.

The potential reward, as his Angelina would have said, was worth every measure of the risk.

He trespassed for his son's future.

In Salvatore's dreams, his mind slid into dark recesses he had glimpsed long before. He had found this portal a long time ago and realized soon that it gave entry to the misty realm of the Wyvern. Somehow he'd stumbled upon it in his dreams. Maybe it was undefended, since the current Wyvern was just a child. Maybe it was accessible to him because he himself was close to death. Salvatore didn't know, and he had no intention of asking questions.

He didn't want anyone to realize the treasure he'd found. He eased closer to those hollows, knowing full well where they led. He'd entered them only once before, then retreated when he realized his location.

He'd known where he was because he'd had a glimpse of the future. He'd seen Drake—the leader of the Dragon's Teeth Warriors and a mysterious *Pyr* in his own right—holding the darkfire crystal that was secured in Lorenzo's hoard, wielding it and commanding it. Salvatore had understood that he'd seen this because it was his task to give the stone to Drake.

Maybe the current Wyvern had allowed him to enter her realm so he could do her will. Salvatore didn't know, but he respected the power of this place. The point of access was a secret to hold in reserve.

Until now.

Salvatore let his breathing slow and his pulse weaken, hoping against hope that he could once again find his way. He had need of the Wyvern's wisdom and vision. She was, after all, the prophetess of the *Pyr*, the one who saw into the realms of dreams and possibilities. He slipped into those dark crevasses, felt his way by instinct, and passed through a glimmer of quicksilver.

He recognized the realm of the Wyvern as soon as he entered it. It could be nothing else, a parallel world radiant in possibilities, in glimpses of past, present, and future, a glorious visual feast of shadows and might-have-beens. In this realm, they lingered, possibilities all.

Salvatore made himself as small as possible and tiptoed deeper into forbidden territory. He could have been surrounded by stardust. By snow. By the glittering, infinite light of the moon. He felt large and clumsy and that his presence was ridiculously obvious.

Perhaps she did know that he was in this place. Perhaps he'd found it because he'd been invited.

Either way, Salvatore dared not tarry. He dared not be caught.

He was in search of a memory.

Salvatore worked on instinct, assuming this was the way the Wyvern herself utilized this realm. He spied a veil of gossamer, one that rippled in a wind he could not feel. It seemed to snare his gaze and beckon to him. On impulse, he stretched for it, seized it, closed his eyes when it would have enfolded him. It was the memory he sought. He willed it to be a dream and felt something change in the hand of it.

Salvatore flung it through space and time, filling his mind with the intended recipient, hoping his aim was true.

Then he ran for refuge, abandoning the marvels of this realm before he was made to pay for his intrusion.

He could only hope with all his heart that he had succeeded in his quest.

Locked in Lorenzo's car and wrapped in his leather jacket, Cassie dreamed.

She dreamed more vividly than she had ever dreamed before. She was used to dreaming in color, but this dream was astonishingly clear and lucid. She felt like she was living it.

Or remembering it.

Even though she knew it wasn't her memory.

She might have been in the painting again, but this time, the room around her was empty. It felt more tangible, maybe because of that.

She could feel the floor beneath her feet and smell the salt tang in the air. She could feel the damp wind that made the curtains drift. She could smell the food that had been eaten and the wine that had been spilled. She could smell the candles that had been snuffed.

She heard the calls of the men echoing from below and went to the window. On the pier not thirty feet below the window, half a dozen men joked as they staggered into their respective gondolas. The water was as dark as ink, barely rippling, and the windows facing the scene were dark. High overhead, the silvery moon was no more than the barest crescent. It rode high in a dark sky lit with a thousand stars.

When the men pushed away, shouting farewells to each other, Cassie heard a woman's voice.

Singing a lullaby.

Cassie moved through the abandoned house, following the sweet sound of the woman's song. She entered a bedroom, one occupied by a large curtained bed and illuminated by the flames in the fireplace. The shutters were closed against the night, making the chamber appear to be an intimate refuge. The entire room looked to be gilded with the fire's light, nothing appearing more precious than the woman who rocked a baby in her arms.

Angelina.

Her hair was unbound and she wore only her sheer pale shift. The makeup that had tinted her features was gone, and her bare feet were held out to the warmth of the fire. Her bed was turned down, but she was alone with her son.

Lorenzo.

He couldn't have been a year old. Handsome even as a baby, he already had that dark wavy hair and that smile. He clutched at a tendril of her loose hair, locking his little fist around it as she sang to him.

Cassie hovered in the shadows, uncertain whether she could be discerned or not. They were so peaceful together, so joyous in each other's company, that she didn't want to interrupt. She could have stood there for hours, just watching.

Thinking. She felt the power of Angelina's love, so fierce and so passionate. Would she feel the same way about any children she had?

Would their son be such a healthy and handsome child? Cassie had to admit that she didn't mind the idea of having a baby—she'd just never thought to raise a child alone.

Angelina cooed to her son and sang to him, so obviously enchanted with him that Cassie had to smile. She did not doubt that his mom had adored him, and whether she had planned for his conception or not, she delighted in his presence.

Would the experience be similar for Cassie?

The tranquillity of the scene was suddenly shattered by a pounding. Angelina started and looked to the window. The pounding continued, as if someone demanded entry.

But it was the middle of the night.

This could not be good.

Angelina got to her feet, Lorenzo held close against her chest. She must have suspected trouble because she barely opened the shutter to peer at the canal below. She slammed it shut quickly, but not before Cassie glimpsed brilliant orange light.

A maid had knocked at the door, her expression terrified. Angelina gave her terse instructions, her eyes flashing, and the girl raced away. Angelina shouted at the girl, probably to hurry. Cassie heard men shouting in anger from the wharf below, and two words became clear in the cacophony.

Puttana.

Diavolo.

She remembered enough rudimentary Italian to translate those two words.

Whore.

Devil.

Angelina put the baby on the bed, fussing over him with agitation. She looked around the room in obvious fear, then seized a box on a table. She opened it and Cassie saw the glitter of gemstones. Angelina took a handful of gems and swallowed them, grabbing a glass of wine to wash them down. She had done this twice by the time the girl came back, then spoke to the maid, who repeated the act.

Meanwhile the shouts became louder.

The maid swore softly at the sound of wood shattering in the lower part of the house. Angelina flung the rest of the gems into the fire. She barred the door; then the two women pushed a trunk across it to barricade it.

Angelina then went to one of the paneled walls and felt along the edge. Somehow she opened a panel, revealing a narrow winding staircase. Cassie could smell wood burning, and she heard the reception room being trashed. The men's shouts were louder.

Angelina and her maid fled through the opening, Cassie right behind them. Angelina shut the portal, urging the girl up into the darkness. Lorenzo was clutched to her chest. Moments later, the two women emerged on the roof. Cassie was awed by the view; all of Venice spread at their feet, the red clay roofs and domes touched by shimmering moonlight.

Angelina wasted no time on the view. She raced to the chimney on the far side of the roof, tugging a loose brick free. She removed half a dozen bricks and Cassie saw that there was a recess in this chimney, one bricked from all sides.

Angelina's breath caught in a sob. The maid cried out and slammed the trapdoor closed at the top of the staircase. Angelina whispered something in Venetian, perhaps a prayer, kissed her son, and slipped him into the hidden space.

She replaced the bricks with shaking hands, tears running down her face. Then she looked skyward, crossed herself, and prayed again.

Cassie didn't need a translator to know what Angelina was praying for.

The men burst onto the roof just as Angelina joined the maid. They fled to the opposite side of the roof, and stood together, defiant and fearful. Backed by half a dozen men, their leader spoke to Angelina in a tone that was far from flattering.

She gave as good as she got, making a show of being undaunted as the men circled. Cassie could see the flames leaping from the windows below, lapping at the stone facade of the house.

Angelina spoke quickly to the maid, then stepped in front of her. She said something daring to the man, gesturing to his crotch. Cassie assumed by his outrage that she had insulted his masculinity.

He swore. He flung his torch across the roof to let it burn wherever it landed. He unfastened his trousers and advanced upon Angelina. She never blinked. She never retreated. She just kept taunting him. Two men seized her and pushed her to the ground. They held her down as the other man mounted her.

She laughed when she saw his manhood.

Then she spat in his face.

He struck her hard, making her nose bleed, but she mocked him even more. He mounted her in a fury, beating her with his fists, and Cassie was horrified by how intent he was upon hurting her. When he was done and stepped away, a beaten Angelina smiled at him again.

"*Syphilide*," she whispered, indicating that he would contract a venereal disease from her. Then she laughed and laughed. He kicked her. He beat her. He struck her so many times that every bone must have been broken. Her face was a bloody pulp.

But what none of the men had noticed was that the maid had fled.

She had jumped to the next roof and run while the men were occupied. Cassie saw her far away, at the end of the block of houses. She glanced back one last time, then dove off the roof. Cassie heard a splash and knew the girl would be safe.

Angelina had planned it that way. She had sacrificed herself to ensure the survival of those she cared about. Cassie was awed by the power of her love.

But the baby cried just as the flames began to emerge from the trapdoor in the roof. The men looked around, seeking the source of the sound, and Cassie prayed for Lorenzo's survival.

Even though she knew he had survived.

It was all so real though, as if she were there in the moment, and she feared that Angelina's plan would come undone at the last second. The men began to prowl the roof, seeking the child they now knew was there. She heard her heart pound in terror.

But that was when she saw the silvery dragon descend out of the sky, breathing fire and fury. His eyes flashed, and his talons were extended. He was magnificent and livid, his scales gleaming like silver in the night.

But Salvatore was too late to save his beloved.

For Angelina lay in a pool of her own blood, stilled forever.

Erik leaned over the makeshift cradle, watching his daughter sleep. The hotel room was secure enough, Erik supposed, his dragonsmoke barrier woven thick and deep around it. He could hear the traffic on the Strip and could see the flashing lights even through the curtains.

He couldn't sleep.

He couldn't leave.

He knew that Lorenzo believed he didn't need the *Pyr*. He knew that Lorenzo was determined to do things his own way. But Erik had a niggling sense that Lorenzo failed to understand the full truth of his situation, of the dangers a firestorm could draw. He feared that if he left, Lorenzo would need him and he'd be too far away to help.

He'd smelled Balthasar's arrival, but that *Slayer* had been defeated before Erik could get to Lorenzo's home. Probably better that way. Still, he sensed other forces, forces that were less easy to identify.

Who else was in town?

Erik suspected he couldn't feel the most dangerous ones. Those *Slayers* who had drunk the Elixir could disguise their scent at will, and Erik worried that he had no idea where they had all hidden themselves.

He paced the width of the hotel room, watching his partner sleep and casting glances at his daughter.

"*No point pestering her,*" a familiar voice said in old-speak and Erik jumped.

He pivoted to find his dead son, Sigmund, leaning

against the wall. Actually, Sigmund's shoulder slid partway into the wall, as if it provided no real barrier to him.

Erik sat down and braced his elbows on his knees as he confronted his son. *"I don't suppose you've come to do more than annoy me."*

"Why change now?" Sigmund asked with a smile.

Erik exhaled with irritation. He might have paced again, but Sigmund cleared his throat.

"Come on, Pops. Have a bit of faith."

Pops? Erik glanced back to find a woman standing beside his dead son. She was no more substantial than Sigmund, although she was beautiful. She was richly dressed, her red-gold hair coiled in elaborate braids and a pearl as big as his thumb hanging from each ear lobe. Her décolletage was as creamy as ivory, her lips as red as blood.

"Meet Angelina," Sigmund said.

"Dead like you," Erik guessed.

Sigmund nodded. *"Dead like me. She wants to tell you something, but I know you don't speak Italian."* Sigmund arched a brow. *"Venetian, actually."* Angelina looked back and forth between then, her fingers toying with her rings in agitation.

Erik caught his breath and guessed again. *"Lorenzo's mother."*

At the sound of her son's name, Angelina's features lit up.

"The very same," Sigmund confirmed.

"What does she have to tell me?" Erik demanded.

"Hey, don't go falling all over yourself thanking me for my help."

"What does she have to tell me?" Erik asked again, his old-speak even more emphatic than it had been.

Angelina confided in Sigmund, her words spilling in

her haste to be heard. Within moments, Erik was verifying that he understood everything when Lorenzo's oldspeak unfurled in Erik's mind.

"I need your help."

Erik was so stunned that he pivoted and looked in the direction of the sound of Lorenzo's voice. Was it a trick? He glanced back to find Sigmund grinning.

"Lorenzo wants my help," Erik echoed in amazement.

"Well, who says old dogs can't learn new tricks?" Sigmund asked and Angelina smiled.

"Is he sincere?" Erik had to ask.

Angelina nodded, her eyes shining, and gestured for him to go. Erik checked the power of his dragonsmoke barrier, kissed his partner and his child, then went to his old friend.

Just before he left, Erik glanced back toward his son and found Sigmund standing alone. His son was looking into the distance, a slight smile on his lips. Erik followed his gaze and saw two shadows. One was Angelina, and she was laughing up at a dragon that hovered over her.

The dragon shimmered blue, the glimmer of change sliding over his body from snout to tail.

One last time.

Erik knew he was glimpsing the future, his gift of foresight telling him what would be. He understood that he would soon feel the fading of one *Pyr* in the great network of dragons in the world. There was no doubt in his mind which *Pyr* it would be.

If anything, that just made Erik's mission more imperative.

Chapter 13

To Lorenzo's relief, Erik came quickly, and he wasn't laughing.

Although that didn't mean Lorenzo was home free.

Lorenzo sat on the summit of the rock in his human form and watched the onyx and pewter dragon descend out of the night sky. The moonlight gleamed on Erik's dark scales, illuminating how he moved with powerful surety.

It had been a long time since the two had first flown together, since they had lingered together in Venice. Lorenzo smiled at the longevity of their friendship, regretting that he had turned his back on it in recent years.

Erik landed beside Lorenzo and shifted to human form. He sat down beside him, his gaze sweeping over the site. Lorenzo kept silent, knowing that his old friend was checking for foes.

"Surrounded by your smoke," Erik said, as if surprised. He slanted a look at Lorenzo, one that seemed to see right through to his heart. "Help with what?"

By way of reply, Lorenzo recounted the prophecy.

"Flashfire lights the solitude
Of the Pyr *with most to lose.*
Firestorm plus an ancient spell
Fuels lust that sees his sense dispelled.
Flashfire's promise is a lure
To cheat the Pyr *of his true power.*
Will he see through the disguise
Forget the song, seize the prize?
The future hangs upon his choice
Between life and love, or sacrifice."

He watched Erik think about it, ponder its references. He handed Erik the piece of parchment. "Is it genuine?"

"Where did it come from?"

"Cassie got it from Angelina, in a painting at my lair."

Erik blinked but recovered himself. He almost smiled. "Darkfire," he murmured, then nodded. "I had heard that a prophecy about you had been entrusted to your mother. That was long ago, when Salvatore was considered to be less than reliable."

"Who made the prophecy?"

"Sophie, who was Wyvern then. She feared it would be lost if she entrusted it to Salvatore but refused to give it to me. She said it was rightfully yours. She believed that Angelina should be its custodian, which was in defiance of everything I believed, but Sophie insisted upon her way. I assumed it had been lost along with Angelina." He slanted a look at Lorenzo. "I wasn't sure why she consulted me, since she was not prepared to discuss it. Perhaps she saw your mother's future and wanted to ensure that one of us knew."

It should have been destroyed in the fire that ruined his mother's home. Somehow darkfire had enlivened the painting and made it possible for the prophecy to pass to Lorenzo.

Darkfire had changed everything.

Lorenzo frowned.

"What is flashfire?" Erik spoke idly, as if the question were unimportant to him. "Do you know?"

Lorenzo wasn't quite ready to surrender all of his secrets. "Don't you?"

Erik shrugged. "I know it is specific, provoking change for a single dragon. Darkfire, in contrast, introduces unpredictability for all of us." He eyed Lorenzo, who avoided his gaze. "I thought you might know more."

"Why?"

"Just a feeling."

Lorenzo admitted a different truth. "You should know that I had the third darkfire crystal in my hoard for centuries."

Erik's gaze brightened at that. "Had?"

"It's gone."

"You *lost* it?" Erik was incredulous.

"No!"

"You gave it away?"

"No." Lorenzo decided he would have to tell Erik all of his suspicions about the crystal's disappearance. "On that day you came to ask my help, during Rafferty's firestorm, another *Pyr* came to my lair. I smelled him, couldn't identify him, but that was when the crystal disappeared. My father gave it to that *Pyr*."

"Describe the scent." Erik wasn't even blinking, he was so intent upon Lorenzo. Lorenzo did, trying to put into words how evocative that *Pyr*'s scent was of the past. Erik nodded. "Drake. It could only be Drake. The Dragon's Teeth Warriors would not have come without him, although their scents are similar."

Lorenzo met Erik's gaze. "I thought my father was feeble and hibernating, but it appears that he has been meddling."

"He had access to the hoard," Erik guessed.

"We kept our treasures together." It pained Lorenzo to admit the truth. "He has been incapable of breathing dragonsmoke for a number of years. I breathed the perimeter mark where it was necessary but allowed him permission to cross it."

"You have cared for him."

Lorenzo shrugged, disconcerted to hear the pride in Erik's tone. "I had no choice."

"Did you not?"

"He is not what he was."

"We always have choices," Erik said with resolve. He nodded and looked over the site again, but Lorenzo could sense that his mood had improved. "So the crystal is in Drake's possession, wherever he has gone."

"You're relieved."

"I have been unable to sense them since the darkfire was released. I have been worried."

"Marco came to me. He seemed to know where the crystal had gone and left in pursuit of it."

"Interesting." Erik frowned. "It seems I must delegate this concern, at least for the time being." He turned to Lorenzo and smiled slightly. "So, *Slayer* or *Pyr*? What's your choice?"

Lorenzo averted his gaze, not willing to confess all of his intentions just yet. "First explain the verse to me. What ancient spell?"

"Dragon Bone Powder," Erik said without hesitation. "The *Slayer* Chen used it during Niall's firestorm, to heat the flames of the firestorm and distract Niall from pending attack."

"But my firestorm was sated."

Erik shrugged. "It fires the lust in all of us to some extent, feeding that primal desire to mate. So close after your firestorm's spark, it could fuel yours more." He spared Lorenzo an inquiring glance and Lorenzo frowned.

"Yes. That must be it." He hated the idea that his desire for Cassie had been manipulated and might be false, but Erik seemed to anticipate that concern.

"Niall says the distraction ended but not his desire for Rox. He says without the Dragon's Bone Powder in his nostrils, he can defend her as he should."

Lorenzo was relieved. And here was proof that the experience of the other *Pyr* wasn't entirely useless to him, as he had preferred to believe. He still felt vulnerable, as if some dragon had targeted him as prey. Could Erik and the *Pyr* truly help him out of this closing trap? Or was he simply paranoid because of his love for Cassie?

"What's the threat?" he asked.

Erik considered him. "Have you been attacked?"

"Pursued," Lorenzo allowed.

Erik nodded. "Chen had a brand, which he used to enslave the shadow dragons—those dragons raised from the dead by Magnus to be his slaves—and force them to his will instead. The brand was broken and the shadow dragons destroyed, but he is not one to accept defeat. I believe he has a plan to put himself in charge of all of us, with the use of that brand. It is ancient magic. He has targeted Thorolf in the past, although I'm not sure why. It is possible that he has similarly targeted you. I would not be surprised if he possessed some ancient magic unknown to us. He is far older than any of us."

"Like the Dragon Bone Powder."

Erik nodded again.

Lorenzo considered the vista spread before them, then decided he had more to lose by *not* confiding in Erik. "Balthasar is here."

"I know." Erik was unruffled by this news.

"He attacked the house last night."

"I know."

"He had offered to give me the keys to claim Magnus's most treasured artifacts if I joined the *Slayer* side."

Erik's eyes gleamed as he watched Lorenzo. "You declined?"

"And he attacked last night, presumably to change my mind."

Erik drummed his fingers on the rock, deep in thought.

"There is another *Slayer* here, named JP."

"The brother of Lucien," Erik said. "Long slumbering and indifferent. I smelled him here. I wondered who or what had roused him."

"I met him when he was with Cassie."

Erik was surprised by this. Lorenzo knew by the way he turned suddenly. "You have had many visitors."

"Including you." Lorenzo shrugged. "Grand Central Terminal."

"Because so much hangs in the balance." Erik watched him, and Lorenzo had the sense he knew more than he was telling. He was keenly aware that he had ducked Erik's question about flashfire, and suspected Erik was, as well. "What of your father?"

"What of him? He is evidently more capable of making trouble than I had believed. Perhaps you know more of his game than I do."

"Perhaps he is trying to ensure your happiness."

Lorenzo smiled at the idea.

But then, the prophecy had come from Angelina.

Maybe his father knew of it and was helping him to fulfill it.

Or maybe he was helping to propel Lorenzo toward the choice Salvatore—and Erik—would have made easily. He felt his own resistance to the notion of commitment dissolving, because he knew that Cassie was different.

He loved her.

He would do whatever was necessary to defend her.

It was nearly sunrise, the sky lightening in the east behind them. "What are you going to do?" Erik asked softly, and Lorenzo took a deep breath.

"Trust and hope for the best." He looked at Erik. "I have a plan, but I'll need your help."

Erik smiled and offered his hand. "Anything in my power to give is yours, my friend."

Lorenzo knew he'd been given a gift beyond expectation, maybe one he didn't deserve.

He could only hope he hadn't asked for it too late.

Cassie nearly jumped out of her skin when the car alarm beeped softly. She heard the locks disengage but only had time to sit up before Lorenzo slid into the passenger seat beside her.

It wasn't quite dawn, the eastern sky just faintly tinged with light. He was wearing jeans and a hoodie, dressed more casually than she'd ever seen him.

"Sleep well?" he asked with his usual composure.

"No. You?"

"Not at all," he admitted, then glanced directly at her for the first time. He did look haggard and his expression was wary. She wondered where he'd spent the night. Watching over her maybe? The idea gave her a thrill.

She remembered her dream then and thought she understood why Lorenzo had such a low opinion of humans. "Is that why you hate humans? Because of the way Angelina died?"

He turned to look at her so quickly that she thought he'd get whiplash. "Who told you about that?"

"I don't know. I had a dream."

Lorenzo frowned and looked out the windshield again.

"*Puttana*," she said quietly and he caught his breath. "*Diavolo*."

Then he bowed his head and pinched the bridge of his nose.

It was true. Her heart clenched for him.

"It was awful," Cassie said, wanting to comfort him but not knowing how. "And you were so young. Do you remember it?"

He inhaled and exhaled slowly. She could almost feel him composing himself. When he turned to face her, his gaze was clear. She knew he would tell her the truth. "I have nightmares about fire." He swallowed. "And about being trapped in darkness."

"But you use fire in your show," Cassie protested. "And you do escapes. You're going to be buried alive here. Doesn't that terrify you?"

Lorenzo nodded. His eyes glittered and his manner was suddenly intense. "I refuse to have my life and my choices shaped by fear."

Cassie could relate to that. She smiled. "The best thing to do when you fall off the horse is to get right back in the saddle?"

His smile was cautious. "Something like that."

"It was my mom's favorite saying. She told us that all the time."

"Us?" Lorenzo asked. Cassie was glad he didn't mention that her mom hadn't followed her own advice after that last disappointment.

"Three older brothers. We're not that close." Cassie looked out the windshield, but felt Lorenzo's scrutiny.

"They took your father's side," he murmured, guessing the truth.

Cassie nodded and changed the subject, knowing she did it clumsily. "Your dad came too late." She looked up at him. "At least he came. My father didn't come at the end."

"Some humans are vermin, then," Lorenzo said quietly.

Cassie smiled sadly and nodded.

Lorenzo reached out and took his hand in hers. His thumb moved back and forth across her skin. His hand was warm and his touch was comforting. He sighed. "The thing is, the entire incident was his fault."

Cassie was surprised. "How so?"

"Salvatore taught me to beguile. He's very good at it, perhaps the best at beguiling ever in all the *Pyr*. He liked to gamble in those days, and he liked to win."

"He cheated," Cassie guessed. "With the beguiling, he could cheat." She was astonished that Lorenzo was confiding in her. Something had changed in him, something was compelling him to share more of himself with her.

Cassie didn't know why, but she would meet him halfway.

She turned her hand so that their fingers interlaced. She had a new and potent sense that they could be good together.

A team. She'd never had a partner or confidant before, not like this, and Cassie liked the prospect a lot.

Lorenzo's smile was rueful. "He wasn't temperate. He

always won. Every time. Every *single* time." He sighed. "If he'd mixed it up a bit, maybe people wouldn't have become suspicious." He shrugged. "But he had to win. In those days, anyone who was very lucky was assumed to be in league with the devil."

"*Diavolo*," Cassie whispered.

Lorenzo turned to look at her. "He beat the wrong man too many times. It was only a matter of time before someone figured out that he always came to my mother to celebrate his triumph at the tables, and eventually someone saw him shift. When he was seen changing shape on the roof of my mother's house, the die was cast. He should have known what would come of it. He should have understood enough of human nature to see the future, but no." He frowned. "He left her alone. Undefended."

Lorenzo looked out the window and Cassie wondered how much he knew of what his mother had suffered. She hoped he only knew that she had died.

She suspected, from the taut line of his mouth, that he knew every detail.

She squeezed his hand and he squeezed hers back. "And when they came for her, he was too late."

Lorenzo nodded, his gaze locked on their hands.

"Then he raised you, after that?"

Lorenzo smiled sadly. "Oh no. He taught me to beguile as soon as he could." He glanced her way. "That way, he could abandon me without guilt, for I could get whatever I wanted from human society in his absence."

Cassie was horrified. "Why would he abandon you?"

Lorenzo shrugged. "He was a gambler and a bon vivant. A small child did not fit with his view of his life, and there was always a game to be joined somewhere."

"How did he come to be with you? It sounds as if you weren't close."

"We weren't. But one day, he ran out of lust for the game. He sought me out, and I saw that the flame had left him. He cared for nothing. He was a different dragon." Lorenzo sighed. "I wonder now whether he realized at that point that there was nothing he could do, no party he could join, no win he could make, that would fill the void of losing Angelina."

Cassie watched him closely, hearing the implication in his words. Knowing her had given him more understanding of his father, and that put a lump in her throat. "Yet even so, you've taken care of him."

"We *Pyr* are loyal, despite appearances to the contrary." Lorenzo shrugged. "Salvatore is my father. He did save me that night and he did raise me—well, as much as anyone did. That ability to beguile has allowed me to earn the funds to support us both. And I cannot say that I am completely without flaws."

He turned to look at her then, and their gazes locked and held. Cassie knew she'd seen his secret heart, the part of Lorenzo that was no illusion. He hadn't been fooling her—she'd been seeing his truth all along.

And she liked it a lot.

She could understand that it might freak him out to realize how much he'd revealed to her.

Plus Cassie realized that she no longer felt so upset about bearing his son. She stared back at Lorenzo, lost in his steady gaze, her heart beginning to pound.

"I came to tell you that you're right," he said, his voice gruff. "You already know that, but I had to come to the realization. I've been thinking about it all night. There's bad and good in every kind. I haven't been fair in calling all humans vermin. I appreciate you challenging me on it." He smiled slowly. "Not many of my acquaintance would."

"People or dragons?"

"Either." He grimaced and she had the sudden sense that his life must have been very lonely.

She was starting to think that a future with Lorenzo by her side would be all the adventure she could ever want. She was starting to think that maybe, just maybe, things could be different than her expectations.

"But that doesn't matter now," he said. "What's important is that we ensure the future."

"Whose future?"

He gave her a look. "Yours." His gaze flicked downward. "His."

Cassie had a lump in her throat. She'd been right about him taking care of those he cared about.

Including her.

She dared to hope about that future.

Lorenzo smiled. "I have some things to tell you, but let's get this done first." She must have looked confused because his smile broadened. He conjured her unused camera from his pocket and presented it to her. "Let's find a good spot while the light is right."

Cassie was so shocked that she was sure she must be misunderstanding him. "You're not going to let me photograph you shifting shape."

"I am." Lorenzo nodded with resolve. "With the rising sun behind me, my identity should be hidden for at least a couple of days. I don't much care if anyone figures it out next week." He eyed her, as if uncertain of her reaction. "How much were they going to pay for the images?"

Cassie exhaled, her heart beginning to pound as she understood. "Child support," she whispered.

"Insurance," Lorenzo said flatly. "You're right—things can go wrong and—regrettably—I don't control everything."

Cassie smiled.

"And I can't put anything in my will because I don't want you haunted by fans. I know that you don't want to come with me, so I'm trying to find another solution."

Cassie's heart clenched.

Lorenzo continued. "I would appreciate if you don't tell everyone about my being the father, although you can tell our son whatever you want. He'll have to learn to keep secrets, anyway."

"You could tell him yourself," she whispered.

Lorenzo flicked her a look. "I know nothing of parents. It would be worse for me to be in a child's life than to disappear."

Cassie didn't believe that for a moment, but she saw that Lorenzo did. The pictures weren't half of what Cassie wanted from him, but it was already more than she'd ever expected him to give.

He was changing, and she dared to hope that there would be more changes.

Besides, she wasn't nearly finished with him yet. She'd take what he offered for now and hope for far more. She could see that it wasn't easy for him to make concessions—to surrender control.

But then, he was going to be a parent, like it or not, so he would have to get over that.

And Cassie thought he'd be an awesome dad.

Cassie took the camera. "What about Balthasar?"

Lorenzo's features turned to stone. "I'm still managing that detail." He shot her a glance, one that was filled with such passion and fury that she knew she was glimpsing his dragon again.

And she knew that Balthasar would be toast, either before Lorenzo's feat or slightly afterward.

It wasn't all bad having a dragon protector.

"You want to drive?"

Lorenzo settled back in the passenger seat with apparent ease. "No. Kind of a different perspective from this side. And you'll know the location you want when you see it."

"You've never ridden as a passenger in this car, have you?"

He flashed her a roguish smile. "Never. Might be my last chance." And he winked, his cavalier manner making her smile.

Even though she was worried by the possibility lurking beneath his words. She had too many questions, questions that would take too long to discuss, and the light was changing. Before the spectacle, she'd ask him for more. That was a given.

Cassie started the car, adjusted the seat, and shot out of the parking spot. She heard Lorenzo inhale sharply, but he didn't move or say anything.

Even if his eyes were glittering like cut glass.

She knew exactly where she wanted to take the shots, and the sun was just cresting the horizon. There wasn't much time to get there.

If nothing else, Cassie was driving the perfect car to get the job done.

Cassie couldn't have planned the shoot better if she'd had weeks of notice. She drove deeper into the park, where the stone formations were most striking. The rock had been carved by water aeons ago, leaving the red stone in fabulous curved shapes. Those stone pillars and hollows seemed to be afire when touched by the light of the dawn.

She chose a spot with interesting stone outcroppings. Some of them blazed with orange light and others remained in dark silhouette. She was aware of Lorenzo watching her as she paced off the distances and checked different angles through the viewfinder.

When she turned to beckon to him, she was surprised to find him nude. His tan was perfectly even and his grin unswervingly confident. He strode toward her, his strength and grace taking her breath away.

And that was nothing compared to the gleam in his eyes.

He touched his fingertips to her chin, bent to kiss her cheek, and Cassie closed her eyes in anticipation of his kiss. She was burning for him, all over again, as if she never would get enough.

"It is treacherous for a dragon to reveal the place where he hides his clothes when he shifts," he murmured, his words so low that they made her shiver. "So I'll just leave them in the car." Then he kissed her ear, his lips sliding over her skin in a slow caress that made her forget everything except the chance of making love to him again.

Lorenzo, fortunately, remembered the business at hand. He took the position she indicated and pivoted in place, checking the view. It was perfect. Through the viewfinder, Cassie could see that he was in silhouette.

His facial features were in shadow.

"Ready?" he asked.

"I want a little bit more sunlight," Cassie said. "To ensure that your face is in total shadow." She saw the flash of his smile, but focused on the image in the viewfinder. "Three, two, ONE."

Lorenzo dropped to a crouch, spinning in place as Cassie clicked wildly. He had his back to her—a great PG-13 shot—but was all male, the sunrise gilding his muscles. As he turned back toward her, he flung his arms skyward. She saw the shimmer of pale blue, even through the viewfinder, and felt a shimmer of energy.

He was going to shift shape. She locked down her finger so the camera would take as many shots as possible in rapid succession. And then she watched, in awe, as the transformation claimed his body.

This was real.

This was what she wanted to do.

Cassie understood the truth with shocking vehemence.

Then she abruptly realized that he'd be much larger in dragon form. Cassie had to reset the zoom quickly, to ensure that his dragon figure wasn't cropped from the shot.

In a heartbeat, it was over. A massive gold dragon stood before her, his eyes glittering as he watched her. He breathed a puff of smoke and the sunlight reflected on the magnificent gold of his scales.

"Gimme some action," Cassie said, and heard Lorenzo chuckle.

"With pleasure," he rumbled, his voice similar but deeper in his dragon form.

She changed the angle of her shots, walking in a circle as he preened before her. He stretched out his wings, which were enormous, casting a long shadow across the desert. The contrast between the golden sunlight and the metallic gleam of his scales against the black shadows was fabulous. Cassie clicked and clicked and clicked.

He arched his neck, turning his head to fix his gaze upon her. She got some great shots of him closing fast, leaning in as if she were going to be his lunch.

"Fight poses!" Cassie demanded. They worked together as if they'd done it a thousand times and she felt that wonderful connection with her subject. He seemed to anticipate her requests, and she knew his moves before he made them. Every shot was perfectly framed and dead in focus. Not just because Cassie was good—because they understood each other.

Like the shoot was destined to be.

Could this be the kismet Stacy always yearned for? Cassie wanted to believe.

Lorenzo thrashed with his talons. He swung his tail. He reared back and breathed a stream of fire that was almost as long as he was.

Then he took flight, those massive wings beating with force. He posed in the sky, twisting his body and breathing fire.

It was amazing. Cassie was sure that every single shot rocked.

She was glad to have upgraded the memory card.

Then he swooped down toward her, descending out of the sky with such speed that she feared the shots would be blurred. He snatched her up and carried her high into the sky. Cassie kept snapping shots, ensuring that the car was outside of the field of view of each one. She got his talons and his tail and his scaled belly, as well as a close-up of his face.

He looked both real and terrifying.

"Wow," she said, looking down at the view spread beneath them. "No wonder your mom was hooked on this."

Lorenzo laughed. He raced toward the horizon, the wind tearing through Cassie's hair. She felt exuberant and alive—yet completely safe. Lorenzo's golden talons were locked around her waist and she knew he wouldn't drop her.

She turned to ask him about flying, and that was when she saw the scale on his chest. It hung askew, dangling lower than the others in that row and at an odd angle.

She touched it, wondering what was wrong with it, and at the merest touch, it freed itself from his hide.

It fell into her hand, glimmering like a piece of armor.

Lorenzo didn't seem to notice, so Cassie figured this happened all the time. She put the scale in her pocket, unwilling to lose something so beautiful. She could see a bit of skin exposed where the scale had been, but maybe another would grow quickly in its place.

He dove then toward a high outcropping of rock, landing on the top with grace. He folded his wings behind himself, put Cassie down, and inclined his head to her. She thought she saw a mischievous gleam in his eyes, but then he took off again, circling her high perch.

He rocketed down toward the earth, the sun still behind him. Another shot with lots of contrast. Cassie clicked and clicked. She saw the blue shimmer of light surround him just before his feet touched the ground.

One minute he was a dragon on final approach.

The next moment, a naked man stood on the desert. He pivoted and glanced up at her, his muscles flexing. Even with his features in shadow, Cassie knew Lorenzo was grinning at her.

Then she realized why. There was no way down from this pinnacle of rock, not without a lot of gear she didn't have.

"Hey! You can't leave me up here!" she shouted, and he laughed.

"Got everything you need?" he asked.

"And then some. Memory card is full to the brim." Cassie turned off the camera and tucked it into her pocket. "Are you going to make me jump?" she demanded, not believing it for a moment. It had to be two hundred feet down.

Lorenzo leapt into the air instead of replying, shimmering and shifting and soaring straight for her in his dragon form. He snatched her off the top of the rock, pivoted, and shot down to the earth again, more agile and more exciting than any theme park ride.

"A girl could get used to this," Cassie teased when they stood beside the car again. Lorenzo flashed her a smile, then tugged on his jeans and boots, his gaze never leaving her.

She offered him the camera. "Have a look. Delete anything you don't want to go further."

He seemed to be startled. "You're kidding."

"No. We had a deal. There's got to be six hundred shots there. Even if there are fifty you don't like, there are a lot left."

He smiled then, the expression dawning slowly over his face. Cassie realized that she'd never seen Lorenzo smile with real pleasure, not the way he was smiling now, as if she were the most remarkable creature on the face of the earth.

She had the evidence in her camera of how remarkable he was.

And she knew then that she could love this man, this dragon shifter, for the rest of her life, with all his complexities and enigmas. Forever wouldn't be nearly long enough to work all of those stories free.

When he smiled at her like this, she was warmed right to her toes. She wanted to be with him for the duration. She wanted to figure out a way to be with him after his spectacle.

Because she not only could love him—she already did.

"You're good at this," Lorenzo said. He was flipping through the images on the camera as Cassie watched, her obvious delight with her work rising by the second. He could feel her pulse leap every time a good shot slipped into the viewfinder. The sun was warm on his back, and Cassie's presence by his side was sweet.

Friday.

One more day.

He suddenly, irrevocably, did not want to go alone. It wasn't just his duty to be with Cassie for the duration. He wanted to be with her forever.

"I am," she agreed with obvious pride.

She should be proud. The shots needed no cropping or touch-ups. Virtually each one was perfectly composed, even though she'd shot on the fly. She'd done it instinctively, intuitively, because she was talented.

He couldn't reconcile that skill—never mind her pleasure in what she'd done—with the fact that she was thinking of giving it up.

"Then why do you do this paparazzi stuff? You're too good for it." He watched her closely, not needing his sharp perception to notice how she flinched. She didn't like talking about herself any more than he did, and was even more reluctant to share her secret thoughts.

"You don't know that," she protested, but her heart wasn't in it.

Instead he heard longing in her words.

"It's not what you really want to do, is it?"

Cassie exhaled and folded her arms across her chest. "Can we just talk about the shots?"

"No. Let's talk about why you don't believe in yourself, when you have so much innate talent. Let's talk about why you take chances to get shots you can sell, but sell yourself short."

"Ouch," she said, giving him a hot look, and he feared she would shut him out completely.

But he sensed that this was important.

"I know you don't want to talk about it," Lorenzo said quietly. "And I understand your wish for privacy." She looked up at him then, her eyes dark. "Think of it as fair trade." He smiled, hoping to encourage her.

She averted her gaze, blushing a bit when she looked back at him. "I guess I do know a lot of your secrets."

"I guess you do."

"Okay." Cassie leaned her hips against the car and Lorenzo did the same beside her.

She looked relaxed and happy in a way that hadn't been the case the first time he'd seen her. Her hair was free of its ponytail, dancing around her face in a most enchanting manner, and the sunrise was reflected in her eyes. Her shirt was untucked, and he could glimpse the lace edge of her bra. Those appalling boots were dusty, but not without their merit in this particular place.

If anything, the contrast made her look more feminine.

Lorenzo could have stared at her all day, but mindful of her uncertainty, he turned to watch the sun as well. He tried to content himself with the soft press of Cassie's arm against his and the faint scent of her skin, but failed.

He wanted more.

"Tell me," he urged quietly, and she did.

Chapter 14

"**O**kay, here's the story," Cassie said, her tone resolved. "I was supposed to grow up to be a mom. My parents thought that's all that women were good for. I wanted more. I was good with a camera. The short version is that we fought, I left as soon as I was legal, and I was determined to make it and prove them wrong."

"Sounds reasonable," Lorenzo said.

"Celebrity shots pay the best. When I started in the paparazzi business, I had a mentor. He was one of the greats, but he'd left the field to become an editor. He saw promise in me or something, and he took me under his wing, right from the beginning. He'd give me tips and it took me a while to realize that he didn't share those tips with all the freelance photographers. It took me years to realize that he was deliberately helping me build my portfolio."

"And what did he want in exchange?" Lorenzo could imagine what Cassie had thought he'd wanted, given her family history, and he hoped she'd been wrong.

Cassie smiled. "It's always a negotiation, isn't it? That's what I thought, so I confronted him one day and asked the very same thing. He wanted to go for a drink in some quiet bar, where no one in our business hung out."

Lorenzo felt his eyes narrow.

"I thought I knew what he wanted then," Cassie said. "But I was wrong." She laughed at Lorenzo, and he knew his surprise showed. "He wanted to give me advice."

"Really?" Lorenzo knew his skepticism showed.

"I know," Cassie said, "but that was it. He'd been there, in Paris, the night that Princess Diana died. I didn't know until we had that drink that it had been his last night photographing. He told me that I would have to decide which side of the line I was on, and he wanted me to remember that there are things more valuable than a photo credit. Or the check it generates. He told me that one day, I'd have to choose, and that I needed to remember that I had enough talent to do anything I wanted to do."

"That's it?"

She sighed and looked across the desert. He heard her breath catch. "He was dying. He knew it, but no one else did. I think originally he just thought I had talent and wanted to help me out, give me the break he hadn't necessarily had. But in time, I think he saw some of himself in me, and he had to talk to somebody, so he talked to me. He was dead a couple of weeks later. I was in Kenya on assignment and didn't even know for a month."

He saw her throat work, and let her take the time she needed. No wonder she was good at being alone. She'd lost a lot of people who had been important to her.

"I miss him. I miss how blunt he was. I miss how he would always push for a bit more, even when you thought you'd given your all. I miss how he laid out truths that you never expected, or maybe didn't even want to hear, but that later, those truths seemed so obvious that you couldn't believe you'd overlooked them."

"He was more than a mentor," Lorenzo suggested quietly.

Cassie nodded. "In a way, he was the father I never had. He understood me, and he didn't hold that against me. He didn't try to change me to fit his own ideas of what or who I should be." She cast him a sidelong smile, if a sad one. "And I wouldn't be who I am without having known him."

"And so, did that day come?"

Cassie nodded. "About a month ago, I was chasing a shot." She named a child star who was often in the news. "She'd been out of sight for a while, which wasn't characteristic, and the tabloids were hot for shots. Dead, alive, sick, whatever. They just wanted images. I'd met the housekeeper and she let me in, even let me park my car inside the compound."

"Because she liked you?"

Cassie rolled her eyes. "Because I paid her. Some of these people with millions and millions of dollars are so cheap with their employees. It's shocking. And, of course, it makes them vulnerable, because a couple hundred dollars solves nearly anything. And if you're going to get a couple hundred thousand for the shot, that's pocket change. Just a cost of doing business."

Lorenzo was suddenly very glad he'd always ensured that his help were well compensated. He'd done it because it was right, not because he'd thought of the security risk of doing otherwise.

"So I was there, hiding in their back garden, when they came out of the house. The girl and her mother.

And they had the family dog. The dog was clearly unwell, and not a young dog either. The girl was crying. The staff were scurrying, clearing out the limo, while the mother frantically called the vet. And I knew right then and there what was happening, that on this day, this famous child star was just a kid who was losing her pet. And that maybe it was a little bit worse for her, this day that every kid goes through sooner or later, because maybe that pet was the only friend she had."

"And you chose," Lorenzo suggested.

Cassie nodded. "There were paparazzi everywhere outside the gates of their home. I knew they couldn't drive out without being photographed a thousand times. It was a moment where they needed their privacy. I revealed myself, but before I could offer them anything, the mother turned on me. Oh, she called me a lot of things—'fucking parasite' is one that I remember—and would have had me thrown out, but I couldn't look past that kid's tears."

Cassie took a breath and swallowed. "I tipped the batteries out of my camera and threw them in the grass. I told her about the number of photographers outside; I told her that I had my Jeep and that the windows were tinted. I told her that everyone knew my car and that they'd ignore it, that she and her daughter and her dog could hide in the back and I'd take them wherever they wanted to go."

"What happened?"

"She didn't believe me. But the kid did, and she begged to have Patches stop hurting. So we did it." Cassie nodded, her eyes filled with tears. "It worked like a charm. Their security guards even made a show of kicking me out, which made the other photographers laugh. I helped them into the vet's, and then I left." She shook her head. "Never bought new batteries for that camera. That's when I decided I needed a vacation."

"Maybe you need more than a vacation," Lorenzo suggested softly. "Maybe you need to retire."

Cassie nodded slowly. "And start all over again."

Lorenzo watched the play of emotions on her face. This mattered a great deal to her—but he saw that she was afraid of pursuing her dream, whatever it was. "Sounds like you know what you want to do."

Cassie sighed. "From the first moment I held a camera, I dreamed of being the next Ansel Adams. Later I thought maybe the next Edward Burtynsky. I want to photograph moments to remember. I want to take pictures that *matter*."

"So?" Lorenzo prompted. "Do it."

Cassie grimaced. "I'm not sure I have enough talent."

"Your mentor thought you did."

"My dad didn't."

"What do you think?" Lorenzo asked softly. He leaned over and tapped her heart. "What do you believe in your heart?"

She watched him for a long moment. "I'd like to think I could do it."

Lorenzo scoffed, suspecting that would prompt a reaction from her. "But you're afraid to take a chance on yourself? That doesn't sound like you."

"It's different when it matters."

"Bullshit. It's always mattered to you."

She glanced up at him, surprised, but he could see conviction dawning in her eyes.

Lorenzo indicated the camera. "Do these shots count as real?"

She smiled at him, her gaze warm. "You're about as real as it gets, Lorenzo di Fiore."

"And you are the best photographer I've ever known, Cassie Redmond," Lorenzo said. He tipped up her chin with a fingertip. "Life is about risk. Taking chances is the only way any of us know that we're alive."

She smiled. "I guess you live by that credo."

He lifted a brow. "I think you do, too. Aren't you the best at getting a shot? I think we have that in common." He smiled. "I believe in you. And I know you're a great photographer. You just showed me the evidence. Quit playing it safe. You owe it to the world to take a chance on yourself, Cassie."

She stared at him, tears rising in her eyes, and then she smiled. "Thank you."

"No. Thank you."

There was nothing else to do then, nothing but bend down and capture her lips with his. He had no idea what the scheme was against him, much less whether he could thwart it. The *Slayers* weren't in their vicinity, but Lorenzo knew that wouldn't last. This was only a reprieve. He'd die fighting in Cassie's defense, although he'd prefer to live with her by his side.

He just had to figure out how.

No matter how it shook out, Lorenzo wanted to taste her one last time.

Cassie felt once again that Lorenzo was reading her mind. His eyes seemed more gold in this light, but he was no less intent upon her. His gaze danced over her, as if he'd memorize her features, and she swallowed at the heat in his eyes.

She wanted him.

She didn't care if he knew how much.

There was nothing left to say.

The sun had cleared the horizon and its light was becoming less rosy, more yellow. The desert and the rocks appeared to be glowing still, but not touched with fire. There wasn't a sound in their vicinity except the low murmur of the wind, the shift of sand. The sky was a perfectly clear blue, a single contrail streaking high overhead.

They were alone, as alone as two people could be, and Cassie didn't want it to be any other way.

When Lorenzo reached for her, she didn't resist him. He speared his fingers into her hair with a proprietary ease that made her shiver and drew her closer. She was his to claim, his to take, and Cassie realized with a start that she always would be.

She would never know another man like Lorenzo.

She never wanted to.

The warmth of his hand cupped her nape as he bent and kissed her. Thoroughly.

There was something different in his kiss. It was more hungry, more demanding, less reserved.

Because this might be the last time.

Cassie was just as determined as he was to make it count. She slid her arms around his shoulders in complete abandon. She stretched to her toes and arched against him, wanting everything he could give. She wouldn't hold back, either. They'd both have the memory of this morning.

And not one regret.

"Slow," he murmured. "I want this time to be slow."

"We've done slow before," Cassie whispered against the heat of his skin. She spared him a glance, knowing her eyes were twinkling. "Let's be wild."

He smiled that slow, sensuous smile and arched one brow. "Dragon style?"

Cassie nodded. "So hot and powerful that everything is left shaking afterward."

"Deal." He grinned, and she knew by the light in his eyes that he'd take her dare and then some. He scanned their surroundings, then scooped her up in his arms and headed for a hollow carved out of the rock. Cassie kicked off her boots as he walked.

"Good riddance," he muttered.

"I like my boots," she protested, knowing that they had become a joke between them.

"I like your feet better." He sat on the rock, tipped her backward, and caught one foot in his hand. His other arm was locked around her waist, holding her captive against his bare chest. Cassie couldn't resist him. She touched him, running her hands over his muscled shoulders.

Lorenzo ran his thumb along the bare arch, his gaze simmering, then kissed her instep with deliberation. Cassie shivered. He locked his fingers around her ankle, his tongue both tickling her and arousing her. She squirmed and found his erection beneath her buttocks, the size of him arousing her even more.

He closed his eyes at her move and she did it again, wanting only to ensure that his desire was as great as her own.

"Tease," he muttered.

"You should talk."

His smile flashed again. "I'll show you teasing."

He ran his fingers around her ankle, his tongue and teeth making her ache for more of him. A steady stream of kisses and nibbles made her keenly aware of every inch of her skin—and make her want to feel him against every bit of it.

Cassie quickly undid her jeans and peeled them off. Lorenzo stopped his caress while she removed them, then bent to kiss the inside of her bare knee. She wriggled, because that tickled, too, then saw the mischief in his eyes.

He watched her through his lashes as he kissed his way closer to her panties. He could have been a different man, one less refined and more driven by his passions. He had a day's growth of dark beard and it prickled against Cassie's skin, reminding her that Lorenzo wasn't all polish all the time.

At least not with her. His eyes shone golden, reminding her of the powerful dragon he could become, and Cassie's mouth went dry.

Then he locked his hands around her waist and slid them down, taking her underwear with them. His thumbs moved against her skin, making her tingle with anticipation. He cast the teal-green panties aside without a backward glance, gripped her hips and bent to taste her. His tongue was more relentless this time. He drove her to the cusp of orgasm at least four times, easing off just before she climaxed, cheating her over and over again. Cassie could have screamed in frustration, but Lorenzo only chuckled, his breath warm against her thighs. She was burning with desire for him, her need far greater than it had been even with the firestorm.

Because Lorenzo himself was casting the spell over her.

If she was beguiled, Cassie didn't want to break free of his enchantment.

But she would get even. She moaned in frustration when he withdrew the next time, leaving her vibrating on the cusp of orgasm. He smiled a wicked smile, and she took advantage of his distraction to pounce on him. Lorenzo fell backward, surprised but still cradling her fall.

"Payback time," Cassie declared, then closed her mouth over his erection.

He gasped. His hand locked in her hair. She heard him exhale shakily and felt him get larger. She caressed him with both hands as she teased him.

She loved how he whispered her name.

When he was just on the verge of exploding, she stopped. He groaned and she flicked her fingertips across him. He arched his back and ground his teeth. She loved how much he wanted her and how he didn't mind showing it.

He made to reach for her, but Cassie held up a finger. "Don't move. I'm not done with you yet." He lay back with some reluctance, his gaze locked upon her. She peeled off her shirt and preened for him as she had once before. Lorenzo's eyes shone. She reached back and unfastened her bra, tossing it toward him. He caught it in one hand, rubbed his thumb across the cup that was still warm from her body, his gaze never leaving her.

She straddled him, let him look, then slowly crouched atop him. She lowered herself onto his erection, taking his strength inside of her in one smooth move. He inhaled sharply, his gaze brightening.

"You're not allowed to come before me," she murmured, then began to rock on top of him. Lorenzo groaned.

Then he grabbed her hips in his hands, coaxing her to a steady pace. Cassie watched him even as he watched her. She felt him become even bigger inside of her. She felt his thighs flex beneath her. She saw the sunlight touch his skin with gold. She saw his eyes darken and she knew he was close.

He slid his hands over her, the brush of his fingertips driving her to distraction. She felt her whole body begin to tingle, the cumulative desire rising to a fever pitch.

She felt a trickle of perspiration on her own back and saw the same shimmer on Lorenzo's tanned skin.

He reached up and caught her face in his hands, pulling her down to him. Their kiss was openmouthed, hungrier than ever before, almost bruising in its intensity. He moved inside of her with power. Cassie ground herself against him, letting her tongue duel with his in a ferocious dance.

Then Lorenzo slipped his hand between her thighs. He touched her with surety while he drove deeply into her. And when he pinched her clitoris, Cassie's orgasm flooded through her body with savage force. Lorenzo roared as he found his release as well, his bellow of pleasure enough to shake the earth.

Cassie lay panting, sprawled across his chest, entranced by the thunder of his heart beneath hers. "Again," she demanded, kissing his nipple. He didn't hesitate for a second, but rolled over, easing her beneath him. She was lying on her belly, Lorenzo's heat braced protectively over her.

He pulled up her knees on either side. One arm slipped beneath her, holding his weight even as his fingers closed over her breast. His other elbow was near her waist, that hand sliding through her pubic hair.

She knew how he was going to caress her and spread her legs wider to invite his touch. He slid his strength inside her again and she closed her eyes at the size of him, at the press of his thighs behind her own.

"This time, you can't come until I do," he whispered against her neck, and Cassie couldn't wait for his torment to begin. She rolled her hips, smiling when he growled with pleasure; then his fingers moved and she was lost in his embrace once more.

*   *   *

Salvatore intended to trespass again.

But this would be the last time.

His anticipation rose as he worked his way closer to the hidden portal, easing through the veils of the ages, through the gossamer dimensions that overlaid each other. He let the whispers of other times slip past him. He felt the caress of material items lost and those yet to be possessed touch his skin. He smelled perfume and food and rot and promise, a heady mix of scents that did not belong together outside of this sphere.

It would have been easy to have become distracted in this carnival of sensation, but Salvatore had a destination. His fear was that he would never find it. He didn't care if he ever returned to the world he had abandoned—he had kept his promise and was done with that realm. Salvatore feared only becoming lost in this place, spending all of eternity drifting, like a thief trapped in the house of another.

It was the scent that finally oriented him. The smell of water and of stone, of shadow and of pale light. The smell of fog and salt and mist, and the inside of a woman's elbow. He knew that elbow. He knew that woman.

She was why he had risked this intrusion again.

He finally found the threshold to the Wyvern's realm again, although it took him longer than it had before. He had the sense that his back door was becoming elusive, probably because it was closing against him.

But he was through it, that scent drawing him onward to his destination.

Salvatore followed it with diligence, impatient yet needing to move with stealth to ensure that he wasn't discovered. He nearly wept when he found the house. He was shaking when he climbed the stairs. He swallowed when he heard the music and the laughter.

And smelled one distinctive perfume.

His first tear broke after he knocked for admission, when he heard the achingly familiar tread of a woman's foot, when he heard her call back in jest to another in the room.

He feared in the last moment that she wouldn't recognize him, that he was too aged for her to know who came to her door.

Then she opened the portal. His Angelina. She was dressed in sumptuous red and gold, the silk shimmering with its own light, the pearls at her throat gleaming. Her feet were bare, her elegant toes peeping from beneath the hem. She held a glass of wine in one hand, and her hair was still coiled high.

She froze, eyeing him in mingled astonishment, hurt, and hope. "Salvatore," she whispered, her gaze dancing over him.

The evening was young, he realized, his favorite time of the nights he had spent in her abode. No one was as yet drunk; the conversation sparkled; the world seemed to be full of possibilities.

Salvatore knew that he was returned to the moment when he *should* have returned to her, when he had not returned, when pride had kept him away. Salvatore didn't believe he could change the past, but he did believe that he could try to repair his mistakes.

"I am sorry," he said, awkward as always with the dialect that flowed from her lips so eloquently. It was important, though, that he apologize in her native tongue. "I was wrong."

She stared at him for a minute, an endless minute that made him fear her response. She glanced back at the revelers in her establishment, then stepped closer to him. Her eyes were dark with concern, filled with the knowingness that being outside the stream of time gave her. "The fire will still happen on this night?"

He nodded. "I cannot change it. I can only make my peace with you."

"And Lorenzo?"

"I kept my promise to you. She is his match, in every way." He smiled, knowing he had done right by his son. "Between us two, we have ensured his future."

Angelina nodded. They eyed each other for a long moment, perhaps both guessing that this might be the last time they met.

Forever.

Would their souls find each other again? Salvatore could only hope as much. Would he see her in whatever afterlife there might be? Again, he could only hope for the outcome he desired.

"How did you come to be here?" she asked. "I did not know you had such powers."

"I don't." Salvatore could not help from glancing over his shoulder. "I don't know how long it will last."

A twinkle dawned in Angelina's eyes. "You are breaking some rules, I would wager." She had always loved making mischief, defying expectation and pushing the limits. "You are cheating again!"

Salvatore grinned, unable to help himself. Then he sobered, guessing his heart was in his eyes. "I had hoped it would be worth the risk."

Angelina glanced back at her patrons, then eased a little closer to him. She offered him the glass of wine, and when he sipped, unable to look away from the majesty of her eyes, she leaned closer to whisper, "Take me for one last ride, my love."

His heart clenched at her endearment. She had forgiven him.

Against all expectation.

"It's too early in the evening," he protested. "People will see . . ."

"It is too late for so many things." She laid her fingertips across his mouth, silencing him with the touch he had yearned to feel again for four centuries. "If you are stealing moments, Salvatore, steal this one for me."

And as had always been the case, Salvatore could deny Angelina nothing. It was how he believed a great love should be.

He knew when he reached for her, when he surrendered to her request, that he would never find his way back through the realm of the Wyvern again.

Salvatore did not care. He had arrived at the destination he had always dreamed of reaching.

And as he soared above the city of Venice with his beloved Angelina laughing in his embrace, far across the ages, the breath caught in the chest of a dragon sleeping in a mansion outside Las Vegas.

The silvery dragon's eyelids flickered as he dreamed.

He smiled.

He shifted shape, becoming an old man once again.

His heart beat one last time, then stopped forever.

Cassie was an addiction. Firestorm or not, Lorenzo was never going to get enough of this woman. Even knowing about the Dragon Bone Powder didn't change his conviction—he understood exactly what Niall had meant.

The magic at root was Cassie's own. She entranced him. She fascinated him. She excited him and surprised him, and Lorenzo dared to believe that perhaps the firestorm had been right. Perhaps it had chosen the perfect partner for him. He liked that she was unafraid of his dragon nature, that she was undaunted by his attitude and that she was prepared to push him to change.

He loved her.

And he wanted to make love to her for the rest of his life. He had to make this work. He had to give them a future.

When she languished beside him after two orgasms, her skin faintly flushed, her smile of satisfaction was all the reward he needed. For the first time ever, Lorenzo was content to lounge with a lover after the loving was done. He stretched out beside her as the sun rose higher, trailing his fingertips over her breasts and belly.

"You could sunbathe nude," he suggested, tracing a tan line with one fingertip.

"Not smart in a world full of predators," she replied.

Her words, though lightly uttered, reminded Lorenzo of unfinished details. Who would defend her in his absence? He frowned, then glanced toward the car. "You could come with me."

She watched him for a minute, then sat up abruptly. "You've got some scheme, I know. You think you're going to survive this feat." She glanced back at him. "But I can't imagine how."

"That's not your job. I'm a professional."

She watched him for a minute, her eyes narrowed. When she spoke, her words were low with concern. "What if you're wrong? What if you do die?"

Lorenzo shook his head, dismissing the idea. "What if you come with me?"

"Where, exactly?"

"That matters less than the fact that you would never be able to look back."

"I'd have to go with you in the car."

Lorenzo nodded. "It's the only way to ensure your

safety." He thought of Caterina, knew Cassie was different from his first love in every way. But there was no point in telling her the destination—she could only go there at his side.

Cassie studied him then, and he wished he could will the words from her lips.

He wanted her to trust him.

He wanted her to join her life to his.

He wanted her to come with him.

But he wanted her to *choose* to do so.

Cassie averted her gaze and he knew what she would say. She shuddered. "I'm not sure I could do that. I'd have to leave my house. My friends." She turned back to him, unable to hide her horror. "I'd have to be buried alive in that car."

Lorenzo nodded. "With me."

She swallowed and shuddered again. "I don't like closed spaces. I don't like darkness, and I don't like being underground." She met his gaze. "I would completely freak out. I wouldn't be rational, and I wouldn't listen to anything anybody said."

Lorenzo averted his gaze. He couldn't even express how much her answer disappointed him.

"You have to tell me how the illusion works."

Lorenzo caught his breath. "I can't do that," he admitted quietly, his chest tight.

To his surprise, Cassie reached out and took his hand in hers. "I can't go with you. Not because I don't trust you. Not because I don't want to be with you. But because I've never faced my fear of darkness, and when I freak out, I'll endanger both of us. Your escape might fail because of me."

Lorenzo blinked. Once again, Cassie had surprised him.

"I could beguile you," he offered.

"Would the beguiling even hold?" Cassie asked. "Didn't you say that beguiling worked best when the suggestion was something the person wanted to believe?" Lorenzo had to nod agreement to that. Cassie smiled, but her smile was rueful. "No one is ever going to persuade me that being buried alive in a car is a good thing." She leaned down and kissed his cheek. "Not even you are that good."

And there was nothing Lorenzo could say to that.

Except to create an alternate plan.

He respected her conviction, her fear, and her choice.

And he'd prove that to her.

That was the only way to win her heart.

What if he met her after the spectacle, after he'd used the flashfire song, after his connection to the *Pyr* was severed? Could they make a life together then? Lorenzo dared to hope.

Lorenzo stood up, returned to the car, tugged on his jeans, then walked around the vehicle, ensuring that the scratch on the rear right fender was the only damage. He'd spent a fortune retrofitting this vehicle for this stunt, and it was more important than ever that he survive.

Balthasar was a problem that had to be solved.

Immediately.

If Cassie wasn't coming with him, if she wasn't his to defend on Saturday, he had to ensure that there was no threat to her. He couldn't rely upon Erik and the other *Pyr*, not over an issue so critical. He had to somehow ensure her safety himself.

Lorenzo peered at the scratch on the rear fender as if it was much more troubling than it was. He was exhausted, but that was irrelevant. Cassie's survival had to be guaranteed. His only chance of a future with her was if they both survived independently, then he sought her out.

He'd find her anywhere. He knew that.

Lorenzo sensed Balthasar's presence somewhere nearby, and tried to target him with old-speak. He wished he were better at it, but even this crude effort might do.

"I thought you wanted a fight," he taunted. *"But then, you were never very effective, were you? That's why Magnus didn't share his secrets with you. You didn't deserve to be his heir."* Lorenzo paused, heard no reply, so added a bit more. *"You've always been a loser, Balthasar. I'm reassured that some things never change."*

He heard the roar of Balthasar's rage like distant thunder and smiled in satisfaction.

Plan B was coming together right on cue.

Cassie couldn't believe it. Lorenzo had invited her to share his life with him, she declined on a technicality, and now he was thinking about his car.

Like his question was no more important than the convenience store being sold out of his favorite beer.

It was too bad that she had scratched the rear fender, but the Ferrari was fine otherwise. She got dressed with impatient gestures. Oh, she was sure that the paint would be hard to match and the entire quarter panel would have to be repainted, but really, even if the whole *car* had to be repainted, Lorenzo could afford it.

He was the one who was planning to bury this car for a month anyway. What would *that* do to the paint job?

Cassie resented that he had just brushed off her refusal, as if it had been irrelevant. Maybe he'd asked her only to be polite. Maybe he thought it would make for a better show if she was buried in the car with him.

No. She nibbled her lip as she watched him, unable to avoid noticing how indifferent he seemed to her presence. Did he really not care? Or was he pretending disinterest to make it easier for both of them? They would have to drive out of this park together, after all. Lorenzo *was* a seasoned performer.

Yes. He was feigning indifference again. He only did that when he really cared. He was managing the details and making a new plan. And she, who liked to control her choices as much as Lorenzo did, needed to trust him.

She watched him closely and saw the signs of his agitation. Then he looked at the sky and she heard thunder.

The sky was perfectly clear.

Was that dragon stuff, too?

She picked up her boots and tugged them back on. Lorenzo hauled on his T-shirt, then put his hand out for the keys. They were shoved deeply into Cassie's pocket, so she dug them out and silently surrendered them. There was clearly no question of her driving. He unlocked the car and held the passenger door for her.

But he was scanning the sky as she got in.

What was going on?

Lorenzo swung into the driver's seat, touched the button for the car to adjust the mirrors and seat to his preference, and turned the key in the ignition. He hit the gas, the rear end of the car fishtailing as he accelerated hard.

That was when she noticed the blue shimmer surrounding him.

"Company coming," Lorenzo said with grim satisfaction, and pushed the accelerator to the floor.

"The thunder," she guessed.

"We call it old-speak. The frequency is too low for humans to hear clearly, but we dragons can all hear it."

He gave her a glittering look and she knew he'd issued a dare.

She could guess to whom.

Cassie checked the mirror on her side, and even looked out the rear window, but couldn't see anything. Then she twisted in her seat to look out the sunroof.

And saw an airborne dragon closing fast.

Talons extended.

He breathed a plume of fire and Cassie spun around to stare forward again. "Balthasar?" she asked, but Lorenzo's only reply was a smile.

A dangerous dragon smile.

Okay. This was good. Cassie tried to convince herself of that. The Balthasar problem would be solved. More proof that she should just trust Lorenzo when it came to matters draconian.

Even though Cassie pretty much believed all of that, she still screamed at the scrape of dragon claws on the car's roof.

Never mind when Balthasar lifted the car off the road.

That Lorenzo swore so thoroughly couldn't be a good sign.

Chapter 15

It would have been nice if someone had shown an iota of consideration for this subtly retrofitted vehicle, which held the entire key to Lorenzo's survival. If the Ferrari was trashed, there was no way he'd be able to replace it by the next day, not with all the expensive modifications in place. His whole plan would have to be scrapped, the spectacle canceled, and all his work would have been for nothing.

So he swore when Balthasar locked his talons around the roof. The two windows on the passenger doors broke and the points of Balthasar's nails curved through the space, jabbing into the roof interior and puncturing the upholstery.

Balthasar lifted the car off the road with a grunt and flew over the desert, carrying them captive. Lorenzo fumed at the inconvenience of it all. He prayed the moronic *Slayer* would at least put the car down gently instead of dropping it on rock. If the undercarriage or the suspension were damaged, he'd never get them fixed without someone seeing the modifications made to the car.

He sincerely hoped that Balthasar strained something from the effort.

Cassie had slid down in her seat. She was clutching the seat beneath her, her eyes round as she stared at those dragon claws. "Hell on the upholstery," she said through gritted teeth, and he appreciated her attempt at levity.

"If he wrecks this car, I will kill him. I will hunt him to the ends of the earth and ensure that he suffers."

She cast him a look. "I thought you were going to kill him anyway."

Lorenzo felt his eyes narrow. "It's so barbaric and primitive. There must always be fighting and killing and bloodshed." Even as he protested against his own nature, he felt his rage grow. He felt himself hover on the cusp of change. He was keenly aware of the threat to his mate and to his unborn child, and the very notion that they should both be at risk made him more livid than he had ever been before.

All because this stupid *Slayer* thought Lorenzo should join his team.

"Why can't any of these fools just take no for an answer?" Lorenzo muttered.

"Seems a bit late to negotiate," Cassie noted.

He flicked a glance her way, and she smiled. Her attitude made him feel better.

And he realized that negotiation was Erik's solution of choice. Only now did Lorenzo appreciate the balance struck by the leader of the *Pyr* and feel a measure of respect for it. Joining forces with Erik not only meant having the help of the other *Pyr* in ensuring Cassie's survival—it meant that he could work against the crude nature of his kind.

It meant that his life could have a purpose beyond

the pursuit of wealth and pleasure. After four centuries, Lorenzo was ready to mix it up a bit. He couldn't exactly provoke Cassie into following her dreams and not pursue a few of his own.

But first he had to survive.

He unfastened his seat belt with purpose.

"I assume you have a plan," Cassie said.

"Not as much of one as I'd like." Lorenzo turned off the engine and put the car in park. Out of habit he engaged the emergency brake, which would have been amusing under other circumstances. "But I'll think of something."

He gave her one last intent look, grasped the roof the car, and hauled himself out through the window. He felt the wind in his hair, saw the glitter of the sunlight on Balthasar's scales, then shifted shape with a roar as he surged into the sky.

Lorenzo leapt high, turned tightly, and buried his claws into Balthasar's back. He ripped, and the *Slayer* screamed. He moved like lightning, giving the wounded *Slayer* no time to respond. He breathed fire until Balthasar bellowed in pain, and the smell of his singed scales filled Lorenzo's nostrils. He smacked his opponent with the weight of his tail, ensuring that he reopened the wound that had barely closed.

When Balthasar snarled and made to lunge at him, Lorenzo saw his grip loosen on the car. He snatched the vehicle away from Balthasar, then raced away from his opponent. Balthasar was right behind him, breathing fire and muttering obscenities. Lorenzo swung the vehicle with all his might, hearing Cassie scream when the left rear fender caught Balthasar in the chops.

The *Slayer* fell backward, losing the rhythm of his flight, a good bit of altitude, and several teeth.

Lorenzo raced toward the ground, set the car down with care, and watched Balthasar approach. He managed to breathe one ring of dragonsmoke around the vehicle, then saw Cassie reach for the door handle.

"Stay in the car!" he roared. She looked at him in alarm, but he had work to do. He leapt into the sky again, intercepting Balthasar. They fought hard, neither of them holding back, spinning through the air as they wrestled for supremacy.

For each blow Balthasar landed on Lorenzo, Lorenzo laid at least two. He was pummeling the *Slayer* and getting no small satisfaction from it. He realized that, for the first time, he was savoring his dragon powers.

That shook him a bit. Had he become a barbarian as well? Was that the legacy of the firestorm? The prophecy echoed in his thoughts and Lorenzo knew he had to find his own way clear of the situation. Balthasar slashed at him while he was distracted and Lorenzo winced at the impact of the blow.

"*Want to join the winning side yet?*" Balthasar demanded in old-speak.

Lorenzo scoffed. "*No team comprised of dregs and losers will ever claim a victory over anyone.*"

Balthasar's eyes flashed and they locked talons, grappling back and forth across the sky. "*You don't even like humans. Except maybe this one. And you've had your firestorm. You've got nothing to lose.*"

"*Just my soul. My dignity. And my red, red blood.*" Lorenzo punctuated his claim with a snarling bite, one that left a gaping wound on Balthasar's side. The *Slayer* howled in pain and his black blood flowed, but Lorenzo didn't release his grip on his opponent's talons.

He could have killed Balthasar, right then and there, but that would have made him no better than a *Slayer*.

He'd eliminate the *Slayer* with his own signature style.

Lorenzo backed Balthasar hard into the rock face, slamming his spine into the rock so hard that Balthasar lost his breath. He sagged in Lorenzo's grip, but Lorenzo held tightly. "Now we negotiate," he murmured, holding Balthasar captive there as his black blood dripped down the rock.

Just as Lorenzo had planned, Balthasar looked up with hope.

Looked right into Lorenzo's eyes.

Lorenzo smiled. He conjured the beguiling flame in the depths of his eyes. He spoke in his lowest, most melodic tone, using old-speak to slide some of his instructions into Balthasar's thoughts.

The *Slayer* offered some resistance, but his mind was malleable. In moments, he was utterly transfixed. He was trapped to Lorenzo's will. He succumbed so easily and so completely that Lorenzo knew his solution was the perfect one.

And when Balthasar was totally in Lorenzo's thrall, Lorenzo told him what he was going to do.

Against her every urge to run as far and as fast as possible, Cassie followed Lorenzo's instructions. She stayed in the car.

Fidgeting.

Watching.

Fretting.

At least until Lorenzo slammed the other dragon hard into the rocks and held him there. She could have cheered that he was taking the upper hand, and expected him to finish off the dragon that was a threat to her very existence.

But Lorenzo seemed to be talking to him.

Cassie couldn't figure it out. She watched, incredulous, as Lorenzo released his opponent. Balthasar, who was bleeding profusely, fell like a rock. He wasn't dead, though, because he managed to beat his wings a little bit and soften his own landing. He shifted shape immediately then, becoming a dark-haired man in a halo of blue light. He sat down and buried his head in his hands, moaning in pain.

Lorenzo, in contrast, landed with elegant grace, shifting shape just as his toes touched the ground. He strode toward the car with purpose, ignoring Balthasar completely, and his expression was grim. He wrapped the hem of his shirt around his hands and pulled out the safety glass from the two front windows, chucking it on the ground.

Balthasar looked up just as Lorenzo opened the driver's door of the car. Lorenzo didn't so much as glance his way; he simply got in and started the engine.

As if they'd been to the mall.

"He's not dead!" Cassie cried, pointing to the other man who had now pushed to his feet.

"Of course not," Lorenzo agreed with taut composure. He accelerated furiously, leaving a cloud of dust behind them. "I assume you'd prefer to go to your hotel?"

Cassie looked between him and the rearview window in astonishment. "I thought you were going to kill him."

He shot her a glance and she noticed how dark his eyes had become. He spoke, though, with precision, his tone level. "I was, but you changed my mind."

"Me?" Cassie said. "I thought you were going to kick his butt."

"His butt has been kicked." Lorenzo winked at her. "And you did notice that I had need of a corpse to make my illusion complete."

"I can't believe he volunteered for that."

Lorenzo slanted her a glance, a smile curving his lips. "No. So I spoke to him about it." His eyes were twinkling, a reaction that she didn't think the situation deserved.

"Oh, you spoke to him. Wonderful. That will solve everything. I feel so much better."

Lorenzo chuckled.

Wait a minute . . .

"You beguiled him."

Lorenzo's smile was wicked. "It is said that we cannot beguile our own kind. Rumor is not always true."

"That's why you didn't believe about the baby."

He grimaced and shook his head. "So much PR and so little of it based on fact."

"I suppose I shouldn't ask you how the illusion is going to work."

Lorenzo only smiled and took the turn onto the highway. When he sped up, the wind ripped through the broken windows, tossing her hair into her face. Cassie disliked that he wasn't confiding in her. "Don't you think I have a right to know?"

"Illusionists keep their secrets close."

Cassie folded her arms across her chest. "Is that really it? Professional discretion? Or don't you trust me?"

He didn't answer that, but he frowned.

"Here's the thing," Cassie said. "I need to know whether I'm ever going to see you again. I need to know what happens next."

His lips tightened. "You should trust me."

"You should trust me."

Lorenzo simply drove. Cassie turned to look out the window, frustrated with him.

"Too bad about the car," she said, unable to keep a bit of snark from her tone.

"Windows I can have fixed today. It's only nine, after all."

Cassie eyed him, his proprietary tone convincing her that maybe she was missing something. She surveyed the interior of the car, but other than dragon battle wear and tear, it looked perfectly normal. "Is there something special about this car?"

He gave her one of those sidelong glances. "Everything I covet is special," he said in a low voice, one probably intended to make her shiver with desire.

It did.

"You need to trust me, Cassie," Lorenzo murmured as he entered the city and slowed down. "Everything hangs upon that." They stopped at a red light and she saw his fingers drumming on the gear shift.

Once more Lorenzo was uncertain.

Hiding it well, as she'd expect, but nervous.

When she looked at him, he was regarding her steadily. Cassie swallowed and took a chance. "I'm just not used to falling in love with people who don't play straight with me."

Lorenzo arched a dark brow. "I'm not used to falling in love at all. Once was enough to cure me of that inclination."

Who had he loved before? What had happened? Nothing good, Cassie would guess.

"Who was she?"

Lorenzo sighed. "A beauty. A temptress. A woman who overwhelmed me with desire." He flicked a glance at Cassie. "Not unlike you."

Cassie's mouth went dry. "And?"

"And it was a trap. She had been sent to reveal me, to entice me and snare me, and she nearly succeeded."

"How?" Cassie could understand why this would

make him cautious about women, and she had a new appreciation for his openness with her.

He swallowed. "It was the first time I had planned to disappear and reinvent myself in a new identity. I was maybe fifty, in Venice still, and there were suspicions about my apparent perpetual youth. I made plans, and then I met her. I never saw the link to the timing until it was too late."

"You loved her."

He sniffed. "She ensured that I did. I learned later that she was insincere, but I adored her. And I wanted her to come with me. So I explained to her all of my plan."

"She tricked you," Cassie guessed.

His eyes narrowed. "She did not meet me alone." He glanced at her, his expression cold. "I barely escaped with my life."

And Cassie understood why he was so concerned about sharing the details with her. "I won't ever do that to you," she said quietly.

He tapped out a rhythm on the gear shift, considering. The light turned green and he shot into the intersection. "Old habits are hard to break," he murmured.

"You've had a lot of time to get set in your ways," Cassie teased and was rewarded by the flash of his smile.

"The point is that the less you know, the safer we both are." He shook a finger at her. "Not because I don't trust you. Because I don't trust *them*."

Cassie could understand his point, but she needed more from him than this. She needed proof of his trust if she was going to believe in a future. "Tell me where you're going."

Lorenzo's jaw tightened. "I'll come for you, once it's all resolved."

"No." Cassie was adamant, her heart pounding as she challenged him. This was one detail he couldn't control. "Tell me now and I'll meet you there. Otherwise you won't need to bother coming for me."

She heard him inhale sharply. Lorenzo pulled into the drive of her hotel and braked so hard that the tires squealed. A doorman reached for Cassie's door, but Lorenzo waved him off with impatience. The doorman stepped back, leaving them in comparative privacy. Cassie met Lorenzo's gaze and wasn't surprised to find his eyes glittering.

As they did when he felt strongly about something.

"I want you to know, right to your marrow, that I will defend you for all time. I have seen the result of a failure in that—"

"Your dad not defending your mom."

Lorenzo nodded. "And I will not repeat his mistake. You have my word of honor on that." He caught her hand in his and lifted it to his lips, his gaze locked upon her as he kissed it. "And I will come for you."

Even the touch of his lips on her fingers was enough to make her mouth go dry. "I told you, don't bother."

He smiled crookedly. "Then I'll come with you now and change your mind." His grip tightened on her fingers and he looked worried. "Come with me in the car, Cassie. It's the best way to ensure your safety."

"But you won't force me."

"I want you to choose."

Cassie nodded understanding and tried to slow the crazy gallop of her heart. "I still think it's too risky for me to be in the car. I don't want my freaking out to be the reason your feat fails."

Lorenzo drummed his fingers on the steering wheel. "I don't think you should be out of my presence."

"I'm sure I'll be fine."

He gave her a hot look. "I respect your choice. I think you are stronger than you believe and that it would be fine, but it doesn't matter what I think. The choice must be yours."

"Even if it's killing you."

His smile flashed. "I hope it doesn't come to that. Maybe the fact that you challenge expectation is part of the reason I love you."

Lorenzo loved her.

They stared at each other for a long moment. "You could cancel the spectacle," Cassie whispered. "We could just go to my house in California and you could hide out there. No one would know. I'd make sure of it. . . ."

"I will not hide," Lorenzo insisted. "I will not cower in the shadows and sacrifice my freedom. I will *make* the future I want to have." He reached out and took her hand. "I would like that future to be with you."

Cassie thought about the car. "How long would we be buried in the car?"

His eyes glinted. "Less than an hour."

An hour. An eternity. She would feel every excruciating second. She'd probably go insane.

Cassie exhaled. She could get some kind of relaxant from Stacy, maybe. Not a sleeping pill because she'd probably have to be mobile, but something to mellow her out. Something that wouldn't hurt the baby.

"I have to make the deal with the pictures first—"

"Fine." Lorenzo interrupted her firmly. "There is another choice. If you can't go through the spectacle with me, even though everything should go according to plan, I want you to be under the protection of someone I trust."

"The British guy," Cassie guessed. She appreciated that he was trying to find an alternate solution.

Lorenzo nodded. "Erik Sorensson, leader of the *Pyr*. We have been friends longer than we have been at odds."

"Okay. I want to get my things, sell those pictures, and check in with Stacy. Shower and change. Is it safe?"

Lorenzo scanned the hotel, inhaled deeply, then nodded slowly. "I sense no *Slayers* in the vicinity. But be quick. I need to defend you until the spectacle begins, whether you intend to join me or not." He looked at his watch. "I'll get the windows in the car fixed and be right back." He gave her a look. "Be here, or I'll come and find you."

Cassie was convinced of that.

Once Cassie was in the hotel—away from Lorenzo's persuasive presence and his conviction—she felt the return and redoubling of her doubts. How much did she really know about Lorenzo, anyway? She knew he was great in bed. She knew he was an illusionist. She knew he had lots of ambition and even more secrets than should be humanly possible.

She also knew that he wasn't human.

Was he really going to leave his successful life behind and start anew? If so, where? She nibbled her lip, thought about that house and the adoration of his audience, and doubted he would be happy living the quiet life of a recluse.

Had he really accounted for every possibility in his planning for this feat? To face her own deepest fears, all simultaneously, on trust seemed like a lot.

On the other hand, his own past meant that it was hard for him to compromise, even as much as he had. Cassie had to believe that if they could both get past their issues, the reward would be worth it.

She had to take a chance on that future.

But right now, she had work to do. She needed to sell those images of Lorenzo before someone else made that editor happy.

This was the first step to her creative future, a bridge between what she had done and what she wanted to do. The pictures of Lorenzo weren't fake and they weren't just for PR—they were the closest images to reality that Cassie had ever taken, and she knew they brought her to the threshold of a change.

She wasn't entirely sure what she'd do next, but she was excited by the possibilities.

Maybe a fresh start in a new location would be just the ticket for both of them.

Lorenzo had given her this chance, and she was going to make the most of it.

Cassie knew she needed a laptop with an application to crop images. Hers was at her house in California, but she was due for new hardware anyway. She'd hole up in the business center of the hotel until she'd finished her work and made the deal.

Then she'd go back to Lorenzo.

All she had to do was build her nerve to get into that car. Darkness. Falling earth. Closed spaces.

Cassie shivered.

Lorenzo and the future. When she focused on that, it felt more and more like a risk worth taking.

Lorenzo intended to head right back to Cassie, but he didn't have a choice. He received a panicky call from his housekeeper as soon as Cassie had disappeared into the hotel. His father, it seemed, remained locked in his room and refused to answer any summons from her.

Lorenzo heard what she didn't say—she feared Salvatore had died.

Lorenzo wasn't at all convinced of that. He assumed that his father was—yet again—making mischief. But there was nothing for it. He'd have to go home and check.

He dropped off the car for the repair and got a loaner, speeding to the house as the minutes ticked by.

At the house, Lorenzo went directly to his father's room. He tapped in the security code and the door opened. It was silent and still inside. His own dragon-smoke barrier was thinning already, and Salvatore looked as if he'd fallen asleep on the couch, in his human form. That alone was a warning—Salvatore always slept in his dragon form.

Lorenzo took a cautious step into the room.

His father was smiling slightly.

Utterly still.

Because he was dead.

Lorenzo checked his pulse twice, even though he knew the truth. Then he stood with his hands shoved into his pockets and tried to imagine his life without the obligation of caring for his father, without their constant differences of perspective, without his father's tendency to make trouble.

He couldn't.

But he wouldn't have to imagine it. That would be the reality of his life from this point forward. Lorenzo supposed he should be grateful that they'd had so much time together—so many years to argue!—but he felt cheated.

He had wanted to take his father back to Venice, back to the house he had bought and restored, back to the place Salvatore had yearned to be for so long.

And now he had lost the chance. He couldn't fulfill his father's only dream. He'd waited too long to try.

Lorenzo felt like a failure.

He touched his father's face one last time, then shook his hand in farewell. He sensed that his father's spirit was gone, although he hoped the old man might be watching from some other dimension.

Lorenzo wondered whether Salvatore had guessed that his time was ending, that he didn't have to follow Lorenzo's plans for the future because he wouldn't be a part of it. It was said that many old *Pyr* could sense their own demise. Maybe that had been true of Salvatore, too.

Either way, it was done.

He left his father's apartment and spoke to the housekeeper, then went to his office to make the arrangements. His father's body would have to be exposed to all four elements before it was incinerated. Lorenzo had to ensure that no *Slayer* could turn his father into a dragon zombie, so rituals had to be followed.

Even though they were inconvenient in daylight in human society. He tapped his fingers on the desk, then decided he had no choice but to call Erik.

Again.

Lorenzo used his cell phone and was glad that Erik answered immediately.

"I know," Erik said by way of greeting.

"How?" Lorenzo was surprised.

"I feel the presence of all of us, which means I also feel the absence of any one of us."

"You knew last night."

"He promised her he'd ensure your happiness," Erik said. "He had no more reason to live."

"He told you that?"

"Angelina came to me. Since the darkfire, I can see the dead. I saw a dragon with her. I guessed who it must be." His voice dropped low. "I am sorry."

"I need your help," Lorenzo admitted.

He heard the smile in Erik's reply. "I know."

They agreed that Erik would pick up Salvatore's body, posing as an undertaker, and that Lorenzo would meet him in the desert at midnight to ensure that Salvatore's remains were properly destroyed. Erik was going to summon the other *Pyr* to help ensure that Salvatore's body was treated correctly.

For the second time that day Lorenzo was glad to have a friend in Erik, and once again, felt a sense of common purpose with the leader of the *Pyr*.

It turned out that there were things he couldn't manage on his own. For once, he was very glad of Erik's commitment to the *Pyr*—and for the *Pyr*'s commitment to him.

For the first time, he wondered at the price the flashfire might demand of him. Was he truly ready to surrender all of his dragon nature? It might be a good idea to have some dragon power in reserve if he was going to be with Cassie.

Was there a way he could find out exactly what he'd have to give up? Lorenzo didn't like loose ends, and flashfire was looking like a big one.

Lorenzo informed the housekeeper of the arrangements, then turned to survey the large painting in the main room. He had an idea. He surveyed it quickly, knowing that he could not leave it behind when he left this place.

The housekeeper followed his gaze. "Your father loved that painting, sir. Even in the few days I've been here, I often found him studying it."

"He did love it," Lorenzo agreed. "There's been a collector wanting to buy it for years, but I wanted it to be here for my father. I think I'll call that collector today, though."

"It was kind of you to keep it for him, sir."

Lorenzo nodded politely. "Kind" didn't really explain his relationship with his father. "I'll confirm the arrangements, but if past dealings are any indication, this collector will have his team of movers here before the day is through."

"Very good, sir. I hope you have a good performance tonight, sir."

"Yes, thank you." Lorenzo shoved a hand through his hair. The odds seemed to be getting longer, but he had only one more show to get through.

He had to do it.

He called Cassie, but apparently her BlackBerry wasn't getting service inside the hotel. He'd have to stop by the hotel and find her, never mind the time.

It was later than Cassie had hoped by the time she raced back to the hotel room she was sharing with Stacy.

She was deciding whether or not to confide in her friend—because she knew that Stacy would tell her to join Lorenzo for the spectacle, and because she was pretty sure she shouldn't be telling anyone about Lorenzo's plan—when the door to their room was hauled open.

Stacy stood there, dressed from head to toe in vivid blue with eye makeup and nail polish to match. She gave Cassie one look, tapped her booted toe, then marched back into the room and threw herself into a chair.

Cassie knew this expression. It was Stacy's version of a woman scorned.

"Trouble in paradise?" Cassie ventured.

"JP stood me up! I can't believe it." Stacy got up to pace the width of the room. "He came back here last night and it was awesome, and when I woke up he was gone." She fixed Cassie with an accusing glance. "You, too."

"I'm sorry. When I called, I thought you'd be busy all night."

"You must have been." Stacy glared at her. "Did you have fun, at least?"

Cassie sat down. She couldn't tell Stacy what she'd been doing, because that would have revealed Lorenzo's true nature. "Yes and no." She forced a smile. "Kind of like you."

"He left a note," Stacy said, shoving the note in question at Cassie. Cassie read JP's suggestion that they meet for breakfast, then glanced up at her livid friend. "He stood me up!" Stacy said, flinging out her hands. "He wasn't there. He'd never been there. I waited an hour and he never showed." She was so agitated that her feet didn't stop tapping. "He never called. He's not in his room, or if he is, he's not answering the phone. I can't believe this! I thought he was different."

Truth was that Cassie had thought so, too.

She remembered that blue shimmer around his body when Lorenzo had approached them. She'd forgotten about that. Did it mean that JP was another dragon shifter? Or had he just learned some of their tricks?

Maybe being a dragon shifter was how he'd learned their tricks. He had been the one to tell her *Pyr* lore.

So why had he been here? It seemed too much of a coincidence—and also could explain the animosity between him and Lorenzo. What was JP's real plan?

"Maybe something happened to him," she suggested with care.

"Like what?"

"Like an accident, or a health issue." Cassie couldn't stop thinking about that blue shimmer.

How many dragon shifters were in town, anyway? Was this unusual, or were they everywhere, all the time? That defied belief, given how many people were trying to get pictures of them.

She frowned at the note.

Was JP targeting her?

Or Lorenzo?

If so, why had he disappeared?

Stacy dropped down to sit beside her. "I asked the concierge. I asked the maître d' at the restaurant. I asked the doorman. No one has fallen ill in the hotel for two days. No one has needed medical assistance. And no one has been hit by a car."

"It could have happened outside the hotel."

Stacy flung out her hands. "Why are you defending him? You're always the one who says I shouldn't trust guys so fast. I thought you'd be smug because you'd been proven right again."

"Well, I feel bad. I thought he was different, too."

Stacy made a face. "As if." Then she turned a bright eye on Cassie. "What about Lorenzo? Where have you been and what have you been doing? Was the sex good?"

"Awesome."

Stacy watched Cassie for a moment, sighed again. "Yeah. At least there was that. Before he gets buried alive for a month." She grimaced and bounced to her feet. "Come on, let's get something to eat. I need a frilly drink and I need one right now. You look like you could use one too."

"I need a shower." She was supposed to meet Lorenzo. Cassie pulled out her BlackBerry, intending to tell him that she'd be late. She couldn't bail on Stacy now.

But there was a message from him, asking her to meet him at the theater. She sent a quick reply, explaining the delay. She liked that he answered her instantly. That gave her the sense that he was watching out for her.

What did he know about JP? Cassie was going to ask, then realized something. The fact that Lorenzo hadn't said anything to her about JP indicated that he'd solved the issue—and, after all, JP was gone.

Lorenzo was cleaning up the details to keep her safe. The truth of it made her smile.

"Come on, Ms. Workaholic." Stacy rolled her eyes. "Hurry up."

Cassie headed for the shower.

"Hey, I forgot to tell you," Stacy said, snapping her fingers. "There's this guy looking for you."

"What guy?"

Stacy produced a business card. It was from a federal agency, which made Cassie's eyes widen. T. Chen. "Did you talk to him?"

"Yeah, he's investigating these dragon guys. I guess the feds think they're involved with some black market stuff." Stacy gave Cassie a hard look. "Making things disappear."

"Things?"

"Illegal immigrants. Drugs. Those kinds of things."

Cassie had a bad feeling. "What would I know about that?"

"Probably nothing and he admits it, but he's trying to talk to everyone who was at that show of Lorenzo's. I guess they figure that a dragon guy in the business of making things disappear could be a ringleader."

"Not Lorenzo! He wouldn't be involved in anything illegal." Cassie knew that right in her bones.

He was a dragon shifter.

He took care of his dad.

He was an awesome lover.

He was confident, cocky, gorgeous, clever, and secretive.

Lorenzo was a lot of things, but not a criminal.

Stacy shrugged and bounced on the bed. "Then tell this guy so. I just told him that I thought it was a great trick."

Stacy bounced a little harder on the mattress. "Don't just stand there. Hurry up already. You can call this Chen guy from your BlackBerry in the bar."

Lorenzo arrived at the theater, hoping to get a bit of sleep in his dressing room before his final evening performance. He also hoped that Cassie would be there. He was exhausted. He had several small wounds to dress. He needed time to find his composure once again.

His wishes were not to be.

Cassie wasn't there. He still couldn't sense *Slayer*, but he had a very bad feeling.

Was he just worn out?

The python had gotten out of its enclosure again, a disappearing act that it had mastered recently and was repeating with increasing frequency. It had simply gotten too big for its enclosure. Lorenzo knew it, but he'd hoped to get through the day without having to make changes.

No luck. The animal control people had been summoned and arrived right after Lorenzo. The python could not be found in the theater and was assumed to have escaped into the hotel. The backstage area was crowded, Fred and Ursula trying to defend the area, the clock ticking down to showtime as the animal control people argued with the hotel management.

It was left to Lorenzo to find the snake ASAP.

He got a call from Erik in the midst of this.

"They're not coming," Erik said, his tone grim.

"Who?" Lorenzo asked, but he already knew. It was traditional for the *Pyr* to gather for a firestorm, to help the *Pyr* in question to secure his future when *Slayers* attacked.

"The others," Erik said crisply. "I forbade Quinn and Donovan to come, because JP is here and is likely seeking vengeance. Rafferty is in the Middle East with Melissa, so too far away to arrive in a timely fashion." He paused. "Niall and Delaney declined to join us." He forced a smile. "Brandt is coming, though."

Lorenzo couldn't really blame the other *Pyr* for refusing to help him. He'd never helped any of them.

Even so, his heart began to pound.

"You have to remember that everything changed with the darkfire."

Lorenzo knew it was more than that.

He wished he was in Erik's presence, so he could try to discern more of Erik's thoughts. He had the definite sense that Erik wasn't telling him everything.

Erik cleared his throat. "Sloane and Brandt will arrive shortly. Sloane is going to take Eileen and Zoë to Donovan for me."

"I thought maybe you'd leave, too," Lorenzo said.

He heard Erik's voice warm. "We have been friends longer than we have been at odds, Lorenzo."

"What's really happening?" Lorenzo asked. "What have you seen in the future?"

Erik was quiet for so long that Lorenzo didn't think he'd answer. "I see only a shadow," he admitted. "A darkness that engulfs everything around it."

Lorenzo looked at the floor, trying to put a positive spin on what Erik had glimpsed.

He couldn't.

Neither apparently could Erik.

He also couldn't quite drive the flashfire song from his thoughts.

"Midnight, as planned?" Erik said, obviously trying to sound optimistic.

"Midnight," Lorenzo agreed, holding up one finger for the hotel manager who was tapping his shoulder. "We'll be fine."

"Of course," Erik agreed and then cut the connection.

Lorenzo immediately called Cassie's hotel and was connected to her room. The phone rang and rang.

He reminded himself to believe in her.

He told himself that she was probably finishing the sale of those shots, just as she'd planned.

He breathed deeply and didn't smell *Slayer*.

That should have reassured him more than it did.

Meanwhile, the gathered experts were debating the possibilities of the snake's location. In the plumbing? In the walls? In the basement? The elevator shafts? They hadn't come to any kind of consensus when there was a loud scream from the lobby of the hotel.

"Found," Lorenzo said firmly. He marched away to beguile the creature into submission once again.

At least one item on his list was resolved.

Then he'd go to Cassie's hotel and find her.

Chapter 16

Mr. Chen looked like a typical bureaucrat. He was dressed in a forgettable cheap suit and his hand actually trembled when Cassie shook it. He wore thick glasses and stammered when he spoke. He couldn't look either Cassie or Stacy in the eye.

Cassie couldn't imagine a less likely individual to bring down a smuggling organization, much less to battle dragon shape shifters with an illegal agenda.

She took that as a sign that the feds were wrong and relaxed.

Stacy rolled her eyes and sipped her drink, crossing her legs and spinning on her barstool to check out the view. There were a number of good-looking men in the bar already, and Stacy's heartbreak over JP appeared to be healing fast.

Then Mr. Chen began to ask questions and Cassie had to pay close attention. His soft-spoken manner meant that she had to lean close to hear him over the din in the bar. He asked for her full name, her occupation and home address, as well as her contact information.

Then Mr. Chen flipped through his notes. His hands were still shaking and he hadn't looked up at her yet. Cassie didn't think she was quite that terrifying. "Am-am-am I correct that you saw Lorenzo become a dragon d-d-during his show on Wednesday?"

"Yes, but I thought it was an illusion."

He shuffled his notes, frowning as he scribbled something. "Do you st-st-still believe that?" He shot her a furtive glance.

Should she lie? To a federal agent? Everyone would soon know that she had taken those pictures.

But they wouldn't know who the subject was. Cassie decided to defend Lorenzo's privacy.

"Yes." Cassie spoke with resolve.

Mr. Chen pushed his glasses up his nose and peered through them at her. The lenses were smeared and so strong that he looked buglike.

Cassie held his gaze unflinchingly.

Mr. Chen flipped through his notes with nervous fingers. "But you were p-p-picked up by the dragon at the show."

"Yes. It seemed that way."

Mr. Chen appeared to find this an exciting admission. "Seemed?" he echoed.

Cassie shrugged. "It was an illusionist's show. It must have been a trick."

"And wh-wh-what happened then?"

It struck Cassie that Mr. Chen's interviewing technique wasn't very organized. But then, he wasn't very organized either. Maybe he was really junior. Maybe if the feds were assigning an agent like this to the case, it wasn't very serious.

Mr. Chen murmured something, then looked expectant.

"I beg your pardon?" Cassie leaned closer. Things were getting a bit rowdy at the bar. There was a game on the televisions and Cassie assumed that some team or another had just scored. The guys at the bar were shouting and making bets with each other.

Mr. Chen murmured again, wincing and scratching his chin, then flipped through his notes again.

"I still can't hear you. What was the question?"

Mr. Chen looked irritated as he glanced at the partying crowd at the bar. "We must go elsewhere. I must finish this interview."

"How long will it take?"

"I'm starving," Stacy muttered.

"Only a few m-m-minutes," Mr. Chen insisted. "It is very important. You may have seen s-s-something."

"I don't think Lorenzo is involved in any illegal activities. . . ."

Mr. Chen became very agitated, so agitated that he dropped both his notebook and his pen. "There is pr-pr-procedure! Please. I must do my job to the b-b-best of my abilities."

Cassie didn't think that was a very high standard, but she would do the right thing. "Be right back," she said to Stacy, who sighed and waved for another drink. "Is there a quiet room in this hotel?"

"Right over here," Mr. Chen said, showing surprising purpose as he guided her across the lobby. "I used this r-r-room earlier."

Cassie's confidence was bolstered when a security guard waved Mr. Chen into a locked service area. His identification must have been validated by the hotel. She was thinking it was a bit sad that the feds were employing people who appeared to be so incompetent, thinking that it was no wonder that criminals got away with so much, and wondering just how long this would take when Mr. Chen shoved her through a doorway.

He pushed her so hard that she stumbled.

"Hey!" Cassie protested in surprise, just as she heard the door lock behind her.

"Cameras are out," JP said from one corner of the room.

"Excellent," Mr. Chen said, his voice much more confident than it had been. Cassie stared at him as he smiled and ripped off his glasses.

There were flames dancing in the pupils of his eyes.

"No!" she shouted, but JP seized her from behind. He clapped one hand over her mouth and held her head so that she couldn't look away from Mr. Chen. She might have closed her eyes, but Mr. Chen began to shimmer blue.

He shifted shape right in front of her, becoming a massive red dragon with gold talons. He smiled and seized her chin, his eyes widening so that she could see those mesmerizing flames.

Cassie tried to avert her gaze, but his first words captured her attention. "You want to save Lorenzo," he said in a melodic tone.

Cassie couldn't help but agree. She nodded and JP uncovered her mouth. "I want to save Lorenzo," she heard herself saying. She fought against the beguiling, but felt her willpower losing ground to his.

Mr. Chen smiled more broadly. "So you will do exactly as I say. Or Lorenzo, you, and your unborn child will die."

Cassie didn't want to agree with him. She didn't want to echo his words, but she couldn't deny her desire to save Lorenzo.

"Promise me," Mr. Chen said. "You will do exactly as I say."

"I will do exactly as you say," she echoed, and saw Mr. Chen's dragon smile flash.

"Sleep now, mate," he murmured and Cassie felt her eyes drift closed. She felt JP relax his grip upon her, and felt her body slide onto a sofa.

A cell phone rang and she was vaguely aware of JP answering it. Her sense of time was out of whack. She had to fight Chen's influence.

Cassie fought against exhaustion. She fought against the beguiling. She tried to stay awake, tried to listen to their plans.

Maybe there was a way she could warn Lorenzo.

"That was the housekeeper," JP said with satisfaction. "She delivered the inside info, just as we anticipated she would." His voice could have been coming through a fog from Cassie's perspective, or from the other end of a long corridor. She fought the urge to sleep, determined to listen. "The old dragon is dead. The body is being picked up this afternoon."

Salvatore was dead?

"Excellent," Mr. Chen said. "I do enjoy when a plan comes together."

"You're going to make more Dragon Bone Powder, aren't you?"

Cassie struggled to hang on to consciousness. What was Dragon Bone Powder?

"I like to have some inventory." Mr. Chen sounded far more purposeful and clever than he had in the bar. "Get rid of the other one and come back here."

"You don't want me to intercept the hearse?"

"No." Mr. Chen seemed to be thinking. "I sense Erik Sorensson's presence and I wonder what his role in all this will be."

"But Lorenzo isn't allied with the *Pyr*," JP protested.

"Erik doesn't care. He stands by all of his kind."

His kind. Cassie remembered that the British guy was Erik.

Mr. Chen chuckled. "And if he is custodian of Salvatore's body, then I will have even more Dragon Bone Powder in my inventory."

Mr. Chen was going to kill Erik, too. Just when Cassie thought the plan couldn't get any worse, it did.

"And then," Mr. Chen said with glee. "And then, it will be time to spring the trap."

Cassie wanted to hear the rest, but she lost her grip on consciousness. Darkness closed over her. She was lost and there was nothing she could do.

Not to save herself.

Not to save Lorenzo.

Erik fought a sense of doom all day long.

He'd actually sensed it since he arrived in Las Vegas. It just kept getting stronger. Some plan was coming together and he wished with all his heart he could figure out what it was.

At least Eileen and Zoë were safe.

The sun was setting, smearing the sky with orange and red. He had the visor down on the hearse as he drove back from Lorenzo's mansion toward the city. Salvatore's corpse was in the back and Erik was wearing a dark suit.

He'd rented the hearse, no questions asked.

But then, Las Vegas was an amazing place in more ways than that.

He was checking the presence of the other *Pyr* in the world, confirming their locations and welfare. He could sense the other *Pyr* and when he was troubled, Erik went through his inventory of dragons.

He was pleased to ascertain they were all pretty much where he expected them to be. As far as he could tell, they seemed healthy enough. Lorenzo was beginning his last performance, albeit in a sour mood.

He knew that Balthasar was in Las Vegas and that Lorenzo had beguiled him for some purpose. The *Slayer* wasn't very active, which perhaps was part of Lorenzo's plan. He couldn't sense JP anymore, which was worrisome. Where had he gone?

He had the definite sense that something was being hidden from him.

Slayers who had drunk the Elixir could disguise their scents. How many were left? Balthasar, who was evidently too drunk to bother. Chen. Just the thought of that *Slayer* troubled Erik. Jorge. That *Slayer* had been buried alive in Wales in December. Erik had a hard time believing that entombment would kill Jorge, or that the vicious *Slayer* would stay put. As he had done repeatedly since December, Erik reached down the conduit in his mind for that cave on Bardsey Island.

But this time it was empty.

Jorge was loose. Erik's eyes widened in shock.

That was when he saw the woman picking her way along the side of the highway. She looked like she was drunk, her path weaving from one side to the other. There was no sign of another vehicle, but Erik worried that she would be hit if she kept wandering like that.

He stopped the car and backed up on the shoulder. He was shocked to realize that it was Cassie.

Lorenzo's mate.

She was shaking her head and moaning.

What had happened to her? Erik was out of the car in a heartbeat.

She took one look at him and ran.

He raced after her, catching her easily since she was so unsteady on her feet. "Nooooooo," she said when he took her elbow. She fought against his grip, but seemed to be sedated.

"Cassie!" he said crisply. "I'm Lorenzo's friend, Erik. You must come with me."

"No!" She fought against him with renewed strength.

Erik had little trouble tugging her toward the safety of the car, despite her protests. His mind was filled with questions. How could she be drunk? How had she gotten here? He urged her into the passenger seat and just before he shut the door, she flung her purse into the desert.

He went after the purse, seeing too late that Cassie had used it as a diversion. She stumbled out of the car as soon as he left her side and went in the opposite direction. What was her problem?

Erik swore. He snatched up her purse and pursued her, catching her up against his side as she fought him. He turned back to the hearse in time to see a red dragon descending out of the sky.

Chen.

His heart sank.

"Sorry," Cassie moaned, as if fighting her way free of a sedative.

Or a beguiling.

Erik understood with sudden clarity.

She'd been beguiled, and sent to distract him. "Stay here," he instructed, putting her down beside a large rock. She clutched his sleeve, struggling to tell him something.

"Dragon Bone Powder," she managed to whisper.

Erik was shocked. "He wants Salvatore," he whispered.

Cassie poked Erik in the chest with a heavy fingertip, her expression anguished. It was killing her to not be able to communicate.

It was amazing that she'd managed to fight the beguiling so well.

Erik looked into her eyes. "Sleep. You have helped Lorenzo," he murmured, and he felt her shudder with relief. "Sleep."

And somehow Erik would save her.

Chen spiraled down toward the hearse as Erik shifted shape and leapt into the sky.

Lorenzo was exhausted when he took the stage for his last performance in that theater and he was rattled. Where was Cassie? He'd called the hotel time and again, but she hadn't been in her room. He'd gone to the hotel, but hadn't been able to find her. Her scent just disappeared, as if she'd been snatched up by fairies and carried away.

Where could she have gone? Why would she have gone without contacting him?

Had he read her intention so inaccurately as that?

Or had someone taken her?

Who?

There were still no *Slayers* that he could sense in the vicinity, other than Balthasar, who had been beguiled. JP must have left town.

Lorenzo had to return to the theater and arrived just as the music was swelling for his performance. There was no time to compose himself.

One last show. He was caught between the obligations of his contract—and the implicit contract with his audience, most of whom had paid outrageous prices—and his duty to Cassie.

On the other hand, she was a woman who knew her own mind. And he respected her. He wouldn't be a barbarian who forced her to do what he wanted her to do. He wasn't that kind of man or that kind of *Pyr*.

He'd find her right after the show.

Even if he had to take her to his father's funeral.

Lorenzo took the stage, trying to calm his nerves.

But he was aware that his agitation showed. He was a bit slow, a bit less charming, a bit less polished. Ursula cast him a questioning glance or two, but he soldiered on.

Half a performance to go.

One hour until his future.

The lack of polish grated at him, but Lorenzo wasn't frightened until he screwed up. He usually slid his thumb quickly beneath the shackles on his wrist, that digit giving him an extra increment of space with which to work himself free. He was too slow. He missed his chance.

Ursula did her job perfectly, tugging the restraint tight with showy flair before she locked it securely. He couldn't signal her, didn't dare interrupt the performance.

He had to make it work.

Even if the restraints were too damn tight.

She tied him in the sack, then tipped him into the tank, right on cue, oblivious to his distress. Lorenzo fell into the dry tank behind the LED screen that showed the recorded image of him in the water. He landed on the foam, fighting already against his bonds.

He thrashed, but the restraints just cut deeply into his skin. He knew the timing of this trick as well as he knew his own name. He heard the "splash" of his impact and the bubbles he supposedly blew. He tugged the interior cord with his teeth and freed himself from the sack. But he couldn't get his hand through the shackle.

He knew Ursula and Anna were taking the keys across the stage.

He heard the snake hiss.

He heard the clock ticking.

He started to sweat. He should have been free by now, but he was still securely bound. He saw a glimmer of real alarm in his assistants' eyes as they turned back to feign dismay. He should have been below the stage already. He should have been peeling off his clothes, running through the shower left on for this illusion, and running through the underground passage to the back of the theater.

He should have been calling for intervention.

Lorenzo tried again to break the restraints but failed. Ursula and Anna were watching, but there was nothing to be done.

He wasn't scheduled to die for one more day.

Lorenzo gritted his teeth and began to shift shape. He let the shift go far enough that the bonds were broken, then forced his body back to human form. He seized the bonds on his ankles and ripped them free, flinging himself toward the trapdoor on the stage. He was under the stage, running for the back, peeling off clothes as he went. The crowd was really agitated and he realized they would think that he had made a mistake.

Well, he had.

But there was no reason not to work with it.

He tried to catch his breath before he stepped into the theater. It took him a moment to summon the last vestige of his composure. He could see Ursula and Anna gaping at him and knew his secret was finally revealed.

Well, they had probably wondered anyway.

Did he have the strength left to beguile them?

He would find it, Lorenzo resolved. He would beguile them immediately and control the damage. It was the last show and he was done. He strode down the aisle, revealing himself to wild applause. He leapt onto the stage, hoping no one saw that he was shaking, and took his bow. He was sure he had covered reasonably well, that he could get through this last bit, when the old-speak snapped in his mind.

"*So close to disaster,*" whispered a voice he didn't recognize. "*What an artful game.*"

Lorenzo's blood ran cold. He scanned the theater in terror. He didn't smell any *Pyr*. He didn't smell any *Slayers*. Erik wasn't present and neither was JP. Balthasar was drinking himself to oblivion in a bar in a hotel across the street. Lorenzo was sure that Marco had left him alone forever.

Who was this?

"*So nice to finally meet you,*" that old-speak continued with oily smoothness. "*Especially since I'm going to raise your son as my own.*"

Then the dragon laughed.

It was a dark chortle, one that made Lorenzo's blood curdle.

Still Lorenzo couldn't pinpoint the origin of the old-speak. Was this dragon in his theater? Was he broadcasting his old-speak from a distance? Lorenzo scanned the rapt audience in rising fear. Why couldn't he sense the presence of this other one?

Lorenzo nearly fell backward at the sudden vehement scent of *Slayer*. The smell of rot and decay and darkness was so strong that it nearly made him stagger.

Then it was gone again.

Lorenzo was shaken. He still didn't know who it was, but it had to be a *Slayer* who could disguise his scent at will.

One who had drunk the Dragon's Blood Elixir.

And that couldn't be good.

Now he really needed Erik's help.

He just hoped he hadn't asked for it too late.

Lorenzo bolted out of the theater, his shirt open. He'd decided against beguiling Ursula and Anna. He was in too much of a hurry to get to Cassie. He'd been able to smell the arrival of another *Pyr* from inside the theater, although he wasn't sure who it was.

There was a guy leaning against his car, a buff guy with auburn hair and an unwelcoming expression. He had his arms folded across his chest and he gave Lorenzo a glittering look.

He was *Pyr*.

"Brandt," he said without putting out his hand. "Can't say as I'm delighted to make your acquaintance." His accent was Australian.

Lorenzo didn't know this *Pyr*, but he knew of him, thanks to Erik. Brandt was the one with the botched firestorm, the dragon who had ensured that he hadn't had much to do with the *Pyr* after his divorce.

"Where's Erik? I thought he would be here."

"Waiting for us, I hope." Brandt's eyes narrowed. "You'd better hope nothing goes wrong."

Lorenzo was pretty sure it already had. "We might be late for the funeral."

"What do you mean?"

"I have to find Cassie," Lorenzo said, unlocking the car from the remote.

"Don't you know where your mate is?" Brandt was incredulous.

Lorenzo didn't want to explain himself to this dragon with attitude. "She wanted some time. I gave her what she asked of me. Now she's missing."

Brandt gaped at him. "You gave her some time," he echoed, his astonishment obvious. "During your firestorm, while there are *Slayers* in town." He shook his head and opened the passenger door.

Lorenzo realized the other *Pyr* might be a good source of information. "Which *Slayers* can disguise their scent?"

Brandt shook his head. "You don't even know?"

"I know they must have drunk the Elixir, but I don't have a list of names."

"Even I know their names," Brandt said.

Lorenzo gritted his teeth. "Why don't you show your brilliance and tell me?"

"Chen." Brandt snarled the word. "Old, nasty, and sneaky." He counted off another on his finger. "Balthasar." Lorenzo wasn't worried about him. Brandt tapped a third finger. "And Jorge, although he's out of commission."

"Who? Where?"

"Buried in Wales. Probably dead."

So that was probably Chen he had smelled in the theater.

Had Chen really captured Cassie?

What would he want in exchange for her freedom?

Lorenzo got in the car and started it. "Chen must be here, then."

"Oh, that's good news." Brandt got into the passenger seat. "What'd you do to attract his attention?"

"Have a firestorm?"

Brandt shook his head. "No. It's got to be more than that."

Lorenzo put the car in reverse. "He says he'll raise my son as his own."

"Bait," Brandt said with a shake of his head. "He's after bigger fish than that."

"What do you mean?"

Brandt spread his hands. "That guy's got more tricks than you can believe. Always changing the rules. Always digging another secret out of his stash."

Lorenzo's competitive spirit soared at this news. "Sounds like he and I might understand each other."

"Yeah, well, why else would he come to your fire-storm?" Brandt asked with unexpected scorn. "Maybe he thinks you're two of a kind. Everyone always said you were half gone to the *Slayer* team. Maybe he's looking for a partner."

Lorenzo glanced at the other *Pyr*, surprised by his hostility. "What have I ever done to you?"

"Nothing. Nothing to me and nothing for me. That's the point, mate." Brandt looked him right in the eye and the air crackled between them. "But if I were looking for a *Pyr* to turn *Slayer*, you'd be my first stop. Your reputation has preceded you."

With allies like this, Lorenzo didn't think he needed enemies.

He slammed the car into reverse and peeled out of the parking spot, squealing the tires as he raced to Cassie's hotel. He cut in and out of traffic, in perfect control despite the speed.

Brandt's tough facade slipped. Only a *Pyr* would have heard the way the other dragon's heart skipped a beat at the speed of his driving—much less the way he caught his breath—but Lorenzo heard both.

And he liked spooking Brandt just fine.

Cassie was still gone, as surely as if she had never even been at the hotel. There was no trace of her scent, as if it had been surrounded and disguised. No trail to follow. Just as it had been earlier. Even her friend Stacy had checked out and gone home. There was no hint of JP, much less of Chen.

"Dead end," Brandt said. "Pun intended."

Lorenzo scanned the lobby, thinking. He could smell only one other dragon besides the one in his company. He tried to call Erik, but Erik's phone just rang and rang and rang. Cassie's BlackBerry said that she was unavailable.

He had a definite sense that a trap was closing around him.

How much did Chen know of his plans? How could he find Cassie? There was only one individual who might know the answers.

Balthasar.

Who was sitting in a bar, drowning his sorrows, precisely as he'd been instructed to do by Lorenzo.

Marking time until he followed Lorenzo's next instruction.

The beguiling had worked perfectly, and Lorenzo didn't like the idea of messing with it at this late point. He wasn't entirely sure what would happen and feared that Balthasar's mind might snap under the duress.

But he had to know more.

He'd have to take a chance.

But then, risk was what proved he was alive.

"We're gonna be late," Brandt said, tapping his watch. "Even in that car."

"I'll meet you there, then," Lorenzo said. "I have one more thing to check."

Brandt's eyes narrowed. "Why don't I trust you?"

Lorenzo realized that the other *Pyr*'s resentment might make his ploy sound even more plausible.

And who knew who was listening?

"Probably instinctive," Lorenzo said and smiled. "Because I feel the same way about you."

"Hey, I've come to help you. . . ."

"Tell me, is it true that most Australians are descended from convicts? Oh wait. You *were* a transported convict yourself, weren't you? I remember now."

Brandt's eyes flashed. He shimmered slightly around his perimeter. "Turn your back for one second," he growled. "I'd love to kick your ass."

"But?"

"But Erik thinks you're worth defending. Who knows why, but I keep my promises."

"Minion," Lorenzo sneered, deliberately provoking the other *Pyr*. "I prefer to make my own choices."

Brandt looked to be on the cusp of shifting shape to fight, but Lorenzo turned to walk away. "You can only come with me if you wait in the car," he taunted. He was starting to develop a plan. It was daring. It was risky.

It just might be perfect.

Brandt followed him. "You gonna tell me what you're doing?"

"No." Lorenzo smiled when they were both in the car again. "You'll just have to trust me."

That was when he heard Brandt laugh for the first time.

Balthasar was almost too drunk to be useful. Lorenzo slid into a barstool beside him and ordered a double Scotch, the same thing Balthasar was drinking.

"What do you want now?" Balthasar asked, his speech slurred. "And what did you do to me?"

"Nothing." Lorenzo smiled. "You seem to be recovering well enough. How is the Scotch here?"

There was an inconvenient gleam of suspicion in Balthasar's eyes. Lorenzo's drink came, he paid, then indicated a quiet booth. "Let's talk privately, shall we?"

"About what?"

Lorenzo had to hold the *Slayer*'s elbow to guide him to the table, where Balthasar fell onto the bench. He didn't spill his drink, though, so there was hope. "Magnus's library, of course. Teamwork."

Balthasar glanced up in surprise. Lorenzo took the opportunity to summon the flames of beguiling in his eyes. Balthasar tried to look away, but his will was weakened and he was readily snared. Lorenzo liked that his game hadn't slipped that much.

He was the best.

"Magnus's library," he echoed.

Balthasar twitched.

Lorenzo changed tack. "Then tell me about Chen."

Balthasar flinched.

Lorenzo lowered his tone another increment. "You will tell me about Chen."

Balthasar became agitated. "Too much. Too much." He winced and pressed his hands against his temples.

Lorenzo eased back a bit, even though time was of the essence. "You're both *Slayers*," he said softly. "You must have a great deal in common."

Balthasar snorted.

"You must want the same things."

"Want the same thing," Balthasar agreed. There was a glint in his eyes, a flash of ambition and Lorenzo guessed.

Of course.

"There is no leader of the *Slayers* with Magnus dead," he said quietly.

"No leader," Balthasar agreed and threw back some of his drink.

"Chen wants to lead the *Slayers*?"

"Chen wants to lead the *Slayers*," Balthasar agreed.

He averted his gaze and took a ragged breath. "Magnus's library."

"But you have the key to the library," Lorenzo said. "Which means that you are the rightful heir to Magnus."

"Rightful heir!" Balthasar looked up at Lorenzo with bloodshot eyes. "Rightful heir."

Lorenzo leaned closer, bending his will upon the *Slayer*. "What does Chen have?"

Balthasar's mouth opened and closed again.

"Secrets?" Lorenzo guessed.

"Secrets."

"What secrets does he hold?"

Balthasar fidgeted, struggling to release his gaze from Lorenzo.

"Tell me what secrets Chen holds. Tell me. You want to tell me. It's the only way that I can help you to become Magnus's heir."

Balthasar's eyes flashed with hope. "Help?"

"Of course. You were right all along. I should join you."

"Join me."

"We would make the perfect team."

"Perfect team."

"But I must know what we are up against. You must confide in me to guarantee your triumph."

"Guarantee." Balthasar stared deeply into Lorenzo's eyes. "Triumph."

"Magnus's heir," Lorenzo assured him with a smile. He felt the battle within the *Slayer*, the tentative grasp his adversary had on sanity. He could push too hard and lose everything.

Lorenzo exhaled and released him.

For a moment.

Balthasar slumped on the table, exhausted by the power of the beguiling. Lorenzo could have snarled in frustration that he had so little to work with. He glanced across the bar, ensuring that no one was paying attention to them, and found Brandt watching him closely.

The *Pyr* hadn't even ordered a drink to give some disguise to his interest. Lorenzo shot him a scathing glance—he deserved no less—and the *Pyr* turned abruptly away.

"Dragon Bone Powder," Balthasar murmured sleepily. "Chen has Dragon Bone Powder."

"I know that," Lorenzo said with some impatience. "It stimulates desire . . ."

"Using so much," Balthasar murmured. "He must need more."

Lorenzo stared at the besotted *Slayer*. "Where does it come from?"

Balthasar opened one eye and giggled. "Where do you think?" he asked, his words slurring. "Dead *Pyr*."

Lorenzo's eyes widened in horror. He knew with sudden certainty where he'd find Chen—at his father's funeral. It was close to midnight now. Had the *Slayer* already attacked Erik, alone in the desert with the corpse? Was that why Erik wasn't answering his phone? Lorenzo lunged to his feet.

Balthasar lifted his head. "And the brand," he added groggily. "He has the brand." He tugged at his own shirt collar. "See? I'm still free." He giggled again, lost his balance, and slumped in the booth.

Lorenzo could make no sense of that. Maybe Balthasar was delirious.

Lorenzo had no time to spare. He had to help Erik. Because if Dragon Bone Powder was made of dead *Pyr*, Chen might be able to double his supply tonight.

Lorenzo wasn't going to let that happen.

He had to hope that where he found Chen, he'd find Cassie.

He raced out of the bar, Brandt fast on his heels.

"Consorting with the enemy..." Brandt began to chastise, but Lorenzo raced to the car.

"Get your ass to the designated spot yourself."

"Changing teams?"

Lorenzo spun on his heel and roared at the other *Pyr*. "I'm not feeling the love of the *Pyr* here."

"I knew it!" Brandt shouted. "I knew you'd take care of yourself first. I knew you were half *Slayer* already...."

Lorenzo seized his collar and gave him a shake. "I do whatever I have to do," he said in a low, deadly voice. "You might want to keep that in mind." Then he left Brandt in the lobby.

The illusion was coming together beautifully.

With any luck, it would be his last one.

And he would complete it in time.

Chapter 17

Cassie was cold and stiff.

She lay still for a moment, keeping her eyes closed and her breathing slow while she gathered as much information as possible. She could smell rock and felt a wind on her face. She thought maybe she was in a cave. Her hands were tied behind her back, her ankles were bound together, and she was on her side. Her left arm had gone to sleep and was all pins and needles. She could hear another person breathing in close proximity.

That person moved. Slowly.

Cassie jumped when she felt fingers on the bonds at her ankle. Her eyes flew open and she found Lorenzo's friend Erik surreptitiously untying the cord. He shook his head and frowned, holding a finger to his lips.

Cassie bit back her question.

He tapped his ear and she understood. There were others who would overhear them. She had a thousand questions, give or take, but didn't want to blow whatever plan he had.

Where were they? Where was Lorenzo? What was going on? How were they going to escape?

What Cassie could see was that they were in a cave, just the two of them. The opening showed only night sky. But there had to be someone guarding them. Erik certainly acted as if that were the case, and Cassie knew to trust keen *Pyr* senses.

He retied her bonds so they looked just as tight but actually were loose. She guessed that he was waiting for a specific moment. He gave her a questioning look and she twisted her ankles, proving that she could slip free. Erik made a little flourish, like she was a great apprentice of Lorenzo. They shared a smile.

He moved forward to do the same to her wrists. Cassie watched him, unable to read his emotions from his expression. She'd gotten him into this situation, even though she'd tried not to. She felt horrible for that.

She caught his eye and mouthed the word "Sorry."

He shook his head and shrugged. "Beguiled," was his silent reply.

The he gave her a hard look. "Trust me?" he mouthed.

Cassie wasn't sure what to think of that. She shrugged and Erik leaned closer. His eyes were a very clear shade of green. He opened them wide and she knew what he was going to do.

And she did trust him, because he was Lorenzo's friend.

Those flames danced, brilliant orange against the darkness of his pupils. Cassie felt his will bent upon her. She felt as if he were pushing clarity into her thoughts— and with that clarity came the fear that they could be discovered.

"Your mind will be your own," he said softly, his words low and melodic.

Her own. Cassie was tempted to echo the words. They rose to her lips and she wanted to shout them, she was so glad to be thinking clearly. But Erik laid a fingertip across her lips in warning.

She mouthed them instead. "My mind will be my own."

"Your mind is your own again," he murmured.

"My mind is my own again," Cassie mouthed, knowing it was true.

Erik glanced suddenly at the opening and Cassie understood that someone was coming. He leaned against the wall, suddenly looking much older and more defeated. He gave her a warning glance and she closed her eyes, as if she were still out cold. She let her mouth hang slack.

"Help Lorenzo," Cassie murmured, as if she were still beguiled. "Help Lorenzo . . ."

"Don't waste your breath, Erik," JP said, his tone mocking. "You can't undo a beguiling of Chen's."

"You're right," Erik admitted, sounding weary and defeated. "But I had to try."

"Valiant to the end," JP said. "Or is that—stupid to the end." He laughed. "You won't have to wait much longer now."

Erik moaned as if in pain and slumped lower on the wall.

JP chortled to himself and left.

When his footsteps had faded, the illusion was shattered. Cassie looked at Erik and he winked at her.

She needed to know more. "Salvatore?" she mouthed. "Dead?"

Erik winced and nodded.

That reality saddened Cassie. She wondered how Lorenzo was dealing with that loss, and suspected he hadn't had a lot of time to think about it. Yet.

Erik was close beside her again, his manner intent. He held up four fingers. "Elements," he mouthed, his gaze flicking to the opening. Cassie guessed that JP hadn't gone far.

There were four elements. Cassie nodded agreement. He started to count them off, glancing at her when he touched his first finger. If this was a test, she could pass.

"Fire," she mouthed.

Erik mocked breathing fire. Cassie understood that to mean that the *Pyr* could generate fire.

"Air."

He gestured around them, then took a deep breath. Okay, that was covered.

"Earth," Cassie added as Erik raised his third finger. He patted the ground beneath them with approval.

"Water." That was the last one.

But Erik glanced around, apparently puzzled.

Cassie understood. They needed water, although she wasn't sure why. "Mead Lake," she mouthed. They had been near the state park when the *Slayers* had dropped her off to snare Erik, and if they hadn't gone too far, there should be a spur of that lake in the vicinity.

Erik nodded, apparently satisfied with her answer. He pulled a set of car keys from his pocket and pushed them into her hands.

Car keys. He'd been driving the hearse. These must be the keys to the hearse.

Which would have a corpse in the back.

"Salvatore?" Cassie mouthed.

"Mead Lake," Erik mouthed again.

Okay. Cassie had a job. She didn't understand it fully, but she knew what she had to do and that was good enough. She made a gesture as if she'd get to her feet, but Erik shook his head. He settled back against the wall as if intent upon waiting.

But for what?

How would she know when to go?

"Lorenzo?" she mouthed and Erik grimaced.

Cassie didn't like that he wasn't sure of Lorenzo's fate. But then, maybe she could show him something that would make a difference.

She glanced at the doorway, then slipped free of her bonds. She pushed the keys to the hearse silently into her pocket, but found an obstacle there. She tugged out the golden scale that had fallen from Lorenzo's hide, the one she'd shoved into her pocket and forgotten about.

Erik's eyes lit at the sight of it. It had some importance because he nodded enthusiastic approval, then gestured for her to put it away again. By the time Cassie had done that, Erik was looking into space.

He stared for a long moment, his attention apparently captured by something she couldn't see. Then Erik smiled slowly, whatever it was giving him great pleasure. Cassie was both encouraged and intrigued.

When she finally caught his eye, she indicated her confusion.

He smiled. "Darkfire," he mouthed. He held up both hands and made a gesture like opening eyes. He mocked a gasp as if beholding something, then tapped the keys in her pocket and made his fingers do the walking. He pointed out the opening of the cave.

So when she saw the darkfire, she should run, snag the hearse, and drive to Lake Mead. Cassie nodded, just as a tread echoed outside the opening. They both resumed their previous positions, and she hoped JP couldn't hear her thoughts racing.

Too bad she didn't know what darkfire was.

Cassie could only hope she'd recognize it when she saw it.

*   *   *

Lorenzo left the car in the state park, not wanting to risk its welfare. He parked in the shadows, raced into the protection of the shadows, then leapt into the night. He shifted shape with a roar and flew toward the spot he was to meet Erik.

He sensed Brandt far behind him. The other *Pyr* hadn't flown as quickly as Lorenzo drove.

There was the reward of motivation.

The night was dark and still, the sky like black velvet above them. The moon glowed so brightly that its silvery light cast shadows across the desert. There was almost no wind, which made the scene below them look timeless and unreal. Lorenzo felt sharp despite his exhaustion, adrenaline kicking his *Pyr* senses into overdrive.

This was a test of his abilities, the greatest test he'd ever faced.

Because Cassie and his future with her hung in the balance.

Lorenzo saw the hearse that Erik had rented, the black paint gleaming in the moonlight. It was parked exactly where they had agreed to meet.

But there was no movement around it.

He couldn't discern any movement inside it, either.

His sense of pending doom became stronger.

Lorenzo could smell Erik's scent, proof only that the leader of the *Pyr* had been there. He could smell JP, although he couldn't see that *Slayer* either. He caught Cassie's scent and relief nearly made him lose the rhythm of flight. He inhaled greedily, grateful that he could discern that she was alive.

It wasn't nearly enough.

Suddenly he caught a whiff of the scent he now knew to be Chen's, an odor so strong that it made him falter slightly in speed.

He knew it had been deliberately revealed to him.

A taunt.

Lorenzo was ready to deceive the old *Slayer*. He scanned the ground, hunting a detail that would give Chen's location away.

He saw the flash of a red salamander on the ground. It was as red as Chinese lacquer and embellished with gold.

Lorenzo guessed instantly who it was, although he was astounded that the *Slayer* could take that form.

Chen was supposed to have a lot of secrets.

Lorenzo would show the ancient *Slayer* a few of his own.

He dove and snatched for the small reptile. The salamander turned just as Lorenzo's claw was closing over it. He saw the flash of Chen's eyes and a telltale blue shimmer.

Chen shifted shape into a red dragon with gold talons and horns. The pair collided. Everything in Lorenzo urged him to fight, but he deliberately held back. Chen spun, his eyes flashing, and landed a ferocious blow on Lorenzo's head.

Lorenzo took the hit, and let himself sprawl in the dirt. He pretended to be far more injured than he was and shook his head as if addled. He opened his eyes to find Chen before him, eyes snapping and talons raised.

"No wonder you get so few recruits," Lorenzo said, rubbing his head.

Chen froze and surveyed him. "*Recruits?*" he echoed in old-speak.

The word echoed in Lorenzo's thoughts, sounding ominous. He refused to be rattled by the *Slayer*'s powers—or at least to show his reaction. He smiled slowly, and picked himself up with care.

If he'd been in human form, he would have taken the time to brush the dust off his clothes.

As it was, he shook out his wings and ran a claw over his mailed chest. He felt the gap where he'd lost a scale, but deliberately hid his surprise. He left his claw over the gap. "If you beat the crap out of anyone who comes to talk to you, I understand why your numbers are dwindling."

Chen's eyes gleamed.

Lorenzo snorted. "Here I thought it was Erik's doing. You need better PR." He flashed a wide dragon smile, confident and hungry. "Or maybe you just need me."

He held the astonished *Slayer*'s gaze for a potent moment, sensing Brandt's approach. He had to admit that he was looking forward to this part of his deception—although he had to ensure that Brandt wasn't overly injured.

That's why he had to attack the *Pyr* instead of the *Slayers* doing it.

He glanced upward and swore. "*He followed me!*" Lorenzo roared in old-speak, then leapt into the air. He rocketed toward Brandt, whose yellow and orange scales shone like a flame in the night.

If nothing else, Lorenzo had surprise on his side.

"They're down there," Brandt cried at the sight of him, ready to attack Chen.

Instead Lorenzo tackled Brandt. He flew sideways and snatched the other *Pyr* out of the sky, tumbling through the air with Brandt.

The other *Pyr* swore and spun in his grip, struggling for release. "What the hell are you doing?" he demanded, then clawed at Lorenzo's face. His talons dug deep and drew blood.

"Changing teams," Lorenzo snarled and decked Brandt.

He was keenly aware that Chen was watching him closely, that this was but the first test to gain the *Slayer*'s confidence. The last thing he needed was his red blood spilling when he was trying to persuade the *Slayers* that he'd joined them. Lorenzo was annoyed that Brandt had nearly blown his cover and his irritation showed in the force of his blow.

He couldn't even beguile Brandt, because Chen would overhear.

The other *Pyr* fell back in shock as much as pain, then leapt at Lorenzo. The two locked talons, grappling for supremacy. Lorenzo pounded Brandt with his tail, aiming for bruises instead of cuts.

As a matter of principle.

Brandt, though, didn't hold back. He was livid and bent on destroying Lorenzo. He bit. He slashed. He breathed fire. He inflicted as much damage as he could, probably trying to score a victory for the *Pyr* side.

Lorenzo could have done without his misguided nobility.

When he was cut deeply across the chest, Lorenzo lost his temper. He slammed Brandt into the rocky outcropping so that the *Pyr* was momentarily stunned. Then he landed a trio of blows on Brandt's gut, backhanding him so hard that the *Pyr* lost a tooth. Then he closed his claw around the *Pyr*'s throat and squeezed.

"*Say good night, Brandt,*" he murmured in old-speak.

The tips of his talons pricked the *Pyr*'s hide. Brandt struggled, inflicting damage on himself as Lorenzo held him tightly against the rocks. Lorenzo continued to tighten his grip, cutting off Brandt's air supply, silently cursing the fact that this particular *Pyr* was even tougher than he looked.

Or maybe more stubborn.

He should have passed out by now. But he was still fighting, his tail still lashing, his claws leaving a thousand little scrapes in Lorenzo's hide. Lorenzo clenched his throat and Brandt flailed.

Then went still.

He was a dead weight in Lorenzo's grip.

Lorenzo, thoroughly pissed off, dropped him. It wasn't that far to the ground. Brandt probably wouldn't break any bones on impact, but the feat would prove whether he was conscious or not.

There was a resounding thud as Brandt hit the ground.

"Bravo," a woman said. Lorenzo looked down to find an attractive Asian woman applauding him. There was something sardonic in her expression and a challenge in her eyes.

Was this another form that Chen could take?

Lorenzo suddenly felt the lack of his knowledge about his own kind.

He'd just have to work with it.

Cassie pretended to be unconscious when she heard the flap of leathery wings. The floor of the cave vibrated as a great weight was tossed into the cavern; then she heard the steady sound of breathing.

She dared to peek and found a dragon of red and orange and yellow had joined her and Erik. This dragon looked broken, as if he'd survived a fight. He was out cold, and right before her eyes, he began to shimmer blue. He became a man, a muscled man with auburn hair, and then a dragon again. He flickered between those two forms so quickly that she had to avert her gaze.

Erik was slumped against the wall, like he was still out cold, but she could see a gleam of green as if his eyes weren't quite closed. Watching.

Silhouetted against the night was a dragon of luminous yellow, his scales so bright that he seemed to be generating his own light. He looked as if he were made of yellow topaz or citron, set in silver, and nearly radiant.

Was this JP's dragon form?

There was a mark on the side of his neck, like a dark tattoo. It was a spiral and the scales there looked as if they were dead.

He was breathing slowly and deeply. Cassie couldn't figure out why. He moved his head back and forth as if directing his breath.

It was some kind of dragon stuff. Cassie was sure of it.

He stood there, exhaling steadily for a long time, then leapt into the air and flew away. When she was sure he was gone, Cassie looked at Erik.

His expression was grim.

The new arrival stirred, moaning. He had stopped shifting in human form and opened his eyes with an obvious effort. He looked between Cassie and Erik and winced. "Bastard took me down," he muttered, then looked steadily at Erik. "Lorenzo is turning *Slayer*. You were wrong about him."

Erik said nothing, but his eyes glittered.

The new arrival forced himself to a sitting position, shook his head, and looked around their prison. "He asked me about turning *Slayer*, then went to talk to Balthasar instead of coming right here. If he hadn't been screwing around, we would have been in time to help you."

Cassie would have argued Lorenzo's case, but Erik flicked her a quick warning glance. What did he know? She decided to trust him and keep her mouth shut.

And keep pretending that Chen's beguiling was holding.

"So, now here we are, trapped behind JP's dragonsmoke barrier," the new arrival said with disgust. He grimaced as he got to his feet and approached the opening of the cave. He jumped back as if he'd been burned and gave Erik a resentful look. "You backed the wrong horse, mate."

Erik smiled coolly. "I'm sure you have a better suggestion."

"Send her through the dragonsmoke. It won't hurt her. Maybe she can change Lorenzo's mind before it's too late." He shoved a hand through his hair. "Before we're all dead."

"She's been beguiled to do Chen's will," Erik protested smoothly. Like Lorenzo, he was good at hiding his feelings, but Cassie understood that he was maintaining their cover story.

There could be only one reason.

He knew that Lorenzo joining the *Slayers* was an illusion and he was ensuring that the spell held.

Cassie could help with that.

"So we're all screwed." The other *Pyr* threw himself against the opposite wall and glared at Erik. "If either one of us gets out of this, you owe me."

Erik inclined his head but still said nothing.

"If." The other *Pyr* bit his lip and stared into the night.

Lorenzo stood before Chen as JP took Brandt's fallen body away. He feigned indifference, but he watched the *Slayer* from the corner of his eye, keeping track of where he went.

Cassie would be there.

Probably Erik too.

What was the mark on JP's neck? Lorenzo was sure it hadn't been there before.

Chen was in the form of an old man now. He turned

a piece of steel in his hands. It was round and looked like a swirl cast in metal, and it was mounted on a steel handle. Chen twirled it with a dexterity born of familiarity. Lorenzo recalled Balthasar's warning about the brand and wondered.

What was its power? Nothing good, he was sure of that.

"So, you would join me," Chen murmured, his eyes shining.

"I like to back the winners," Lorenzo said.

Chen chuckled. "Then you have no objection to a rite of passage?" he asked. His voice had become louder, as if he were excited. He turned the piece of metal with more agitation.

Lorenzo watched it turn in the old man's hands. "What kind of rite?"

"Nothing important. Just a little tradition of mine." He spun the brand, held it by the handle, then shifted shape to a dragon. He breathed fire on the brand and there was a dangerous glint in his eyes. The swirl responded with amazing speed to his dragonfire, heating to a brilliant yellow immediately. It matched the new mark on JP's neck.

It was a brand.

And he intended to mark Lorenzo with it.

"I'm good with tradition," Lorenzo said quietly, needing the old *Slayer* to come closer. He heard JP breathing smoke and knew he didn't have much time.

He'd have to surprise Chen.

"What did you have in mind?" he asked mildly.

"A little gang mark," Chen said, unable to hide his anticipation.

"I've always wanted one," Lorenzo agreed easily. "Where? On the arm?" He pushed up his shirtsleeve.

"On the side of your neck."

"Oh. Here, you mean," Lorenzo said, indicating the place where JP had a mark.

"Exactly."

"Let's do it, then. Get the details out of the way. I'm ready to help rule the world."

Chen grinned.

He pounced, the brand held high. But Lorenzo shifted in a blaze of light blue and snatched at the *Slayer's* claw. Chen obviously thought that Lorenzo wanted the brand himself, for he struggled against his grip even as he breathed more fire on the steel. It heated to a white that glowed in the darkness.

But Lorenzo had other plans. He caught Chen by the chin and stared into his eyes. He had to work fast. He summoned the beguiling flames and lowered his voice to that melodic pitch.

"You will give me the brand."

Chen stared at him in shock. "You cannot beguile me!"

That was exactly what Lorenzo was going to do.

If he could find something to work with.

What had brought the *Slayer* here?

What did he want?

"I will not permit this," Chen roared, fighting against Lorenzo's grip. He bellowed for JP.

"You need me," Lorenzo guessed and felt Chen's defiance waver. He'd found something. "*You need me,*" he repeated in old-speak, letting the flames leap high in his eyes.

Chen tried to look away.

He closed his eyes tightly.

He shifted shape to a woman again, but Lorenzo held fast.

"*You need me,*" Lorenzo repeated with more confidence.

The *Slayer* struggled. He shuddered. He bit off the words, saying them aloud. "I need you."

"You came because you need me," Lorenzo said.

"I came because I need you," Chen agreed with obvious reluctance. He still wasn't under Lorenzo's spell, but each statement that they could agree on drew him closer.

"You came to my firestorm for a purpose," Lorenzo said.

"I came to your firestorm for a purpose," Chen admitted, his eyes flashing with anger. Even he could probably feel his will surrendering to Lorenzo's.

"You want me to ally with you."

Chen snorted and blinked.

Lorenzo tightened his grip on his chin. "You want to control me."

"I will control you!" Chen said.

Lorenzo laughed. The *Slayer* was startled. Lorenzo turned and exhaled dragonfire on the upheld brand. It glittered and glimmered when he did so, a blue-green spark dancing along the metal. Something had changed because of his dragonfire. Lorenzo ran on instinct. He ripped the brand from Chen's grip and took flight with it.

"No!" Chen roared. He shifted shape to dragon form and leapt into the sky after Lorenzo. JP was closing fast from the other direction, answering Chen's summons. Lorenzo flew straight up into the sky, breathing dragonfire on the brand at every possible interval.

"No!" Chen screamed.

Lorenzo pivoted abruptly and dove back down toward the pursuing *Slayer*. He saw Chen's shock, then caught him by the wing. He swung the *Slayer* around, bringing his neck toward the glowing brand. He wasn't at all sure his ploy would work, but given the choice, he'd happily risk Chen's health and welfare over his own.

"You are mine!" Lorenzo bellowed and pushed the brand against Chen's neck.

There was a blinding flash of blue-green, as if lightning had struck the brand. Chen appeared to be electrified before Lorenzo's eyes.

He fell toward the earth, unconscious. He shifted between shapes in rapid succession, a sign of his distress. He became a woman, an old man, a young man, a salamander, then a dragon again. It was enough to make Lorenzo dizzy.

"Now you're mine!" JP declared as he abruptly caught Lorenzo from behind. Lorenzo swung and hit the *Slayer* with the brand, catching him across the temple. He smacked him again and again, until the *Slayer* fell back stunned.

That was when Lorenzo saw the woman running across the desert below him. She was headed for the hearse, which told Lorenzo exactly who she was.

Cassie.

His Cassie.

He hooted, then breathed dragonfire at JP.

It was payback time.

Cassie heard thunder, even though the sky was perfectly clear. She remained on her side, waiting for the cue of darkfire—whatever that was.

In the end, she couldn't have missed it.

There was a brilliant flash, as if lightning had struck a tree right before her eyes. But the flash illuminated three dragons who were fighting in the sky.

Erik gave her shoulder a distinct nudge.

Cassie flung off her bonds and ran out of the cave. She felt a slight tingle against her legs, but she didn't stop. She could see only three dragons: one was falling to the earth and the other two were fighting furiously in the sky.

Were there more?

She scrambled down the rock face, focusing on speed instead of stealth. The falling dragon hit the ground with a tremendous thud, but he didn't move again. Cassie heard the dragons battling overhead, but kept her eye on her goal.

About twenty feet from the car, she realized that the interior light would go on as soon as she opened the door. That would attract the attention of anyone in the area, but there was no way she could avoid it.

She'd just have to move fast.

Cassie did. She eased up beside the car, her breath coming quickly. The hammered gold dragon was pounding the crap out of the yellow one, which worked for her in a big way. Lorenzo was fine and he was winning. She checked the door of the car, confirmed that it was unlocked, then opened it and swung inside. She closed the door as quickly as possible and kept down low.

She was panting when she slipped the key into the ignition. The engine started right away. She crawled up into the driver's seat, put the car into gear, then looked out the windshield.

There was a large lacquer red dragon in front of her.

Chen.

And he'd survived the fall. He looked a bit singed around the edges, thanks to the darkfire. He looked furious. His eyes shone with malice. He breathed a vivid orange plume of dragonfire, then flew directly toward the car, talons extended.

Cassie figured she had one chance to survive. She squeezed her eyes shut and pushed the gas pedal all the way to the floor.

There was a thump when she hit the dragon and the car swerved dangerously. All she could see was Chen's scaled belly, covering the windshield. Cassie didn't take her foot off the gas.

She didn't figure she had much to lose.

There was a GPS on the dash. Since she couldn't really watch where she was going, she punched up Mead Lake as her destination.

"Turn right," said the GPS, so Cassie did.

She turned hard, hard enough that Chen slipped to the left. She could see a bit of sky on the right end of the windshield. They hit a ditch and Cassie bit her tongue. The car's shocks took a hard hit, but she didn't slow down.

Chen meanwhile smashed the glass on the driver's door and reached inside with his claws. Cassie lunged for the passenger seat, keeping one foot on the gas. What she needed was a brick to hold that pedal down. She let go of the steering wheel and rummaged in the glove box. There was a flashlight and a map. She silently thanked the rental agency for nothing.

Chen snatched for her, his claws ripping through the air. Cassie ducked and he missed.

Barely.

Then one large dragon eye peered through the broken glass into the car.

Cassie turned the flashlight onto its highest setting and shone the light in his eye.

He blinked and she yanked hard on the wheel.

"Turn left in .6 miles," the GPS said.

Cassie chose to turn left immediately. She leaned over and cranked the steering wheel hard to the left, sending the car into a spin. Chen's eye disappeared and his talons scratched across the roof of the car.

"Turn left in .2 miles," the GPS said.

Cassie leapt back into the driver's seat, pulled the car out of the spin, then slammed on the brakes.

The scales of Chen's belly slid across the windshield.

Cassie hit the gas.

She heard him scream, then kick out the window on the passenger side. Broken glass fell all around her. She could see through the windshield again, so Cassie just drove.

She saw the highway and raced for it, aware that Chen was scrambling for a grip. She drove in a weaving pattern, much to the dismay of the GPS, trying to ensure he didn't get that grip on her.

She heard the back window break. Something ripped the gate of the hearse off its hinges and Cassie could have guessed it was red and had claws.

To her horror, she saw the coffin begin to slide backward.

She wasn't going to lose Salvatore now!

Cassie hit the brakes so hard that the coffin slid forward and bounced off the back of her seat.

Chen dropped to the ground behind her and took the form of an agile young man.

Cassie put the hearse in reverse and floored it.

She hit something.

Or someone.

"Turn right," advised the GPS.

Cassie ignored it. She spun and braked, put the car in gear and accelerated again. She aimed directly at the dark shape on the desert and hit it with two tires. When she looked in the rearview mirror, the lump that was Chen wasn't moving.

She could see the reflection of water ahead, assumed it was Lake Mead, and raced for her destination.

"Turn right," advised the GPS.

Cassie peeked out the window and saw the silhouette of a dragon overhead. She shouldn't have been surprised when he fell across the hood of the car with a thud.

She was surprised that he was bleeding so profusely.

"Turn right," insisted the GPS.

The dragon on the hood was vivid yellow, his scales almost translucent. Like topaz. There was a brand on his neck, one that looked like a swirl. He wasn't dead, but he was moaning, on the verge of consciousness.

He shimmered blue, then shifted shape, becoming JP right before her eyes.

"Turn right," said the GPS.

Cassie heard a rush of air as Lorenzo lunged through the window, shifting shape with elegant timing.

"Well done," he said, granting her a smile. His tone was easy, as if she'd just made a good shot at billiards.

Cassie grinned. "You weren't too shabby either."

"Turn right!" insisted the GPS. "Turn right!"

Cassie hit the brakes instead.

JP slid off the front of the car; then there was a splash. The hearse came to a halt with the front tires sinking into the soft shore of the lake.

Mission accomplished.

Cassie turned off the engine and exhaled with relief. Lorenzo reached over and squeezed her hand, and she was sure that he must be able to hear her heart pounding.

She could hear his.

He reached for the door handle, but she stopped him with a touch. There was something she had to say.

"I know that you don't think you have the stuff to be a good dad, but I'm sure you're wrong. The firestorm changed everything. And no matter how you look at it, a dragon boy is going to need a dragon dad to show him how it's done."

Lorenzo smiled at her, his eyes lighting with pleasure. Cassie felt like she could look into his eyes all night long. He didn't say anything, but leaned over and gave her a sultry kiss that curled her toes. When he was done, he touched his finger to her lips as if to keep her from saying anything, and his eyes shone as he watched her.

"It wasn't the firestorm that changed me," he whispered, and kissed her again.

It was a few moments before they got out of the car, and Cassie's heart was thundering like crazy.

Lorenzo fished the unconscious JP out of Lake Mead and gave him a shake to wake him up. He held up the bedraggled *Slayer* so that they were looking each other in the eye. JP struggled, but it was clear that he was outmatched.

"Why don't you change the permissions on your dragonsmoke?" he suggested, his voice low and silky. There was a rumble of thunder then, and JP twitched.

The way Lorenzo smiled told Cassie that he was getting exactly what he wanted.

And he hadn't even needed to beguile anyone.

Chapter 18

Cassie touched the wounds on Lorenzo's face and shoulder, but he shook his head. "I'll be fine," he said with a smile.

"I've got to tell you that right now I'm very glad you're a dragon shifter."

His smile broadened. "So am I."

"Even though it's barbaric?"

"Barbaric works, on occasion."

She could see that he was thinking about something, but trusted that he'd tell her when it was time. "Why are we here, anyway?"

"A dead *Pyr* has to be exposed to all four elements to ensure that his body can't be roused again." Lorenzo glanced at the sky, then nodded approval.

Erik arrived first, with Brandt behind him. That *Pyr* was still muttering about Lorenzo being sneaky, although Erik seemed to be amused by his complaints. They pulled the coffin out of the back of the hearse and opened it.

Cassie caught her breath at the sight of Salvatore

dead. He looked to be sleeping, but she knew better. Lorenzo heaved a sigh and she touched his shoulder. "Maybe he's with Angelina again," she suggested, wanting only to console him.

"That's what Erik says." Lorenzo shrugged. "I hope it's true."

Cassie watched as they did their dragon business. Lorenzo lifted his father in his arms with great tenderness, then laid him on the ground for a moment.

Earth, Cassie thought.

Lorenzo gathered his father into his embrace again, then shifted shape and took flight. He soared through the air with his burden, the other two dragons right behind him.

Air.

He flew high over the lake, then dropped his father's body. Cassie covered her mouth with her hands. But the three dragons circled around the falling body, breathing fire that was radiant against the darkness of the night. Salvatore's clothes caught fire and he looked like a fireball falling to earth.

Fire.

They followed his descent, still breathing fire, all the way to the surface of the lake. Lorenzo was the last to pull away and there wasn't much left of Salvatore's body to break the surface of the lake.

Water.

The splash was smaller than she would have expected. Lorenzo hovered there for a moment, his golden splendor reflected in the dark mirror of the lake.

When the surface was still, he came directly to her side, the other dragons following him.

"You have to come in the car tomorrow," he said, his

terse tone revealing the intensity of his feelings. "I'll beguile you if you want, but it is not optional."

"Chen is still at large," Erik said, proving that he agreed with Lorenzo.

"And JP isn't dead enough to suit me," Lorenzo said.

Cassie nodded and took a deep breath, knowing what she had to do. "No beguiling," she said. "I'll face my fears once and for all. You're not the only one getting remade by the firestorm."

The only reward she needed was Lorenzo's smile of pride. He took her hand and tugged her against his side, and she heard from the pounding of his heart that he was concerned as well.

"I'll try not to freak," she whispered.

"I'd appreciate that," he said, then winked at her.

By the time Lorenzo drove his orange Ferrari into the state park—right on time—he was running on fumes. The car was fine, but Lorenzo couldn't remember when he'd last slept. His current state of mind was about as far as possible from where he had wanted it to be at this point in time.

The key to a successful escape was planning and composure. Lorenzo had thought his planning had been superlative, but with so many things changing in the past twenty-four hours, he was no longer confident that he'd accommodated for every variable.

He had no composure left.

His sole triumph was that Cassie was with him.

Even if her presence made him more nervous than usual. JP was in Erik's custody, but Lorenzo didn't trust Chen. He didn't want to be paranoid, but he wouldn't believe Cassie was safe until Chen had been incinerated and exposed to all four elements.

And that hadn't happened yet.

"You can do it," Cassie whispered. She was tucked into the space in front of the passenger seat, a dark blanket over her.

He cast her a confident smile. "So can you." He gave her a look and she nodded, touching her finger to her own lips. She took a deep breath and squared her shoulders, composing herself for the ordeal ahead.

Lorenzo paused on the mark as scheduled and scanned the crowd. It was a good showing, a better crowd than he'd hoped. The weather was perfect and the timing was dead on. The sun was just beginning to set the rocks aglow, the shadows drawing long. The mood was festive, orange banners on all the bleachers and the massive mounted video screens alight with clips of Lorenzo on stage.

The fireworks were arranged and would be the perfect send-off.

The site looked exactly as he'd envisioned it, every detail in place. He'd gone over the car in obsessive detail this morning and was sure it was perfect, despite the scratch on the fender and the new windows. Cassie was the one factor left to chance. She hadn't wanted to be beguiled, and while he respected that, he also worried about her facing her fears at such a key moment. She was the one who had insisted she'd freak out.

He hoped she was wrong.

He could smell *Slayer*. That should have reassured him more than it did. He could smell *Pyr*, as well, and narrowed his eyes to scan the crowd again. Erik stood near the pit, watchful as ever. Lorenzo knew that Brandt was also close by.

He was amazed by how much it reassured him to be part of a team.

Lorenzo supposed he should have asked Erik to do the pyrotechnics display since that was Erik's specialty and occupation, but he hadn't thought of it until this very minute. He smiled then, certain that Erik would have refused such a request six months before.

But this firestorm was about fresh starts. It was about seeing things clearly for the first time in a long time, knowing one's priorities and understanding everything in a flash of pure insight.

One last feat.

He wasn't going to screw up now.

Cassie brushed his hand with hers.

For luck.

Just as she'd said she would.

Lorenzo revved the car and the crowd cheered. The music poured from the speakers mounted on all sides, its pounding rhythm calculated to build excitement. Lorenzo drove to the side of the pit, then stopped with a flourish, sending a plume of dust into the sky.

The music soared, then faded as he stepped out of the car. He ensured that the door didn't swing wide open, lest Cassie be revealed. He was dressed more casually than usual but with a measure of flair. His jeans were black, as was his leather jacket, but his shirt was as orange as flames.

He bowed to enthusiastic cheers.

"Welcome to the final test!" he said, gratified when the speakers picked up his voice precisely as planned. "I bid you not farewell but *au revoir*. Meet me here in thirty days to witness my survival of the greatest test of all time."

He bowed and waved. The operator who had installed

the video feed on his arrival stepped back from the car, his movement crisp and smart. He nodded once at Lorenzo and shook his hand, as if wishing him the best.

Lorenzo could feel the anxiety in the crowd.

He waved with exuberant confidence.

He swung back into the car and drove it over the network of chains laid ready for it. He opened the window, gave a thumbs-up to the operator, then closed the window and turned off the car.

On the massive screens mounted on either side of the viewing area, the video feed showed his face, ten feet tall. It was a good signal. He winked, the image of confidence, and the crowd cheered encouragement. Lorenzo changed the angle of the seat back, unfastening his seat belt, ensuring he could stretch out. He folded his arms across his chest and began to breathe slowly, as if preparing himself for the ordeal ahead.

Actually, he was listening to the patter of the announcer coming through his ear bud and watching the spectacle unfold. He kept one eye on the second hand sweep of his watch, ensuring that every detail happened on time.

He was listening to Cassie's breath and her heartbeat. She slipped a hand over the console and touched his knee, contact helping her composure.

He was reassured that her pulse slowed slightly.

The chains were lifted around the car and locked in position, and he liked how the sun glinted off them. They were oversized and looked impressive. The arm of the crane swung into place, and Lorenzo was glad that the operator had remembered to wear his wraparound sunglasses. It made him look impassive, maybe inhuman, and added to the drama.

The car was lifted with a lurch, right on time. It swung

out over the pit, spun slightly, then was lowered into the yawning darkness of the hole. The announcer was rolling through the statistics that Lorenzo had provided about oxygen and water, doing a passable job of presentation. His own concern echoed in his tone, a nice touch.

Lorenzo felt the chill of the earth as soon as the shadow passed over the car. He waved two fingers at the video feed and heard the response of the crowd. The car settled in the bottom of the pit and he steeled himself for the part he dreaded the most.

He heard the backhoe move into place. He heard it scoop the first load of dirt. He fought not to wince as that load of dirt landed on the roof of the car. Cassie's fingers tightened around his leg and her breath hitched.

He refused to think of darkness, of being trapped, of being condemned with no chance of escape. He wanted to remind her to be strong but couldn't say anything.

He breathed steadily and evenly, forcing his heartbeat to remain slow. He tried to lead by example. He heard her try to do to same breathing exercise.

The wig he wore itched.

He watched the dirt cover the windshield, enclosing him in darkness, but refused to twitch. He eyed the luminous dial of his watch, then touched the LED installed on the dash to illuminate the car. He smiled with confidence for the crowd, hiding his discomfiture as well as he was able. The announcer chattered on and on.

It seemed to take forever to bury the car. That was the point. It should look overdone, escape should appear to be impossible, the weight of earth too great to allow Lorenzo to ever be free again.

Finally, he heard the bulldozer roll away. He heard the announcer cue the clock and encourage the onlookers to participate in the vigil. He heard the music soar and the fireworks begin. He heard Cassie start to panic.

And then he moved.

Lorenzo touched the lever installed below the dash, flipping it with his left knee. The video feed should change, with only a slight flicker, shifting from the live feed to a prerecorded file. Lorenzo waited and listened, but the announcer made no comment upon the display changing, and the fireworks burst overhead with enthusiasm.

The perfect distraction.

He waited ten minutes to ensure that the switch had been made and was flawlessly done. It was the longest ten minutes he'd ever endured. He counted them down with the tapping of his foot, just as he'd promised Cassie. She clutched his leg like a lifeline.

When he was sure it was safe, he bent and caught her face in his hands. She was trembling but not freaking out. He smiled at her, then kissed her quickly. He arched a brow and she swallowed before she nodded.

She gave him a thumbs-up.

Lorenzo kissed her harder, to hell with the time.

Then he folded down the passenger seat of the car. He removed the panel behind the seat, revealing the hatch that led into the trunk. He squeezed himself through the gap, pulled back the carpet on the bottom of the trunk, and slid open the panel installed in the floor. He wriggled along it, feeling Cassie close behind him.

The exhaust had been slightly reconfigured to allow a narrow span for escape through the bottom of the trunk, one that just barely allowed Lorenzo to slide through. He was glad he'd had it made a bit bigger on impulse, given the modification to his plan. He pulled on leather gloves and plunged his hands into the dirt, hoping the car had been positioned as precisely as planned.

For a minute, he couldn't find the cord buried in the dirt. He fought against his panic, searched again, and his fingers closed over it a little more to the left than he'd expected. He pulled the cord hard, heard a small explosion below the car, then the dirt abruptly fell away.

The fireworks continued far above.

Lorenzo was down the hole and into the hidden passageway in record time. He crawled its length with haste, uncertain precisely what he'd find at the end of the tunnel. Cassie was close behind him, her breath hitching in her fear. But she was moving. She was keeping to the plan and she wasn't freaking out. He didn't think he'd ever been prouder of another person.

Lorenzo could smell *Slayer*, so he knew Balthasar had come as bidden.

What he didn't know was whether his beguiling had held or not.

Had Balthasar's mind come unhinged? Was he still beguiled? Or had Lorenzo's last-minute interrogation jeopardized everything? Cassie's safety depended upon his success, but in his current state of exhaustion, Lorenzo wasn't as confident as he wanted to be.

He'd have to make it work.

And that was when he realized precisely what he could do with the flashfire spell. It was his to use, just once, and Lorenzo was going to make it count.

He wasn't going to give up anything.

Balthasar was sullen.

And hungover.

Lorenzo decided that was better than other alternatives.

"I knew you weren't going to spend a month in that car," Balthasar sneered by way of greeting. "Nothing is as it seems with you." His gaze flicked over Cassie, who was leaning against the wall of the tunnel, her knees weak with relief. "What's with her?"

"Not your problem." Lorenzo dropped his voice to the low tone ideal for beguiling. At the same time, he brushed dirt from his jacket. "Everything is real if you look closely enough."

Balthasar eyed him warily.

"It's those who only look at the surface who are easily fooled." Lorenzo smiled.

Balthasar didn't. "I don't know what I'm doing here. . . ."

"Of course you do. You came because you wanted to." Lorenzo closed the distance between them, backing Balthasar into the wall. He stared into the *Slayer's* eyes, checking. The beguiling was holding, but just barely. He was fairly sure that the *Slayer* wouldn't attack him, but beyond that, there were no guarantees.

He had work to do. He summoned the flames in his pupils.

Balthasar caught his breath and stared.

Lorenzo smiled. "You came because you had something to bring me."

Balthasar's fingers twitched as he fought the beguiling, but he succumbed. His mind was becoming soft, like butter, but Lorenzo didn't want to push him too far. "I'm not sure I like your terms," he said by way of protest, some corner of his thoughts recognizing the truth.

Lorenzo made those flames burn more brightly. "But we will be allies," he lied.

"Allies," Balthasar agreed.

"And you cannot break the code alone."

"I cannot break the code alone."

"Without me, the legacy of Magnus will be completely lost."

Balthasar swallowed. "I'm not sure . . . ," he said, looking away.

Where was the key? Lorenzo seized his chin, compelling him to look into his own eyes. "You are sure. You know what is right. You know what Magnus wanted."

"I know what Magnus wanted."

"You know his legacy belongs to you."

"I know his legacy belongs to me."

"You know that only I can help you claim it."

"Only you."

"Because we will be allies." Lorenzo put out his other hand. Balthasar caught his breath. He stared deeply into Lorenzo's eyes and Lorenzo feared it would all come apart in this last moment.

He pushed. "Allies," he murmured again.

"You a *Slayer*," Balthasar whispered, as if trying out the idea.

Lorenzo smiled. "You and me, together. Allies. *Slayers*."

Something changed then. Lorenzo felt it. Balthasar began to fight hard against the beguiling. "No, no, it's a lie, it's a trick, it's an illusion. . . ."

Lorenzo seized Balthasar by the chin, compelling the *Slayer* to hold his gaze. He had to work with the *Slayer*'s doubts to get around them. "You're right," he said, even as he let the flames burn higher and brighter in his eyes. Balthasar stared into his eyes with awe. "We will not be allies."

"Not allies."

"You will be my minion. You will do as you are bidden."

"I will do as I am bidden."

Lorenzo was relieved that this idea made sense to Balthasar. Of course, Lorenzo would want to be in charge. It was what Balthasar wanted. "You are nothing without me."

"Nothing."

"You cannot unlock Magnus's secrets without me."

"I cannot unlock Magnus's secrets without you," Balthasar admitted and Lorenzo knew he believed this.

"So you will do whatever I command you to do."

"I will do whatever you command me to do."

"Where is the library secured? Tell me!"

Balthasar dug in his pocket and offered a key, like the key to a safety-deposit box. "Caymans, all digitized," he admitted, then surrendered the name of the bank and the password.

This legacy of information was what Lorenzo needed to repay Erik. He smiled in triumph as he took the key. Erik had stood by Lorenzo and come to his firestorm, despite years of animosity between them. Erik would have Magnus's library of ancient documents as his reward. It was only right that these secrets, whatever they were, be in Erik's responsible claws.

"*You are my minion,*" Lorenzo said in old-speak and Balthasar's lips worked. "Swear it!"

Balthasar trembled. He swallowed. Some vestige of him flickered in defiance, but Lorenzo had no tolerance and no time. He pushed even harder. He let his hand change shape, let the dragon talons lock around Balthasar's neck and pierce the skin. Black blood slipped over his nail.

"Swear it," he demanded again. "*You are my minion.*"

Balthasar's eyes widened. His mouth opened and closed. Lorenzo let the flames in his eyes leap higher. He began to sing the flashfire song, the song that the Cantor had given him, the song that he had intended to use to sever his own connections with the *Pyr*.

But he directed it at Balthasar, severing that *Slayer's* connections to the other dragons in the world. Balthasar was as good as dead anyway.

Lorenzo knew the moment Balthasar's mind snapped.

It was the same instant that the flashfire song ended, and Balthasar's connection to his kind was eliminated.

The *Slayer* went slack in his grip, a bit of spittle dribbling from the corner of his mouth. He murmured the word "minion" over and over again, which would have to do.

"What's happened to him?" Cassie whispered.

"His mind is gone." Lorenzo grimaced. "I pushed too hard."

"It'll all be over soon," Cassie said and flashed him a thin smile.

It was over already, his commitment to his kind reinforced, but Lorenzo would tell her all about it later.

He peeled off his own clothes, while Cassie removed those of Balthasar. He dressed in Balthasar's clothes, finding the keys to the rented Ferrari in the pocket of the *Slayer's* jeans. He forced Balthasar into his clothes, then hauled him down the narrow passageway to the car with Cassie's help.

He'd hoped to command the *Slayer* to get into the car, but he was almost unresponsive now. There was no room for Cassie to help and besides, he thought she could do with the time in the tunnel to regain her composure.

He didn't like leaving her behind in the tunnel, but he reasoned it would be for only a moment.

And Erik was here.

It wasn't easy to haul the limp Balthasar through that opening in the trunk, much less to get him into the driver's seat of the car. A man who was not a contortionist and escape artist would never have managed the feat.

Lorenzo barely did.

He fussed over the collar of the orange shirt, ensuring that it was just so. He checked his watch obsessively, knowing that he had only moments left to complete his escape. He replaced all of the panels in the car, hiding all of the accesses, then dropped down into the passageway again.

He retreated, then filled the space beneath the car with the bags of dirt stacked farther down the passageway. He worked double-time, moving at lightning speed, dragging them into place. He was sweating by the time he was done. He stood in the passageway where he had met Balthasar and detonated one last small explosive device, one that would compel the earth to settle behind him and disguise what he had done.

Lorenzo had time to think that far before he heard the old-speak.

"*Nicely done,*" Chen said. "*And how kind of you to eliminate an outstanding annoyance for me.*"

Lorenzo pivoted to find Chen in the form of a young Asian man, holding Cassie captive in front of himself. His right hand was a dragon claw, his sharp gold talon held against her throat like a knife. It astounded Lorenzo that the *Slayer* could hover between forms like that.

"A trade," Chen said out loud. "Her life for my brand."

"Don't give it to him," Cassie said.

Chen grabbed her more tightly and her eyes widened in pain. Lorenzo saw a trickle of blood run from her throat, where the sharp point dug into her flesh.

He wanted to destroy Chen for that injury.

Chen smiled. "I've always wondered how early a *Pyr* could turn *Slayer*. Maybe your son will be the youngest yet."

Lorenzo held his ground, knowing he needed a plan and had very little time to concoct one.

Cassie couldn't believe how fast the *Slayer* Chen could move. One minute she was alone, quietly hyperventilating, hearing Lorenzo get Balthasar into the car.

The next moment, she heard a soft footfall.

Then there was a dragon claw against her throat and a strong arm locking her arms to her sides. She knew she couldn't free herself from his grip.

Because she tried.

Lorenzo came back quickly, but not quickly enough. She saw how he tried to hide his fear and wondered whether the *Slayer* knew how troubled he was. She trusted Lorenzo completely, and braced herself for him to do something unexpected.

He took a step closer and shrugged. "If that's the choice, you can have her," he said. He pulled the circle of the brand out of his pocket and tossed it in the air, catching it easily. Lorenzo had broken off the handle earlier to make it more portable, but Cassie didn't know where he'd put it.

"I'd rather have the brand," Lorenzo said with that breezy confidence. Cassie knew he was scamming Chen, and could only hope Chen didn't get it.

"It is not yours!" the *Slayer* protested.

"Sure it is. Finders keepers." Lorenzo tossed it again, easily snatching it out of the air. He slid it back into his pocket and grinned as Chen snarled. "So, we're agreed then. Don't worry about sending me pictures of the kid." He moved as if he'd step past Chen and leave.

Cassie felt the *Slayer's* surprise.

His uncertainty.

Then she saw the blue shimmer. Lorenzo suddenly leapt at Chen, shifting shape faster than she'd ever seen him do it. She drove her elbow into Chen's ribs, simultaneously driving her heel up into his crotch.

He didn't even flinch.

But he roared and shifted shape himself. The pair of them breathed fire in unison and Cassie smelled her hair burning. Then Lorenzo flung the circle from the brand down the tunnel.

Chen gave a cry and leapt after it, Cassie tight in his grip. Lorenzo leapt onto his back, tore his wings, and buried his talons in the *Slayer's* neck. Chen screamed and stumbled. Lorenzo ripped Cassie from Chen's grip and practically flung her toward the opening of the tunnel.

Then he blocked the passage, massive and ferocious, seething and ready to fight. Chen looked between him and the rolling brand, then dove after the brand.

Just as he might have snatched it up, the tunnel was suddenly lit with a strange blue-green light, the light of darkfire. Cassie saw the spark dance around the perimeter of the brand. She heard Chen shout in dismay; then the pieces crumbled from his claws.

"You!" he said, spinning to breathe dragonfire at Lorenzo.

"Me, actually," another man said. Cassie found a dark-haired man standing beside her. He had a large quartz crystal in his hand, one that seemed to have a similar blue-green spark trapped inside it. He pointed it at Chen and made a blowing gesture.

A blue-green spark erupted from the point of the crystal, firing down the length of the tunnel like a shot. It hit Chen right in the chest, making a fearsome crack on impact. He fell, shifting shape as he dropped so that an attractive Asian woman landed on all fours.

She looked up at the stranger, glaring in fury. "You will not turn the darkfire against me. I loosed the dark-fire. It answers to *me*!"

"No. It responds to your attempts to pervert it," the man said calmly. Lorenzo shifted shape and backed toward Cassie in human form, still barricading the *Slayer* from her.

The stranger fired his crystal again, and this time Chen fell. Cassie backed away, glad to have Lorenzo de-fending her. The air shimmered blue as Chen rotated between forms, shifting from the woman to the young man who had held Cassie captive to an old man, then a dragon.

He became a red salamander.

Then he fled into the darkness of the tunnel.

Cassie exhaled, realizing there was a lot she didn't know yet about dragons.

"Marco," Lorenzo said as easily as if they'd met at a cocktail party. He took Cassie's hand and led her to the other man. "Good to see you again."

The stranger inclined his head and smiled serenely. "It's useful to hear the thoughts of the *Pyr*," he said, then walked to the back of the tunnel. "Not to mention the flashfire song."

What was he talking about? Cassie looked between the two of them.

"Could you have reclaimed it?" Lorenzo asked.

"Of course. But you needed it." Marco smiled. "I knew you wouldn't use it to sever your own connections to the *Pyr*, but you needed to come to that conclusion yourself." He smiled at Cassie, as if she were responsible for this change. "You did keep the other crystal safe for a long time."

Lorenzo's gaze brightened. "Then you know where it is?"

Marco smiled. "Of course."

"Did you get it back?" Lorenzo asked.

Marco's smile broadened. "It is not yet ready to come to my hand again." He picked up the pieces of the brand, examined them, and tucked them into his pocket. "Part of the darkfire," he said by way of explanation.

"Thus your department?" Lorenzo said.

Marco nodded.

"What about Chen? I marked him with the brand."

"Yes." Marco smiled, as if at a private joke.

"What does that mean?" Lorenzo asked.

Marco didn't answer. "Have a good trip," he said, then strolled out of the cave.

"Trip?" Cassie asked. "I thought this was more permanent."

Lorenzo caught her hand in his. "It is permanent, if you'll have this old dragon."

Cassie smiled and turned her hand to grasp his, but she still had questions.."What does he mean about the flashfire?"

"Flashfire was a spell that came into my possession. It would have severed my ties to other dragons and possibly taken my powers away." He smiled at her. "But you're right. A dragon boy needs a dragon dad. I don't know much about being a parent, but I intend to try."

Cassie laughed and threw her arms around him. He caught her close, and she reveled in his embrace, fiercely glad at having found him.

But when he pulled back, there was that glint of mischief in his eyes, a light that hinted at some secret scheme.

"You have a plan," Cassie guessed.

"Of course." Lorenzo smiled. "But we have a stop to make on the way." He patted his pocket where he'd put the key from Balthasar. "Feel like a vacation?"

"Where?"

"The Caymans?"

"Don't give me that," Cassie teased. "You're not switching sides."

"No. I'm giving the library to Erik, so we can learn more of Magnus's secrets." He held her hand tightly and led her toward the exit, tugging off his wig and shoving it into his pocket. The sight of him shaved bald still made her smile.

"And then?"

"And then, Signor L. Rossi will move into the villa he's restoring in Venice, the one that's on the footprint of an old courtesan's home." He flicked her a look and she sensed his trepidation. "He's hoping that there will be a Signora Rossi joining him there."

Cassie grinned. "Any particular candidates in mind?"

Lorenzo grinned right back. "I believe the lady in question will be very interested to learn that Italians make wonderful lingerie."

Cassie laughed. "Does Signor Rossi have identification?"

Lorenzo scoffed. "Do you really imagine I'd overlook such an important detail?"

"No. And we're in the perfect place for a quick wedding."

"Honeymoon in the Caymans?"

"Sounds perfect to me. Let's go."

Lorenzo donned Balthasar's sunglasses and pulled the keys to the rented Ferrari out of the pocket of Balthasar's jeans. He and Cassie marched out of the tunnel, leapt down the rocks, and headed for the temporary parking lot. The black Ferrari was at the edge of the lot, presumably because Balthasar had arrived late.

The fireworks were just ending when they got into the car.

"I'm just curious," Cassie said. "Who would you have left in the car if Balthasar hadn't shown up?"

"Some details can't be planned," he admitted. "I had a feeling the perfect candidate would turn up, and I trusted my instincts. If he hadn't, I would have thought of something."

"I thought you liked to control every detail."

"Sometimes, even old dragons need to learn new tricks." He winked. "Otherwise, I'd never have won the prize offered by my firestorm. That would have been a tragedy." He leaned over and kissed her thoroughly. They shared a smile; then Lorenzo merged the car into the departing traffic.

Their future had begun.

Epilogue

A month later, Cassie and Lorenzo had a houseful of guests and a raging party. A massive flat-screen television had been installed in the largest room of the Venetian palace Lorenzo was restoring and the room was full of dragons, their mates, and their children.

All the *Pyr* had come to witness Lorenzo's big finish. As a bonus, Lorenzo and Erik had given Cassie permission to share the truth with Stacy, and Cassie's best friend was also staying with them in Venice. Stacy was awed by the dragon shifters, and as much in pursuit of kismet as ever. Cassie was glad to have the air cleared between them and doubly glad to have her friend visiting.

The unearthing of Lorenzo's car was scheduled for dawn, which meant the show made a good prelude to dinner in Venice.

Cassie really liked the other dragon shifters and their partners. They had arrived gradually, some staying with Cassie and Lorenzo in the palace and enduring the dust of restoration, others staying at nearby hotels. She liked that they hadn't all descended upon Venice at once, so she'd had time to get to know them each a bit.

She wasn't surprised by how much she liked Melissa Smith—having seen her on television made the reporter seem like an old friend. Rafferty was impossible to dislike, his calm and charm making him someone who was easy to have around. Their adopted daughter Isabelle was lovely and had explored the house with Cassie.

Cassie wasn't surprised by how much she liked Eileen Grosvenor, either, given her admiration of that woman's partner, Erik Sorensson. Their daughter, Zoë, was adorable and just as inquisitive as Isabelle.

Sloane, the Apothecary of the *Pyr*, had arrived with Marco. Cassie liked Sloane's quiet competence, although she still found Marco quite enigmatic.

Donovan, the Warrior, was charismatic and energetic, also impossible to dislike. He and his partner, Alex, had taken daily forays into the city with their son, Nick, seemingly determined to explore every corner in their time here—and this despite the fact that Alex looked about ready to drop their second son. She was due at the beginning of August.

Quinn, the Smith of the *Pyr*, was watchful and protective of his family. Cassie liked the consideration he showed for his partner, Sara, who seemed to be still tired from her last pregnancy. She'd delivered her second boy in February and they'd named him Ewan. She disappeared into Lorenzo's library with the new baby every day and had pronounced it perfect.

Delaney and Ginger had come from Ohio, leaving their organic dairy farm in the care of trusted friends and neighbors. The *Pyr* were teasing Delaney that their son, Liam, needed a brother and Cassie noticed that the couple had been taking regular moonlight strolls in Venice.

There was no more romantic place on earth, she was

convinced. She also suspected that Stacy would be visiting a lot in the future.

Niall and Rox had come from New York with their twin sons, who were just four months old. Quinn and Sara had done some babysitting for that pair as they delved into the nightlife of the city. Cassie hadn't even realized there was a tattoo parlor in town, but Rox had found it and befriended the artists there.

Having the *Pyr* visit with their partners and kids was like suddenly inheriting the enormous, affectionate, extended family that Cassie had never had. Cassie loved it, and she knew Lorenzo did, too.

Brandt had arrived last, still somewhat unhappy with Lorenzo's deception. They had spent a day closeted with Erik, probably negotiating a truce of some kind, and he'd been thawing toward Lorenzo ever since.

He was also making a sizable dent in their inventory of brandy. Cassie saw Sara try to speak to him several times, but Brandt brushed her off. Cassie was sure she'd find out in time what the issue was.

Apparently there was one *Pyr* missing, a guy named Thorolf. Although Rafferty expressed concern for him, the others consistently changed the subject when his name came up.

Cassie wasn't feeling too badly, other than the morning sickness that had her running to the bathroom. She had no doubt that she was pregnant, although she'd only gone for the blood test a few days before and had not yet received the results back from the lab.

In Venice, she'd decided that the Ansel Adams plan wasn't for her. Nature was beautiful, but not as surprising or as revealing as she liked. Cassie was intrigued by people and liked to capture that perfect candid shot. She recalled an image she had seen years before, of a clown backstage removing his makeup and his facade with it. She'd hunted it down on the Internet and bought a print for inspiration.

Since then, she'd been hunting glimpses behind the veil, documenting the truth behind the illusion. She had a good two dozen shots, about six of which she thought were fabulous, and a real sense of pride in what she was doing. It wasn't easy and it wasn't quick, but Cassie was having a wonderful time.

And Lorenzo was her number one fan. He was determined to get her a show in Venice to showcase her work.

It wasn't as if either of them had to worry about money. The shots of Lorenzo that she'd taken that morning in the desert were throwing cash beyond her highest expectation. It seemed that every publication on the planet wanted rights to print them; there were T-shirts, umbrellas, tote bags, and a touring gallery show in the works; Melissa Smith had integrated some of the shots into her own program, paying for exclusivity on a couple of very nice shots; a digital artist had used morphing software to animate the change, stringing together the shots into a seamless video display. Cassie was carefully investing the money, ensuring that their son would have a secure future.

From the look of it, the kid would be able to start his own Ferrari collection when he got his license.

Life was good.

The *Pyr* jostled each other for a view as the music swelled.

"Here it comes," Quinn said.

The music rose to a crescendo and the scene unfolded in brilliant color across the huge flat-screen television. The view was stupendous with the sun rising over the desert, touching those red rocks with fire. The sky was perfectly clear.

"Fantastic resolution," Donovan said with admiration. "We should get one of these."

"I like having windows instead," Alex said, and he grinned.

"Great reception," Sloane said.

"Dish on the roof," Lorenzo supplied.

Cassie watched Lorenzo's eyes narrow as he scanned the image. She knew he wanted every detail to be perfect.

Stacy shivered elaborately. "It's so exciting."

Cassie saw Lorenzo smile at her friend's reaction.

"And here we are," the announcer said. "Finally at the day of unearthing Lorenzo's greatest spectacle. Let's review the feat."

They ran footage of Lorenzo's arrival at the site, his confident wave, the car being buried. Cassie was glad to see that her presence was completely invisible. She put her hand in Lorenzo's and he squeezed her fingers.

"That's one great car," Delaney said.

"Shame about the paint," Niall murmured.

Lorenzo smiled as the video shifted to the feed within the car. He looked calm and composed, closing his eyes and settling back as if he'd sleep for the entire month.

Serene.

They saw the fireworks from that night for the first time, and Cassie thought about what they'd been doing while the world was entertained. She shivered, glad that Chen's brand was destroyed for good.

The shot changed to one announcer, who looked concerned. "Of course, we were all shocked when there were technical glitches with Lorenzo's feat. The batteries died in his cell phone two weeks ago, so he's been out of contact. His team, though, was determined to not intervene."

The announcer pivoted and gestured to another screen. "The video feed from the car also died two days later. No one knows what's happened in that car in the past twelve days. No one knows Lorenzo's status. The people gathered here today have come to see the truth with their own eyes."

"Is that what they'll see," Erik said softly, and the *Pyr* all laughed.

The second announcer took up the patter, speculating on the possibilities and reviewing Lorenzo's amazing career.

Meanwhile, the camera panned in on the site of the spectacle. Cassie was surprised to see how many people had gathered. There must have been ten thousand people and their agitation was palpable. She was pretty sure that waitress and her kids were there, despite the hour.

"Great turnout," she said to Lorenzo, tightening her grip on his hand.

His smile was quick. "The more witnesses, the better."

They split the screen then, showing a slice of the expectant crowd on one side, and the large, shiny bulldozer rumbling into position.

"Should have gotten a bigger one," Lorenzo murmured.

The bulldozer dug into the earth, the crowd seeming to hold their collective breath.

"An amazing feat, if he does survive it," one announcer babbled. "What do you think his chances are, Ed?"

"Not very good, I'm afraid. It's been unusually hot this month here in the desert, with record-high temperatures recorded almost every day for the past two weeks. Even buried in the sand, the car would have become very hot."

"There were sensors linked to the car, weren't there, Ed?"

"There were, and they've recorded a consistent temperature within the vehicle between 90 and 110 degrees. There's a very real chance of dehydration, as Lorenzo had only a small amount of water enclosed in the car with him. If, of course, he didn't run out of oxygen first."

"But until the video feed failed, Lorenzo appeared to be sleeping quite comfortably in the driver's seat of the car."

"Appearances can be deceiving," Rafferty murmured, and Melissa smiled. She'd been sworn to secrecy on the truth of Lorenzo's feat, just like all the *Pyr* and their partners. Given the speculation about Cassie's photographs and the identity of the man in those images, Lorenzo needed to lie low for a few years.

The announcers continued. "Well, there are people, Bill, who can lower their metabolic rate. This means that they require less air and less water and burn less energy. I wouldn't be surprised if Lorenzo could do that. On the other hand, I'm not sure it would be enough to ensure his survival under these circumstances."

"You're not optimistic, Ed."

"I fear that Lorenzo has reached too far this time."

"Well, let's go down to the ground and find out. I can see the orange metallic paint of the car roof, and the crowd is becoming restless."

"That is one beautiful car."

Gears moved on the massive cranes and the enormous stainless-steel chains groaned. The car was lifted out of the hole, sand slipping away from it on all sides.

The car was spun slightly—Cassie was sure every move had been choreographed by Lorenzo, and his smile of satisfaction convinced her that she was right — and turned over the crowd.

The car was set down and then brushed off by Ursula and Anna, Lorenzo's stage assistants. They had enormous feather dusters for this job and took their time, steadily building the suspense.

"Can you stand it?" Stacy whispered, then gave a squeal of anticipation.

On screen, Anna held up her hands, beginning to clap a steady rhythm. The crowd quickly copied her gesture, the sound of their applause almost deafening.

She knocked on the window, as if to awaken Lorenzo from a long sleep.

There was no reply or movement.

She turned to the crowd, spreading her hands as if asking them what to do.

"Open it!" one man roared and the crowd took up the cry.

The announcers were chuckling. "Always the perfect showman," Ed murmured.

The *Pyr* grinned.

Ursula held up a car key dangling on a ring, one with a Ferrari logo. When the sunlight touched it, the crowd started to cheer. She touched the button to unlock the doors. The car's lights flashed once.

Encouraged by Anna, the crowd began to chant Lorenzo's name.

Beside Cassie, the man himself folded his arms across his chest and watched with undisguised satisfaction.

Ursula opened the door on the driver's side with a flourish, gesturing to the man within.

Then she stumbled backward in such obvious horror that the crowd fell silent. She put her hand over her mouth, obviously gagging.

"Another false alarm, Ed?" the announcer asked, his tone jovial.

"Just part of the show, I'm sure," Ed replied.

But one camera zoomed in, capturing an image of the man in the driver's seat.

Who was very, very dead. In fact, he had decomposed to the point that he wasn't even recognizable as Lorenzo.

But he was wearing the same leather jacket and orange shirt that Lorenzo had worn when he'd been buried in the car.

The *Pyr* gathered in Venice broke into applause.

"Balthasar?" Brandt guessed. "Is that what happened to him?"

Lorenzo just grinned. The announcers were chattering away in their excitement at an unexpected development, but Lorenzo turned off the sound. He stood in front of the television and took a bow, for the greatest disappearing act of his career.

"And now we have a surprise for you," Erik said.

Cassie enjoyed the sight of Lorenzo's confusion. "What surprise?"

She went to the sideboard and got his lost scale, the one she'd kept and hidden away from him. She offered it to him on both hands, smiling at the sight of his surprise.

"Erik told me that you need to get it repaired. That's why they're all here. That's why Quinn is here. To fix your armor."

And she saw that, as much as he might have preferred to hide it, Lorenzo was overwhelmed.

Cassie had surprised him one more time. Lorenzo was honored that she was his partner and knew he could never love another woman the way he adored her.

He hoped she would never stop surprising him.

Quinn murmured satisfaction as he took the scale. He turned it over in his hands, checking it for damage and obviously pleased with what he'd found.

Meanwhile, Cassie pushed the button that closed the drapes. This room had sixteen-foot ceilings and was enormous. Lorenzo knew it had once been a ballroom, with such dimensions. It had a long line of tall windows that opened to a balcony over the canal.

The drapes—of navy Fortuni velvet with light-blocking linings—had cost a fortune, but Lorenzo had wanted to ensure their privacy. Now he was glad to have them. At the touch of a button, they rode on an automated track, too heavy to be simply tugged across the glass.

He liked how precisely and neatly they closed.

Centered on the opposite wall was the enormous painting of his mother and her place of business.

This same property.

Although Lorenzo had bought adjacent buildings and expanded upon the footprint. He'd been quietly restoring it, as L. Rossi, waiting for the chance to make his escape.

It had turned out far better than even he'd hoped.

The massive chandeliers hanging from the ceiling glittered. They were gilt and hung thickly with glass drops, as well as each being six or eight feet across. He'd scoured half of Italy for them, and they were perfect. There were nearly a thousand bulbs burning in this room and he appreciated every one of them when the *Pyr* began to shift shape.

This was the true spectacle.

The light caressed the sapphire and steel scales of Quinn, the Smith. It danced over the lapis lazuli and gold scales of Donovan, the Warrior. It gleamed on the ebony and pewter hide of Erik, the leader of the *Pyr*. The light flashed on the amethyst and silver scales of Niall, the Dreamwalker. It lit the emerald and copper scales of Delancey. It glimmered on the opal and gold scales of Rafferty, the new Cantor. It twinkled on the brilliant tourmaline scales of Sloane, the Apothecary, highlighting the way the color shifted over his length from green to purple and gold. It flickered on the orange and yellow scales of Brandt, making him look like a dragon made of flame.

Stacy's eyes were round.

Lorenzo roared and shifted shape, knowing the light would glow on the hammered gold of his own scales. He cared only for the way Cassie's eyes shone as she stood before him.

"Show-off," she teased, and he grinned. He caught her in his embrace and reared back, baring his chest to the Smith. Quinn breathed fire, heating the scale that he held in his talons; then he cast a glance at Cassie.

Lorenzo was appalled to realize that he didn't know what the Smith wanted.

Quinn put out a claw.

Cassie knew, though. She offered him a pearl as big as her thumb, which was set in a gold pendant.

"A gift willingly given from the mate is required to heal the scale," Quinn said.

"I saw it in a shop here," Cassie said. "It reminds me of those earrings your mom is wearing in the painting."

Quinn reared back and breathed more fire, heating the gold setting of the pendant, then fusing it to the scale. He worked deftly and quickly, his older son watching raptly as he worked.

Then Quinn turned to Lorenzo and lifted the glowing scale toward the gap in his armor. "Fire," he said, heating it again.

"Earth," the *Pyr* and their mates cried, pounding their feet on the floor. The kids enjoyed this part and continued to stamp.

Lorenzo bared his teeth and growled as the scale was pressed into place and his skin seared.

"Air," the *Pyr* said and Cassie blew on the wound.

Lorenzo held her close, his throat tight with the goodness she brought into his life. He had the definite sense that he'd finally arrived home, after a long journey. He glanced up at that painting and thought he saw Angelina smile and nod approval.

He knew he saw her glance over her shoulder, her smile filling with satisfaction. He followed her gaze and found a younger, more handsome version of Salvatore lounging at a table, watching her. The room was empty, save for the two of them, the heat of their smiles telling him everything he needed to know.

Lorenzo shed a tear, a tear of relief that his parents were united in some dimension. He felt Cassie lift it from his cheek with a gentle fingertip.

"Water," she murmured and put that tear on the repaired scale. It sizzled on contact. She looked up at him and he saw the tears shining in her own eyes.

She was the treasure he'd sought all his life.

And winning her heart was the greatest feat he'd ever performed.

"Kismet," Stacy pronounced with satisfaction and not one soul in that room would have dared to disagree.

Lorenzo shifted shape and caught Cassie close, kissing her soundly as the others hooted approval. The future was everything he'd ever hoped it might be.

Because of the firestorm.

Because of Cassie.

Author's Note

Balthasar's rental car, the red Ferrari 360 Spider, is available for rent in Las Vegas from Dream Car Rentals. At this writing, the going rate is $750 for five hours or $1,050 per day—probably not inclusive of taxes and insurance. Lorenzo's prize Ferrari—the 1963 Ferrari 250 GT Berlinetta Lusso—is the same as one owned by Steve McQueen, which sold for $2.3 million dollars in 2007. Only 350 of these cars were made, and the V-12 engine (even if it burned oil) would be the stuff of a car lover's fantasy. I have to think that Lorenzo's car would be a more flashy color than the metallic brown "Marrone" of McQueen's.

Read on for a peek at the next exciting installment in
the Dragonfire series by Deborah Cooke,

Ember's Kiss

Coming from Signet Eclipse in October 2012.

Oahu, Hawai'i
Friday, December 9, 2011

The sun was setting over the ocean, painting the sky
in rich shades of orange and indigo. Brandon was
standing outside his favorite beach bar in Kane'ohe
with a few buddies, talking about the best curls of the
day, when four cars pulled into the dirt lot. The guys
turned as one, curious about any new arrivals, and
watched the group spill out of their cars. Brandon and
his friends had made the drive to Kane'ohe, after all,
because Matt had insisted they needed new scenery.
Their usual haunts on the quieter North Shore were
filled with familiar faces.

About half of this group were in their thirties, as was
Brandon, but were conservatively dressed, as he and his
gang were not. Many of them didn't know each other,
judging by their body language, and they exchanged a
lot of polite smiles. More than half of them wore glasses.
The rest of the group was older and had a scholarly look
about them. There was one older woman with gray hair

wearing a vivid pink Hawaiian shirt who seemed the most gregarious. She put her arm around a dark-haired woman who may have been the youngest of the group and shepherded her toward the restaurant.

Brandon noticed immediately how pretty that woman was. She was wearing a lei of yellow plumeria, black capris, and a white top. He guessed from the lei that she had just arrived on the island. The woman in pink must be trying to make her feel welcome. He smiled at that and noted that she needed a pair of flip-flops to even begin to blend in.

The younger woman was slim with curves in all the right places, was taller than most, and had delicate hands. Her hair was long and thick, with just a hint of wave to it. He thought it might curl more in the island breezes. She would be stunning when she got a bit more of a tan, and he wondered whether she'd brought her bikini.

"Fresh bait," Matt teased, as crude as usual.

Brandon gave him a poke. Matt was a good surfer, but a jerk with women. "Don't be a pig. It's not just about sex," he said.

Matt and Dylan laughed. "What is it about, then?" Dylan demanded.

Brandon shrugged, watching the woman. "I don't know. Romance. There's got to be more going on to make it special."

"From thirty feet away, it's about sex," Matt concluded, then finished his beer. He was cocky, the way he usually was when he'd had a couple of beers and wanted to show off. "Tell you what—let's square it off between sex and romance. Let's see who gets results first."

"What are you talking about?" Brandon asked, although he already could guess.

"Let's go for your brunette. She can choose sex or

romance. Whoever gets lucky doesn't have to buy to-morrow night." Matt stuck out his hand. "Deal?"

The very idea annoyed Brandon. He had been raised to respect women, and the brunette's quiet manner made him feel particularly protective of her. "You really are a jerk, aren't you?"

"Either that or you know you're going to lose," Matt countered with a grin.

Dylan started to laugh.

Meanwhile, the party moved into the bar. Josie, the waitress, pulled tables together for them, and there was a lot of jostling as they chose seats. The older woman in pink seemed to be in charge, or at least she bossed people around in a genial way. The brunette hung back, indecisive. Her gaze flicked to Brandon and he impulsively smiled at her. She blushed and averted her gaze, then took a seat in a hurry.

"She's not going to know what hit her," Dylan commented.

"I'll tell Josie to give her the extra large mai tai," Matt said with satisfaction. "On me. It'll smooth the way."

"Wait a minute. You can't just target her," Brandon objected. "That's not right."

"Right?" Matt seemed to be amused by this idea. "Look at her—she just got here. For all we know, I'm exactly what she wants on her vacation. All those mainland girls are looking for action." He preened a bit and smiled at the brunette.

Her eyes widened slightly and she shook her head, as if disinterested in Matt's attention. Her gaze flicked to Brandon again and he rolled his eyes, as if despairing of his buddy.

She smiled then, a real smile, one that brightened her features and made her look young and pretty. Brandon's heart thumped and Dylan chuckled. "You're on," Brandon said to Matt, who moved to the bar to order that drink for her.

Brandon didn't even know this woman, but he was annoyed by Matt's behavior. He was going to defend her from his friend, whether she was ultimately interested in him or not.

It was just the right thing to do.

One thing was for sure—the men were gorgeous in Hawai'i. Liz couldn't believe how many hunks were at the beach bar, lounging around with their shirts open, looking fabulous. They were all tanned and handsome, completely built. She'd never been in a place so filled with gorgeous men.

"Surfers," Trudy confided with a sniff. She was a contemporary of Liz's mentor, Maureen, who had invited Liz to the islands. Maureen had blossomed here, but apparently Hawai'i hadn't made Trudy relax at all. Her dark hair was tightly pulled back and she spoke more quickly and decisively than the others. "Completely self-indulgent," she added, then sipped her mineral water.

Liz found herself sneaking a peek at the auburn-haired guy again, the one who had smiled at her a couple of times already. Unlike the others, he didn't seem predatory. She found his confidence appealing, as if he was comfortable in his own skin—exactly the way she was not. There was a tattoo on his chest, although she couldn't fully see what it was, and she glimpsed part of another on his arm. He was drinking beer, chatting with his friends. She heard him laugh and liked the rich sound. His eyes twinkled when he caught her looking and he toasted her with his beer before he took a swig.

Liz developed a fascination with the menu.

"The shrimp are good," Maureen said, bossy and kind, just as Liz remembered. "They're farmed locally."

Before Liz could answer, the waitress put a large drink in front of her. "With the gentleman's compliments," she said, gesturing to a dark-haired guy at the bar. He also was incredibly handsome, but his smile had a roguish tinge that reminded her a little too much of her ex, Rob.

Liz pushed the stem of the glass. "Thanks, but no. Please give the gentleman my thanks."

"You sure, honey?"

"I'm sure."

"It's the jumbo mai tai, house specialty."

"I'd just like a glass of white wine, please."

The waitress shrugged. "Suit yourself." She picked up the drink and the guy at the bar scowled. Liz peeked and saw that the auburn-haired guy was debating something with his blond friend, as if he hadn't even noticed. He turned and gestured to the sky beyond the beach and she admired the breadth of his shoulders, the unruly tangle of his hair. It was long, long enough to tempt her to touch it. And that tan . . .

She was losing her mind. Liz took a gulp of her wine as soon as it arrived.

She finished the glass before the food arrived and Maureen ordered her another before she could argue.

It tasted even better than the first one.

The party loosened up as it got later. They didn't drink much, Brandon noticed, but what they did drink loosened their inhibitions. They laughed more and were obviously having fun. The brunette kept glancing his way, but he wasn't in that much of a hurry to make a conquest.

She seemed different from the women he usually met. She looked like she had a job, like she had it together in a way that the girls who hung out at the beach seldom did. She looked as if she were serious about life, something that he didn't see often. She wasn't interested in Matt—she'd made that clear—which also set her apart.

He wondered what she was looking for in a guy.

He wondered whether he had any chance of delivering it.

When her group spilled out onto the beach in the wee hours, he trailed behind them.

"I tell you, we'll be able to see the eclipse," insisted one guy, tapping his watch. "Any minute now."

"It's supposed to be quick this time, just an hour from start to finish," added another guy.

Brandon remembered that there was supposed to be a total lunar eclipse, and there was no better place to see one than on a beach. The night was clear, the dark sky filled with stars and the glowing orb of the full moon. He stood with his feet in the warm sand, listening to the lap of the waves, and stared at that radiant moon. The warm wind tousled his hair and he could smell the plumeria in the brunette's lei. His heart was filled with an affection for this island where he had chosen to live.

"There we go!" cried one of the women, and Brandon saw the first increment of shadow slide over the full moon. The group stared upward, enraptured.

Brandon would have happily stared as well, but he felt something strange. His hand was warm, but tingling. He glanced down to find orange sparks dancing over the fingers of his right hand, the hand closest to the brunette's group of friends.

At first he thought his eyes were deceiving him, but

the flames grew larger, becoming orange tips that outlined his entire hand. The fire slid up his shoulder, spreading over his skin like a bonfire. At the same time, a warmth slipped through his body, turning his thoughts to pleasure.

Brandon glanced around, but no one else had noticed the fire.

And no one else had the same corona of flames around his body.

What was going on?

When the flames danced down his side, he felt himself become sexually aroused. He spread his hands, looking down at his feet as they were illuminated by the strange orange fire; then a spark leapt from his fingertip.

It cut a blazing arc through the air, colliding with the shoulder of the brunette. She jumped, then turned to look at him. Her eyes rounded in surprise and her lips parted. Their gazes locked and held, and he felt as if they were all alone, standing outside of time, as the flames cavorted between them.

And that was when Brandon knew what was happening. He was having his firestorm. He'd heard about it, but only vaguely, from his parents. He'd never really thought it would happen to him—or that if it did happen, it would be centuries from now. But as he stood and felt the burn of the firestorm, he felt everything become clear.

This woman had seemed special and different to him because she *was* special and different. She was his destined mate, the one human woman who could bear his son. He had a duty to fulfill the firestorm, which meant he had to seduce her.

Without spooking her by revealing the truth about his other nature.

The firestorm gave Brandon purpose.

He smiled and stepped toward her, offering his hand. She stared at those flames, glanced at her friends—who were so busy staring at the moon that they hadn't noticed anything odd—then took a cautious step toward him. Brandon felt like they had a secret, a magical connection, and then realized they did.

The firestorm.

She frowned slightly as she surveyed the dancing fire; then her hand was in his. The flames spread over her skin, dancing over her, making her eyes brighten in awareness. She would have asked a question, but Brandon didn't want to risk the loss of the magic.

He tugged her so that she was against his chest. Her hands fell on his shoulders and she looked up at him, his desire mirrored in her blue eyes. That was all the encouragement he needed to bend his head and claim her lips with a kiss.

And the firestorm surged through his veins, filling him with commitment and desire, persuading him that it knew best.

About the Author

Deborah Cooke has always been fascinated by dragons, although she has never understood why they have to be the bad guys. She has an honors degree in history with a focus on medieval studies, and is an avid reader of medieval vernacular literature, fairy tales, and fantasy novels. Since 1992, Deborah has written more than thirty romance novels under the names Claire Cross and Claire Delacroix.

Deborah makes her home in Canada with her husband. When she isn't writing, she can be found knitting, sewing, or hunting for vintage patterns. To learn more about the Dragonfire series and Deborah, please visit her Web site at www.deborahcooke.com and her blog, Alive & Knitting, at www.delacroix.net/blog.

DARKFIRE KISS
A Dragonfire Novel

by DEBORAH COOKE

Rafferty Powell has resolved to destroy his hated arch-nemesis, Magnus Montmorency. The pair have exchanged challenge coins, and their next battle will be their last. But Rafferty never expected to meet a woman whose desire for Magnus's end matches his own—and whose soul sparks a firestorm within him...

<u>Also available in the series</u>
Whisper Kiss
Winter Kiss
Kiss of Fate
Kiss of Fury
Kiss of Fire

Available wherever books are sold or
at penguin.com

S0318